UNENDING

Also by Ivelisse Housman

Unseelie

IVELISSE HOUSMAN

UNENDING

Quill Tree Books
An Imprint of HarperCollinsPublishers

HarperCollins Children's Books,
a division of HarperCollins Publishers,
195 Broadway, New York, NY 10007

HarperCollins Publishers, Macken House,
39/40 Mayor Street Upper, Dublin 1,
D01 C9W8, Ireland

Quill Tree Books is an imprint of HarperCollins Publishers.

Unending

harpercollins.com

ISBN 978-1-335-01004-9

25 26 27 28 29 LBC 5 4 3 2 1

First Edition

For everyone who waited for this one,
but mostly for Sam.

PART ONE

Gossamer remembers the dizzying, bittersweet taste of what it feels like to be mortal—and right now, he's wishing he didn't. Those fleeting, entangled moments when he and the changeling fought for control of her magic, her mind, her hands—worse, the moments when they shared them—are like an ink-dark poison, seeping into the smooth white perfection of his own nature. He dreams of them, trapped in an endless cycle of thoughts and, more disturbingly, feelings.

In a way, this is more merciful than his last imprisonment: those long centuries trapped in that cold, iron-wrapped statue, aware of every passing second. Now, embedded so deep in the changeling's head that even he forgets he's there until she sleeps, he doesn't have the luxury of time to boil angrily and plot revenge. He exists in dreams, pacing her mind at night like a caged animal.

He only needs her to slip up once.

If Gossamer knows one thing about mortals, it's that they're endlessly fallible. But if he knows anything about Iselia, it's that she's . . .

Stubborn. Unpredictable. All but impossible.

She tricked him into this unfortunate situation, after all, and she's only one mortal, compared to the dozens it took last time. He thought he'd win her over with pretty words and sharp-toothed smiles, but he's the one who didn't see the truth all along.

She's just as ruthless as he is, if for different (boring, selfless) reasons. He underestimated her.

He's waiting for his chance to escape—to claim control of her frail mortal shell so that he can eventually return to a body meant for a glorious creature like himself. And when he does (he will, he's certain, and he repeats this to himself over and over as the stars wheel overhead), he isn't sure if he wants to rip her throat out with his bare hands or take her apart piece by piece, gently, as one might with a butterfly they wanted to study.

Either way, there'll be a lot of blood to look forward to.

chapter one

ISOLDE

The sun sets early on Wintersol, but I've never minded the dark. In summer, it would still be light out now, the sky a glowing treasure box of ruby and gold. Today, on the shortest day of the year, night has fully set in, and only candlelight illuminates my twin sister sleeping with a dragon on her chest.

Even though I'm glad to see her resting for once, my heart sinks. We have a very tight schedule to keep if we're going to pull off our escape. "Seelie," I call as gently as I can. Seelie (who has been sleeping in light, troubled bursts, trying unsuccessfully to shield me from the nightmares of the Unseelie Realm that haunt her every time she closes her eyes) startles awake with a gasp. She's sitting up in the same instant her eyes fly open, dumping the dragon unceremoniously in her lap.

The dragon has a perfectly fine bed of his own, but he insists on sleeping on my sister instead. Which is fine for now, if not ideal, but definitely a habit that needs to be broken before he's a fire-breathing monster the size of a cottage. He teeters a little, balancing himself with his undersized wings, and lets out a groggy screech of complaint.

"*Am-I-late?*" Seelie pants, all in the one breath. Her fingers run in a staccato pattern over Egg's pearly white scales, and the dragon—still cranky from being woken up so suddenly—nips at them with his needle-sharp teeth. His tail lashes around, like he's absorbing her panic and multiplying it.

Just *looking* at her stresses me out. But I don't say that. My twin doesn't handle the winter darkness as well as me. Seelie is all summer, bursts of sunlight between fits of storms, and she's been on the edge of a gale for days now.

The Wintersol Ball is already in full swing, but if we hurry, we can get her there before anyone notices she's missing. I was only stopping by our shared room to check on her, to go over the plan one more time, to soothe my own guilt for leaving her to handle Leira Wildfall on her own. Not that I'd be much help against the heir of the last shapeshifters, an enchanter so rich and powerful she's managed to keep me trapped here for months now, but I wish I could at least be there for moral support.

"A little late," I say with a wince.

Seelie flies out of bed, her knotted hair whipping wildly around her in an uncontrolled swirl of wind. Egg rolls onto the floor and stays there, twisting on the smooth stone with uncontrolled toddler energy. In her frantic swirl of movement, Seelie doesn't even seem to notice the dragon underfoot.

"Fate, I'm so sorry," she says, still breathless, hopping over him. "I don't know what happened, I just—I got so tired, and it was the middle of the afternoon and nearly dark already, and I—" She tosses her hair over her shoulder, nudging him aside with her foot and nearly tripping in the process. "I didn't mean to go to sleep. How long have I been out? Is the plan ruined? Did I ruin the plan?" She grabs for the dress she's meant to wear like it's going to try to escape her if she doesn't catch it quickly enough.

"Slow down. Nothing's ruined," I say, taking a deep breath of my own. Trying to convince myself that this is not a bad omen for the rest of the plan.

It's a good plan. I've been puzzling over it from every angle for weeks, and I think we can pull it off if we're lucky. The only thing better than a heist is an elaborate escape plan, the kind that relies equally on luck, scheming, and skill. One where each piece fits into the next, like tumblers in a lock clicking into place. It was almost fun to have something to work on, instead of being cooped up on my own while everyone else keeps busy, knowing I'm only here so Leira Wildfall has leverage over my sister.

"Nothing's ruined *yet*," Seelie grumbles, struggling to pull her Wintersol finery into place.

Egg, offended at being ignored, retreats to me to nurse his pride. The dragon looks up at me with those big molten-metal eyes, leaning hard against my leg. He's hot to the touch and denser than you'd think: almost heavy enough to knock me over. I guess he has every right to be upset, since, technically, this is his room—we only ended up sharing because someone needed to keep an eye on him, and he burned the fingers off anyone else who tried to touch him.

It's hard to connect that monster with the sweet baby creature blinking up at me now. With a sigh, I heave the dragon up into my arms. He's only a few weeks old, and already the size of a small dog. Soon, he'll be too big to carry.

"Can we help you, Grumpy?" I ask Seelie pointedly, wiggling Egg's floppy weight with the words as if he's speaking with me.

"I'm not grumpy, I'm panicked." She whirls past us to the mirror across the room, wrapped in a windstorm that blasts my hair into my eyes as she goes. The touch of her magic makes

Egg restless, and he wiggles out of my arms, dropping to the floor with a *thump!* that vibrates in my boots.

I am already in the Wintersol outfit provided by Leira Wildfall without any input from me, just like everything else in this room. The gown is flashier than I'd like, with heavy gold brocade that feels like a mockery of everything I don't have, but at least it's mostly black. Its sleek, heavy fabric swirls around my legs, a tide pushed by my constant movement.

Seelie huffs at her reflection, her hands slapping at the outrageously pretty ball gown as if it's made of spiders. "This is wrong," she growls, twisting around like she'll catch the back of her reflection if she moves just a bit faster. Her long hair is loose and tangled, random strands trapped under the pale silk bodice. "I can't do it. I can't do this. I'm wearing something else, they'll just have to—"

"Easy," I interrupt. Her hands shimmer with heat, and we're seconds away from the gown's long puffed sleeves bursting into flames at the cuffs. Her once-suppressed magic has been slipping free, like the familiar power is some shapeless, liquid thing she can't catch hold of. I've seen the way sparks follow her movements, and irritated gusts of wind brush anyone who stands in her path.

I should probably be scared of getting burned when I push myself off the wall I was leaning on to grab her hands, forcing her frantic movements to still—but my self-preservation instincts have never been strong. "Let me help."

Seelie's breath escapes in an angry sound through her nose, but she doesn't fight me. Her skin cools from burning to merely feverish as my eyes sweep over her, fitting her into the part she's meant to play tonight. The dress *is* a bit much—layers of frothy fabric, dark green embroidery crawling over its length like midwinter ivy. It's something Seelie would never pick for herself, and that's what makes it perfect. At tonight's ball, Leira is hosting enchanters and wealthy families from the city of Auremore and beyond. If Seelie isn't over-the-top, it will be noticed. And tonight, above all else, she needs to be forgettable.

After a moment of examining, I realize what's wrong with the dress. It's meant to be loose and flowy, but a few inches of lacing up the back draw the waist tight without the need for tailoring. The laces are all twisted, digging into her back, but after fighting with the strings for a moment, I manage to free them, then tie them into an inelegant bow.

"There," I say, smoothing the fabric. "Better?"

Seelie's lips press together, but she nods, gazing at her reflection. Or maybe at *our* reflections, side by side. Her bruised, shadow-smudged eyes and my short hair are the only things that set us apart. My hands work absently, freeing the trapped sections of her hair, then trying to loosen some of the knots. My sister tenses, holding her breath. She's never liked anyone touching her hair.

Our mother always liked to dress us up for Wintersol when we were little, preparing us to make a good first impression on the new year. Seelie would sit still for Mami's gentle hands, let her tease each tangle free and twist tiny braids into her long, dark hair. If we were home—

I cut the thought off before it can fully form. If we were anywhere but here, trapped in a gilded cage under the thumb of one of the world's most powerful enchanters, a lot of things would be different.

A loud *clink!* startles me out of my thoughts and makes Seelie jump. We both turn to the candle, which has burned down enough that the nail I set there earlier to help track the time just dropped into the metal pan below. Eight hours past noon—time to set the first stage of our plan into motion.

Seelie jerks forward, barely avoiding tripping herself on her long skirts. "*Late!?*" It's between an exclamation and a question, high-pitched and screechy.

Egg, who I'm afraid may be absorbing her high-strung personality, lets out a defensive yelp and bounds over to her side. He stands at the hem of her fluffy skirts, his undersized wings raised in what I'm sure he thinks is an intimidating posture.

"It's okay," I soothe, running through a quick checklist in my mind. "You're dressed. Your hair is . . . fine. Do you have the bottle?"

In response, Seelie fishes into a pocket she sewed within her full skirts, pulling out the little vial Olani gave her this morning. The potion inside sloshes around sluggishly.

"Good. Are we forgetting anything else?"

Seelie sucks in a jagged little breath. "One thing."

I watch her sweep self-consciously back to her side of the room, a chamber almost the size of our childhood home deep within Wildline Manor. As far as prison cells go, it's nice. We have comfortable beds, tapestries on the wall, and a fire that magically maintains a comfortable temperature. Leira Wildfall needs us right now—needs Seelie, at least, and I'm just collateral—which means we're treated well enough. It's almost like being a guest, except for the constant, unspoken threat:

If we stop being useful to her for even a second, things will get very messy, very quickly.

It feels wrong to see Seelie's side almost as chaotic as mine, instead of everything impeccably ordered and sorted into categories, and she has to dig through the piles for a moment before finding what she was looking for. She emerges with a circlet of dried flowers, and refuses to make eye contact with me as she asks, "Can you help me put this on?"

I can *feel* my eyebrows shoot up, but I bite my tongue. I know what it is. Dried flowers are part of the celebration for Wintersol, collected all through the rest of the year—but the circlets are special. Exchanged by sweethearts to wear to the midnight celebrations, a promise of fidelity through the dark and cold winter days.

Seelie holds hers up, trying to balance it on her head. She's still not looking at me, possibly embarrassed or shy—more likely avoiding a conversation she knows she won't enjoy. Because we both know that Seelie, who is reserved and withdrawn and doesn't particularly like most people, has never had a sweetheart.

I sigh, giving in first. My hands brush hers away, straightening the circlet atop her head. The papery petals crinkle against her hair as I tie the ribbon at the back of her head, securing it in place.

"So, where did this come from?" I let the words slip out casual and light, fighting back the urge to tease or scold her for thinking there was any chance I'd let it go without comment.

Seelie hesitates, gnawing on her lip. It's already raw, skin irritated by the cold and by all the times she's done that. Finally she says, in one short exhale, "Raze."

"Hmm," I say. I don't say *I figured*, or *You've been spending a lot of time with Raze lately*, even though both are true. I can't fault her—I'm sure making it through the Unseelie Realm and back is a bonding experience—but I'm not sure he sees their time together the same way she does, and I don't know if I should worry about that. It would be a lot easier to be all vicious and protective and sisterly about it if he wasn't so damn likable.

"It's not like it *means* anything," she adds quickly, giving her reflection one last wide-eyed glance. Despite it all, she looks pretty. Even exhausted, even messy, even with her dark eyes glittering a little too brightly. It adds an unsettling edge to the softness of her face, in a downright faerie way.

"Hmm," I say again. True, Raze is an incorrigible flirt, but he's different with Seelie—less flash and more substance. I've noticed how he reaches for her hand, how he exaggerates his own steady breathing for her to mimic when she's spiraling, how he lights up the second she enters a room . . . even if she, apparently, still hasn't. "He said that?" I ask a little sarcastically.

That makes her turn back to me, hunching up all awkwardly defensive. The eerie fae creature vanishes, and she's just my sister again. "Well . . . no."

"Ohhh," I say, as if that wasn't already obvious. Part of me feels the littlest bit guilty for messing with Seelie when she's already in so far over her head. Then again, she's the one making things difficult for herself.

"Stop smirking," Seelie snaps, meeting my gaze with that tiny wrinkle she gets between her drawn brows.

"What? I'm *smiling*," I say innocently.

She glares harder. "Well, don't do that, either."

I lean back, crossing my arms. "So now I'm not allowed to be happy?"

"Not like that, you aren't," she mutters, brushing past me. "Don't we have somewhere to be?" Even though her voice is more affectionately irritated than annoyed, I can tell she's definitely in a Mood.

The plan does not account for a Mood.

Seelie's hands continue to flit restlessly as we make our way through the lantern-lit halls, followed by the pitter-patter of Egg's claws on the shiny floors. It's strange, being prisoners without bars or locks. Moving deep within the manor, where there are no windows to let in the moonlight or the winter wind, is almost like being in another world. In theory, we could just slip out a back door, and no one could stop us.

But they would come after us. And we've failed to outrun Leira Wildfall too many times now. As it stands, nothing holds us here but our own good sense, our fear of retaliation if we upset the delicate balance of our situation. Servants scurry around, acknowledging us with a nod as they pass, as if we're honored guests. Seelie ignores them, lost in her own mind, but I try to smile back.

I know we make them nervous—not because of anything we did, but because our presence sets their employer on edge, and any source of tension in Leira's already-fraught domain is one more thing everyone has to worry about.

Hopefully, that's a burden that will ease tonight. It's a few flights of stairs down to the manor's grand hall, but even from far away I can hear the faint rumble of music and conversation. Seelie's fingers skim the cool stone walls as we spiral down a back stairwell, like she's absorbing the vibrations of the sound.

"Nervous?" I ask, since we're alone again in the dark, cool space. Well, alone except for the firedrake that's managed to get his front paws wedged between us.

She hums noncommittally. "Not for myself," she says, voice distant. "But Egg . . ."

"Will be fine," I finish for her. Seelie's thoughts have been occupied by the dragon hatchling even more than usual lately. His presence makes everything more difficult, but it's not like we can leave him behind without risking his life or the lives of thousands of others.

I sigh. All I wanted was to steal some treasure, see my parents set up in comfort, earn enough riches to keep throwing myself into adventures without worrying where my next meal would come from. *This* has all gotten far too complicated for my taste.

"Taking the long way around?"

The high-pitched, purring voice yanks me from my thoughts. Seelie stops short at the bottom of the stairs, and I barely manage to stop myself from crashing into her. Over her shoulder, framed through the layers of Seelie's circlet, a pair of icy green eyes meet mine.

Aris smiles serenely, like she's delighted to catch us sneaking around. Leira Wildfall's distant niece and her obedient little pet, Aris is a powerful enchanter only a year younger than Seelie and me. Aris may be intimidating in a fight, but the ability to shapeshift that runs through their family seems to have passed her over—and she seems to have decided to make that everyone else's problem. It's sad, really. No one should find that much delight in making my life harder, especially not for the bare scraps of approval Leira throws her way.

Not that we're really doing anything wrong—using the servant's entrance to the banquet hall is as easily explained by Seelie's aversion to crowds as by anything else. For example, being closer to the firedrake so she doesn't miss her cue.

"Are we?" Seelie asks, voice just a bit too snappy to be masked in faux innocence. "I still get so lost in here, I swear, everything looks the same."

Aris's smile tilts smugly as she looks down her nose at us. She's only a couple inches taller, but somehow, she makes it work. "Don't worry," she says. "I'm happy to guide you."

Seelie glances at me, thoughts written clearly on her face—*If we're being watched this closely all evening, things are going to be a lot more difficult.*

I try to offer her a comforting smile, stepping down to loop my arm in hers. "Lead the way," I say, steadily meeting Aris's gaze.

"As if I'd turn my back on you." She scans me, head to toe, as if she can somehow sense the gold-plated letter opener, string of pearls, and tiny silver jewelry box stashed deep in my pockets. It's amazing what people leave lying around in a place like this. "You two first, with the firedrake. Just to make sure no one gets lost. Tonight's a big night for him."

We all look at Egg, who has done his best to shrink into the shadows. He recognizes Aris. She's one of the many enchanters Leira has called in to figure out how his bond with Seelie works and to shatter it. I can't imagine the experience left a great impression on him, or on my sister.

Aris crouches, holding her fingers out to him like he's a stray dog. Her tone tries for gentle, but it sounds strained. "Come on, you. There's nothing to be scared of. Tonight's your big night."

"Tonight?" Seelie repeats. "Like, *tonight* tonight?"

I elbow her, though I'm also struggling to deal with this news. I knew Leira was eventually going to have to boast about being in possession of the world's last firedrake, which she sees as an incomparable weapon. I just couldn't have imagined it would be so *soon*. She can't control the firedrake herself—she can barely touch him. Besides that, his fire-breathing abilities haven't shown themselves yet. I know that firedrake flame is more than just *fire*, but I have no idea what that means. I don't know if Leira does, either.

But none of that matters right now. I need to focus on dealing with this sudden twist in the plan. We were leaving before midnight, so it doesn't really change anything. Except that it does. It means that if we fail, there will be no second chance. Because once Leira reveals Egg's existence to the collected enchanters and wealthy families of the scattered cities that make up our world, it'll be impossible to disappear with him.

Aris smiles smugly. "Let's just say that this little one will be starting the new year off with a *big* change." Even I can tell she isn't giving Egg enough space. His ears are flat against his head, his lips pulling back in the beginning of a snarl. I'm struggling to formulate a snarky reply, watching Seelie panic-spiral from the corner of my eye.

Seelie, impossibly, stands even more stiffly. "What do you mean?"

"Why do *you* think Aunt Leira was keeping her possession of the world's last firedrake a secret?"

Seelie, who tends to think out loud when she's stressed, breathes an answer before I can remind her that it's more strategic to play dumb. "Because she couldn't control him."

As if to prove her point, Egg finally loses patience and lunges at Aris's extended fingers, his disproportionately large, pointy teeth snapping. She shrieks, automatically firing off a blast of light that narrowly misses him and successfully blinds us all.

"What did you do that for?" I snap, trying to sort out the sounds around me.

Aris, for once, sounds shaken. "I- It was an accident! He scared me!"

I blink to clear spots from my vision and see Egg tumbling back, just as disoriented. He turns and sprints in the other direction. Seelie makes a dive for him, but between her impaired vision and regular lack of hand-eye coordination, she misses by a long way. The dragon's claws scrape the expensive floor as he disappears like a shot. I try to picture my mental map of the manor, to narrow down the number of corridors that connect to this one, destinations where he could end up. There are too many options.

I curse, rubbing my eyes hard to ease the burning behind my lids. "And there he goes. Do *you* want to explain that to your aunt?"

Egg bolted once before. He was barely a week old, and one of Leira's hound-sized guard dragons suddenly decided that the firedrake was a threat when he showered its mistress with sparks. The guard dragon lunged, teeth snapping. Egg slipped out of Leira's grip, and the whole pack of them chased him out of the room.

We found Egg within a few hours, but I haven't seen any of the guard dragons since.

"Oh, no, no, no, no," Aris mutters.

"Don't just stand there!" Seelie says. I turn to see her hands running over her folded arms, eyes watering. As she shifts the fabric of her sleeves, it lets glimpses of her lightning burn scars show through, bright flashes against her brown skin. Our eyes meet, and we make a silent agreement: *Stick to the plan*. She'll go after the firedrake, and I'll complete my part of the mission. Leira never has to know.

"We should split up," I say authoritatively. Seelie is already in motion, skirts swishing around her as she brushes past Aris.

"Oh, no you don't," Aris says. "I'm not letting you out of my—"

I smirk as she passes, chasing after my sister. "Unfortunately, there's only one of you—" I pause, watching her freeze, looking quickly between Seelie and me, before I lean back.

"and two of us," Seelie finishes for me.

And then we take off in opposite directions.

chapter two

seelie

The mortal world seems to me just as confusing and strange as the faerie ones—the only difference is that, here, everyone pretends the games make sense.

I don't look behind me to see if Aris is following or give Isolde any hint that I'm doubting her plan more with each passing minute.

I don't look at the people who stop and stare as I enter the ballroom, whispering about why I seem to have found Leira Wildfall's favor. The stakes were already high enough, but I'm glad Aris let it slip that Leira plans to unveil the firedrake tonight. In a few hours, either we will all be gone without a trace, or all will be revealed.

And I don't meet Raze's eyes as I cut straight through the room to his side, though I can feel them on me, tracing up my face to the circle of dried flowers on my head. I touch it again, as if making sure it's still in place. I could have left it behind—perhaps I should have. I can tell myself that I just didn't want to throw away a gift from a friend, but we both know I wore it because I knew he'd like it. Because I wanted him to know that it meant something to me, even if I *cannot* give him the satisfaction of acknowledging that.

They say changelings don't feel love, which is obviously untrue—but there's a huge difference between friendship or family ties and *romance*. The latter implies a set of expectations that someone like me could never fill.

If Raze brings it up, I'll tell him that. Probably. If I don't lose my nerve.

The problem with mortal games, aside from how nonsensical they are, is that there's no way to win.

"We have a problem," I say to Raze's shoulder, as soon as I'm within earshot. Still not making eye contact.

"You look—" he's already saying, overlapping my words until their meaning sinks in. "Wait, what?"

"I lost him," I mumble, so quiet even I can hardly hear myself. Aris is catching up to me already, and in another moment, her spiky presence invades the bubble that always seems to surround us when it's just me and Raze talking.

He looks from me to her and back, brows drawn together. "What?"

"She lost the dragon," Aris snaps, keeping the phrasing intentionally vague in case someone is listening in. There are plenty of domesticated dragons around the manor, tame little things no more frightening than scaly hounds, and no one needs to know we're not talking about one of those. "He got startled and ran off, but he can't have gotten far."

Raze is, for a moment, too stunned to speak.

I take the opportunity to weakly joke, "You haven't seen any mythical, long-extinct creatures running around here, have you?"

His jaw snaps shut, and he matches my wry smile. "Can't

say I have." Ignoring Aris to the best of his ability, he offers his arm in a dramatic sweep. "Care to take a turn about the hall to search?"

I slip my arm into his, resting a hand on his elbow, but shake my head. "He doesn't like people. He wouldn't be in here."

"There's people everywhere," Aris snaps—a fact I am far too aware of.

Raze considers this for a moment, then looks down at me. "Well, if it were you, where would you go?"

I look around, considering. The space glows with the light of an irresponsible number of candles, dimming everyone's winter finery to deep jewel tones. The room's tall windows show a dark, glittering winter night, but in here, the scents of warm wax, rich wine, and sharp evergreen sap hang heavy in the air.

According to my childhood stories, back before the faerie and mortal realms were divided, faeries of the Seelie Court would bring gifts from their land of unending summer to cheer up the mortals trapped in winter's chill. I was told only children who were very good and very lucky would receive these gifts, but having experienced the Seelie Court's idea of generosity myself, I can safely say that *goodness* had nothing to do with it. They value order and politeness and, above all, spectacle.

I was also told that on Wintersol, faeries from the Unseelie Court wandered the snowy countryside looking for naughty children to spirit away to their land of chaos and misrule, but that was hardly different from any other night. Long after humans stopped visiting, we still had ballads and tapestries about the Seelie Realm. The Unseelie was painted in whispers and shadows, a place of vicious faerie beasts and tricks that trapped you there forever.

Now that our realms move independently of each other, threads pulled apart but not severed, I don't know what use faeries have for the solstice. Their magic doesn't fizz in the air as it does on the equinox, when the veil is thin, and they no longer visit us for good or ill on the longest night of the year.

I've been waiting for this night, and not just because of the escape plan. Each day, shorter and darker than the last, has been like climbing a steep hill. At midnight, our world will stand balanced at its peak for just a moment before we go tumbling down into a new year. For us mortals, it's a fresh start—but for the faeries, counting the passing of years is like counting heartbeats.

I've always found Wintersol a confusing holiday. Besides the shifting of magic and the promise of new beginnings, it's a yearly celebration of warmth and the sun. Winter's dullness is chased away with dried fruits and flowers, candles are burned with reckless abandon, and we all invite warmth back into our lives. It seems like a contradiction, since the main fixture of the holiday is a gathering celebrated at midnight on the longest night of the year, but that's just it—Wintersol is supposed to be a reminder that even the darkest, coldest night has an end.

Or, more realistically, people just want an excuse to get drunk enough to forget there's painfully few hours of daylight and it's cold and miserable all the time. My eyes skim over the floral arrangements and the people milling around, landing on the double doors thrown wide to an equally decorated courtyard. One I know from experience opens up to the manor's walled-in grounds. It should make the whole hall freezing, but an enchantment has been cast to keep the cold out, which makes the air around the door spiral in never-ending clouds of steam, billowing up into the open air and clear sky.

I gesture to the door with my head, already pulling Raze along. "This way."

Aris lets out a heavy sigh, far too world-weary for someone who's only sixteen years old, but neither of them argue as I walk at a clipped pace across the ballroom.

As we force our way through the party guests, I hear

whispering, wild speculations on the surprise Leira Wildfall has already teased for tonight, empty glasses sparkling in the candlelight with their gesturing hands.

A snort escapes me. They could guess for a thousand years, and I doubt they'd ever land on the truth: that Leira Wildfall has the last living firedrake, a creature whose kind was hunted to extinction for glory and for their ability to generate magical energy. Or that the only thing standing between Leira and total control of the firedrake is the same thing that gives her any influence over it at all: me. Unveiling him tonight is a bluff I can't quite understand, a threat cloaked in celebration.

"Does Isolde know?" Raze whispers without looking at me—barely a movement of his lips. It's a fairly subtle question, but I think he's really trying to ask if our escape plan is still on.

I nod before remembering he isn't looking. "Yeah. Nothing changes."

That's all I dare to say with Aris breathing down our necks. I force myself to breathe deeply, ignoring the little breeze that winds around us in response. As long as we grab Egg before Leira realizes he's missing, it's the truth. Nothing changes.

I know I'm digging my fingers too hard into Raze's arm, but I can't seem to make myself stop. Every sound feels magnified in the crowded ballroom, the hundreds of candles illuminating the room all blurring into fractals of light, the pressure of being surrounded by this many people a sensation I'd almost forgotten after being trapped in the manor for so long. I can feel them as much as hear them—the heat of their bodies and the rustle of their clothes and the crushing, prickly awareness of their magic.

My eyes squeeze shut against my will. I don't know if I've ever seen so many enchanters in one place before.

Suddenly, I realize we've stopped moving. Raze's other hand closes over mine, which is probably clawing his arm painfully tight. I can feel his face close to mine, but he doesn't say anything.

He just breathes.

After a moment, the room's swirling seems to slow. I let out a long exhale and slowly open my eyes. It's still chaotic and loud, a full city block compressed into one enclosed room, but I can manage it.

"Sorry," I sigh, looking up at him. Then I realize he's looking over my shoulder, watching the people around us.

Across the room, out of earshot, Leira Wildfall stands out less because of her scarlet dress, and more because of all the people in orbit around her. I recognize some of them—enchanters and the wealthiest inhabitants of Gilt Row: frequent guests to the manor always hoping to impress her. With them, she smiles and asks questions and laughs at all the right moments. She reigns the conversation like a benevolent ruler, and when someone says something she finds distasteful, she frosts over so quickly that they seem to shrink away, others immediately taking their place in her presence. I wonder if people even realize they're being pulled to her. I don't think it's an enchantment, but it still feels like magic.

Someone greets Raze as they pass us, and he offers a tight smile that drops the instant their back turns.

"Raze?" I say.

He swallows hard, not moving. I'm not even sure he heard me. I reach up and start to touch his face, then realize that I shouldn't, which turns it into an awkward brush of my fingers beneath his chin. Still, it gets his attention, and he turns to me.

"What is it? What's wrong?" I whisper, afraid to look behind me.

He shakes his head. "I know some of these people," he says quietly. "From . . . before."

Before. Before our adventures together, before he schemed to break into Leira's study and steal back his family's greatest treasure, before she gave up on ever torturing more powerful magic from him and tossed him out on the street.

I wonder if they had even met before his parents died in a

suspicious accident and he, a six-year-old just starting to show a talent for the shapeshifting magic passed down by their shared maternal line, went to live with her. I doubt Leira Wildfall ever wanted children, that she ever truly saw Raze as hers, but that doesn't change the fact that she raised him. She must have, at least once, picked him up and wiped tears from his eyes, soothed his soft pink cheeks with a brush of her fingers. She trained him, kept him under her roof, gave him anything he asked for—and then, when he was no longer of any use to her, she threw him away.

And no one—least of all the people in this room who must have known him, even respected him, as the Wildline heir once—did anything about it.

I don't know much about that gap, I realize. Those months when he started scheming, when he and Olani began working together in earnest, when the boy who had everything suddenly found himself with nothing. It makes sense that he wouldn't talk about it.

And yet, I *want* to know.

"I'm sorry," I say again, in an entirely different tone.

He shrugs, shifting back into his normal, cheerful self in an instant. "It's fine."

"No, it's not." My fingers are digging into his arm again. I force myself to loosen them.

"It will be," he says with such determined optimism that I can't make myself argue. Unlike faeries, humans can lie. They can say something they *want* to be true with such conviction that, for a moment, it is.

I, who am still not sure if I'm human, faerie, both, or neither, do not possess this ability.

And just like that, I realize we've made it to the doors. I let out a long exhale as the crowd clears up, everyone subconsciously avoiding the enchanted door exactly as they would if it actually were letting the chill in. I hesitate for a second before plunging through, warmth clinging to my skin for a moment until the enchantment releases me, like a popped bubble.

Cold winter air bites at my face, slipping in the cracks between my cloak and my braided hair to raise bumps along my neck. I've been slightly feverish ever since our return from the Unseelie Realm, a side effect of taking Gossamer's power for my own. I try not to think about him, too afraid of summoning the faerie with a distracted thought. Ever since I dug an iron dagger into my own palm, he's been silent, and I'm too suspicious to be grateful for it. I breathe in the stinging cold like a balm, banishing the thought. On the exhale, my breath curls in a steaming cloud that swallows all three of us.

The Wintersol Ball isn't just a party. It's a self-contained festival within the manor's walls, spilling out from the courtyard. Unlike most of the city, Wildline Manor has its own grounds, composed of meticulously maintained gardens, stone paths winding through velvety green grass, and multiple outbuildings that I'm not allowed inside, including a menagerie. Decorated for the solstice and lit by torches, it's as bright and as crowded out here as it is in there. I let out another long breath, dense enough from the warmth of my magic to fog over the whole path, obscuring me and Raze.

"Cut that out," Aris snaps. She's burrowed so deep into the fluff of furs sewed into her collar that her voice comes out muffled.

"Breathing?" I take in another deep breath, tossing my hair away from my face as I turn to give her a look. The cold rushes in all around me, like the whole world is gasping at the chill. This time, I push my magic intentionally, heating it so that Raze and I are briefly bubbled in a cloud warm as a summer day.

"You're doing it on purpose," she says through gritted teeth.

I shrug, turning back to the garden ahead. Frost shatters under my boots with each step along the slate path, and before I can antagonize Aris any more, Raze angles his arm to pull me closer. "That's a good trick," he says. "Do you think it'd work indoors?"

"Whatever you're planning, the answer is no." I squeeze his arm, looking over our shoulders. His longer legs cover more ground than mine, and keeping up means I'm not technically running, but only barely. It leaves just enough space for Aris to feel like we're within reach, without her listening in too closely.

"How about when we get to the booths by the menagerie?" he asks, looking pointedly at the glowing buzz of activity ahead. It's a modest crowd, but filled with all sorts of distractions and hired entertainers. You could get lost in the colorful swirl of cloaks, overlapping chatter, and bursts of flame in the shapes of dragons.

I sigh. "I suppose I could make an exception for that. Since it's Wintersol."

Without looking, I can clearly picture Raze's responding grin. A thrill of excitement runs down my spine.

My eyes are still searching every shadow for the hint of white scales, the warm yellow of glowing eyes. This is stressful and awful, and I shouldn't be enjoying myself, not even a little bit. But it will be easier to search—to talk openly—without Leira Wildfall's lapdog on our trail.

We're almost to the arch of greenery that separates the garden into its parts, and Aris is still several steps behind. I suck in a huge breath, watching the mesmerizing back-and-forth of the crowd in the torchlight as if it's one living thing, rather than dozens of individuals.

"Three . . ." Raze whispers, giving my arm one more squeeze as he prepares to run.

I hold my breath, chest expanded, heart racing. My palms are getting sweaty, but I'm not sure if it's from nerves or magical energy.

"Two . . ." Our arms slip apart, cold rushing into the gap between us. "One . . ."

My muscles tense, preparing to run. The warm air filling my lungs is restless as the wind, pressing at my lips with barely restrained force.

"Now!"

I let all the air out at once, sending white fog billowing all around us. The cloud swallows Raze, and for a second I'm lost and unanchored. Then his hand clamps around mine, pulling me so hard I nearly fall over, and we go sprinting through the fog.

"Hey!" Aris shouts. "Stop!"

There's something so absurd about the futility of her commands that a laugh rises up my throat. I grip Raze's hand tighter as the fog fades, the Wintersol festivities blurring around us. We weave around people and twist between booths at random, giggling like little children until, finally, the cold catches up to us.

Out of breath—and out of earshot of wherever Aris is most likely still yelling for us to come back—we sneak around a dark, uninhabited corner and fall back against a wall, choking on the last of our laughter. I gulp for air with frost-burned lungs, suddenly realizing that my skin is cold. I put all my warmth into the fog, and it'll take the magic a while to build to a fever pitch in my system again. My whole body feels frozen.

Well, all except my hand, still gripped in Raze's.

"I think we lost her," he wheezes as we finally settle down, folded in half and still puffing for air. My head twists so I can meet his eyes, that deep blue lake color. Then I focus on his auburn eyebrows, just above them, the one freckle closest to his left eye, the bottom corner of his mouth. Anywhere but his eyes. My stomach flutters uncomfortably, and I squeeze my hands into tight fists.

This feeling is dizzying and a little nauseating, like standing over a tall cliff, and it's the reason I've hardly spoken to him for weeks now. Only when necessary. Only when I can address him without directly addressing him, like to a group. Only when

I'm not near enough to see the specks of gray in his eyes and feel the air stir with his breath.

Wind tosses loose strands of hair into my face, and I lean into our twined arms to steal more of his warmth. "Think we're going to be in trouble for that?"

"No more than usual." He pairs this statement with a carefree grin I haven't seen in weeks, more mischievous than his genuine smile. When he sees my face, though, his eyebrows jump up to his hairline. He turns into me so that our joined hands fall at our sides. With his other hand, he reaches out to brush my cheek. "Your face is red."

My mouth twists. "So is yours." It almost always is, with his pale complexion. When his only response is a worry line at the corner of his mouth, I let out a breath. "I'm just cold. That spell used up all my body heat." My face feels frozen stiff, but his hands are so warm. I want to lean in closer and absorb every bit, like a plant facing toward the sun.

His fingers linger there until my skin is tingling under their touch, then lightly slide away. He reaches for a strand of loose hair that blew into my eyes as we ran, gently tucking it back from my face. "I'll keep you warm," he promises, squeezing my fingers tight.

All of a sudden, I realize I've been holding eye contact with him for . . . I'm not sure how long. Certainly too long. I swallow hard, gaze darting over his shoulder. "Come on," I say, ignoring the frantic gallop of my heartbeat. "We still have a firedrake to find."

After one last peek around the corner to make sure Aris isn't waiting for us, we emerge into the garden and are instantly folded into its chaos. Without any faerie guests, it's a different energy from the frenzied crush of Revelnox, though so much is the same: overlapping chatter, the sound of someone singing a midwinter ballad, fire crackling on all the torches. The mingled scents of food vendors' carts twist through the air on clouds of steam—cheese buns and candied oranges and cinnamon-sugar-dusted pine nuts.

My stomach growls loudly, reminding me that I haven't eaten anything today. I'm pretty sure I skipped dinner last night, too. It's been hard to remember trivial things like eating regularly.

"Should we keep an eye out for that bear I hear as well, or . . . ?" Raze teases, looking around us in exaggerated confusion.

It's convenient that I'm still tucked in close to his side, because it makes it very easy to elbow him in the ribs. "You're not funny."

"I know plenty of people who would disagree. Including you, when you're not so starved that you're grumpy."

"Grumpy?"

He nods.

"I don't get grumpy. It sounds so . . . undignified."

"Sorry, Iselia, but the whole terrifying-beacon-of-magic thing loses a lot of dignity once you've seen a person trip over their own feet a certain number of times. You're grumpy." Before I can launch another argument, he's already turning to one of the carts. "Do you want food or not?"

I do, which is why I let him hand me one of the cheese buns, still warm even though it must have been baked hours ago. All the food is paid for already, each vendor here part of Leira's celebration, so there's nothing to do but gently untuck it from its paper and devour the soft bread as we look for Egg. Say what you will about Leira Wildfall—she may be cruel, cold, and power-mad—but she knows how to throw a party.

This is taking too long. If we don't find Egg soon, we're going to miss the rendezvous Leira expects, and the one she doesn't expect, and everything is going to be ruined, and we're never going to escape her clutches.

"Is something wrong?" Raze asks, startling me out of my wandering thoughts. "I mean, besides the obvious."

It's an impossible question to answer. Of course something's wrong. But I don't want to give it a voice, don't want to stop pretending that this one beautiful moment exists outside all that. A needle prick of ice stings my nose, and I realize that—as if on cue—it's started to snow. It's not a stormy, blowing snow—just a dusting. Fluffy flakes drift lazily down from the sky, like the clouds are trying to kiss the ground as gently as possible.

Raze tilts his head back to the sky and laughs open-mouthed, trying to catch snowflakes as they fall. His eyes sparkle as he looks back to me. "Is this you?"

I allow myself a half smile as my head tilts up, watching wisps of cloud as they drift over the moon. It wouldn't be the first time I influenced the weather. Still, this feels different from the blood-pumping, stomach-churning energy that called storm clouds into the sky at my command. I wrap my arm around his, burying my grin in his shoulder to hide it. "I don't think so."

The snow starts to collect in glittering drifts, glazing the streets in a sugary coat. A group of small children in heavy velvet cloaks race by with ice skates slung over their shoulders, screeching like crows. The sound of someone playing a stringed instrument takes over the garden, notes sliding up and down the bow.

We keep walking, our wide circle slowly taking us closer to the manor again. I'm starting to worry that Egg somehow found his way outside the walls, that he truly is lost and not just throwing a little draconic fit for attention, that he's in danger and it's all my fault.

Raze interrupts my thoughts, leaning in so close his nose brushes my hair away from my face. "You're overthinking again, Iselia."

He's the only person who calls me by my full name instead of its (admittedly unfortunate) shortened version, which is equally annoying and endearing. I fight not to flinch at the startling closeness, staring up at him instead. "I believe the word you're looking for is *thinking*."

He scoffs at that. "Thinking is overrated." He says it with a look that is so painfully sad and dazzlingly happy at the same time, I can't make heads or tails of it. Then he stares at me like he's waiting for me to figure something out.

I don't look away, and neither does he.

Until movement catches in my peripheral vision, and my eyes drift away to a spot beyond his shoulder. A light dusting of snow crusts the stone path, except under a table draped with a long cloth. One side of it is as frozen as everywhere else, but the other half has melted in an inexplicable warm patch. My focus shifts, and I stare harder—just in time to catch the twitch of a pearly-white scaled tail.

"Egg!" I exclaim, interrupting whatever Raze was about to say next by diving past him toward the table. Egg scrambles out from under it in a flurry of claws and scales, bolting into the crowd. Unsure what else to do, I lurch to catch my balance and chase after the dragon.

Egg looks back at me gleefully, weaving between ankles and leaving a trail of melting snow everywhere he goes.

"Get back here!" I snap. The irony of yelling at the dragon after laughing at Aris's useless commands earlier is not lost on me. I might as well be shouting at the Harrow River to stop running.

A family with three young children passes between us, and I briefly lose sight of the firedrake. He's obviously not frightened of the crowd, so the only reason he could possibly be acting like this is to mess with me. I manage to catch the gleam of scales again just as he disappears from sight, and I sprint after it.

I've only made it a few steps when my boot lands in a patch of ice and slides out from under me. I scramble in place to keep my balance, but I only manage to plant my other foot on the ice. My legs slip independently of each other, and I realize that the fall is inevitable.

I land with a crash that feels like it bruises all the bones in my body. I hear a few people snicker, but the crowd just keeps moving around me. Honestly, I can't blame them—if I'd seen that fall, I would probably laugh at me, too. Breathing heavily, I let myself lie there on the quickly melting ice for a moment. My loose hair is wild and snarled around my face, and I can feel the flower circlet coming loose from the top of my head. At least I didn't lose it.

A hand pushes into my field of vision, and I turn to look up to see Leira Wildfall.

My stomach drops as I try to figure out how long she's been there. How much she saw. How much she knows. Raze stands behind her, looking as stunned as I feel. His hand is still outstretched, like he was on his way to come help me when she stepped between us. It takes me a moment to realize that the lump on the ground between them isn't a pile of snow. It's Egg, wrapped up in a bright silver chain and completely motionless, like he's sleeping. Any previous attempt to restrain him has ended in thrashing, biting, and scorched fingers, which means that whatever it is holding him must be enchanted.

The sinking feeling grows, like I'm plummeting through endless darkness, with nothing below to catch me except more darkness. Whatever that chain is, it's a very bad sign. It means she's figured out a way to handle him without me.

Leira—who is in her thirties, only a few inches taller than me, plain with pale ginger hair—has no right to elicit this deep and sickening a reaction from me. On the surface, when she smiles that practiced pleasant smile, she seems like she could be friends with my mother. I mean, except for the deep crimson dress glimmering with jewels. Her fingers, decked in rings, twitch, and I have to bite the inside of my cheek not to flinch.

Leira Wildfall doesn't have to hit you to hurt you.

"Changeling," she says, still smiling that pasted-on smile. I can almost convince myself that she is just as afraid of me as I am of her, but I can't stop myself from flinching when she extends a hand to help me up. I keep sitting there, feeling foolish as I stare at her before finally taking her offered hand. The biting chill of her rings digs into my palm. "I believe a discussion of our arrangement going into the new year is in order. Walk with me?"

It isn't a question.

chapter three

ISOLDE

Olani wears her hair in two long, raised braids these days. Tonight, they're pinned up to circle her head like a crown, which only makes her already-statuesque features look even more imposing. Her high cheekbones, arching brows, and long, curled lashes seem excessively elegant for someone whose neutral expression makes her look like she wishes you'd stop talking. The curve of her neck stretches into a smooth, uninterrupted line as she tilts her head back, lips pressed to a strange little flask.

I didn't mean to eavesdrop, but Olani was already deep in conversation with someone by the time I made it down to our meeting point in the manor's carriage house. Someone facing away from me, so all I could see was his shaved head and skin a half shade lighter than her rich, dark brown.

I hesitated as I approached, not sure if I should interrupt or not, and it wasn't until I crept close enough to hear what they were arguing about that I realized I absolutely did not want to get in the middle of this.

And—okay, *then* I started eavesdropping. Ducked behind one of the carriages, I can see most of the conversation without standing in plain sight of them. The smooth wood against my cheek makes my heart ache with homesickness for the *Destiny*, the enchanted wagon that Seelie and I called home in all our years away from home, lost when we passed through the faerie realms. Enchanted wagons are rare, but if anyone would have one, it would be the wealthy enchanters attending tonight's ball. Which is why Olani and I are supposed to be using her magic and my lockpicking skills to steal one—not having conversations with strangers.

She lowers the little bottle, wipes her mouth roughly, and attempts to hand it back to the stranger. When he just keeps staring at her, arms folded over his chest like a disapproving statue, she huffs a sigh and pockets the bottle instead.

At least I can get a good look at the man from this angle. He seems about ten years older than us, with handsome, angular features and a sharp intelligence in his honey-brown eyes. He and Olani stand at exactly the same height, and both of them are obviously annoyed about it—which tells me, before I even hear a word of their conversation, that this must be one of her brothers.

"You're acting like a child," the man says calmly. So far, he's said everything calmly. He must have the heart rate of a hibernating bear.

Olani—who is usually the calm one, but at this moment seems like a kettle fighting against its boiling point—breathes sharply through her nose. "I'm not going to respond to that," she mutters. "You are making things very difficult right now."

His eyebrows raise a fraction, which would be barely perceptible if not for the slight wrinkle it causes across his forehead. "Oh, *I'm* making your life difficult? Would it be better if you thought I was dead? Not that you'd bother to check, of course—"

"Hawn, that's enough," she snaps, interrupting his bland stream of mild sarcasm. How long has it been since she's spoken to her family? I knew she was letting them believe that she'd found an apprenticeship in the family trade of healing magic. That's why she told them she came to Auremore, after all. Her plan was to get work as an adventurer and tell them the truth once she was successful enough to prove it was a real career.

Instead, she got stuck working as hired muscle for Leira Wildfall. And then betraying Leira Wildfall to go on a wild-goose chase of a treasure hunt with the Wildline family disappointment, Raze. And . . . well, the rest is history. Still, I thought she'd at least send them a note to let them know she was still alive—or just to keep the ruse running with any believability.

And that's why you *always* make sure you get your friends to double-check your lies for you. I snort at the thought as it flits through my head, and the slight sound is enough to make Olani forget what she was about to say next. She and her brother both look up, startled, waiting for someone to stroll in.

My muscles lock, freezing me in place. I don't want her to know I was listening in on what is obviously a delicate situation. But since this is Olani, who is observant and clever and not great at subtlety, she's probably going to figure it out anyway—in which case, it might be better to turn myself in now. Then again, I don't want to make her any more annoyed with me than she already is. I can't bear to see that disappointed little crease at the corner of her mouth.

After a second, they dismiss the interruption, turning back to each other, and I can breathe again.

"I told you," Olani says, her voice tight with restrained anger, "I'm *not* coming home. I couldn't even if I wanted to. I'm sort of . . . tied up in something."

"Working for Leira Wildfall, you mean? Was *any* of it true,

Olani? I can understand lying to Mom and Dad, but if you had at least told *me* what was going on, I could have had your back! Did you ever think of that?"

Her bottom lip dimples as she bites down whatever she's feeling. "Well, I . . ."

"You owe someone money?" People don't usually interrupt Olani. She's always so confident, so put together, each word carefully weighted. Standing in her brother's shadow, I'm reminded that she's barely a year older than me—still just a kid, really. Hawn continues, voice rough with worry. "How much? Do you need me—"

"No!" Olani says sharply, startling them both (not to mention me) with her increased volume and pitch. "No. It's—it's something else. I just *can't* leave right now, and honestly, it would probably be safer if you weren't here, either."

I don't know why, but that strikes me as kind of sweet. Technically, after the firedrake hatched, Olani could have left at any time. She and I were only hostages to stop Seelie and Raze from interfering with Leira's plans for the dragon—not that *that* really worked out for anybody. Still, she chose to stay, even after the mess we found ourselves in got a hundred times more tangled, because she knew anything she did would be taken out on us. She could walk out that door right now, take her brother's hand and never look back—but she's trying to protect us.

Probably mostly Raze. Realistically. After all, they've known each other the longest.

A pause stretches out. My hand clenches tight, flexing in and out of a fist. Maybe I should stop hiding. Maybe it's way too late for that now.

Finally, Hawn lets out a sigh. His voice softens, so pitying and full of devastated fear and disappointment that I can taste the bittersweet emotions at the back of my throat. "Oh, Olani. What did you do?"

Another pause. When I dare another glance, her shoulders are slumped, making her seem impossibly small. "I can explain everything," she finally says. "Just not tonight. Name the place, and I'll meet you first thing in the morning."

Olani's brother stares her down. It's like watching two walls having a silent argument. After a long time, he finally concedes with a "Hmm."

They hug, and he tells her the name of the inn where he's staying, a place in the not-expensive but not-too-shabby Market District. I used to haunt the tavern next door to pick-pocket patrons too distracted or intoxicated to notice. Olani promises again and again to be there. He gives her one last searching look, pursing his lips.

Then he turns, shoves his hands in his coat pockets, and leaves the carriage house with a heavy sigh.

Olani watches her older brother leave with her usual flawless posture, back as straight as the quarterstaff gripped in one hand. After he disappears into the winter night—and then another count of ten—she lets out an even bigger sigh, slumping so that only the quarterstaff is holding her up. Her back goes to the wall, and she finally lets herself feel.

My stomach turns. I'm not supposed to be seeing this. It feels wrong to see Olani vulnerable like this without her knowing I'm here.

Which is ultimately what decides it for me. Steeling myself for another unpleasant conversation, I take a deep breath and push out of my hiding spot.

"Hi."

She doesn't even look surprised to see me, which damages my pride more than it should. She only watches me warily, her eyes the only thing moving as I approach. "How much of that did you hear?"

I hesitate before deciding to tell the truth, offering a little shrug. "A lot of it. Are you okay?"

She doesn't answer, which is as close to admitting defeat as Olani gets. She just stares at her hands, clasped around her knees, like something new will materialize there.

"He seems nice," I try again, closing the distance between us. It feels weird looming over her, so I fold myself down onto the ground next to her, my back against the wall.

She lets out a frustrated groan. "He's here because our parents sent him to drag me home like a misbehaved child," she snaps. "As if I can't take care of myself. As if I don't know what I'm doing. I don't even know how he *found* me. I don't know what I'm going to tell him."

"Tomorrow?" I ask, a question nested in another question. *As soon as we're free of Leira, are you going to leave us? Leave me?* I can't say what I really mean, because if she says yes, then I'm going to have to admit that I'll wait for her. Despite the danger of being followed or recognized, I'll linger in this city as long as it takes.

I get the feeling Olani understands anyway. "Mind making a quick stop?"

"Whatever it takes to help you lie to your family." I try to make a joke of it, to hide the truth. But when she flinches, the smile drops from my face, the gravity of the situation setting in. "Why don't you just . . . you know, tell him?"

"The truth?" She laughs, harsh and a little high-pitched. "Are you out of your mind?"

I shrug. "Maybe?"

Olani squints at her bootlaces, shifting to adjust the left side so that it matches the right's perfectly symmetrical knot. "You don't know my family. The truth is not an option. They still think I'm apprenticing as a healer—where would I even *start*? Which is why I stopped replying to their letters, which was obviously stupid and shortsighted and I—I feel terrible about it, but I still don't want to talk. How can both those things be true at once? It doesn't make sense."

In the silence that follows that uncharacteristically long stream of vulnerable truth, I stare at her. If I could somehow contact my parents, I'd be able to write hundreds of pages on what's happened since the last time I saw them. They wouldn't like a lot of it—especially the illegal and/or life-endangering parts—but I'd let all those secrets go for the chance to hear from them. To tell them I'm still alive, and I still love them.

But I can't do that, because the whole reason Seelie and I ran away from home was to protect them. Because she used enchantment to alter their memories so they wouldn't remember their daughters and throw away their lives trying to track us down and protect us. Because the tiny glass vial that held their memories shattered months ago, crushed under a boot as I fought capture by Leira Wildfall's goons, and it was all my fault.

It's been three and a half years since I saw my parents, and some part of me is stone-cold with certainty that it was the last time.

"How many?" I whisper, my voice unsteady.

She turns, one hand dropping to the floor. "What?"

I forget about our surroundings, about the mission, about the plan. Instead, I look up at Olani. "How many letters have you not replied to?"

"Thirteen."

"That's bad."

"I know that."

"Like, really bad. Thirteen?"

"Plus a few just from Hawn."

"Olani!"

"I know!"

I stare helplessly at the open panic on her face. "Okay, well, no wonder they're worried. If it was *me*, I wouldn't have let you off the hook that easy. I'd be dragging you home right now so the whole family could celebrate together that you aren't spending Wintersol lying dead in some back alley in the Twilight District."

"No offense, but you are potentially an outlier when it comes to your sibling's well-being. If it were *you*—" Olani stops mid-sentence, her eyes going wide. Her cheeks pucker, like she wishes she could suck the words back in. After another sharp exhale, she swears quietly under her breath.

"No, go on." This feels all too familiar, dizzying me with a blend of emotions I don't have time to deal with right now. My head fills with echoes of our argument from weeks ago, the one we're both still stewing over. The one neither of us ever apologized for. "You were saying?"

"Fate, Isolde, I shouldn't have said that." Olani chokes a little on the sentence, still struggling with her composure in a way that's all too rare for her. Seeing her brother must really have her shaken.

Despite my best effort, the anger swirls into a confusing blend of sympathy and confusion. My head tilts as the spiky feeling fades away, giving me space to breathe again. To sigh, and really look at her. "Are you . . . okay?"

She blinks, her swiftly moving thoughts obvious behind a pained expression. "Hawn's cursed faerie-tongue potion," she says darkly, as if that explains everything. At the face I pull, she quickly adds, "It doesn't actually have faerie tongue *in* it. It's named for the effect. I didn't know how else to convince him I wasn't lying. It seemed harmless, just to get him off my back until I—I—" She breaks off, and I realize that she isn't sure what she's going to do next. After a moment, she starts over. "Anyway, I probably took too much. It should wear off in a couple hours."

I feel bad for Olani, I really do, and I'm aware that this might complicate our mission . . . but the possibilities are already flying through my mind. I can't help but give in to the little intrigued thrill that instantly lightens the mood. "So, just to be clear, anything I ask you for the next several hours, you have to answer honestly?"

"Or I can not answer," she says, a bit too quickly. "But I have to think about it to hold back."

Our eyes meet. I let my eyes widen innocently before saying, "Could I pull off a shaved head?"

"Could you? Probably. *Should* you? Absolutely not."

I cackle at her immediate honesty. I can already feel the fiendish grin creeping over my face, despite my best efforts. "Oh, that's *good.* Your brother makes that? Doesn't sound very healer-y to me."

Olani snorts a half laugh, slightly bitter and homesick. "Hawn's magic has always been a bit different. He's the oldest. The most like me."

"Ohhh." I dig back through my memory, searching for the reason that sounds familiar. "He's the one who taught you how to do that . . . shield thing?"

"Yeah." Her mouth quirks into a faint smile. I've only seen Olani's shielding magic once before, when we first met—when it was me and Seelie against her and Raze, and she knocked my sister out with her own lightning magic reflected back at her. It's a powerful enchantment, one Olani can only do with a month or so of rest between charges.

But it's extremely cool.

"Come on," Olani says, standing. She seems a bit steadier now. Maybe confiding in me took some of the weight off her shoulders. "We have work to do."

"One more." I know I'm testing my luck, even as I hoist myself up with her offered hand. "What's your favorite color?"

She sighs. "Yellow."

"I *knew it*!" I crow, trying not to be too loud in my excitement. I've been haunted for weeks over the time Olani said she didn't have a favorite color. I knew it was a lie.

There are dozens of carriages and wagons here, all gleaming and expensive and well-kept. They all pretty much look the same to me, and if they carry their own enchantments to make the horses faster or deter robbery, I can't sense it. All I'm looking for is a hitch for horses—or rather, the absence thereof.

Neither of us is an expert in carriage construction, so there are a few false alarms. When we think we've found an enchanted wagon, Olani places her hand on its side, using her magic to sense if it has an enchanted mechanism like the *Destiny*. Her face screws up in concentration—then goes flat with disappointment. She shakes her head, and we move on, avoiding the grooms dashing in and out and the guards patrolling at wide intervals.

After we've nearly done a full circle of the carriage house, I start to worry that we won't be able to find one, and it'll be useless. Maybe we could still get away drawn by horses. We'll have a head start, after all. Maybe I should have built in more backup plans.

And then something deep within nudges me in the right direction—an instinct I've been ignoring far too long now. It's the same feeling that's guided me into countless reckless, impulsive decisions, saved me on multiple occasions, drawn me to the best stolen hauls. I followed that pull on the night Seelie and I first broke into the manor and stumbled across its greatest hidden treasure. Seelie calls it luck, but I feel like there's a better word for it, one of those words you forget mid-sentence and have to circle in synonyms instead.

Whatever it is, I'm tired of ignoring it.

Tucked away in a corner, as if to hide it from notice, sits a wagon that's smaller than the *Destiny*, made of plain brown wood in different shades. It's almost comically exaggerated in its minimalism, and I don't have high hopes when Olani reaches out for it.

But this time, her face lights up.

I pick the lock and take a peek around the inside of the wagon, which is just as bare. We crawl over and around the wagon, looking for its fueling mechanism. In my experience with enchanted wagons, they generally drive better when the driver's magic is running it. All Olani needs to do is give it a little spark of hers, and it'll be ready for us when we return with Seelie, Egg, and Raze.

The *Destiny*'s mechanism was on its underside, but this one is on the roof, which means we have to awkwardly climb up the carriage to reach it. Olani's height makes it easier for her to swing herself up, and she lands with an easy lightness. I start to follow, stuttering at the stab of pain that shoots through my ankle when I lift onto my toes. I try to mask it, but it must show on my face, because Olani reaches down to help me up.

I ignore her hand, pushing onto the healed ankle despite the pain. I've pushed harder through worse. Olani gets to work on the lock, and I get to work rolling the stiffness out of my ankle and getting lost in wandering thoughts.

I broke my ankle escaping from the faerie realm, and it was still broken when Leira Wildfall captured me and Olani less than a day later to force Seelie and Raze to give her the firedrake egg. She'd promised to free us if they did as she asked, but I knew even then that she was lying.

It's strange—I can't pinpoint the moment the four of us became a unit, much less when that unit split into a new formation: Seelie and Raze, Olani and me. I know it was before we were physically separated. When I think back to those days on the road, my thoughts are drawn to a night that feels so long ago now. The early autumn chill in the air as we huddled around a fire in the shelter of an abandoned city. The ruins, a familiar sight everywhere we'd traveled, took on a new shade as Raze mused about what they'd once been.

I'd accepted that the Mortal Realm had always been as it was—fragments of civilization with wide swaths in between—but it hadn't. We'd had kingdoms once. Before a rogue faerie from the Unseelie Court tried to claim our world as their own, and Raze's Wildline ancestors somehow managed to get both faerie courts on our side to fight them off. It was called the War of the Realms, and it shaped our world into the broken thing it is, but we—the regular mortals, not descendants of wealthy and powerful shapeshifters—eventually forgot about it. Memories only last so long, and the world moves on.

The war might have been forgotten entirely, if not for the relic passed down from those long-ago shapeshifters to their descendants. They called it their family legacy, an enchanted compass that pointed to what was supposed to be a mysterious hoard of treasure called the Mortal's Keep. That relic was Leira's most priceless treasure, a puzzle she had dedicated her life to unlocking so she could reclaim the priceless treasure that had been deemed too dangerous to exist in our world.

That relic was what we stole when we broke into her manor on the autumn equinox, and honestly, it's all been kind of downhill from there.

The "priceless treasure" turned out to be the firedrake egg, last member of a species that breathed flames of pure magical energy. An unmatched weapon, and way harder to fence than, say, a pile of rubies the size of my fist. Before Seelie returned, before Egg imprinted on her like a baby duckling, Leira didn't try to hide what she wanted. She openly discussed political strategies and battle plans, how she would use her and the firedrake's combined might to bring our scattered world from chaos back into order.

Which sounds noble and all, until you realize that *order* means under her rule. Her ancestors saved the world, after all. Why shouldn't she claim it? Even I have to admit she'd be a good queen. A good, harsh queen who would earn obedience through fear and punishment and cruelty. Who wouldn't hesitate to burn whole cities to the ground to send a message.

"Would you really have left?" I ask abruptly, swinging my feet over the side of the wagon so I can lean back propped on one hand. "Without Raze and Seelie? Without even knowing where they were?"

She looks up with a tense frown. "I thought we were done with that conversation."

"*You* were done with that conversation," I shoot back. "I never got a choice." And now I'll have the truth.

"I don't know what you want me to say. Obviously, it would have been a mistake. I was wrong. But with the information I had, the likelihood that they were still alive after disappearing for that long was—"

"Exactly what I told you! But you didn't want to listen to me."

"And you didn't want to listen to reason."

After that, the silence hovers over us like heavy clouds, like a weight bound to drop at any second. Olani and I exist at opposite ends of a spectrum, an unstoppable force and an immovable object. I doubt we'll ever be able to truly understand each other.

And yet I still want to try.

"You didn't trust me about Seelie and Raze surviving. You didn't trust me enough to tell me about your family. You don't trust your brother to—"

"Leave my family out of this," Olani snaps, apparently down to the dregs of her reserves of patience. Patience I thought was an endless resource, but I do tend to have that effect on people.

I sigh, not rising to the heat of her tone. "My point is, you keep everyone at arm's reach. What are you so afraid of?"

Olani's jaw trembles, neck muscles going taut. "Noth—" she starts to say, but the word is choked off.

Because it's a lie.

She keeps glaring at me, as if it's somehow *my* fault she downed a double dose of truth potion and now can't keep pretending she's fine all the time and doesn't need anyone else.

I meet her gaze steadily, refusing to back down even though there's only a few inches left between us. She's used to people shying away, but I'm not going to cave. And I'm not going to get distracted wondering if she uses her healing magic to keep her skin so clear, or if it's just naturally flawless.

"Well?" I push, raising an eyebrow.

"Hey! What are you two doing up there?"

The voice startles us. Both of our heads turn automatically to the guard—no, *curses*, it's a whole pack of them—as we share a gasp in one mingled breath.

"Stealing!" Olani calls back, loudly and confidently. It hasn't even finished echoing before her eyes go wide, and our eyes lock in matching horror. Because she *could* hold in the truth, but only if she focused on it—and she was focused on entirely the wrong thing.

After that, it goes pretty much how you'd expect. We're escorted at swordpoint by several burly individuals to a room that locks from the outside. We don't fight it, because I *did* plan for this, and if either group ran into trouble before we met back up, starting a huge fight would jeopardize the other half of the plan—better to go quietly and salvage what we can.

I sit in the dark, in the opposite corner from Olani, and we don't talk, and I hope with every ounce of my being that things are going better for Seelie right now.

chapter four

SEELIE

There's something deeply troubling about seeing Egg so still, his constant frantic energy reduced to the sluggish rhythm of his breaths. His eyes flutter open at random, so I can't tell if he's awake or not. I can't tell if he's just as peaceful as he looks, or silently suffering.

The warmth of the hall and all its burning candles feels suffocating after so long outside. Leira guides us through a door I didn't see before—probably because it's shielded from view behind a row of thick velvet curtains behind the musicians, who are so close I can feel each note vibrating through my head. She carries Egg with both hands, stroking his scales almost tenderly, in a way that would seem sweet if I didn't see a sinister edge to everything she does.

"It was an accident, I swear!" I grind out again, wringing my hands. "He bolted. We were just trying to bring him back."

"Nevertheless," Leira says, and it's a whole sentence on its own, final as a stone settling to the bottom of a pond. Shifting Egg gently to one arm, she walks over the plush rug to a large, covered object. Based on shape alone, I already know what it's going to be before she whips the cover off dramatically.

Fabric slides into a puddle on the floor, revealing a gleaming brass cage. At my side, Raze sucks in a pained gasp, and I can sense his posture going rigid with—

Fear? Familiarity?

"Nephew, you're dismissed," Leira says without even looking at him. In one motion, she pulls a key from a pocket hidden in her full skirts, twists it in the lock, and deposits Egg into the cage. His chains fall loose with a gentle shake, and she pulls her hands free as he gives his first fitful stir. His tail lashes against the bars the second after they click shut.

"Thanks." Raze doesn't move to leave, but just in case, I reach out a tentative hand to keep him here with me. My pinky brushes his, and when he doesn't move away, our fingertips meet, hands sliding together like a key in a lock. With our fingers intertwined, Raze squeezes my hand.

I squeeze back.

The bottle tucked into my pocket feels like it's growing heavier by the second, but that might just be the weight of trying to salvage our escape plan falling onto my shoulders. I fight the urge to drop my other hand into my pocket and run my fingers over the glass, grabbing a fistful of my skirts instead. Back here, it's just her and us. This was the first step of my part in the plan, anyway. *Get Leira Wildfall away from her guards. Knock her out with a whiff of Olani's sleeping potion. Make her forget that any of us ever existed.* I might not get another chance.

Leira turns, pinning me with an icy look as if she can read my thoughts. "Your usefulness is waning. Do you understand? Perhaps you have control of the firedrake now, changeling, but it's only a matter of time before he's *mine*."

"I don't have *control* of him," I snap, crossing my arms. We've been over this time and time again, and the conversation always goes in circles. "We just . . . listen to each other." Which is not exactly true, but my thoughts feel like a swarm of words in my head right now, and I can't grasp them long enough to force them to take shape.

"And that's how the firedrake managed to slip away from you this evening? Listening?" Her mild sarcasm is accompanied by a delicately arched brow.

"Well . . ."

She interrupts before I manage to craft a reply. "Aris told me what happened. And whose fault it was. You were distracted."

In his cage, Egg rolls over, shaking his head as if to clear it. He's confused, but it's only a matter of time before he realizes he's confined and absolutely loses it.

Leira continues, not paying his distressed little sounds any attention. Her focus is solely on me now. "I worry, Seelie. You have enough struggles of your own without having to worry about your sister's. Your magic is so special, and you hardly know how to use it—how much of that is because of distractions like the ones she's constantly stirring up?"

I don't respond, biting the inside of my cheek. I can force myself to look into her eyes as long as I need to, no matter how much it makes my skin crawl. I can stare and stare until the watery blue almost seems disconnected from her face, not a threat trying to pry open all my secrets.

"Of course, I know how *attached* you are. Still, I can't help but wonder if you would be the one to benefit should you two be separated—and if she acts like this because she knows it." Before I can fully swallow that grim statement, she turns to run a finger over the cage's brass bars, offering me the wicked curve of a smile over her shoulder.

Should you two be separated.

Isolde and I are two halves of a matching set. We belong together. Even back home—back in Rurava, the village where we grew up, no one dared to challenge that. Leira doesn't have to speak the threat plainly to know that she's envisioning one or both of us thrown in a dungeon. Or Isolde kidnapped while we're asleep, hidden away so I couldn't retaliate. I *know* my sister can protect herself, but—

My heart forgets how to beat. I can't let anything happen to her. If not me, who's going to protect her *from* herself? To tell her the truth about herself that I've been hiding all this time, because I don't know how to say it?

That's when Egg's eyes open fully and land on Leira. I understand now why the cage has been tucked away next to the musicians, behind thick (sound-dampening) velvet. The gleaming brass structure rattles—at least, it would, if it hadn't wisely been placed on a thick, patterned rug—as he wakes with a start, throwing his little body against the bars.

I flinch, automatically stepping forward to comfort him, but Leira stands in my way, her threats as sharp and present between us as a blade. Raze squeezes my hand again, and I step back. The writhing mass of furious, hissing scales slams into the bars again and again, making me twinge in sympathy each time.

Leira grabs the cage and gives it a rough shake. "*Enough!*" she commands, through gritted teeth.

For a second, it seems to work. Egg stops moving, his eyes latched on her, pools of gold that seem to ebb and flow around the black slit of his pupils. Then he launches himself at her fingers with snapping pointed teeth.

Leira's fast, but not fast enough to avoid getting nipped. She lets out a surprisingly high-pitched sound as she yanks her fingers back, staring at the tiny spot of blood that's already welling up.

"Careful," Raze warns sarcastically. Our hands slip apart as he shifts, arms crossing over his chest.

"Hmm." It isn't quite a chuckle, but the sound turns up one corner of her mouth. Her eyes focus on Raze, looking up at him without deigning to tilt her chin. "Raze. I thought I told you to leave us."

It's the same mild voice she uses to correct servants, and hearing it directed at Raze makes me so instantly angry that my stomach turns a little. He doesn't flinch, or even let his forced smile drop. "You did," he replies pleasantly. "And yet, here I am."

She snorts out the tiniest of mocking laughs. "I hardly think the changeling needs your protection, nephew. You're just taking up space."

"I don't—" Raze starts.

"Ah." With that one harsh syllable, she silences him. "Fly away, little bird."

I can't figure it out. She spends so much time acting like he means nothing to her, like he's no more than a stranger, beneath her notice entirely—and then she'll do something like *that*. Invoking the limits of Raze's magic, the whole reason she tired of him, like it's some kind of joke. As if he's less than nothing, filth from the city streets to be scraped off the bottom of her shoe.

And Raze—who always has something to say, always finds the bright side, always laughs the worst things off—lets her. With one sideways look at me, he drops his head and starts to slink away.

A bitter taste fills my mouth as magic tingles its way down my spine, dripping to my fingertips, sparking along my skin. "No," I say, in a voice that surprises even me. It sounds like a growl, like a roll of thunder. Leira only arches an eyebrow, eyes not showing so much as a flicker of interest, which only makes me angrier. I step toward her, and everything else around us seems to fade away. "You do *not* talk to him like that."

Leira laughs with the delicate clarity of a bell. "I'll talk to him however I like. I don't take orders from anyone, least of all *you*, little changeling. Need I remind you how delicate our situation is?" Her hands fold neatly in front of her, motionless except for the twisting of one of her rings. It's a nonthreatening pose, but I know by now what it means when she moves her hands like that. She's getting ready to call on her magic, only a breath away from starting a fight I'm not sure I can win.

"Seelie . . ." Raze warns in a low voice. "Leave it. It's fine."

For some reason, that makes me even angrier. It's like my ribs are one big, hollow space, echoing the emotions around and magnifying them until there's no room left for me to breathe.

"No, it's *not* fine! Nothing is fine! You can't treat people like that! Or changelings, or firedrakes, or—or anyone!" I reach for my pocket again, trying to force my agitated hands to stop trembling. I can feel them getting warmer, ready to burst into a protective flame, but I'm really not trying to catch my gown on fire right now.

I find Olani's potion, but my fingers slip on the glass when I try to uncork it one-handed. I contemplate abandoning stealth, ripping the bottle open with both hands where Leira can see, but before I can decide if that's a good idea or not, she's already moving.

There's no time. My hands fly up automatically to defend myself, and I turn the motion into grabbing Leira's face. She isn't expecting it, and she barely has time to wiggle once before the magic starts to flow between my fingertips. She tries to pull away once, twice . . .

And then goes still.

At least, I think she goes still. The world gets fuzzy and faint as the spell kicks in, as my focus shifts to the tangled threads of Leira's memories.

This is *so* much worse than last time.

At least with my parents' memories, I knew what I was looking for. I was *in* most of them. I plucked at the bonds that tied us together, that made us family, and altered it so thoroughly that no one who knew us would remember Isolde and me as their children at all. Every second of it hurt, but it was shockingly quick and simple.

This time, a blur of Leira's past and present runs through me, an unwelcome tide I could get lost in if I'm not careful. I don't know if she's conscious enough to be fighting me, or if her mind is just *like* this. I set my jaw and fight to concentrate on what I'm here for—

Egg, as he is now. Small and weak and pathetic. Egg, as he might be someday. A massive monster of teeth and scales, a thundering roar, blistering-hot magic. In her dreams, the flames roll over and through her, and she directs the power with the expert touch of a surgeon.

I shudder, but don't turn away. I hold on to that one.

There's me and Isolde. Useful, but not that interesting. She's eager to dispose of those thoughts. Memories of Olani pull free almost as easily.

I hesitate, but there's no helping it. I plunge deeper into her mind and find a flood of Raze's past. There's no need to touch all of it, only what happened after she kicked him out.

She knew he was going to cry, but she didn't know it would make him look so young. So much like that boy she took under her proverbial wing. It was a shame things had to be like this, but there was no use for it: Raze was a waste of time and resources, and he had to go. At least he didn't beg. At least he didn't ask why things couldn't be different. At least he got angry, and started shoving over antiques and ripping down tapestries on his way out, destroying everything he could touch.

Perhaps that was a bit too poetic, but it made it easier to be done with him.

I force that specific memory away, nausea coating my tongue. Leira Wildfall's mind is a deeply unpleasant place, and there are some things I don't want to see. I have to be more careful about my own thoughts, or she'll keep dragging me through those.

Continuing to wade through her memories is difficult and

tedious and feels like it takes hours, though I know it can't be more than a few minutes. Time is all jumbled up in here anyway, following the threads of her thoughts over the course of years. The compass we stole from her—the enchantment that led us to the Mortal's Keep—that was her life's work. It's not easy to remove. But the more pieces I leave, the more questions she'll have. The more likely she'll hunt us down.

Deep breath. Keep searching.

Don't get lost in her dreams for the future, in the feeling of security that comes from knowing no one can best you, at finding everything in this world stronger than you and crushing it beneath your heels. In visions of dancing flames overtaking anyone who would stand in your way, and magic stronger than any mortal enchanter should be able to wield.

It doesn't feel like that. Something I know from experience, from taking control of Gossamer's—

Gossamer.

I don't intend to have the thought, much less to follow it, but once I do, it's like being pulled by a current. I'm powerless against being swept years away into the past, a memory buried deeper than I meant to go. I want to cringe away, but I have to look.

Leira Wildfall sees her reflection in the compass, the freckled face of a girl no more than eighteen. She's in charge now, the sole keeper of her family's treasures and magic, and it's a heavy burden. One she knows she has to protect, at all costs. The metal is cold against her manicured fingertips, which are going white from holding on so tight. Her heart pounds in her ears, each beat weighted with the decision before her.

"Find me," the cold voice says. "Once I am freed, we will be a team the likes of which your realm has never seen. When you have no other allies left, our power will be combined."

She squeezes her eyes shut against what she's about to do.

"It's a deal," she says, in her frail young voice. On the last word, she opens her eyes to look up into a translucent faerie face.

Gossamer smiles at her, and the layers of history and memory strip away.

Gossamer smiles at me, and the world flips upside down. I was already lost, but suddenly I'm powerless, too. Every memory I've gathered scatters as fear overtakes my magic. He's not supposed to be here. I defeated him. I'm in control now. I'm in *control.*

I can salvage this, I can pull the spell back together, I can do it—if I can just remember what I was trying to do. Why it was important. My mind goes blank, trying to escape, but I don't let it. I can't let myself give up that easily. I won't—

Air fills my lungs. When did I stop breathing? I'm falling backward, chest constricted, and I automatically start fighting it off before I realize it's just Raze dragging me away. My knees fold, legs giving out as I slump to the floor. Raze tries to support my weight at first, then gives up and crouches next to me. He's calling my name, but the sound seems distant. I feel weak and overspent, and I'm still trembling with fear.

I thought it was over. I thought I'd won.

Leira takes a few fumbling steps back before catching her balance on the cage and forcing herself upright. She's breathing just as hard as I am, blinking rapidly, but she recovers quickly. Her eyes burn with indignant fury when they meet mine, which is a much more personal kind of hatred than I've seen in them before.

She whips her hands through the air, and Egg's discarded chains fly in response, wrapping around my wrists before I can rally myself enough to defect. I just keep looking up at her, feeling foolish and useless, as the weight of metal drops my hands solidly into my lap.

chapter five

seelie

Isolde and Olani are, conveniently, already in the cell when we arrive. At the sight of us, and the sound of my chains, Olani swears loudly and creatively, for longer than you'd think.

Aris scowls at the guard who shoves me roughly inside. "Shouldn't we separate them?"

The guard shrugs, slamming the heavy door behind us, which muffles her reply: "Orders are orders."

Wherever we are, it's not really a cell. We're in the first part of the manor I ever saw, all those months ago before this mess started. I might not have recognized it, except that we passed Leira's old study just down the hall, now boarded up in addition to its overly complicated lock. Yellow-green moss spills like bile from the lock's openings, and the shiny gold decorations on the door are tarnished. Flickering white light peeks through the crack below the door, hinting at the portal to the Unseelie Realm still swirling within.

This room is only two doors down, and it would be relatively comfortable if not for the dark hearth and the unlit candles . . . and the stains of rot seeping through the paint on the side closer to the old study. If I close my eyes and focus, I can smell traces of magic and forest air.

I've done my best not to think about it, because then I start remembering things that happened and things in nightmares and it's not like there's anything I can do to fix any of it anyway.

When I first woke up fully from my feverish, faerie-magic-induced haze, they took me to the room that used to be Leira's personal study before I wrecked it with a sloppy portal from the Unseelie Realm. I was supposed to close it up like a door behind me, but without the guidance of the faerie who helped me create it, I couldn't do it.

The portal has remained, glowing white around the edges, a gash in the border between worlds. Egg's help with the spell sealed it up enough to stop anything living from passing through, but the room is unrecognizable. Magic seeps through the open tear like a slow drip of water through a roof, suffocatingly thick in the air. Last I saw, before it was locked off for good, the bookshelves and plush carpet and shiny desk were all still there, but now ghostly trees seemed to hold the ceiling up with silvery-leafed branches; now the carpet was an impossibly patterned moss instead of wool; now the books chattered and whispered among themselves.

Another one of my mistakes.

"Why did you pull me away?" I whirl angrily on Raze before anyone else has the chance to speak. "I almost had it!" It's not necessarily true, but I want it to be.

"No, you didn't." He snaps back, but his anger is more subdued—which only makes me more upset. "Trust me, if anyone knows what pushing your magic too far looks like, it's me."

My hands ball into fists. "I didn't even pass out this time!"

"No, you just started shaking uncontrollably and stopped breathing!" The heat in Raze's tone sizzles against the cool concern of the words themselves. "And even after that, I waited—but then the magic went . . . wrong. *That's* when I pulled you away."

Suddenly, it's hard to swallow. I know exactly what made the spell go wrong, and the thought that Raze could sense it—sense *him*—makes me sick. My voice goes low through the tightness of my throat as I spit out another wishful truth: "I could have *handled* it."

He and Isolde exchange a look over my shoulder, and I hate it. Since when are the two of them allied against me?

"It's what I told him to do."

I stare at her in disbelief, and she stares right back. She's making her stubborn face, all hard lines and sharp angles. I can't believe she went behind my back with any part of the escape plan, even if it was to protect me. Did she think I couldn't handle the spell? That I couldn't handle having a safety net? Was I always doomed to fail?

She must see the hurt creeping into my expression, because she adds, "I knew you would push yourself too hard. And—after last time . . ." Last time I attempted that spell, it gave me a headache so bad I could barely stand. The spots didn't clear from my vision for days. What if I'd passed out there, and the spell hadn't worked? Would Raze have dragged my unconscious body through the ballroom? Isolde's voice softens. "I just . . . didn't want to risk it."

Maybe—*maybe*—she has a point. But I don't like being babysat.

"I can take care of myself," I mumble. Now she's the one wearing a hurt expression, and I can't blame her, because I know I'm brushing her off. I'm glad Isolde cares enough to worry about me. I just don't want to be seen as someone who always needs to be worried over. Isolde is filling the role she always has, watching out for me. It's my turn to return the favor.

Oh, is that why I won't tell her the truth? The thought is bitter and sarcastic, fed by my worst fears, but I keep my face blank. I've never been good at keeping secrets, and there are things I've been keeping from Isolde. She still doesn't know everything that happened in the Mortal's Keep; she doesn't know what I learned in the Unseelie Realm.

She doesn't know the truth about herself.

I know it's not fair of me to keep it from her. My sister is a changeling, and no amount of stalling will change that. I glance at her from the corner of my eye, all messy hair and stolen jewelry and sparkling eyes.

Our whole lives, we thought we knew the story of how our family came to be: how Isolde was born, snatched out of her cradle by faeries, and I was left in her place. How our mother traveled to their realm to bargain for her original daughter safely returned, and refused to give up the changeling double.

But we were wrong—not just about our origins, but about all changelings. I was a changeling from the moment I was born, a human baby with a spark of faerie life. Isolde was created by the faeries to trick our mother, a faerie-made body brought to life by the mortal soul I might have had. They never dreamed that a young exhausted mother would outsmart them, unleashing both of us on the Mortal Realm.

We're not pieces in a set, a mortal girl and her changeling reflection. Her magic is different, since it doesn't come from within, but she's just as much a changeling as I am.

I can't keep it from her forever. I know that. I'm just waiting for the right moment.

"It's done now," Olani says. "So where do we go from here?"

It feels hard to breathe in this room, but maybe that's just my imagination. I run a hand absently over the patches of magical rot on the wall, fingers tingling with the brush of the Unseelie Realm.

"Not so fast," Raze says. "You still haven't told us how you two ended up here."

Isolde sighs, tossing something into the air—a tiny dagger. The rest must have been taken from her before they were locked in here. "Olani, do you want to fill them in, or should I?"

Olani groans.

It only takes a few minutes for the two of them to fill us in on Olani's truth potion, the wagon they found, and the run-in with the guards. I should have protested more when Isolde suggested that if anything went wrong, we should weather the punishment and wait for a better opportunity. After what I saw in Leira's head—and the cage, the chains, the obvious threats—I don't think we're going to get a better opportunity.

"But you *did* find a wagon." Raze's optimism earns him an immediate, chilling scowl from Olani, which I appreciate. I don't think any of us want to hear it right now.

"Yes," Isolde confirms, smirking. "One we can't use—"

"Because we're locked in here now?" I finish for her, hoping that's where she was going.

Isolde shoots me a look, letting out a little snort. "Please. I could have that door open in two minutes."

"Because Leira's going to retaliate," Raze says, voice a little too tightly controlled. "She's figured out a way to subdue Egg, and . . . uh . . . she seemed pretty mad."

That's an understatement.

"Maybe we shouldn't give her the chance." Everyone turns to look at Olani, who shrugs. "What? We've tried being sneaky and cautious. I'm starting to think it might not be our strong suit."

She has a point. But if we're not escaping in an enchanted wagon at top speed, our memory fading from Leira's mind, what other options do we have?

The wall seems to crackle at my touch, and I jump back as if burned. Blood rushes in my ears, drowning out the rest of the world, until there's nothing left but me and the locked door in the back of my mind. Magic surges through me again, through my clenched fists, surrounding them with the shimmer of heat that comes before a fire.

I take a deep breath.

"I . . . have an idea." It's my voice, words forced out before I can stop to think about them, examine them, pick them apart. "Something we haven't tried. But it's . . . kind of a last resort." Everyone goes still, staring at me. I'm going to lose my nerve if I keep hesitating like this. "How opposed are you to traveling through the faerie realms?"

"Deeply," Isolde says immediately. "But I'm low on options." Her tone is mild, almost bored, but there's a look in her eyes I don't like. It feels as if she's trying to stare *through* me.

I look away, accidentally meeting Olani's eyes—and find the same expression there, the slow realization that something isn't adding up. "You mean travel through a portal?" she asks. "Can you even do that?"

I thought that we'd built trust together, that we'd gotten past our initial suspicion of each other's motives. I know we did. I also know that if there's anything carving cracks into that trust, it's my own fault for keeping secrets. And now my own fault that our chance to escape is dead before even being fully formed.

Raze isn't quite so jaded, but his arms fold over his chest. "I thought it was a fluke. No one can do magic like that."

I swallow hard, fingers twisting in my skirt. He's right—sort of. Mortals can't perform portal spells. Only faeries have the power to walk between the worlds at will. I was only able to do it because I bargained with one of them, tricked him into giving me control of the spell halfway through, and locked him away in my nightmares. I still have access to the faerie's magic, a constant stream that swirls around me now instead of pulling me under, but without his knowledge, I can never be sure I'm directing it in the right way. I'd be taking a wild guess—but I *have* done it before.

"Seelie?" Isolde sounds concerned. I know I look tense, possibly like I'm about to explode, and it's hard to tell if she's concerned for me or about me. The last time I lost control, I summoned an out-of-season thunderstorm that nearly blew half the city away.

"I don't know. It would be dangerous." I stand up, turning away from everyone, and start to pace. Even after getting this far, the pressure in my chest is no less, the thrumming in my head no quieter. I've kept this secret for so long out of the fear of what would happen when it was set loose. What if this changes everything?

What if I don't take the chance, and Leira changes everything anyway?

"Dangerous . . . how?" Raze asks tentatively.

I rub my hands together, twisting my fingers. The fire sparks and catches, and I don't put it out. Letting it hop from finger to finger gives me something to focus on, a sensation besides the building dread that shadows me.

"There's something else I haven't told you."

I swear, you could hear a faerie's footsteps in the silence that follows. No one so much as breathes. Oh, Fate, this is really happening. I'm going to do this.

"I thought I could handle it myself, but I saw something I don't think I was supposed to see in Leira's memories, and it's the reason I screwed up, but you can't get mad, because it might also be what saves us, and I just—I just want you all to know that I didn't mean for it to go this far." The words come out in one quick stream. I'm not even confident I'm breathing anymore.

I can do this. I can't *not* do this any longer.

"There's a faerie trapped in my head." It comes out in a

rush. "I mean, not physically. Magically. I'm not exactly sure how it works."

A long silence follows that announcement, prickly and brittle, like they're all afraid to be the one to break it.

"Okay," Raze says eventually. When I glance at him, his brows are all twisted up into a thoughtful knot. I wait for him to say more, but nothing follows.

I swallow hard. "It—it started on Revelnox. The faerie was trapped in the Mortal's Keep by the Wildline shapeshifters. When I picked up the compass, I absorbed the fragment of his power they put inside it to guide us to the treasure. It seemed like just a spell—like it was just nightmares, and—and I didn't really think about it after that, with everything else going on." By everything else, we all know that I mean weeks of frantic travel running for our lives, teaching myself how to control my magic, slowly learning to trust each other. "But I—I saw him in my dreams. I heard this voice in the back of my head, egging me on, and I—I just ignored it."

"That's all?" Olani says, never one to mince words. "That doesn't necessarily mean a faerie. Could be a weird curse—"

"No," I interrupt, pushing away from Isolde to start pacing again. "No. That's not all."

And then I tell them *everything*.

Well . . . almost everything.

I tell them about being drawn to the faerie, imprisoned in a statue in the Mortal's Keep, about freeing him with a bargain, how the deal trapped us both into being stuck with each other. How he made me see things that weren't there in an attempt to trick me into letting him control me until he could get his own body back. How I saw him, spoke to him, almost lost myself to him in the Unseelie Realm. How I bargained with him again, mingled our magic, and then banished him with an iron dagger cutting deep into my palm. That I stopped seeing him, stopped hearing his voice, that all that remains of him is the magic I can't seem to shut off. That even though I managed to banish Gossamer's voice, I'm not sure he's truly gone.

I don't tell them about the other faerie—Briar. The one I killed. The one that wore Isolde's face and spoke in her voice.

I don't tell them about the nightmares.

I don't tell them that even without Gossamer's voice in the back of my mind, I still feel destructive anger building in me every day.

When I finally wind down, fire still flickering on my fingertips, no one says a word. I stand there shaking, relieved and exhausted and terrified by the truth, ears ringing in the silence.

Raze is the first to meet my eyes. His hand is still on his dagger, flexing restlessly. "You were talking to yourself when we were in the Unseelie Realm," he says. He has that thoughtful look again, but his eyes are glassy with—hurt? "To him."

I nod, suddenly unable to speak. Some of my thoughts, directed at the faerie, slipped out when my defenses were down.

He shakes his head, voice coming out a little raw. "He almost killed you there. And I—" His voice breaks off. During my final stand against him and the Unseelie courtier that would have killed us both, Raze was unconscious, ensorcelled by faerie magic and unable to move. I don't hold it against him.

Isolde is not as hesitant to confront me. Her hand wraps around my scarred one, holding it up so she can see. "Why didn't you *tell me*?"

"I couldn't," I say, voice tight. It isn't exactly the truth, but it isn't a lie, either. I don't want to tell them I was too frightened, that I care what they think about me so much I'd rather risk dying than jeopardizing that.

Olani speaks through gritted teeth. "Maybe we could have helped you *avoid* bargaining with a faerie if we'd known. Just a thought."

Great. Now everyone is mad at me. Exactly like I knew they'd be.

"I'm fine," I force myself to say. "But . . . I made the portals with *his* help. I'm not sure I can do it alone, but I'm willing to try."

"Forget escaping!" Isolde cries, which seems a little dramatic. "Don't you think we should be worried about getting rid of it?"

"Sure! Let me go ask Leira if she has any advice." I feel bad for the sarcasm in my voice immediately, but we have less than an hour until midnight, when Leira plans to unveil Egg to everyone. If the world knows she has the firedrake, freeing him—and ourselves—is going to get much more complicated. I sigh, trying to rein in my tone. "Sorry. I just don't think staying here is going to help anyone."

"She's right," Olani says decisively. I must perk up a little too much, because she adds, "But I'm still not happy with you."

Raze takes a deep breath, trying to shake off his stunned expression. "We can't leave Egg with my aunt."

"Obviously." I look around the room at each of them. "We're going back for him first."

Silence follows that, each of us wondering who's going to make the first move. Then it's broken—by the slow creaking of the door.

"That's quite a story, changeling." Aris stands in the doorway, a miniature sun suspended in the air before her. "Is any of it true?"

The fire jumps back to life in my hands, and Isolde is somehow already standing in front of me, dagger drawn.

"Wait a minute, how long have you been listening?" Isolde asks.

"Long enough," Aris replies, smirking.

"Stay out of this," Olani says. "It's four to one, Aris. Do the math."

At that, Aris sighs. "That's not what I was told to do, though, was it? I was ordered to keep you out of trouble until midnight. And I don't really need to fight you. I can just tell Aunt Leira what you're up to . . . and everything you've been hiding from her."

"Aris," Raze says, his voice low enough that I can't tell if it's begging or threatening. "Don't. Please."

Her eyes move between us, coldly calculating. "Then lie to me," she says, leaning back. "Why don't you convince me that none of what I heard is worth repeating?"

I don't know what to tell her—she knows too much already. Then Raze takes a deep breath, and I know he's about to say something either totally brilliant, or horribly ill-advised.

Please let this one be good, I silently beg.

"We're going to take care of Seelie's problem," he says, standing up taller. Back straight, jaw squared, he radiates confidence and commands attention. "We're going to escape. And you're going to help us." I feel my own spine stiffen, my heart pounding faster. It's a gamble, but I trust Raze. He's known her since they were little.

Aris lets out a laugh that isn't a laugh, brittle and sharp. "Why would I do that?"

"Because then we'll be out of the manor, and we'll do everything in our power to make sure Leira forgets about all of this. Everything can go back to how it was." He pauses, tone softening. "That's what you want, isn't it?"

The silence that follows is so full and deep I can hear my own heartbeat. I can see her teeth grinding together as she thinks, her ever-moving gaze flicking back and forth between each of us. After a moment that feels like forever, Aris extinguishes her ball of light. "So, just to be clear," she says, in a voice dripping with derision, "your plan is to make Leira forget the firedrake ever existed, then take off into the night with the most valuable weapon in the Mortal Realm?"

"He's not a weapon!" I insist. I wouldn't call the thoughts whisking around my head a *plan*, necessarily—but I wouldn't call egg whites a meringue, either. Both still need a few ingredients, a little time to cook . . .

"But otherwise, yes." Raze offers her a sort of self-deprecating smile that should be at odds with his cool, reasonable tone, but only manages to magnify the effect. "And you'll never see us again."

Aris stares at us a second longer, then nods. "You have yourself a deal."

Is she . . . *agreeing* with Raze? Agreeing to help us? I can't understand why she would turn on Leira, if all she's ever wanted was . . .

Leira's approval. Leira's attention, on her and her dazzling magic, not distracted by a changeling and a family disappointment and the firedrake that overshadows all else. With us out of the picture, Aris will be the last enchanter of the Wild line. She may not be able to master shapeshifting magic, but she's powerful enough. Leira will take her back under her wing, and the two of them will live happily ever after.

The thought of someone who's caused Raze and countless others so much suffering living *happily ever after* makes me grind my teeth, but it's a thought I can live with if it gets us out of here in one piece.

Aris extends her hand to shake, but before Raze can accept, Olani pulls him back by the sleeve. "Not so fast." She digs around in her pockets before producing another bottle like the one with the sleeping potion. She uncorks it and forces it into Aris's hand in one smooth motion, indicating for her to drink with a slight raise of her chin. "Faerie-tongue potion. I want to hear that you're not planning to double-cross us."

I expect Aris to splash the potion in Olani's face, but in the time it takes to blink, she's already thrown back whatever drop is left in the nearly empty bottle. When she speaks, her voice is perfectly even.

"I want you gone more than I want Aunt Leira to have the firedrake. I'm not going to double-cross you. I'm going to help you escape." Our expressions must be suitably shocked, because after one more glance around the room, the grim slash that passes for a smile cuts across Aris's face. "You're going to need all the help you can get."

chapter six

ISOLDE

If we live through this, I'm going to kill my sister.

Okay, that might be a bit melodramatic, but I haven't had time to sit and feel my frustration yet, and it's fermenting into impatient fury. Seelie and I are the last to leave the room. Aris slips out first, Raze and Olani a few minutes later, all timed carefully, a few minutes apart, so no one notices a sudden crowd of suspicious adolescents wandering the manor. Which means, for a moment, it's only the two of us.

Just like it used to be. I miss it, in a strange way—Seelie and me on the road, traveling from city to city, with no one but each other to watch our backs. Bickering and learning how to live together in a small space and crying with homesickness together. Before all the secrets and the lies.

I understand why Seelie made the choices she did, I really do, but why did I have to be on the outside of it all? Some part of me knew she was keeping secrets, but it was hard to convince myself that the Seelie I knew would really keep something important from me. I guess she's grown up. We both have—still, why does it hurt so much more when *she* does it?

And in the moment, I didn't even feel mad. She spilled the truth like blood from a wound, and all I could think was what I must have done to make her feel like she had to keep all that hidden. How thoughtless I was to all the ways she struggled through our journey, because I was finally living out my daydreams of adventure.

"Seelie, we need to talk." My voice sounds scratchy.

She startles out of her thoughts and looks up at me, brow wrinkled. "You know I hate it when people say that."

I let out a pitiful, choked laugh. "I know."

"So? Let's talk." I wouldn't be able to tell that she was rattled, if not for the restless movement of her hands wiping on her skirt.

We stare at each other for a long time, eyes locked. The words are on the tip of my tongue, but it feels like my chest is bound too tight to draw the breath I need to speak them. How do I say that this morning with all of us laughing together might be our last? How do I allow myself to even think it?

Well, I have to start somewhere. We can't just stare at each other forever. I take a deep breath, release my nerves, and blurt, "Why don't you trust me?"

Seelie, who was already frozen, stiffens more, until she looks like a wooden doll. "Wh-What do you mean?" Fate, she's a terrible liar. How she managed to keep this secret so long is beyond me.

It's such an absurd question that just the thought of responding to it makes an irreverent grin hover on my mouth, even though this situation is *dead serious*.

Seelie sighs and slumps into the nearest chair, tucking into herself until she seems impossibly small. With her face buried in her arms, she mumbles, "Because I knew you'd be like this."

I lean forward in my own seat, resting my forearms on my knees. "'Like this'? Worried, you mean? Upset? Fate forbid, *helpful*?"

She glances up from her hiding place just long enough to give me a heavy scowl. "You can't protect me from everything, Isolde. Besides, it's not like you noticed anything was wrong. Not like you *asked*."

"Right, I should have thought to *ask* if you'd been possessed by an evil faerie. And you would have told the truth, obviously. Because you've been so open and honest lately."

Her fingers fist tight in her sleeve, pulling the fabric into a sunburst of wrinkles. "I've been *busy*."

Busy. Of course. Busy taking care of Egg. Busy meeting with Leira Wildfall, following commands even while stewing in silent rage like a gathering storm. Busy shutting all of us out and disappearing into herself. Must take a lot of effort.

But I don't say any of that, because this isn't the important part and I can't get stuck on it. Instead, I stand so quickly that I'm already pacing by the time I realize I'm on my feet, raking a hand through my hair. It's getting too long, falling in front of my eyes. I should cut it again. I should try to explain myself as best as I can, and not just skip straight to—

"Are you sure about this?" I ask, vaulting forward.

Seelie studies me for a second, trying to piece together how I glossed over the parts of the conversation she probably considers to be vital. Finally, she says, "The portals thing?"

"Yes," I say after an awkward pause. "The portals thing." My stomach tightens, flooding me with sickening fear. I've been in the Seelie Realm once before, and it didn't go particularly well. In fact, it went so terribly that just the *thought* of that place makes my skin crawl with the memory of black fur poking out from my pores, the liquid feeling of my bones shrinking, the too-quick pace of a fox's heartbeat in my chest.

I have no one to blame for that particular curse but myself. From the first moment I woke up in the faerie forest after Seelie crashed our wagon into it, my head was foggy with ensorcellment. I was in a strange gauzy gown, surrounded by smiling inhuman faces—and then I saw her. Olani, her smile brilliant in the twilight, glaringly human and impossible to miss. I couldn't remember why we were there, or why it mattered, but I knew I had to get to her.

She was already in the hunting party, all securing their gear and mounting their terrifying horses. I said something to her, feeling like I was forgetting something important. She threw her head back and laughed, turning to the shifting excitement of the hunt about to begin, like I was nothing to her. Like she didn't even remember me. Her glittering eyes scanned the forest ahead for whatever quarry they were after, and I—a fool, though I guess I do have the excuse of faerie magic clouding my head—said, in the presence of *multiple faeries*, that I wished she would pay attention to me instead.

The memory is just as embarrassing as it is terrifying. I was a fox before I knew what was happening, and the whole party of faeries was after me, with Olani in the lead. If it hadn't been for Seelie and Raze accidentally stumbling across our path, I would have *died* there. I can't go back. In a world where every single word is weighted, where each move has to be as carefully placed as game pieces on a board, I'm not smart enough to survive.

Not that Seelie has fared much better when it comes faeries. Is there something about our family that just attracts danger and bad decisions? I have to fight to quiet the voice that asks what else she's hiding from me, if I really know her at all, and how she could keep something like that secret so long.

Seelie is looking past me now, staring at the patterns of seeping Unseelie rot in the wallpaper. "I don't think we have another choice, Isolde."

"Not if we're taking the firedrake with us, no."

That makes her look at me all too quickly. She examines my face like a puzzle in that way of hers that reminds me why people might find her unnerving. I swallow back guilt at the thought—just because I know she means well doesn't mean I have to enjoy her piercing gaze going straight *through* me, like an arrow to the heart. After a long time, she seems to make a decision and stands up.

I chew on my cheek, waiting for her to say something. I don't have much time. I don't have many chances. I don't have the space I need to come up with a better plan than this.

"What are you so scared of?"

I blink. "What?"

Seelie takes a step closer, and the whole room seems to vibrate. *Magic.* I don't know what she's doing, but I'm familiar by now with the pull of magical energy in my sister's hands. "Is it Leira? Did she threaten you? Is it the faeries? Traveling through a portal?"

"No!" I lie quickly. "Nothing. I just thought . . ."

She breathes deeply, hands flicking in the air. A small, steady flame jumps to life. "I won't let them hurt you."

"Good." I can't keep the sarcasm from my voice. I hate being talked to like this, like I'm something delicate that needs to be protected. After all those years of standing between her and danger, it makes me feel so small and unimportant to have the roles reversed. "Since obviously, I couldn't be scared that we're *all* walking into something too big for us to handle."

"I won't let anyone hurt you," she repeats. "But we can't just give up now. That would be letting her win. If we leave Egg behind, things will only get worse for him. And if she figures out how to *control* him somehow—" Her voice breaks a little, and she shakes her head as if to clear away the unthinkable. "But if we keep him safe, if we wait for the right time . . . we could take her down." Seelie is getting more energetic and animated, pacing and tossing the flame in her hand like a ball.

"Take her down?" I echo cynically.

She stops and turns in place, facing me with bright eyes. *Really* bright eyes for someone who's barely eating or sleeping, burning through magic like cheap candles, and burdening herself with the safety of so many. "Don't you see? It's not enough to just *get away*. We need to stop her. Remove her from power. Make it so she can't control us or anyone else, ever again."

"Okay, I love the energy, but Seelie, that's *impossible*. Someone will get hurt."

"That sounds like a fair exchange."

"Are you serious? Is all that magic rotting your mind? You sound like . . ."

"Like what?"

"Are you thinking like a faerie, or thinking like a human?"

I wish I could take the words back as soon as I say them. Our entire childhoods, Seelie tried to hide what she truly was—and when the truth finally came out, it went exactly as poorly as we all dreaded. She never wanted magic, or to be different. She only wanted to be . . . like me.

But she doesn't burst into tears this time. Instead, she studies me, her mouth twitching with repressed anger, her eyes impossibly brighter. Just when I think she's about to storm off without replying, she says, "I'm *exactly* as human as you are."

This time I'm the one who flinches, searching her expression for a deeper meaning. I know she hasn't always accepted herself, but it's not like her to outright deny what she is. Unless . . . that's not what she meant.

What else could she mean?

Before I get the chance to ask, she actually does storm off, flinging the door wide with a gust of wind so strong that it slams into the wall. I'm left standing in our room alone, with my arms wrapped around myself and a dread I can't explain seeping into my bones.

chapter seven

SEELIE

I should turn around and explain myself. Or apologize. Lie, and say I didn't mean what I said. The anger that made me lash out at Isolde cools quickly, leaving nothing but stomach-churning terror in its place. I keep moving at the same quick pace, long strides that make the hallway seem like it's fading away at the corners of my vision.

I should turn around, but I don't.

I'm almost running now, the same reaction strong emotions have always triggered in me: *Run away! Put as much distance between yourself and the threat as possible!*

But what if the threat is something I take with me? Was Isolde only questioning my nature because she's annoyed with me, or because she could somehow sense the ways Gossamer's faerie influence has changed me?

It's not Isolde I'm running from. It's myself. My surroundings seem to fade as I slip unnoticed through the party. I keep my head down and keep moving and don't stop until I'm hidden behind the curtain, listening to Egg's half-hearted escape attempts.

I've calmed enough to start composing the apology I'm going to give Isolde the second all this is over, and debating whether to just try shoving the whole cage through the portal, when the raven swoops in through the open door. The bird lands at my feet, feathers ruffled by the wind, and taps my shoe insistently with his beak.

"Yes, I see you," I whisper to Raze, kicking him gently aside. If only there was enough time to backtrack and talk to Isolde before our escape attempt. If only I could explain the concept of *stealth* to the panicking dragon. If only absolutely everything wasn't going wrong tonight. "You're not supposed to be here," I add, looking down at the bird so I can properly scold him.

Unfortunately, it's next to impossible to make Raze feel shame, in any form. He already knew we were supposed to split up so that we wouldn't draw attention to ourselves, and he flew here to me anyway. The raven regards me with a cheeky little head tilt, feathers fluffing out as if to indicate that there's no one around to see us. Then he hops forward and taps my toe again.

I sigh, dipping down to let the bird hop on to my hand. "*What?*"

His form blurs in midair, transforming into streaks of color that shift again, this time resolving into Raze's familiar human shape. He manages to shapeshift so smoothly that when his boots hit the ground, his hand is still perched on mine, as if we're about to join a dance.

"Sorry," he says. "I just . . . I thought you wouldn't want to be alone. And I wanted to let you know I'm not mad at you. About . . . everything."

That prompts a choked half laugh, half sob. I don't know what I expected him to say, but it wasn't that. Now is absolutely not the time for heartfelt speeches, for forgiveness, for him to be worrying about my fragile feelings. Still, something loosens in my chest, making the world around me feel clearer. Less crowded by my guilt and worry. I let my grip ease, but his hands don't drop as quickly as I thought they would. "Are you sure?"

"I'm sure." He takes a deep breath, motioning for me to do the same. "You got dealt a bad hand, Iselia. We all did. You should stop taking it so personally." When I wince, he quickly adds, "I mean—stop thinking it makes you a bad person. Should you stop bottling everything up until it eats away at you like some sort of horrible potion? Probably. Is it *more* frustrating to those of us who care about you that you don't trust us enough to tell us when something's wrong? Absolutely. But I'm not worried that this evil faerie-statue-whatever is going to change anything about you. I know, because *I* tried to change you, and you burned my eyebrows off. We have you, a firedrake, and a solid plan. He doesn't stand a chance."

I latch on to what is definitely not the point of that statement, but I can't help myself. "You care about me?"

Raze rolls his eyes, then tilts my chin up gently. "Yes, Iselia. I care about you, and water is wet, and the sky is blue. And the worst part is that you deserve it, so the sooner you get that through your head, the better."

I meet his eyes, breath caught in my chest, but I don't move away. Even though it's the briefest of touches, it sets me completely off-balance. Off-balance, and yet, strangely . . . much calmer. I feel like myself again, and it's wonderful and terrible at the same time.

I give him a mock glare. "I liked it better when you were insulting me." When we first met, we hated each other, and that blossomed into a beautiful, barbed friendship full of teasing and mild antagonism. That's the dynamic that I know how to maneuver with Raze. If he starts complimenting me all of a sudden, I might just melt into a puddle.

"I can do that," Raze says. "But if compliments and insults have the opposite effect on you, it would be incredibly inefficient for me to keep calling you stubborn and difficult, when telling you how pretty your smile is would get you much more worked up."

"I can't stand you," I tell him.

Raze's smile returns, crooked and confident. "I know."

I swallow hard and step back, watching his hand drop to his side. But his eyes—a soft blue, like the sky right before it starts to rain—never leave me.

I'm not totally naive—I *know* that Raze is flirting with me. But it's *Raze.* I'm pretty sure I saw him flirt with a potted plant once. It doesn't mean anything.

My heart jumps into my throat anyway, speeding up traitorously. *Does it?*

"But . . . thanks anyway," I manage to say.

He pauses, seems like he's holding his breath for a moment, and then all the tension leaves his frame. His smile looks a bit embarrassed. "Seelie . . . it's okay. I'll really stop if that's what you want." He shifts back ever so slightly, but it makes all the difference. The air around me feels cooler. I can breathe again.

"Thanks," I repeat, looking down. I glance up through my lashes and try to inject my tone with lightness, to make it feel like we're still joking. "I won't hesitate to zap you again if I have to, you know. You should be careful about getting on my bad side."

Raze clutches his chest, and I can't tell if it's a playful wounded gesture or if he's grabbing for the spot where my magic scarred him—when we fought in earnest, and I called lightning down on him. Maybe both. "If you do, I'm sure I'd deserve it."

I just shrug, crossing my arms as we fall into a comfortable silence. That's what this is. Comfortable. I don't want anything about our irreverent push and pull of teasing, running over a current of true support and friendship, to change.

"I got the key." Aris joins us breathlessly, and I don't know if she successfully snuck up on us or if I was just very distracted. She pauses, holding up the beautifully wrought golden key, as her eyes pass between us. Raze and I shift subtly apart under her scrutiny, both suddenly realizing how close we were standing, which doesn't do anything to ease her glare. "Well? Am I interrupting something? What are we waiting for?"

There's a fireworks show scheduled to start just before midnight, a grand finale to this year and dramatic entrance for the next one. We agreed it would be our signal for me to start the portal, and for everyone else to make their way over to me. It also has the added bonus of being a nice distraction from all the light and sound my spell is certain to cause, hopefully buying us a few seconds to get away. Anticipation drives my pulse, a loud thrum in my ears. I don't know how much time has passed, but it must be close to midnight.

Wordlessly, I take the key from her. I don't ask how she got it. Leira trusts her, maybe even enough to hand it over without the need for pickpocketing. At least—she *trusted* her. The future of that trust depends on how well this next part goes.

"I grabbed this, too." There's a light clinking sound as Aris pulls out a length of silvery chain that I've grown all too familiar with in the past few hours. I certainly won't be using it, but I don't trust her to keep it, either, so I silently take the chain and tuck it into my hidden pocket.

Egg goes wild the second I duck through the curtain, and I shush him gently. He's too worked up for us to risk letting anyone else try to open his cage and get maimed in the process, but he lets me approach with barely more than a tremble of excitement. The key slips into the lock, the cage clicks open, and I reach in and grab the dragon before he can make a run for it. He thrashes in excitement, nipping me lightly a few times in the process, until I manage to hold him still and run a calming hand over his scales.

After a few moments, he's calm enough that I can hand him over to Raze, who holds him tight, like a human infant he's afraid of dropping. Not for the first time, I wonder if the dragon somehow remembers the careful way Raze carried his egg out of the Mortal's Keep, wrapped close to his heartbeat for safekeeping. Aris's bright eyes follow Egg, a slight bob to her head the only indication that she's feeling just as nervous about this as I am.

Midnight must be near. The music has stopped, and the crowd's anticipation fills the room with a low murmur. How long do we have left? A minute? Less?

I reach down, pushing through layers of skirts to the worn old boots I wore for comfort and practicality. With practiced ease, my fingers find the dagger hidden there—a small blade of pure iron—and I ignore the prickle of pain as it brushes my skin. The same blade Raze gave me in the Unseelie forest. The same one that gave me the scar on my right hand. The same one I used to banish Gossamer from my mind. Its familiar weight is strangely comforting. Hopefully, I won't need it—but if I do, I'll be ready.

In the last moments before the fireworks start, my eyes sweep the room one last time. Since most of the partygoers are taller than us, it's nearly impossible to pick out Isolde in the crowd, but I see Olani carefully making her way around the edge of the room. I'm sure my sister can't be far behind.

I take a deep breath, squeezing both hands into tight fists.

Then I let it out in a long, controlled burst that mingles with the wisps of winter wind that have managed to seep through the door. The noise of the party blurs into one sound, something distant and unfamiliar. I swallow hard, ignoring the furious thrash of my heartbeat.

What I didn't tell the others is that I'm not quite sure how to get Gossamer's help with this spell. He crept into the background of my mind that night in the Unseelie forest, but I know he's still in there somewhere, that he's been waiting for me to slip up and give him any amount of power. I wait for his voice—slick and treacherous and ice-cold—but there's only silence.

I thought it would be like fishing, my line cast in one of the faerie realms, wrestling with something fighting to escape into the current. Instead, I feel like I've swung my line back too far and accidentally embedded the hook in my own skin. There's a pull, but it's within myself, and it's so fast and deep I'm scared I might drown in it. I focus on the spots of candlelight flickering wildly in response to my magic, struggling for breath as the wind kicks up higher and higher.

I won't let go. I won't stop pulling. I don't know what will happen to us if I do—if he'll be free, if he'll overpower me once more. I'm still holding the dagger like a lifeline, a reminder that I've beaten him once before.

I close my eyes to concentrate on the spell. *Come on,* I think, reaching along that taut fishing line. *I*— The thought fractures like a mirror, reflecting moments I'd rather forget back at me, then forms into a different word.

We need this.

chapter eight

ISOLDE

Wildline Manor's ballroom is full of light and warm enough to forget that it isn't a summer evening. Candlelight flickers in the gold prisms of the chandeliers, illuminating a room decked out in hothouse flowers and packed with people I don't know. With only a few minutes left until midnight, and the anticipation of Leira's big announcement, the room is buzzing with excitement. I just have to hope that our quickly improvised new plan will bring us all back together in time. At least alone, I can slip through the party unnoticed, keeping my eyes and ears alert for danger as I take shelter in the busiest part of the crowd.

It's easier to sneak into the ball than it is to bite my tongue and hold in that I absolutely *hate* this plan. Because being mad at Seelie doesn't make her any less right—we can't stay here. If I had a better idea, I'd suggest it.

I *know* my sister. I may not know all her secrets, but I know who she is. Everyone makes mistakes. Not mistakes that challenge all the known laws of magic and unleash malicious ancient powers, but you know, no one's perfect.

My eyes squeeze shut and I breathe in, trying to reanchor myself in the current moment. The sound of the crowd, mournful midwinter songs plucked out on strings, the scent of evergreen and warm wax. Letting the breath go, I open my eyes again, and the world shifts back into focus. Searching the crowd of strangers around me, I can't pick out Seelie or the others, but that's probably a good thing, since we're trying to remain incognito. In the corner, behind the musicians, I see the velvet curtain that will soon be the center of attention.

All I have to do is be patient. Stay focused, keep my eyes open, call out a warning if something goes wrong or Leira seems to catch on to us. The lookout role feels like a formality at this point. I'm too proud to admit there's nothing for me to do but stand by and wait for someone else's turn to act.

My eyes catch Olani skirting the edges of the room, surreptitiously making her way to the curtain in the corner. At least, as surreptitious as someone her height can be. I force myself to look away so I don't draw anyone else's attention to her, but not before her eyes meet mine. Even though the look lasts less than a heartbeat, the grim determination in their dark depths seems to burn into my vision. I know she's equally frustrated with me and with Seelie, for entirely different reasons, and yet she's still helping us. Maybe, after all this is over, I'll be able to figure out why.

Scanning the room, searching for anything else to look at, I find my gaze drawn once again. This time to Leira Wildfall, who is closer than I realized. I'd be disturbed that she somehow managed to sneak up on me if her back wasn't turned, her hands gesturing as she speaks to someone. This isn't her graceful, speech-making voice, the one that silences a room. It's casual and friendly, sympathetic without being overly sweet. "I can't imagine what you've been through," she's saying, her brow wrinkled in profile as she turns to the person she's addressing.

Everything seems to stop. My mind refuses to process the information right there in front of me, viewing the scene as if it's happening to someone else. Because I *know* the person she's addressing.

Don't I?

Perhaps we already slipped into the faerie realm, and this is all another elaborate glamour, because it makes absolutely no sense for my *mother* to be standing there at Leira's side like she owns the place. It looks strange, her simple clothes so dull they become impossible not to look at against such a rich backdrop, like a moth trapped indoors.

She looks somehow both older and younger than I remember. Years have passed, but the last time we were together, I was a child. I saw both my parents as ancient things, and I'm old enough now to see past that permanence to what she really is: a woman in her late thirties, with light brown skin and dark brown hair and a face starting to bear the faintest trace of worry lines.

And then Papa appears behind her. His black curls are messy, and he's grown out a beard that now has streaks of gray. He reaches out to set a calming hand on her shoulder, which she shakes off, striding forward. I remember their memories of us trapped in a bottle, the shattered glass. They might not even remember us. They probably don't know why they're here.

The air feels so warm and thick it's hard to breathe. This is no faerie glamour—it's really them.

They're here.

"Thank you for the invitation," Mami says.

Leira graces her with a warm smile, the picture of sympathy. "Of course. I can't imagine what you've been through, missing your daughters all this time. When I heard your story, a couple traveling from town to town, asking if anyone had seen a human girl traveling with her changeling counterpart—well, I just had to do something."

Mami's eyes shine with tears, but she keeps her head held high. "The past several years have been . . . difficult."

Papa speaks next, his soft voice nearly a whisper. "We thought we'd dreamed them."

Something hot streaks down my face. Oh. I'm crying. The observation feels like it belongs to someone else. It's like I'm overflowing with every possible emotion, and this is the only way to get any of them out. Part of me urges me toward them, and the rest of me shrinks back like an animal in a trap.

Because that's exactly what this is. A trap. Leira Wildfall, not satisfied with her manipulation of us, raising the stakes by bringing our parents into this game of hers. I've been staring too long. Mami's head turns, thick waves of unbound hair framing her face as her eyes meet mine.

And widen in recognition.

Curses.

For a second, when our eyes lock, I'm almost overcome by the impulse to run to her. To forget all the scheming and the consequences and the past three horrible years and throw myself into her arms. To cry like a child and be comforted like a child. But I'm not a child, and even I am not impulsive enough to abandon the plan and doom us all.

Before Mami can call out to me, reach for me, I turn away, viciously wiping my eyes. I don't have time for a tearful reunion right now. I need to find Seelie, to warn her that there's been a new twist in the plan. I don't know what Leira will do to our parents if we escape without them, and I don't want to find out.

I push my way through the crowd, sniffling pathetically as I try to force myself to pull it together. I didn't expect to see my parents again, much less *now*, much less *here*. There's only so much a person can handle in one night.

chapter nine

seelie

Magic rushes through me, puddling around me—lightning flashing along my skin, a feverish warmth pulsing beneath, long streamers of light struggling to thread between the worlds. I feel all of it and none of it. I can't think clearly. I don't think this is working. I'm trying to pull free something that's truly and completely stuck, and all I'm accomplishing is exhausting myself, burning my lungs.

The wind howls. Isolde is almost close enough to touch by the time I spot her pushing her way through the crowd toward me. She's mouthing something, indistinct words as difficult to read as the glossy look in her eyes. I can't afford the distraction of wondering what Isolde is trying to tell me. She's close enough; I'm sure she'll make it.

Even though it feels like I'm reaching for something impossible to grasp, I can't give up on this spell halfway. I can't do anything with Gossamer halfway. It's always all or nothing.

With another push, I force myself back into the enchantment. Quieting my mind until the rest of the world slips away, until even the colors behind my eyelids fade. Until there's nothing left but me and my magic.

Well, that didn't take long.

Gossamer sounds different—quieter? Weaker? Like he's been shoved to the floor, and is just now managing to lift his head.

"We need to finish this," I say out loud. It's easier this way, even with my voice low and scratchy. I'm vaguely aware of Isolde trying to get my attention, held back by the biting, beating wind. I can't risk letting my focus slip now, not when Gossamer is so close. I force myself to look away from her, to block out her voice, as I close my eyes and start to weave the enchantment. A knot of magic, tying this world to another.

Images flash through my mind. There's a tiny blue flame in my chest, but it burns cold instead of hot. It's the only light source in a completely dark room, but there's nothing here for it to illuminate. Just the frail blue light, and the soft, night-scented dark. And then it flares into a white-hot inferno of anger, stealing the air from my lungs. I know this feeling. I've felt it every night in my dreams—

Except they weren't *my* dreams, were they?

Dread melts into a heavy puddle in the pit of my stomach. He's stronger than I thought. He's been waiting for this. I can't breathe. I grip the iron dagger, hands shaking as I hold it gently to my palm. Its cool metal stings my skin, and reminds me of what I can do. "Don't . . . try . . . anything."

My arm jerks against my will, flinging the dagger carelessly to the side. *Not so fast.*

Raze dodges, but Olani is already stepping in front of him. A swipe of her staff, and the dagger smacks against the glossy floor.

That catches someone's attention, which then draws their eyes to my half-formed portal and me, twitching in place. They scream. More people look. The crowd goes from mildly amused to terrified in an instant, with a horrible crash of sound as they all start moving at once.

This was a mistake. There are too many people, too many ways someone could get hurt. If I'm going to use magic, I need to be controlled. There's no coordinated direction in the guests' movement, which leads to a mad scramble where no one makes much progress at all. But it doesn't matter—it's too late to stop. At that exact second, all the candles in the room flare at once—the sign that it's five minutes until midnight.

"What are you doing?" Aris's piercing voice carries, but even she can't keep the panicked note out of it.

"That . . . wasn't me!" I have just enough time to watch their eyes go wide before my head snaps back around to the half-formed portal. My foot lifts with staccato movement, like a clumsy puppet, and I take one step forward.

Let's try this again, shall we? Just you and me.

I concentrate all my willpower on dropping to the floor and land hard on my knees. I know what it feels like for Gossamer to twist the portal spell. He did it once before, shifting its destination to the Unseelie Realm. But Gossamer is an outlaw there, in the realm that he once called home. He doesn't intend to go back and get captured any more than I do. This time, he isn't messing with the spell. He's messing with *me*. Trying to shove me through the portal alone, without the interference of my sister or friends.

You don't need them, Seelie. I can keep you safe. I can give you everything you want.

The fact that he can say that—that, at least to him, it's not a lie—sends an unwelcome chill down my spine. It feels so long ago that Gossamer told me his plans, what he needed, how we were going to work together so that we could both be free of each other. But it turned out that *working together* meant betraying me and trying to kill me at the first opportunity, so any chance to do this cooperatively is already shot. I don't care what he means, and I don't care about his truths and his lies and his riddles.

Still kneeling, I hold up my hands, struggling to think past Gossamer's voice. I close my eyes, fight the pressurized lump in my throat, and try to call for help. To reach out for the firedrake's magic. Anything, to slow the pull threatening to strand me alone in a faerie realm with the voice in my head and my own worst impulses.

Stop that, Gossamer snaps, trying to force my arms down. I fight the movement, which throws us both off-balance, and we end up face down in a heap.

"Seelie!" Raze calls, but he sounds impossibly far away.

My cheek sticks to the unforgiving ballroom floor, throbbing with a bruise I can already feel forming. I fight to breathe, to calm myself, to regain control. As Gossamer and I clash, we twist against the polished stone, a frenzy of unnatural movement.

Isolde calls my name again, and for a moment, I free myself enough to look up at her. Finally, two clear words push through the confusion: "*They're here.*" She's waving and pointing to something behind her. I knew that Leira would be onto us by now, but luckily, the chaos of the crowd is keeping her from getting to me. Who else could Isolde be talking about?

And then my eyes land on a familiar sight.

For a second, I think I'm seeing things, that my parents are only appearing there because of wishful thinking. But no matter how much I've missed my family, never in my wildest dreams would I have wanted them to be right here, right now. Never could I have summoned their faces so vividly, more detailed and real than any imagining: the lines carved between Papa's dark brows, the reddened cuticles of Mami's short nails. Tiny details that make them real people, rather than characters in my tragic backstory.

They're here.

Why are they *here*? Is this some manipulation by Leira, or did they somehow find us? I thought I'd lost them forever when their captured memories of me and Isolde crumbled to dust. But maybe the memories weren't destroyed, but returned. And maybe they . . .

My body moves without my permission, taking advantage of my distraction to push me back up off the floor. It doesn't matter why my parents are here—at least, it won't, if Gossamer takes control. Now I have to worry about protecting *them*, on top of everything else.

"Give her the knife back," Raze suggests, trying to reach me.

Olani stands in his path. "Too dangerous. She's got to fight it out."

Fight it out. Fight it out.

The candles flare again, and it's midnight. The exact minute that all the worlds shift against each other into a new position. Fireworks boom, sparkling above us. The floor shakes, making another ripple of panic and high-pitched screams run through the crowd.

Okay, usually the world-shifting thing isn't that literal, but I can't question it now. Magic is still humming through me like a flood, and I seize it. This doesn't have to be precise. I stand, posture crooked, arms held up awkwardly. I focus on the magic unraveling all around me, grasping at it with a panic like drowning. I just need something to hold on to, anything, anything to keep us all together in this realm and the next.

My own voice interrupts me. "*Seelie, NO!*" It's more of a howl than words, raw and drawn-out. I hear a gasp I recognize as Isolde's. She's frightened. I'm frightening them.

"*Gossamer*," I say, despite the burning in my throat and the vice grip around my windpipe. "Get out of my head."

And I shove.

I shove with everything—my hands, my mind, my magic, all the magic of the portal and the Seelie Realm and Gossamer himself that I've gathered around me. I shove until I feel something drop, like bonds loosening around me. The line I've been pulling on snaps suddenly in the opposite direction, exploding in a wave of light and magic. It feels like breaking the surface after too long underwater, choking and gasping for air all at once.

The roar continues around me. This isn't over yet.

There's a lightness in my limbs that it takes a moment to place as the lack of Gossamer's presence. Not just squeezed into a pressurized ball of rage, but actually, truly gone. Tears stream down my face, and I'm not sure if it's the relief, or the fact that I'm still staring into the blazing portal, which shows no sign of shrinking.

If anything, it seems like it's getting . . . bigger. Wilder. Its constant swirl is more frenzied and uneven, reaching across the room in fits and bursts.

"What's happening?" I shout.

"You're asking *me*?" Aris yells back, which is the moment the gnawing worry that I've made a huge mistake expands into full-blown terror.

I can still feel threads of magic stretching between us, a pull that goes both ways. It should be closing by now. Why isn't it closing?

And what happens if it gets worse?

The Unseelie Realm has already consumed Leira's study, twisted it into something *else*. I was taught that the difference between the mortal and faerie worlds is that magic flows freely through theirs, while it has to be drawn into ours. What happens when the dam breaks? When those lines are crossed, or worse, exploded by my own carelessness?

I stop caring about doing this right, and start reaching for frantic solutions. My magic has always had a mind of its own, and now that it's been all twisted up with Gossamer's, it's even more unruly. It writhes in the air, wrapping around everything, twisting and knotting the portal like a net. If I can pull it all together, I might be able to stop it from getting any worse.

I strain, with a feral groan of effort, but I'm not strong enough. Light sears my eyes, dancing in colorful sparks over my vision. "*Help me!*" I cry, not sure who I'm talking to.

Then there's a hand in mine. I think it's Isolde's, at first, until the rough fabric wrapped around it scratches my palm. Aris's voice sounds in my ear, more animated than I've ever heard her before. "Tell me what to do."

"Just . . . tie it down." I can't look away from the portal, but I see her other hand rise to join mine, fingers outstretched. A ball of light forms in the air, then crushes around the portal like a cage. Together, we both squeeze, forcing our magic into an unfamiliar shape. Forcing it smaller and smaller, despite the fiery flickering and tiny explosions that roll from its surface.

The portal pushes back with one last burst, flooding the room with light. The warm, green smell of the Unseelie Realm fills the air, the taste of magic on the back of my tongue.

Then the ground shakes again, a terrible rumble like the house is trying to uproot itself and walk away, and the room explodes into dazzling white light that moves like a physical thing, a wave splashing itself up walls and wrapping around people like a predator taking down prey. It's swift and hungry, and it's going to overwhelm the entire ballroom.

I squeeze my eyes shut, but nothing happens. It doesn't slam into my face or burn my skin from my bones. When I finally dare to peek, I see why:

Because Olani has thrown herself over us—Egg and me, Isolde, Raze, even Aris—her shielding spell held high. It's a unique variation of healing magic—turning magic's harm out from oneself. And even though I know she's barely strong enough to cast a spell like this once a month, she's holding it over all of us. I watch the light twist and roll over the surface of the shield, like watching a fire from below. The shield flickers, shrinks, but she holds it steady. Her face is twisted with the effort.

She can't hold it much longer. The shield shrinks again, forcing us all closer to each other. This is my fault. All my fault. The portal was unstable, and I tried to hide it instead of getting help. Aris's light could only hold it for so long, and now it's exploding into the Mortal Realm, an unstoppable blast of chaos.

Egg looks up, light dancing in his wide pupils. A crack carves through the shield, and Olani grunts with effort—or with pain at overexerting herself. He jumps up, ears perking and then flattening, like they do before he breathes flame. But he's never done that for any enchanter except for me. I don't even know if it'll work for anyone besides me.

The dragon inhales deeply, and then his jaw opens to expose all his pointed little teeth, and fire jets out. More than the measured amount he gave me this morning, more than I've ever seen. Pure magical energy sears the air and slams into the shield, splashing along its arc. Egg's magic closes the cracks, strengthens the spell, gives Olani enough support to let out a heavy breath.

All this only takes a few seconds, though it feels like ages. Finally, the explosion disperses, and the shield drops with it. Egg's fire fades, and we all blink dazzled eyes.

When the spots clear, it's to the sight of a dark, lifeless, utterly transformed room.

PART TWO

Gossamer wakes from an impossible sleep to a world of exploding starlight.

As yet another prison unravels, his chest expands in a deep, shuddering breath. A tidal wave of magic bursts around him, plunging him under its current. Tangled in the threads of an unfinished portal, he strains to break free.

That magic. That scent.

The dusty warmth of the Mortal Realm, the syrupy sweetness of the Seelie Realm, a bite of the Unseelie Realm's chilled wind, all drowning him at once. But more than that, the magic here floods his senses with something else:

The changeling.

This is her doing, though he's not sure how. After the burst dam fades to a trickle, then a puddle, he finds that he can stand. The world around him feels strange, like the moment of passing through a portal. Except it doesn't pass.

He breathes again, deeper this time. The tangled threads of dozens of portal spells around him prickle at his skin. The feeling is uncomfortable, but how refreshing it is to feel anything at all. There's a chill in the air, the world around him frozen in more ways than one.

Gossamer stands slowly, taking stock of himself. When he stretches his hands in front of himself, he can see them—his own hands, long-fingered and pale, knuckles blushed rosy and nails coming to sharp points. After so long as a shadow, an idea, a wraith trapped in a statue, it's a novelty for him to be anything at all. He's real enough to push silk-fine hair from his face, but he is still missing something vital. Breathing in the icicle-sharp air, Gossamer tilts his head back and lets himself feel.

Something has changed, but what?

The flutter of excitement in his chest is unfamiliar and unpleasant. He is polished and cool, always one step ahead. He does not hope. *But the thing won't die down, and its thrill spreads through him. Somewhere in the Mortal Realm, just under his nose all these months, there is a portal to the Unseelie Realm. It should never have been left open, but closing it was beyond the changeling's power.*

It's so brilliant in its simplicity that he doesn't know how he didn't think of it sooner. Opening another portal to the Seelie Realm caused a rush of magic into the mortal world, which collided with the leaking remnants of Unseelie magic. Like high and low air pressure meeting in a spectacular burst of thunder. Like lightning splitting an ancient oak down its core, it's pulled him free from the changeling's mind.

Here, he feels as real and solid as he once was, and yet trapped as surely as all those centuries in the Mortal's Keep. Still, this is no mere prison.

Gossamer stands in all the realms at once, and none of them. This is something new. This is everything he's ever wanted. The only thing that stands in his way now is one mere mortal girl.

chapter ten

ISOLDE

I can hear my own heartbeat, racing as it pounds against the confines of my chest. My mind races even faster, trying to make sense of my surroundings.

We're not in the Seelie Realm, and yet somehow, this is worse. The golden candlelight is gone, but the ballroom remains. A faint gray light seems to come from everywhere and nowhere, dawn and twilight holding their breaths at once. In its shadows, the silhouettes of all the party guests, Leira, *our parents*, stand perfectly still, as if they've been turned into statues. They look like stone or ice, color leached from skin and clothes to paint everything in the same cold blue-gray.

For a second, I'm afraid that we're all frozen in the same state, but then Seelie lets out a ragged gasp. I turn to see her, Olani, Raze, Aris, and Egg, all looking around the room with wide eyes.

I've been through portals before, but never like this. All those times, I felt like I was the one moving, walking through the other side to a different world. This time, it's like the worlds moved around us, like we're still standing in the same spot in Wildline Manor, but everything else has changed.

"Are they . . . ?" Raze starts, but trails off, seemingly unable to decide what to even ask.

Olani steps toward the nearest one, trying to disguise the wobble in her steps. Even with Egg's help, she just used a month's worth of magic in a moment. It's a miracle she hasn't passed out. Before I manage to get my arm around her to support her weight, she presses her fingers to the person's wrist.

"They're alive," she says, brow wrinkling slightly. "At least, they still have a living aura. But . . . there's no pulse."

Seelie makes another sound, somewhere between a gasp and a sob—it's hard to tell with her face buried in her hands like that. "This is all my fault," she mumbles into her palms.

"What are you talking about? Where are we?" Aris so rarely seems truly shaken, her icy mask slipping to reveal that she's still just a sixteen-year-old kid. She's the only one of us who's never set foot in a faerie realm, who doesn't know what they look like, and she's even more confused than I am. She looks so young with her eyes wide, fists gripped tight. "This isn't what we agreed to. Fix it, *now*!"

Seelie chokes on a bitter laugh. "You think I did this on *purpose*?"

"I think you could," Aris says. "What did you *do* to them? What kind of magic is this?"

"I don't know!" Seelie's voice rings in an echo around the room.

Someone laughs quietly, and we all look up at each other in the second it takes to realize it isn't one of us. We brought someone else here. I look at Olani, but she seems just as confused. I was certain we were the only ones shielded by her spell.

Movement catches my eye, and I find the source of the

soft chuckle. Someone picking themselves up off the floor, propped up on their hands with a shower of long white hair covering their face. No wonder I didn't realize they weren't frozen—their pale coloring blends right in with our gloomy surroundings. Their head lifts, and inhumanly colorless eyes meet mine. Even though I've only seen it once before, I know that face immediately.

Unlike the last time I saw him, as a translucent vision in the depths of Leira's study, he seems solid. Real. He looks almost like a young man, with features just a little too sharp, eyes just a little too predatory. He is pretty, though, in the same way a toxic flower is pretty. Like an invitation and a warning all at once.

His eyes skip over the rest of us quickly, going straight to Seelie as if she's the only one in the room.

The moment their eyes meet seems to go on forever. Seelie's expression freezes, too stunned and horrified to even show it. She lets out a pained gasp, taking an involuntary step back. "Oh, no," she says, almost too quiet to hear.

All my protective instincts scream to put myself between them. I can feel the dread and fear rolling off her in waves, and no one's allowed to make my sister feel that way.

"Surprised?" the faerie asks. He stands in one fluid motion, head tilting in a mockery of human expression. "So am I."

I'm the first to move, dagger drawn as I put myself between him and everyone else. "Stay back," I warn.

"What a pleasure to see you again, changeling," the faerie says, ignoring the blade. Like I'm not even there. "And all your mortal friends, too. Does this mean we're done keeping secrets now?"

"Quiet!" I snap, cutting him off with a swipe of my dagger. I don't like how he says *we*, as if they're in on something together. What does he know about my sister?

More than you, the useless part of my mind chimes in. He couldn't say it if it wasn't true.

Seelie swallows hard, tilting her chin up to face him. "Did you do this?"

He looks around, eyes glittering. "You know, you're going to have to learn to take responsibility for your actions eventually, Seelie. Do your friends really trust you to protect them? Do they know what you did to me?"

"What *I* did to *you*?" she repeats, forgetting to be afraid. Her voice is pitching up, echoing on the icy stone. "You tried to get me killed!"

"And then I saved your life, and *you* betrayed me!" the faerie snarls, the boom of his voice filling the room like a clap of thunder. "Don't play the victim, Seelie."

He's lying, I'm sure. The words may be true, but I'm sure it wasn't like that. I know Seelie—she's my *sister*. Of course I trust her to protect me. Not that I need protecting.

"Enough games," Raze says. His face looks troubled, but he stands with his shoulders square, facing the faerie. "Just explain what's happening. Now."

Gossamer's mouth twitches into a half smile. "Mortals are always so impatient. Don't worry, enchanter. You have all the time you need here."

"Here?" Seelie repeats faintly. She looks a little sick, color draining from her face. "I don't know . . ."

He rolls his eyes. "You don't know? Or are you just searching for someone to blame for your own recklessness? Was *I* the one making portals I couldn't close? Leaving little holes in the Mortal Realm, fragments of magic propping open doors that were meant to be closed? Was I the one playing with forces I didn't understand and power I couldn't control?"

She steps forward, like she's forgotten he's a threat. "What do you mean?"

"I mean that you've done what I failed at," he says, sounding genuinely excited. "This is something—somewhere—entirely new. An unending portal, sitting in all the worlds and none of them all at once. A prison, for now, but with the potential for so much more. I could never have dreamed such a thing was possible."

I don't like how he's looking at her. I interrupt, raising my voice. "What about everyone else? What did that wave of magic do to them?"

He waves a hand. "Oh, they're fine. They're just trapped outside of time. Not even I can touch them." My distraction failed, because he's still looking at my sister like she's a meal. "Don't you get it? You've done it, Seelie! Your skill—with my magic—it's made all this possible."

"Great," she says. "So I can reverse it?"

When his head snaps up, it's as quickly and fiercely as the faerie hounds catching the scent of their prey, his uncanny eyes wide. "Don't!" He starts to move, and we all take a step back. "This is something truly special. You keep fighting me, but everything you do brings us one step closer. Maybe Fate intended it to be this way all along. If you'd just *work* with me, Seelie, we could—"

Raze interrupts him with a snort. "Is this guy serious?"

Something in Gossamer's posture changes in an instant, patience thawing like ice on a hot stove. Suddenly, he's not looking at Seelie, and his hands move in the air almost like hers do when she's casting an enchantment. Threads of magic shimmer around Raze, and maybe I blink, because the next thing I know there's some kind of golden helmet wrapped around his head. A strange helmet, with no visor to see through and no holes to allow air in or out. His sound of panic is muffled by the metal, and his hands jump to the lock at his throat, scrambling uselessly. It won't come off.

"Stop it!" Seelie shouts at Gossamer. A sudden blaze of white-hot fire swallows her hands, so intense that its radiant heat washes over me. "Leave him alone!"

Raze's panicked yelling stops just long enough for his shape to blur, shifting into a hawk with reddish-brown feathers. He swoops up into the air as the helmet drops, dissolving back into a splash of magic the second it hits the floor.

"Listen to me, Seelie. You're making a mistake. I'm willing to forgive one betrayal, but—"

"No!" She winds back and throws. A blast of fire shoots across the room, slamming square into the faerie's chest. It bounces off him, crackling over his shoulders before disappearing.

Gossamer blinks, brushing away sparks like they're bits of dust. "Think carefully about where all that magic is coming from before making any rash decisions."

"I don't care!" Seelie has always been terrifying when she loses her temper, but now she's incandescent. Fire surrounds her, silhouetting her slender frame and the loose hair blowing around her face. The only bright spot in it all is the twin pinpoints of her eyes, inhuman flat discs reflecting firelight.

His expression shifts to a rueful half smile, just a shade off from an embarrassed human boy. "Well," Gossamer says, voice dropping. "Then I suppose I'm going to need that back."

He reaches out again, and this time, the fire streams to him like he's pulling it into himself.

Seelie's noise of surprise sounds almost pained, which activates my deepest instincts. I draw a dagger from my boot, but before I can throw it, a flash of light zips across my vision.

Aris's magic is like concentrated sunbeams, painful and precise. It leaves a singed black spot over Gossamer's heart, startling him long enough for Seelie's fire to go out. His wide eyes drop to the wound, and his fingertips press over it in shock. They come away smudged black, but instead of being hurt or angry, he just looks stunned. His mouth opens in an inhuman laugh.

I don't wait to ask what's funny. My knife soars with deadly accuracy, burying itself in his throat. The sound of someone laughing *through* a spurt of blood might be the worst thing I've ever heard in my life. What I'd give to be carrying iron on me right now—why didn't I think of that earlier? Gossamer rips the dagger free without a care for the dark blood that follows it, running in a brutal fountain down his white clothing. In his hands, it transforms in an instant into a shining sword, elegantly crafted and wickedly sharp.

I remember what Seelie told us about the tricks he played on her, the illusions that felt as real as they looked. He created her personal nightmare in the Mortal's Keep, a room full of people dead because of her. The blood left her fingers wet—until he disappeared, and all the visions with him.

None of this is real. Not the helmet, not the sword.

"You don't scare me," I say, stepping forward. Seelie is still crouched in pain, Olani and Aris calculating the next clever move, Raze flying around the room. I can't wield magic, but I can put myself between my sister and the faerie bent on tormenting her.

His silvery eyes settle on me for just a moment, his face still bearing a soulless grin like a hat he's forgotten to remove. Before he can decide whether I'm deserving of a response or not, I launch myself in an attack.

I'm not sure what my plan is—just to buy Seelie more time to figure out what kind of magic to use here. To serve as a distraction while everyone else comes up with an actual strategy. It manifests as me drawing another dagger and throwing myself at the faerie, this time aiming for the heart.

Gossamer is quicker than any human, dodging out of the way and raising his sword for a counterattack all in one motion. With my free hand, I reach across his exposed chest to grip the pommel of his sword, wrenching it away from my body. In that moment, I'm thankful for the thick velvet sleeves of my Wintersol gown, because where the illusory blade digs into my arm, it feels . . . surprisingly sharp. Ignoring its sting, I raise my dagger for another attack.

For a second, I think I actually stand a shot of disarming him.

And then he lunges forward. With my hand still gripping the hilt, the blade presses against my ribs. It's just a *dagger*, its point shouldn't *be there* . . .

Except the illusion isn't just an illusion.

I try to let go, to jump back, but it's too late. I feel the cold before the pain as Gossamer surges forward, burying the sword right below my ribs.

Blood.

Red-hot pain tearing through my guts. Several voices screaming. The jarring chill as my knees hit the floor. Gossamer's indifferent eyes watching me fall. My dagger slipping from my hand.

Failure.

chapter eleven

SEELIE

Gossamer looks, for a moment, almost as surprised as Isolde. Instead of batting her away like a cat with a mouse, he crouches to gently arrange her body on the cold floor. Her eyelashes flutter, lips moving with her uneven gasps for breath as her hands curl into the wound.

She's still breathing. Blood is starting to puddle around her, a dark stain spreading out with each beat of her heart. Alive—but not for long.

By the time my mind has caught up with my eyes, my initial scream of shock and rage is echoing around us. I lunge for Gossamer, summoning magic with no idea what I'm going to do with it. I don't make it far before something grips my wrist and hauls me back—Aris, her fingers digging into my skin unflinchingly as stone.

"Seelie, don't. That's what he wants."

Gossamer stands slowly over Isolde's body, still holding his sword. This is it—his chance to finish her off. I fight against Aris, trying to wrench myself free, screaming wordless shrieks. I have to stop him. I don't care what happens to me, to the rest of the world, not if I can spare my sister.

But Gossamer doesn't plunge the sword through Isolde's small, trembling body. He just looks at me, serene sadness in his icy eyes. "They need not all die for you, Seelie," he says. "It's not too late."

He disappears, leaving me reeling. *Sadness*—why would he be sad? He doesn't care about squashing a couple mortals like so many insects in his path. He certainly didn't months ago, when I last faced him in the Unseelie Realm. But he's been lurking in the corners of my mind for months, his power influencing me, making me angry and reckless.

What if I was influencing him right back?

I don't have time to follow that thought to its conclusion. Gossamer shimmers into view—not once, but a dozen times, all over the room. Olani is already running to Isolde. She swings her staff viciously into the Gossamer standing between them, and it passes through him like mist. The second she realizes he's an illusion, in the same swift movement, she lets her staff clatter to the cold stone floor, practically throwing it to the side in her haste to heal Isolde.

"Let me *go*!" My voice is completely unmasked, high and thin and stripped bare of any attempt to sound like anything other than who I am.

Aris, sensing the building danger, finally releases me. "Use your head," she murmurs. Her eyes bore into mine for just a second, a sort of plea in their cool green depths. "Get us out of here." And then she's gone, slicing through the illusions with a narrow beam of light. They all vanish except one, which the hawk descends on, claws first. Raze's talons can't do that much damage, but the attack at least manages to distract the faerie for a moment.

Fighting every instinct that tells me to gather my magic, to rip the world around me apart by the seams and turn all its power on Gossamer, I run to my sister's side. Isolde is unresponsive, shivering as her warm blood pools around us. Olani's face is crumpled in concentration, and I can't tell if the moisture on her cheeks is sweat or tears.

"I don't have enough magic left," she says, looking up at me through damp lashes. "I don't—I don't know what to do."

I stare at her like she's slapped me. Protecting us from the portal's uncontrolled magic took every scrap of power from her, and then some. Still, her hands stay pressed to Isolde's wound. I can sense her magic in the air like a thunderstorm, a hint of power on the back of my tongue. She looks ill. It's not like her to be so reckless, to risk the consequences of pushing the limits of her power when she could still be of use to the group in other ways. She barely wastes a second to glare at me before her gaze returns to Isolde, jaw set, as if she's *willing* my sister's body to heal rather than helping it along with her magic.

"Olani, stop." Isolde's voice interrupts my thoughts, a fragile croak. Her eyes flutter open just enough to pin Olani, and she weakly paws at the healer's hands to move them away.

Unlike me, Olani doesn't flinch at the surprise of hearing her speak. "I've got her," she says to me, totally ignoring Isolde's feeble attempts to squirm away. When I don't move, she finally snaps, "Seelie, are you listening? Cover us. Help Raze. Find something useful to do."

Useful. I can be useful. I'll gather my wits and make us a portal out of here—yes, making a portal is what got us into this mess, but I can't think of a quicker way out. Something went wrong last time, but now that I'm free of Gossamer's influence, maybe I can fix it.

I stand and hold out my hands, reaching for my magic and the magic all around me. It feels *wrong*. Instead of the stillness of the Mortal Realm, or the constant flow that fills the faerie realms, there's a storm. It picks me up and tosses me to the side, physically jolting me back. I land hard, sending a shock up my spine.

The memory of lightning, my own magic turned on me, fills my mind. This is the same pain, the same realization that I can't withstand the same power I wield. The same tension taking over my muscles, pulling them taut in sickening spasms.

Behind me, Raze and Aris still have Gossamer's attention, but not for long.

Ignoring the pain, I force myself back up. I have to do this. For Isolde, for the others. It doesn't matter how the warning sting that precedes the shock runs over my lightning-strike scars, how my hands shake and my stomach turns. I *have* to pull this mess apart, to burn a hole through it if there's no other way. I'm faintly aware that I've already used so much magic today. The price this requires of me might knock me unconscious or worse, and I don't care.

I start the spell once more, teeth gritted, braced for the pain and the pressure. This time, I lock my knees and make it as far as attempting to anchor myself before that force pushes me back again. I try to resist it, but all that accomplishes is a more spectacular blow when my strength inevitably gives out.

Pain shoots up my arms from the flat splay of my hands hitting the stone floor. The taste of blood fills my mouth, and a bruising ache of exhaustion coils around my bones. It hurts to move. If only I could stay here—just for a second—breathing into the grass between my fingers—

Wait.

Eyes shut, I dig my fingers into the ground. It gives slightly, blades tickling my palms. It's like I'm feeling the grass and the stone at the same time, both twisted up in magic. *My* magic.

The first time I cast a portal spell, a desperate bargain with Gossamer at the back of my consciousness, he taught me this: A portal is little more than a string of magic. One end tied around where you are, and the other knotted around where you want to be. Whatever force flows beneath my hands feels more like a tangle in a loom, layers snarled and twisted together where it should be smooth—but it's still my magic.

"Seelie," Isolde murmurs. Her voice sounds like it's being squeezed out of her, like her ribs might collapse and her heart might break. "Get up."

I look back at her, at Olani trying desperately to close her wounds. Egg cowers behind them in the growing puddle of Isolde's blood. Aris is nursing a slash across her shoulder, strained to her breaking point by all the magic she's thrown at Gossamer. She starts to fall, and Raze shifts quickly to human form to catch her, looking just as shaky himself.

Ahead of me, Gossamer is taking his time bearing down on us, sword held lazily in one hand. His clothes are still stained red, but his injuries have closed themselves. His free hand grips the air, pulling magic out from my skin in a glowing stream. It's like watching the life flow out of me, making me weaker with each heartbeat. I know he won't rest until he can drag the last bits of magic I stole from him out of my veins—and I know we can't beat him.

Finally, he stands over me, clearly amused by my inability to rise to meet him. The point of his sword—no less sharp for being an illusion—drags lightly under my chin. "Which will it be, Seelie?" he asks in a voice so quiet I can barely pick it out. A faint sadness soaks into the words, matching the shift in his hollow eyes. "Begging for your life? Or simply goodbye?"

My head is the only part of me that moves, and my stomach revolts at even that. My fingers dig harder into the ground, my arms trembling with the effort it takes to hold me up. With everyone else reduced to a non-threat, the faerie has eyes only for me, and I meet his gaze evenly. "Goodbye, Gossamer," I say, surprising myself with the low, steady flame of my voice.

He smirks, mouth opening to reply, but I'm not listening anymore.

I pull on the magic woven between my fingers with all my might, like a sideshow conjurer might rip a tablecloth out from under a set of dishes. I'm operating purely on instinct, following strands of the half-formed spell that lead to the familiar tug of Seelie magic. As the portal wraps around us, Gossamer starts to realize what's happening, but he's too tangled up in the magic of this place to free himself. He's just as trapped here as he was in my head.

The world spins and disappears and crashes down on us, swirling into a new form before my eyes. The manor's ballroom, along with its ghostly gray glow and its guests and Gossamer's glossy glare, vanishes.

And I find myself—all of us—crashing into a party in a warm, twilit forest. A chorus of birds startles from the emerald leaves overhead, dark feathers flashing between us and the pink sky. My magic snaps back to me, slamming into my lungs and my skin and leaving me gasping for breath in the soft green grass of the Seelie Realm.

chapter twelve

ISOLDE

I am bleeding out onto a tablecloth made of spider silk, fragments of amethyst goblets crunching under the tremors of my last gasps for breath.

It's strange, to be aware that you're dying, but not dead yet. I know I have a body, one that is growing colder and stiller by the moment, but it feels so far away. My fingers twitch defiantly against the impossibly smooth surface I'm sprawled on, restless until the bitter end.

Seelie did it. She got us out, held her own against a murderous faerie, wielded magic I still don't fully understand. I'm so proud.

It's a shame I'll never get to tell her that.

The stunned silence that fell the moment we landed erupts into chatter. I'm not sure if it sounds like speech and birdsong and the hum of crickets all at once, or if I'm just delirious from blood loss. I'd like to sit up and take it all in, but the connection between my mind and body is growing fainter by the second.

There's a flurry of iridescent wings, then a blurry face pops into my field of view. It's similar in structure to a human's, except that the skin is mauve, with dark black streaks and dots like the false eyes on a butterfly's wings. The whole effect is so disorienting that it takes me a moment to realize he's staring at me with expectant, pupil-less eyes and a deeply offended frown.

"Your blood is ruining my dinner," he says in a voice like the groan of a falling tree.

"Oops," I say, and then panic a little, because I'm running out of energy, and I'm going to be absolutely furious if my last word is *oops*.

"Sol?" My sister's voice breaks through the fog. She's battered and weak from overspending her magic, swaying over me with tears in her eyes. Her hand covers mine where it's pressed to the wound, and I see her eyes widen when her fingers come away bloodstained.

"You did . . . good," I manage, even though each sound makes my ribs feel like they're going to collapse.

Seelie shakes her head, and the tears rolling down her cheek drop onto my nose like rain. She opens her mouth, searching for words—something to comfort me, something to apologize, something to make it all better—but comes up blank. Instead, she just throws her arms around me, as if to put the frail barricade of her body between me and anything else that might try to harm me.

I try to hug back, to hold on to her and reassure her that I'm not going anywhere, but it's hard to move.

After a second, Seelie pulls away, looking at me fiercely. "I'm going to get help. Stay here."

I mean, *yeah*. Where does she think I'm going to go? A tiny giggle bubbles up, escaping my lips, and Seelie looks equal parts relieved and annoyed as she stands and starts shouting something I can't make out.

"Well?" I think the faerie with the butterfly-wing face arches a brow, but it's difficult to tell. He's still staring down at me with those ink-black eyes. I try to reply, but all I can manage is a wet cough that rasps my throat and tastes like blood. "Aren't you going to take your blood back?"

"Mortals can't— Cobweb, *help her*!" This voice is lighter and full of nervous energy, accompanied by a surprisingly human face.

"Oh. It's been a while, but I suppose . . ." Spidery mauve fingers stretch out toward me, and the lighter voice keeps talking, but I can't make out all the words.

This is all ruining the drama of my untimely demise, I think, a bit petulantly. If I'm going to be staring at anyone in my final moments, I'd much rather it be someone I know. I'm sure Seelie's going to make it out of this, but I missed what happened to Raze. I'm fairly certain Olani was somewhere over to my right, and I try to reach for her, to turn my head, but my body has stopped obeying me entirely.

"Hold still," the butterfly-faced faerie scolds. His touch cools my cheek, like spray from a waterfall on a blazing summer's day. The feeling runs over me like water, trickling from my face, down my neck, into the spaces between my ribs.

I'm familiar with the feeling of healing magic by now, but this is different from Olani's. Or maybe *I'm* what's different—I've never been so badly in need of healing before. Instead of the slow, soothing flow of power, I feel like I'm being ripped apart by tiny shards of ice. My skin tingles and my stomach boils as my body mends itself at an unnatural pace. I slowly sink back into the world around me, noticing all the details I missed—

My fingers are wet, partly with blood and partly with the faerie wine I spilled. The air is warm, too warm for Wintersol, so warm my clothes feel itchy and restrictive. Seelie is on her feet already, standing defensively above me, yelling at someone. Good. That means she's okay.

Something squeezes my hand tight, ignoring the sticky mess. "Isolde?" Olani's voice, hoarse and breathless. She's worried about me. But at least that means I have her attention. My fingers lock around hers, as if I can use it to drag myself back. Her eyes flick between my face and the wound in my side, where she presses her other hand to stop the bleeding. I thought I was doing that. When did I let go?

I offer the best approximation of a smile I can give right now. My eyes are fluttering shut, exhaustion from the healing magic forcing my wounds to stitch themselves together overtaking any fight left in me.

Bones snap into place. My heartbeat should slow, but instead it's gaining futile speed. Each inhale drags new pain from depths I didn't know I had. A hiss escapes the space between my clenched teeth. The longer you survive a mortal wound, the more it hurts.

"Am I . . . gonna be okay?" I finally manage to ask, wheezing a little with each word.

Olani opens her mouth, and then winces. Which tells me two things, the less important of which is that cursed truth potion hasn't worn off. "You've lost a lot of blood," she finally says. It's not in her calm, steady Healer Voice, which is concerning. I've watched her pull an arrow from her own flesh with barely a flinch, but whatever's happening to me right now has her on the verge of tears.

I'd be worried about that, if I wasn't so tired.

Olani squeezes my hand tighter. "You have to stay awake. Okay? Don't go to sleep." And then she appears in my field of vision, glaring at the faerie, whose touch is starting to burn like ice. There's a blurry haze around her, like something from a dream. In the half-light, her eyes look nearly black, lit from within by a distant fire. The spell breaks when she turns to shove the faerie with a shocking lack of control or self-preservation. "Stop it! Her body can't keep up, you're killing her! You have to pace— Isolde, are you listening? I swear, if you *dare* to close your eyes—"

"I don't like orders," I hear myself whisper, surprised by the softness of my voice. "But for you, I'll make an exception." The words surprise me when they slip out, half silly and half deliriously unsure I'll wake again if I dare to disobey her. I've never been good at being obedient, though. After that, I don't feel any pain.

I don't feel anything at all.

chapter thirteen

ISOLDE

I'm not quite awake, not quite asleep, but the next thing I'm fully aware of is that I'm still alive, and I'm a bit embarrassed over being so melodramatic. There's springy moss beneath me, sinking under my weight and prickling my palms. Something is choking me, weighing down my head, which sends enough of a buzz of panic through me to make me open my eyes.

To a very disorienting void interrupted by two pinpricks of glowing green.

I was already starting to struggle, but I freeze in place, my throat squeezing for a reason besides the paws planted firmly on my neck. It can't be.

"Birch?" I croak.

The creature blinks at me, unfazed. Then it has the nerve to actually yawn, exposing a pink tongue and pointed white teeth. It's a familiar expression—as familiar as its sleek black fur, perked ears, and unsettling green eyes.

It's definitely Birch.

At the sound of my voice, my whole world starts rocking, weight shifting on the bed of moss as Seelie jumps up to loom over me. When our eyes meet, a genuine smile of relief lights up her face. She turns and calls over her shoulder, "She's awake!"

I try to focus on the details of the room beyond the brownie smothering me, but my head is still swimming. I see Olani, Raze, and Aris, and a lot of green.

"Try to stay calm." Seelie forces a cup of water into my hand. "You're—you're safe. How do you feel?"

How do I *feel*? I feel like I've melted, been scraped up off the floor, and scooped back into my own shape. I feel trapped and panicky. Mostly, I feel . . .

"Confused?" I say. My voice is raspy. How long was I unconscious? I accept the cup and sip tentatively, not sure if faerie water is safe to drink but too thirsty to resist. "Where are we?"

They all exchange a look. No one seems sure how to respond to that. I take the chance to look around, combing for details. We're in a room lit by pink sunset light, open and airy with layers of human-made rugs and furniture and trinkets. There are arched windows all the way around, but no glass panes, which makes it feel almost like a gazebo. Through the arches, there's nothing but shivering green leaves. It doesn't feel like it was designed with mortals in mind. It's more like a theater set or an exhibit, a place that is meant to be observed and not lived in.

Eventually, it's me who breaks the silence, fingers squeezed tight around the little wooden cup. "So, obviously, we're still in the Seelie Realm."

Seelie nods, her brows twisted up with worry. I can't blame her, I almost died back there. I'd be wondering if I was okay, too.

"Great," I say, trying to wrap my mind around it. Trying not to let memories of last time I was in the Seelie Realm flood in.

Trying to keep my face and voice casual as I gesture to Birch. "Can someone help me up now?"

"He won't move," Seelie says. "We tried. I don't even know where he came from, he just came running out of the trees and trying to keep the other faeries away. Even when they were trying to heal you."

We practically raised this brownie, brought him in shivering from the cold as a tiny, kitten-shaped thing, shared the wagon that was our home with him for years. We lost him and our wagon last time we were in the Seelie forest, and I thought I'd never see him again—but here he is, alive and insistent as ever.

The warmth of a smile lights me from within. I can feel it transforming my face. "Aww, Birch. If I didn't know better, I'd think you missed me." I lean forward to scratch between his ears, and he tilts his head in acknowledgment. I've missed his furry face and tendency to turn invisible, his ridiculous sounds and occasional helpfulness. I've missed so much that we lost when we started this disastrous quest.

Something nudges my elbow, and I turn my head to see Egg's curious eyes inches from mine. He's never seen anything like the brownie before—and I guess Birch hasn't seen anything like the firedrake, either. They would have been extinct long before his time in the Mortal Realm. Egg snorts loudly, showering us with sparks, and Birch's fur goes all puffy. He rises up—pricking me with his claws as he does—and then uses my throat as a trampoline to launch himself over the firedrake.

Egg gives chase at full speed, both of them dashing in circles around the strange open space.

"Ow!" I complain, which gives me the chance to examine how I feel. Freed from Birch's weight, I prop myself up on my elbows. One hand goes to my ribs, shoving aside the crust of dried blood on my bodice to find . . . smooth skin. Not even a scar. There isn't any pain left, either. I feel alert and energetic, and when I shove my hair back from my face, that feels freshly washed, too.

Faerie magic. I hate it here.

I push myself up, swinging my feet off the bed. Birch meows loudly, in a scolding tone. At first, I think it's directed at Egg, but then I see what I almost stepped on: a gleaming green object that blends in almost perfectly with the moss at my feet. Breathless, I bend to pick it up. My fingers are trembling, my heart beating so fast it feels like a hum.

The emerald-green paint, still sparkly if a little chipped by sharp teeth in places, the impossibly small glass windows, the little door. I wish I could return to it, sit at the wheel, snuggle into my bunk against the back wall. I hold our old home in my hands, shrunk down by a faerie prank. It was Birch's home, too, and he's kept it safe, even if he can't undo whatever spell shrunk it down to dollhouse scale.

"The *Destiny*," Seelie says, crossing her arms with a weary smile. "I thought I saw him with it when we were here before. I haven't figured out a way to fix it yet."

Yet. That means there's still a chance.

"Maybe it would be easier if any of us could remember how it got shrunk down in the first place." Raze's tone is vaguely amused, as if there's anything funny about the last time we crashed into the Seelie Realm, immediately fell under an enchantment that made our minds fuzzy, and lost the wagon.

Okay, maybe I can find a bit of humor in it. With a snort, I stand—but not before bending down to tuck the tiny wagon into my pocket. "How long was I out?" There's a faint wobble before I find my footing, nervous energy spurring me to pace.

"A few hours." Olani grabs me by the shoulder, stopping me in my tracks. "You need to rest."

"We need to go." I shake her off, striding for one of the openings that reaches all the way to the floor, like a doorway.

And stop short, swaying on the edge of an incalculable drop.

We're not just surrounded by trees, we're *in* the trees, high up on a platform among the branches. The constant movement below almost makes me feel like I'm on a boat, crashing waves of brilliant green leaves shifting in the breeze. I reach out to grab the curved branch that forms the arched doorway, leaning out until the space below makes me dizzy. I can see other platforms, other buildings, all clinging to the surrounding trees. Insubstantial bridges thread between them like spiderwebs.

Raze's voice crashes through my awe at the sight of the faerie city. "We're waiting for an audience with the Seelie Queen."

"Oh," I respond, stepping back into the room. My head is buzzing, trying to put together the fragments of what I remember. "Well, if that's all."

I know, vaguely, that each faerie court is ruled by its own queen. The Mortal Realm used to have monarchs, too, but that was a long time ago. I barely have a concept of what a queen is, much less an immortal one who has sat on her throne since before memory, whose life force is inseparable from the magic of her realm, whose will shapes reality around her whims. A faerie that *other* faeries find unknowably old and untouchably powerful. It's like being told we have an audience with the ocean.

"We might be in trouble," Aris adds.

Olani is still staring at me with her jaw set. Enough time has passed that she's had the chance to wash my blood from her hands, but not enough to stop her from looking at me like I'm made of glass that might crack at any second. She catches me noticing her and sighs, obviously forcing herself back into the present. A curve that can't quite be called a smile touches the corner of her mouth. "Apparently, the faeries of the Seelie Court don't love it when mortals crash their Wintersol celebration. Even if it is life-or-death."

chapter fourteen

SEELIE

We end up sprawled in a circle on the floor instead of actually using any of the fancy furniture. Egg and Birch chase each other in a chaotic dash around us, crashing off the walls and rolling over each other, but I'm not going to get in the middle of that battle. They'll figure it out.

Olani and Isolde both sit cross-legged, but Olani remains perfectly still while my sister's knees flutter with nervous energy against the silk rug. Aris lands in a defeated pose, face down. Raze tries to sit with his feet planted and knees in the air, but after only a second he's dropped onto his back with another heavy breath. I find a spot between him and Isolde, where I finally let myself curl up into a ball, arms locked around my knees. It's difficult to do, since I'm still wearing my ball gown from the Wintersol party.

Was Wintersol really tonight? Or—last night? Time feels fuzzy and intangible. All I know is that my parents were there.

They're still there, trapped in a curse of my own creation. Seeing them feels like more of a dream than anything that happened after. I left them behind to keep them safe, but I can't even keep myself safe.

I should be furious and devastated. Instead, all I feel is a numb blankness. Even though I (mostly) understand the events of the past several hours, I can't quite make myself believe that they're real.

Maybe I've felt enough for a lifetime already, and I just don't have any emotions left.

"So," Raze says, still staring up at the ceiling. "Are we going to talk about it?"

I glance down at him, resisting the strange and sudden urge to reach out and—what? Take his hand? Pat his shoulder? Any soft, casual touch that might convey a sense of closeness: all bad options, since I have to imagine his anger over me keeping secrets is going to catch up with us any minute now.

"Talk about what?" I force myself to say, in a voice hollow as a gust of wind.

Aris pops up, propping herself on her elbows. "How about the murderous faerie determined to kill you and/or the rest of us, if not the entire Mortal Realm? The curse you unleashed that could be covering half of Auremore, for all we know? Our pending audience with a faerie queen? What in all the realms we're going to do next?"

"Well, I'd imagine that last one is answered by the faerie queen thing," Isolde mutters. She's still looking around the room, her head tilting quickly in every direction as if she's trying to take inventory for a memory game.

Olani lets out a very long, measured sigh. "Seelie," she finally says, scolding in that mild, even-tempered way of hers. "You put us all in danger."

Coming from her, someone I actually care about, someone I *like*, the accusation stings more. Anger flares up, granting me energy I thought was long gone, sparks jumping to my fingertips. "If I'd had *any idea* that this could happen, do you really think—"

"She doesn't mean that," Raze interrupts. He looks more troubled than anything, blue eyes searching the empty space above us. "It's not the magic, or whatever enchantment you did, or bargain, or—whatever, Seelie. It's that you didn't *tell* us."

All the heated anger comes crashing in on me in an instant, melting into a wave of acidic guilt. My fingers press together, twisting into restless, fidgety shapes outlined in flames. Maybe he's right. Maybe I should have told them. Maybe if I'd told everyone about Gossamer long ago, before we ever reached the Mortal's Keep, then none of this would be happening now. I told myself that I was keeping secrets to keep them safe, but that wasn't really it, was it? I can be honest enough with myself now to see the cold, unadorned truth of it.

My lips part, but I have no defense for myself. "I know," I finally say, my eyes cast down to my hands, still burning and folded together awkwardly.

Raze catches one of my hands in his with the calm swiftness of a child running a finger through a candle flame. The fire at my fingertips fizzles out the moment he touches me, but he doesn't even flinch. He just squeezes my fingers and waits for me to catch my breath and meet his eyes. His features soften to something close to a smile. "No more secrets, okay?"

It feels like a moment meant just for us, not for everyone else to be watching, but I can't summon enough embarrassment to pull away or look at their reactions.

"I'm so sorry." I'm still looking at him, but the words spread and settle over everyone in the room. "I'm sorry I got all of you involved in this."

Olani, who is less given to displays of affection, simply says, "Well, we're here now." I finally tear my eyes away to see her, neatly folding away her anger like she's going to fit it into her medicine bag for later. "So what next?"

Isolde shrugs. "Seems obvious to me."

"Really?" Olani says dryly, raising an eyebrow.

"We have to kill Gossamer."

She says it so plainly that I half expect him to manifest in the room as if summoned by name—which, of course, he doesn't. He doesn't appear behind me like an apparition, either, because he's not in my head anymore. He called the in-between realm a prison, but it's a prison where he seems to be made of actual flesh and blood—or whatever faeries are made of, I should really find out as long as we're here—and gathering strength.

I've gone up against the faerie several times at this point, and I've lost every single fight. Even the time I surprised him with sheer luck was only enough to delay his return. He knows better than to underestimate me now—but I also know something about him.

"Oh, is that all?" Raze says sarcastically. "No problem! Do you want to head back over there *now*, or—"

"We can't go back," Aris interrupts seriously, lifting her head from the rug. "He was drawing power from Seelie. Taking her back with us would just be putting a weapon in his hands. With the changeling *and* the firedrake, we might as well serve ourselves up on a platter."

Isolde crosses her arms, still bouncing with restless energy. "Then who do you suggest should fight him? Going in there *without* Seelie would be a suicide mission. If it's even possible to get through without her shaping the portal."

"We need help." I let go of Raze's hand to stand so I can pace, counting steps across the uncannily cozy room. "They needed help last time."

Isolde is the one to catch my meaning first, finally going still with a sharp breath in through her nose. "And they didn't finish the job."

I nod, running my fingers through the tangled mass of my hair to push it back from my face. "They just locked him away in the Mortal's Keep, kept the story to themselves so his memory would fade, so no one could ever free him . . ." Warmth spreads up my face, prickling my neck. Guilt and anger and determination all in equal measure, impossible to untangle from each other. "But *I* did."

Raze tilts his head, so hawklike I can practically see the feathers ruffling. I think he's catching up now. "*We* did," he says.

"Raze . . ." Aris's confused look matches his for a second, reminding me that despite all their differences, they're related. Unlike the rest of us, they grew up hearing the story of the long-forgotten War of the Realms their ancestors led. In the stories, they were the victors and the victims, rulers over a world that survived, but only as a trampled and transformed version of what it once was. I can almost see the memories of frightening bedtime stories playing out in front of Aris as she asks, "What did you find in Aunt Leira's study on Revelnox?"

He lets out a little snort, smirking half-heartedly. "'The Wildline legacy,'" he quotes. "I guess it sounds better than 'the Wildline prisoner of war.'"

Olani curses under her breath.

"I mean, no wonder he was so excited," Isolde says. She's obviously making an attempt at a joke, but it's *way* too soon to laugh about the fact that I've pretty much delivered Gossamer everything he ever wanted. He tried to take over our world once before, and was locked away before he managed to get a foothold—this time, I've given him a boost.

"We just need to talk to the Queen." Raze looks and sounds confident, and I'm not sure if he's actually this optimistic or if he's just trying to convince himself to be. "We're already here! That's good, right?"

"Maybe . . ." The word draws out slowly. If the fate of our world, our home, our *parents*, is relying on my diplomatic skills—well. I hope it doesn't come to that.

Olani stands, stretching. "So history repeats itself. They

needed both faerie courts to take him down before, so it makes the most sense to start there. Once we have their support, we just charge right in and hope for the best," she deadpans, which does nothing to cushion how lacking the plan is—both in terms of detail and the likelihood of it working out.

"More or less," Isolde agrees. "But this time, we end it for good."

Her insistence on killing Gossamer feels a little bloodthirsty, a little personal, but it's also practical. And something about it bothers me, for reasons I can't place. "There must be a reason they didn't," I mumble.

"Faerie-death," Aris says, almost like it's one word. Like it's an explanation. At my confused look, she sighs. "All magic has to come from somewhere, right?" She holds up her hand, and a small ball of light hovers over her palm. "When it's channeled through something, it either disperses naturally . . ." Her fingers flatten, and little tendrils of light flow out from the ball until it's almost gone out. Then she flicks her wrist, and it flares back to life before exploding in a dazzling puff, leaving spots dancing over my vision. ". . . or it loses shape, and explodes." She pauses, letting her demonstration fade away as she meets my eyes. "Faeries are mostly magic, so when they die, a huge wave of uncontained magical energy is released. Our ancestors probably calculated the risk, and decided the Mortal Realm couldn't withstand it after all the fighting."

I nod as if I'm paying attention, but my mind is no longer on this conversation or the battle ahead. It's in the glittering nighttime of the Unseelie forest, watching a faerie with my sister's face drop into the dirt. My dagger through her chest, dark faerie blood staining my hands and her skin as the life drains from her wide crimson eyes.

Briar was a faerie, and I killed her. And immediately after, as if a beacon had gone off, all the monsters of the Unseelie forest closed in around us. I thought they were drawn in by the scent of her blood, driven to dispose of the corpse in nature's way, but maybe there was more to it. Maybe they were drinking the dregs of her power—as I suddenly surged with enough strength to banish Gossamer to the back of my mind.

I can still smell it. I can still feel the bones snapping.

Nausea boils up in my throat, and I fight it down, struggling to return myself to the present moment. My nails are digging into my palms so hard I can feel them leaving marks. Someone is calling my name, but it's hard to hear over my own pulse in my ears.

"Seelie?" Isolde says again, looking up at me with concern brewing in the depths of her warm brown eyes. I breathe in, and my mind snaps back into place all in an instant. She's here. I'm here. We're okay.

I blink, swallowing hard. "Yeah. Sorry. I was just . . . thinking." I turn quickly so I won't have to look at her—or at Raze, because I can feel his worried gaze on me, too, as heavy as a pack on my shoulders. "We should . . . we should probably plan what we're going to say."

My mind keeps slipping away after that, time blurring as I fight to stay rooted in the moment. They're all strategizing, and I'm standing silently to the side, just like always. Like the shy and shrinking girl I've fought so hard to outgrow. I want Isolde to squeeze me tight in her bony arms, I want Raze to tuck my head close to his chest, I want someone to reach out and hold the pieces of me until they knit themselves together again.

But I'm too much of a coward to ask for it.

chapter fifteen

SEELIE

In the Unseelie Realm, day and night flicker back and forth randomly with no ceremony. I thought the Seelie Realm was endless, unchanging twilight, but I'm starting to realize that it's more like the single hour between sunset and dusk, stretched out into long cycles.

Which is to say, we wait hours for the faeries to return before the stars come out and, one by one, we start dropping into dreams. I don't even realize I'm dozing off until I wake again and the room is silent except for the sound of steady breathing. The sky is a bruised indigo, and Isolde's presence beside me has disappeared.

For a second, I panic, sitting straight up. My breath comes too quickly, my pulse rocketing. I came too close to losing my sister, and even if her wounds are all magically healed now, that fear won't leave me.

But Isolde isn't gone. She's the first thing I see, silhouetted against the opening I've come to think of as the door to this strange faerie chamber, facing out to the trees with her legs dangling over the edge. She turns at the sound of me waking, smiles softly, and presses a finger to her lips, as if to say, *Don't wake the others.*

I nod, slowly pushing up to stand and stretch. Quietly, I pick my way across the floor to my sister's side and sit—several inches back from the edge, with my legs tucked up. Isolde's feet kick in the open air, unbothered by the stomach-clenching drop below.

"Good morning," Isolde murmurs, still facing out. Her eyes scan the trees, and I'm not sure if she's watching for signs of life or simply mesmerized by the rippling movement of the leaves in the breeze.

My reply is just as soft, each word feeling a little frail. "Is it morning?"

Isolde shrugs. "Who knows?"

That's fair. I don't even really know why I asked, except to have something to say. Our shoulders brush, my sister's familiar shape comforting my unsettled nerves. She's here. She's okay.

And I know what I owe her.

"There's something else I didn't tell you," I blurt before I can think better of it. The truth about Isolde's and my origins has been swirling around my head ever since it spilled from Briar's lips, both too important and not urgent enough to focus on. At least, that's what I tell myself. The truth is that I was too afraid to repeat it out loud. To change things forever.

"Do we have to do this right now?"

"Yes," I say, a complete sentence on its own. "Because I want you to hear it from me. Not someone else."

Isolde's brow furrows, but she doesn't pull away. "Okay . . ." she says, dragging out the sound questioningly.

My heart feels like a frog in my chest, jumping around all cold and slippery. Telling Isolde the truth should be easier than anything. She's my *sister*. I trust her more than I've ever trusted anyone, and she knows me better than anyone. Our fates have been tangled ever since the day our mother carried us home from the faerie forest, and nothing can ever change that.

At least, that's what I tell myself. Maybe Isolde won't believe me. Maybe she'll be furious with me for not telling her sooner. Maybe this will crack her trust so deeply and irrevocably that we're never the same again.

"I was—I was really scared back there," I stammer, knowing that I'm stalling. My throat feels thick.

Isolde's gaze softens. "I know," she says. There's a long pause. She swallows, looking off at the trees instead of at me. "Me too."

"I'm really glad you're not dead." The sentence starts off choked in a sob, but ends with a slight giggle as I hear how the words sound, too simple and obvious to deserve being spoken aloud.

Isolde giggles in return, sniffling a little. "Yeah, me, too," she repeats. Then she surprises me by adding, "It's not your fault."

My head snaps up so fast I have to blink hair out of my eyes. "What?"

"I said *it's not your fault*. What happened back there. The curse. Any of it. You were tricked. It could have happened to anyone. I know you're going to blame yourself, but I just want you to know you don't have to."

I snort. "Easy for you to say."

Her fingers slide down to her ribs, to the small gash in the cloth where the blade ran through her. She gives me a half smile. "No, it's not."

I take a deep, steadying breath, letting my fingers dig into the moss carpeting the floor. "Do you remember Mami's story?" It's intentionally vague, my throat squeezing around the details. I need to just *say* it, but I can't seem to push the words out. So going in circles around and around the topic it is.

Isolde, shockingly, doesn't make it harder. "About the faeries?" She nods without looking at me, somehow able to sense what I mean. Of course she remembers the story. Our parents told it to us every birthday, and we shared the telling every year spent running on our own.

When they realized their human child had been swapped for a changeling, our mother went to the faeries and demanded her baby back. The faeries offered her a choice, telling her she could take home whichever child she picked—and she chose both of us.

"But that . . . It isn't the whole story."

Isolde, who up to this point has been casually disengaged from the conversation, snaps around to look at me, confusion drawing lines all over her face. "What do you . . . ?" The sentence fades, trailing off like a breath of fog in the dusky air. Like she can't draw enough breath to finish it.

"I talked to this faerie in the Unseelie Realm." *That's* a kind way of putting it. I bite my lip, forcing myself to keep going. "And we—we—" Every time I stop, I think I'm not going to be able to start again, but I somehow manage to open my mouth and find the words. "We were looking at everything all wrong. Not just about us—about all changelings."

I wait to give Isolde the chance to respond, but my sister, for once, is speechless. She just stares at me in dimly painted shades of a wide-eyed expression I can't read.

"I know it sounds unhinged, but faeries can't lie, and she said it all so plainly—changelings aren't *kidnapped* and exchanged, one for one. We're—we're *born* like this, a faerie spark of life animating a human body. It's all so confusing, but I think the faeries stole away the human spirit that should have been Mami and Papa's child, and when she demanded it back, I already existed, so they had to make a whole new person—the opposite of me. Faerie-made body, with a human spark of life."

There. It's all out in the open, the truth hanging in the warm summer air between us. The words I've been so afraid to speak, because I don't even fully understand them.

". . . You," I finish, as if that wasn't clear.

Isolde keeps staring at me for a long time. She blinks rapidly, almost as if trying to clear tears from her eyes or wipe an image from her mind. "Me," she replies eventually. "And that would make me . . ." I wait. I know the word she's reaching for, but I want to give her the chance to find it first. She takes a long breath, looking more confused than anything else as she finally says, "A changeling."

chapter sixteen

ISOLDE

Hours ago, I thought I was dead. Now I know that my whole life is a lie.

It's been kind of a weird day.

Seelie reaches for my hand. I'm too numb to move, but I let her squeeze her fingers around my unmoving ones. She's peering at me with a worried expression, like she's scared I'm going to be mad at her—and I might be, eventually. I haven't gotten there yet.

I know I should say something, but this new information isn't sinking in. I open my mouth to respond—

And I'm horrified to hear a trembling laugh escape my lips instead. I take a deep breath to compose myself, and the shaky sound just makes me laugh harder. It's too ridiculous, too impossible, too . . . absolutely right.

"Sol?" Seelie says, starting to look concerned. She looks over her shoulder to see if my deranged giggles are waking the others. I clap a hand over my mouth, stifling the laughter into a choked hiss, but I can't get myself under control.

I might be in shock, yet I don't feel surprised. Not really. It feels like hearing something I've always known spoken aloud for the first time. Obviously, I'm not like Seelie—I don't struggle in the same ways she always has, don't have magic, don't fit in among the faeries. I've always felt different, but my differences paled in comparison to Seelie's. I was the *normal* child. The *human* child.

And next to other human children, I was too energetic, too fast and agile, too loud, too *much*. I could fit in, but I never really felt like I *belonged*. There was always some barrier between me and everyone else, something that made others turn away when they got too close. Now I know what that is, and it hurts as much as it feels like a weight off my shoulders, and I am reacting all wrong.

"Sol!" Seelie repeats, looking truly worried now. She grips my shoulder, trying to force me to look at her. "Say something. Please."

"I'm fine," I manage to wheeze, biting my sleeve to fight back another gale of giggles. "I'm—I'm just processing."

So, I'm not what our parents always thought I was. *I* was the one who came second, the one who didn't join the family until Mami carried us home from the faerie forest. Maybe I should be worried that means our parents won't want me anymore—if we ever get the chance to tell them—but after growing up with Seelie, the thought is absurd. I've known my whole life that blood isn't what makes a family.

Taking several deep breaths to calm myself, I finally manage to look my sister in the eye. Her eyebrows are all scrunched up, her mouth set in a very tentative smile. She's been keeping this from me since she returned from the Unseelie forest, holding on to a secret that wasn't hers to withhold. Every strange look she's given me since then, every time she's taken a ragged breath as if to stop herself from saying something . . . it all makes sense now.

"Must feel good for you," I blurt. After a lifetime of fearing that the choice to keep her was ruining our parents' lives, she must feel relieved to know that she would have been there either way.

It was definitely the wrong thing to say, because Seelie looks absolutely appalled. "Of course not," she says, putting a hand over her chest as if her heart will burst out if she doesn't keep a good grip on it. "Sol, if you think—I mean—it doesn't change anything."

Actually, it changes everything, but I know what she means. I didn't mean the words the way they came out, but I still shouldn't have been so harsh. "You're right," I say. Luckily, my voice is finally ready to obey me, and this comes out much steadier. "I shouldn't— Sorry, I just—" I don't usually struggle to speak like this, but I honestly don't know what to say.

Seelie squeezes my arm. "So, you believe me?"

As if I had a choice. I shrug, offering her a little smile. "It's true. Feels right." I turn to face the faerie city, my thoughts spinning. I tilt my head back and try to pick out familiar constellations, but the stars here don't exist in any recognizable pattern. There doesn't even seem to be a sun up there, despite the uniform glow of dusk all around us. I have no idea where the light is coming from.

There are so many layers to this revelation I don't feel remotely ready to unpack right now. For example, the reason I feel so uncomfortable in the Seelie Realm . . .

I let the thought slip past, grasping for the next. "So are there others like me?" I ask.

Seelie shrugs, apparently grateful for the change of subject. "Maybe. Probably. It would be hard to tell, since you're more . . . subtle. Someone like you could go your whole life and never know you're a changeling."

I breathe out another humorless laugh. "Yeah."

"Sorry." She hunches up instinctively, still waiting for the other shoe to drop. "I didn't mean . . ."

"I know."

After a moment of silence, Seelie looks up at me tentatively. "Are you okay?"

No. Yes. Everything feels upside down, and yet it feels like pieces of me are clicking into place. Things I thought would be incomplete and unanswered forever. I have no idea what I'm going to do with this information—if anything. I sigh, kicking my legs so my heels bounce against the tree's trunk. "I will be. I might get mad about you keeping it from me later, though. When all this is over."

Despite my joking tone, Seelie looks worried. Her fingers dig into the moss between us in a way that can't be good for her nails. "You're that sure we're going to make it?"

"We will. Like everything else. Together." I shift just enough to lean a little of my weight onto her. I feel her stiffen, frightened by the slight shift in balance while we're so high up, but she recovers quickly and leans back.

"I hope you're right," she mumbles against my shoulder.

I let out a soft chuckle. "I'm always right."

We don't talk much after that. We just sit in the quiet, watching the sky slowly tint pink and the stars wink out as a new dusk dawns in the Seelie Realm. Seelie—who has never in her life taken so much as a nap without a fight—nods off on my shoulder.

And I remain wide awake.

chapter seventeen

seelie

The faeries return for us just when we've started to worry they won't, buzzing and chattering like insects in tall summer grass. One of those delicate spiral staircases that stretches between trees appears under them, one step at a time, until the vines of its railing curl themselves into our empty doorway. Perhaps I'm meant to feel comforted by the fact that they're led by Cobweb, the butterfly-faced faerie who knocked Isolde unconscious with his clumsy attempt to heal her, and Robin, the changeling who kept up a running chatter the entire time, but I'm not.

There's something familiar about Robin. They look as human as any of us and about our same age, pale as gardenia petals and sandy-haired. They'd blend in to any city street or village market back home . . . at least as much as I do.

Maybe this is how people feel when they meet me. Maybe I just haven't spent enough time around other changelings, and my acclimation to humans has made me pass the same judgment on Robin that I've chafed under so many times.

Once Isolde was stabilized, they informed me of their proper mode of address with an examining look, as if they expected to be the first person I'd ever met whose gender didn't fit in a neatly prescribed box. Even if they had been the first, it never would have crossed my mind to contradict who they knew they were. Honestly, I had far more questions when they followed that introduction with the fact that they had lived here among the faeries for centuries, ageless and disconnected from the mortal world.

Despite the awkwardness, I think we're all relieved to see the faerie procession. Partly because it's a sign that time is still moving, that we can stop pacing in circles, and partly because they brought food. They're toting trays heavy with mismatched dishes—a full tea set with plump cherries rolling around between the cream and sugar pots, rough brown bread topped with delicate marzipan, gleaming Wintersol honey cakes next to fresh midsummer greens. None of the dishes make any sense, but we're all too hungry to care. My stomach growls loudly at the sight of slices of cheese drizzled with honey.

"Is it safe?" Aris asks, managing suspicion even as she gazes longingly at the steaming teapot. Faerie food has a bad reputation in our world, and there must be a reason why. Still, Raze ate a whole meal the last time we were in the Seelie Realm and suffered no ill effects other than an enchantment that made him act like an empty-headed fool—but we all had that, so I'm not sure if the food was really to blame.

Cobweb looks offended—at least, I think so. It's hard to tell with his facial markings. "It wouldn't be polite to serve guests anything unsafe!"

Isolde grins. She's seemed like herself since I woke again, not giving any hints that our conversation last night affected her at all. If I didn't know better, I'd worry that I dreamed it—but there's no mistaking the lightness that comes from releasing the weight of my secrets. "It's a yes-or-no question," Isolde points out, gesturing to a tray with the dagger she's been fidgeting with. "Safe?"

Robin leans over and whispers something in Cobweb's ear. The faerie's shoulders slump as he starts to realize he's not getting anywhere with us without letting some promises slip. "Yes," he sighs. "It's all safe for mortal consumption. There."

We descend on the food with enthusiasm that might be embarrassing in other circumstances. I guess it's been longer than I thought since all that passed on Wintersol, because my stomach tells me it's been empty for some time.

"So you're taking us to the Queen after this?" Raze asks with his mouth full.

All the faeries laugh in harmony, and the tips of his ears turn red. Last time, a picnic wasn't the only thing he tasted. He also had faerie girls draped all over him, flirting with him just like that, kissing him and laughing at him all at once. And then I found him and I was trying to save him, and I . . .

Warmth floods me at the memory of his lips on mine, a hard press, one I didn't appreciate in the moment and have desperately attempted not to think about. Especially since I started wondering if it would be different a second time. I refuse to look at him again, or to look at anyone else, like some part of me is afraid they'll read my thoughts.

"Not like this!" Robin says eventually, still giggling. "You look terrible!"

We all glance at each other. Our clothes and hair look like they've been through a battle, because they have. Isolde's blood has dried to rust-colored streaks on my white skirt, and there's a gaping hole in her bodice with unraveling edges. Next to Robin, who is as lovely and impeccably put-together as any of the faeries, we collectively look like something you'd wipe off the bottom of your shoe.

Olani glares. "You've got to be joking. Worlds are at stake. I think your Queen will be able to excuse our appearance."

The raspy buzz of agitated wings ripples over the faeries. It sounds like they're communicating, but not in any distinct words, just the murmur of a disgruntled crowd. Cobweb quiets them with a smooth gesture, turning to give us a brilliant white smile. "The Seelie Realm is a place of beauty and order. It would be the gravest disrespect to our ruler to appear before her looking like . . ." He pauses, before finally finishing, "That."

Another faerie with apple-green skin and deep black eyes pipes up: "You might not even make it. Folk have been killed by the Queen's Guard for less."

"They sound welcoming," Raze mutters.

Olani's shoulders don't relax, and she doesn't stop staring at Cobweb like she wishes she could burn a hole through him. Isolde reaches out, brushing her arm to draw her attention. "We kind of need them to like us," she says gently. It's not enough to make Olani happy, but she puts on an expression of grim acceptance as she returns to her meal.

Not even in Wildline Manor have I been so helplessly cared for. Once we're all fed, the food is whisked away and the faeries get to work, surrounding each of us. One brushes my hair while another wipes my face with a damp rag softer than silk. It's not an unpleasant sensation, but the feeling of being prodded and grabbed without warning by unfamiliar hands still makes my skin crawl. Next, my hair is yanked back ruthlessly by three different faeries all braiding in tandem. Another reaches out to tilt my chin up, running feather-light fingertips over my face. It feels like healing magic, the bruising soreness fading away around my eyes, blood tingling in my cheeks.

As the faerie leans back to survey her work, I glance past her to see how the others are doing. The room has fallen silent besides the thoughtful hums of hardworking faeries, each of us lost in our thoughts about things that probably shouldn't be discussed with an audience. I only manage to make eye contact with Olani, who has the faraway glare of someone suffering a great indignity. A faerie whose frost-white hair shares the same fluffy, springy texture as hers unbraids her hair with inhuman speed, nimbly teasing each strand free.

One of the faeries tries to polish Egg's scales with a stiff brush, but he hisses and puffs out a shower of sparks, retreating to my lap. His weight is enough to crush my legs and make my feet fall asleep, but I don't move him. He seems to like it when my fingers run over his scales, soothing both of us with the repetitive motion.

"Ow!" I hear Raze whine behind me. "Careful!"

Olani pins him with a look that makes it clear that he's not in any danger. "There's no way that hurt."

"They're *pulling* my *hair*!" he insists, so pitifully that it's hard not to laugh—or to turn around and see exactly how he's being tortured. The faeries behind me *tsk* disapprovingly at the slightest wiggle, turning my head back into place.

Luckily, I don't have to sit still for long. Within an hour, we're all in a line for a final evaluation—and the realization that we're actually being presented to the Seelie Court, to their Queen, finally starts to sink in. My stomach churns with nerves, but I try to stand straight-backed and chin raised, face carefully controlled.

At least our Wintersol clothes seem to be acceptable to them, after any traces of blood and dust are removed with a spell and captured in a jar, which I really, *really* hope they're planning to throw away after this. The faeries drape us in chains of flowers and jewelry, pulling items from their own extravagant wardrobes to make everything just so.

"Oh, you don't have to—" I start when one of the faerie girls pulls an amethyst ring from her own hand to slip onto my pinky.

She shushes me with an ice-cold finger on my lips. "It's not for you," she murmurs with an ironic twist of her lips. Then she pats my cheek patronizingly and buzzes away.

When it's all said and done, there's a collective exhale. We look like . . . ourselves. Ourselves, but better—skin glowing with health, eyes bright, signs of battle and exhaustion gone. Raze's hair, for once, doesn't look messy, instead braided back into a neat coiled bun. Olani's is an elaborate twist made up of hundreds of tiny braids. I have to imagine I look the same as Isolde, dark lashes fanned out to exaggerate our round eyes, lips glossy and pink.

"What are you waiting for?" Aris demands. Her usually neglected curls have been set into ringlets, drawing attention to the brightness of her icy green eyes. Luckily, none of it has done anything to alter her dazzling personality. She's as comfortable ordering around a room of faerie courtiers as she is terrified mortal servants. "Are you taking us to see the Queen or not? Let's go!"

Cobweb finishes a last look at us, hands wringing together nervously. "It will have to do," he finally decides.

"What more does she want from us?" Raze mutters as we file back into a line to make our way across yet another long, intricate bridge from our tree to the next.

I shrug, falling into step just behind him. "Perfection?" I guess.

He turns to look at me over his shoulder, mouth pulled into the faint curve of a smile. I hold my breath, waiting for him to reply, but whatever he was going to say dissolves into a slow exhale instead. His hair is already breaking free of attempts to restrain it, loosening so the shortest strands curl around his ears. I want to say something about it, but I have to focus on the bigger picture. I need to *stop* being distracted by my friend, stop thinking about him instead of about fixing my mistakes and everything that hangs in the balance. The future of the *world* is uncertain right now, much less a future for us.

Stop thinking about it! I command myself, more firmly this time.

It's hard to feel like anything but prisoners being marched to an execution as we're escorted in a spiral down the tree. The winding steps look too spindly to support our weight, and it takes me a moment to realize that the staircase is *alive*, an intricately braided mass of pale vines springing up from the moss to climb the tree.

Walking up to our little room, I was too numb and exhausted and worried over Isolde to really take in my surroundings. The trees here are impossibly tall, even taller than in the faerie forest we visited before. There, lanterns lit the branches, and a huge faerie party spread over the mossy ground. Here, the forest floor seems to be empty, but strange structures curve around the trunks like frilly climbing mushrooms. Bridges as delicate as spiderwebs extend from one platform to the next in a vast network.

The network of living structures and bridges seems to go on forever into an endless expanse of dark green branches. Birch, who vanished at some point before the faeries arrived, seems to have made himself visible again only so we don't trip over him as he weaves between us on the narrow steps. The brownie walks purposefully, as if he would have been going this way anyway, and it's no more than coincidence that we're all headed in the same direction. The trees around us buzz with life, not so different from the hum of the city. If I close my eyes, I can almost hear the voices of people going about their daily business.

I don't have to imagine long. At the first platform, a young man with lacy lichen covering half his face stops and stares at us. At the next, two children with the slitted pupils of a goat point and bleat laughter. It's hard to keep track of them after that, since the forest seems to be getting more crowded the closer we get to its heart—or maybe word of our presence is spreading, and everyone is rushing out to catch a glimpse of the unlucky mortals.

The procession takes us nearly down to the forest floor, and then back up again, a complex web of paths that I couldn't retrace if I tried. It's not a long walk, but the attention of every faerie in the Seelie Court along the way makes it feel unending. We have to walk single file, with the faeries who prepared us for this ahead and behind, which all makes it impossible to talk. Eventually, I start to notice a certain variety of flowering vine growing denser over the rest of the structures. Its glossy, dark green leaves and fragrant white flowers start to overtake more and more of our surroundings, until we finally step onto a huge platform suspended between several impossibly giant trees.

It's impossible to say if this structure is natural or not. The floor is springy moss, covered nearly from end to end with faeries. They glisten like jewels in a thousand different colors. No—more like beetles under a log, a shimmering being made up of hundreds of inextricable individuals. It's better to look at them that way, as a swarm, because trying to focus on each individual's strange, unsettling beauty makes my head spin. Or maybe that's the thick, choking perfume that fills the warm air making me feel dizzy. The fragrant vines weave and drape into a screen all around us, growing into a solid mass from their origin point at the end of the room.

The Seelie Queen's throne room.

chapter eighteen

SEELIE

I worried at first that I wouldn't be able to tell the Seelie Queen from the rest of her court. They're all so dazzlingly splendid, and I was afraid I'd insult her by not immediately recognizing her superiority.

As it turns out, those fears were completely unfounded. Her magic is so powerful that I can taste it in the back of my throat, so strong its thrum in the air makes my head ache. Looking at her feels like double vision:

The face of a beautiful young woman, whose sienna skin and golden hair both gleam like a beetle's shell, an entire rainbow trapped just beneath the surface. Instead of lashes and brows, a living headdress of sunset-hued butterfly wings fans out around her solid sunlight-gold eyes. She's dressed to match the wings, and her expression is pleasant and inviting, like she's eagerly waiting for you to finish the punch line of a joke.

But the longer I stare, the brighter she gets, until she's just a silhouette swallowed by the glare of her own light. I blink spots away from my vision and glance up again, and the first appearance has returned. She's probably sitting on a throne, but it's choked under a thick crush of vines, flowers swaying as gleaming leaves bask in her glow. I understand now why this world doesn't have a sun—because she *is* the sun. A constant source of warmth and life.

I get the feeling that if I get too close, she'll burn me up.

The Seelie Queen extends a hand to us, and I fight not to flinch back. The faeries closest to her stir excitedly, waiting to see what she'll say. Our group presses together a little tighter, until we're brushing shoulders in one big clump. I think I forget to breathe.

Then the Queen smiles with all her brilliant white teeth, terrifyingly lovely. "My mortal guests!" she exclaims, delighted. "It's been so long since we had any human visitors. And just as long since a firedrake has graced our Court. You are lucky to count him as an ally."

We all kind of nod and murmur agreement. I elbow Raze forward, and Olani steers him with a hand on his shoulder so that he's at the front of our group. He stands there stiffly for a moment before composing himself, lifting his chin and smiling so believably that even I am taken in by it.

"It's—" He pauses, clears his throat. "It's an honor to be in your presence, Your Majesty."

She laughs. "So well-mannered. Just like your ancestors, Raze Wildborn. And Aris Halloward, of course." She sighs, placing a thoughtful finger to her lips. "Have we had any mortals in the Court since the shapeshifters came to ask for our aid?"

Are we supposed to answer that?

"No, my lady," a faerie in shining armor says, eyes straight ahead, hand planted on his sword. "It's been over five hundred years."

"Hmm." The corners of her mouth turn up, and she seems to be lost in a fond memory.

Isolde nudges Raze with a poke in his kidneys. He coughs, then says, "That's actually what we'd like to discuss with you, if we may." Awkward pause. "Your Majesty."

"Oh?" Her pupilless eyes skate over us, and I'm not sure if they're actually emanating heat or if I just feel flushed under the weight of her attention.

Raze nods, hands clasped in front of him. I can see him fighting the urge to fidget nervously. "Well—sort of. Ending up here was a bit of an accident, but you see, the—the threat my ancestors faced centuries ago has . . ."

Don't look at me, don't look at me, I plead silently.

His eyes flick to me. ". . . resurfaced," he finally says. "The rogue faerie, Gossamer." A gasp ripples out through the court, and the temperature seems to drop a few degrees. Raze, sensing he's said the wrong thing, scrambles to recover. "But with the aid of the Seelie Court, we feel confident we can end the threat. For good this time."

"Is that so?" It's literally impossible to tell if the Queen is pleased or angered by us so far. Her low, resonant voice fills the air around us, rich and emotionless. "And how do you plan to do that?"

Raze freezes. Who wouldn't, under the full scrutiny of the Seelie Queen and her entire court? No one speaks or blinks. Even the wind stills. After enough time has passed for me to start wondering if he's forgotten how to talk, he says, "Our plans are . . . flexible. Depending on how much aid we receive. You know, there's some—some variation."

The stillness continues several heartbeats more, and then the Queen bursts into raucous laughter with absolutely no warning, shaking the earth like a clap of thunder. The Court follows her on a delay, less enthusiastically. None of us can manage more than a crooked, half-hearted grin.

"I do not forget much, mortals," she crows through the last few chuckles. "But I realize now I had forgotten how entertaining lies can be."

"I'm not lying!" Raze shouts over the Court's merriment. "I'm— We're—"

Silence falls as abruptly as if it was shattered. "I tire of you," the Queen snaps. "Iselia Graygrove, as entertaining as it is, I no longer wish to speak through your mortal pet. Come forward yourself."

At the sound of my name, a shock dances down my spine straight into my shoes. My head remains clear of ensorcellment, but I step forward before I even realize I'm doing it, standing between the rest of my friends and the Queen.

And now all eyes are on me.

"Your Majesty," I manage through a dry throat, dropping into a clumsy curtsy. "We meant no disrespect."

She lets out a sigh like the gust of wind that precedes a summer storm. "After seventeen summers, Iselia," she says, almost sounding sad. I glance up, skin prickling all over. There's something familiar in her voice, something I've heard in dreams or memories. Before the faerie life was placed in my human body, some part of me was here in the Seelie Court. Some part of me was her subject.

Some part of me still is.

That part sings with recognition as she continues, "I have welcomed you and your friends into my Court, cared for your wounds, ensured you had everything your fragile forms needed. You, an utterly unremarkable changeling, who has loosed a terror on our worlds, who has unraveled Fate's boundaries between them, are welcomed home with open arms. You and your friends are invited to enjoy our hospitality as long as you like, and still, after all that, you ask for more."

It's hard not to tremble. I try to breathe slowly and evenly, squeezing my hands to control the tremor that still threatens to show. "Respectfully, Your Majesty . . . I accept responsibility. It was an accident, but it's my fault. I only ask for the means to fix what is broken. I just want everything to—" Here, my traitorous voice breaks, and I have to swallow hard to finish the sentence. "To go back to how it should be."

"I know what you did, Iselia. I can feel the snarl where my realm twists into yours and the Unseelie Realm, teetering on the edge of breaking them all."

If I felt sick before, it's nothing compared to this moment. It can't be *that* bad, can it? I can't stop now, even though all my instincts tell me to bow my head and give in to the Queen, rather than what I actually do, which is face her and say, "Then you know how important it is to set everything right."

"DO NOT PRESUME TO TELL ME WHAT TO DO, CHANGELING." The boom of the Queen's voice is sudden and ferocious, loud enough to hurt my ears. "I interfered in this war once. I took pity on the human shapeshifters, and what did it get me? Hundreds of my forces slaughtered, the relationships that once existed between our people eroded, and an enemy given the chance of centuries to make a second play. What would you ask me to lose this time?"

I'm still trying to recover from the burst of sound, to will myself to stop shaking, to breathe and respond. I will *not* shrink in front of her. I will not give up.

But I can't seem to make myself do anything else.

Isolde steps up before anyone can stop her. "And what will you do when that tangled magic bursts through your realm, and he starts expanding his borders? When he's at your door? You think he'll just give up and leave your people alone then?"

The Queen makes a sound of disbelief, looking down her nose at Isolde. "The Seelie Court protects its own," she says with great dignity. "The other realms are welcome to do the same. I no longer have any interest in them." She flicks her wrist dismissively. "And I no longer have any interest in you."

Her guards start to close in, ushering us out. Isolde scoffs loudly. "Seriously? You're just going to leave the entire Mortal Realm to die because of sheer cowardice?"

I cringe so hard, a spark of lightning snaps down into my fists. Behind me, Raze sucks in a pained breath.

chapter nineteen

ISOLDE

I know I shouldn't have spoken up, but the Seelie Queen hardly reacts. She turns her head lazily to one of her attendants, face tilting up like the flowers all around her. "What is it, do you think, that compels mortals to spend their entire fleeting lives fighting battles they cannot win? They have such a short time already, and they seem determined to waste most of it in misery."

"Our *world* is at stake!"

I'm surprised to hear Olani's outburst, but even she has taken as much as she can bear. Hope is draining away, fast. I don't know how we can do this without both faerie courts on our side. Her eyes burn with the determined fury only a mortal can feel as she faces the Court with her jaw set.

It looks like the Queen would raise her eyebrows at that, if she had brows to raise. As it is, her brow-wings flutter, eyes widening slightly. "Olani Fullbrace," she murmurs. "A human enchanter dealing in Seelie magic. I know you."

Olani squares her shoulders. Even though she's tall and striking, she tends to shrink in a group, preferring to observe rather than get involved in others' drama. Now, with the enchantments on her appearance and her temper flaring, it's hard to believe she could ever go unnoticed.

The Seelie Queen's pleasant smile stretches. "And for your sake, I'll tell you this: I can hold the enchantment stable. My forces can stop it from spreading without risk to ourselves. As long as the borders between worlds are otherwise maintained, this threat can be contained. Your world is safe."

It takes a moment to understand her meaning. "So . . . no more portals between realms?" Raze asks tentatively. "You're threatening to keep us here?"

"I'd hoped you would accept my invitation to stay, and we could avoid any unpleasantness," she says on a wistful breath. Tension draws tight in the air between us as we all realize what she's saying. What we're up against.

Seelie takes another jagged breath, finally managing to speak again. "You can't do that!" Her voice squeaks as it only does when she's too mad to think clearly. "There are people in that space, frozen in time! Our parents are in there!"

"You have no parents," the Queen snaps, finally showing true irritation. "You are mine to do with as I please. And I am keeping you here, where you can't destroy anything else."

The part of me that squeezes in pain, wanting to admit that she's right, is swallowed up by the much larger part of me that feels indignation. We may not be fully human, but we were loved and raised by humans. We have spent the past three years fighting to get back to them, and there is no one in any realm who can make us give up on that now.

"So we're prisoners?" Aris demands.

"You will be treated well," she says, which isn't a no.

"Any mortal would be lucky to experience the hospitality of the Seelie Court." In case she hasn't been clear, she adds, ". . . Indefinitely."

We stand in stunned silence as the chatter of the Seelie Court picks back up around us. I feel suddenly exposed, vulnerable. There's no dark corner to slip away to, no crowd of ordinary people to get lost in. All eyes are on us. And there is nowhere to go.

Something bumps my leg, and I look down to see Birch. His ears are flattened back, his eyes angry green slits trained on the Queen. He doesn't like this any more than we do. This isn't his home, not really. His home—*our* home—was lost the last time we found ourselves trapped in this realm. For all I know, the wagon we shared is still here. Somewhere in the forest . . . in the Seelie Queen's realm.

I step forward while the idea is still half formed, trusting that the details will fill themselves in as I go. "You can't expect to keep us here for nothing in return."

It takes a moment for my voice to carry over the crowd, and then the faeries' conversations quiet to a whisper. The Seelie Queen gives me an appraising look, which is sort of like being judged by the sun. I wonder if I'm going to walk away from this with my skin toasted a nice rosy tan by her light.

There's a tug on my sleeve, and I don't have to look to know it's Seelie. She whispers, "What are you *doing*?" just loud enough for me to hear.

I turn my head slightly, not looking away from the Queen, and murmur back, "Trust me." And I guess she does, because she doesn't say anything after that.

"I feel I've been more than generous with you, *changeling*." The word hisses on the Seelie Queen's tongue, like the drone of a thousand angry cicadas. But she's still a faerie, and there's a different sort of light in her eyes. The inability to resist making a deal, one that will twist me into knots and put me in her service until my bones turn to dust—unless I'm very, very careful. "What more would an Unseelie creature ask of me?"

I feel Olani, Raze, and Aris trying to draw me into their exchanged look of confusion, but my eyes drift away. I'm more focused on that new bit of information the Queen let slip. *Unseelie?* Aren't they supposed to be frightening? Fierce and unpredictable, driven by no code other than their own impulses toward chaos? Meanwhile, the Seelie Court operates based on sameness and its own baffling rules.

The two courts get simplified to good and evil, but that's not quite right. When you look at their differences like that, it seems oddly familiar. I suppose it makes as much sense as anything else.

"Does she mean you?" Raze whispers to Seelie, who is also, studiously, not making eye contact.

"Um . . ." The soft sound Seelie makes is barely more than a hum. "No."

And then everyone isn't just looking in my direction, they're looking at *me*.

It wasn't a secret, only something I hadn't gotten around to saying yet. Seelie shouldn't have held on to the knowledge for so long, but it's hard to stay mad at her now that I've experienced firsthand what an impossible topic it is to bring up naturally in a conversation—*Hey, guys, remember how I'm supposed to be the normal one? Turns out we've been wrong not only about that, but about the whole concept of the very nature of our identities! Pretty weird, right?*

Which is to say, I haven't said anything about this revelation, but I have thought of nothing else. Even I am surprised by how calm I feel as their faces go completely blank, then shocked with the dawn of understanding. The *Unseelie creature* is me. This is who I am.

Whatever that means.

You'd expect the Seelie Queen and her Court to be impatient about our little aside, but their attention doesn't seem to have wavered. Like they've stepped out of their own minds in favor of watching us to see how this plays out. It's more than a little eerie.

Luckily, no one stops me from moving on. There will be time for explanations and questions later. At least, there will if I play my cards right.

"You could keep us here," I admit, turning to the Seelie Queen's radiance. I choose each word as carefully as I can without slowing my speech. "But it would hardly be fair to expect us to cooperate without receiving anything in exchange."

I wait for the Queen's reply, but she keeps staring at me silently. Unblinking as she waits for an answer to her question. I know that I can do this—I just need to be precise with my words, quick, and (most importantly) a little bit lucky. I take a deep breath, feeling the foundations of the plan start to settle into place.

"In exchange for our binding agreement to remain in the Seelie Realm, leaving the borders between worlds intact, I have three conditions."

"*Isolde*," Seelie mutters. I ignore her.

"First, I want a promise that none of us will be killed or placed under any enchantments against our will." I'm not going to risk repeating what happened last time we were in the Seelie Realm.

"With the condition that you offer my people the same courtesy, I give you my word. What else?"

My heart races, but I force myself to stay still and calm as I fish the *Destiny* from my pocket and hold it up on one extended hand. "The last time we . . . visited your realm, something happened to our enchanted wagon. If we are to live here peacefully, I would ask for it to be restored to the state in which it entered the Seelie Realm and returned to us."

As I hoped, the Seelie Queen obviously thinks that we're not worth the trouble of denying the small favors I ask. She simply waves a hand, and the *Destiny* flies from my grip. The wagon grows so fast there's an audible *pop!*, landing heavily enough to shake with the impact.

The *Destiny* looks just as I remembered it—except some chips in the paint and marks gouged by Birch's teeth. It looks out of place in the faerie court, this object that was obviously made by human hands. Seelie and I painted it ourselves, chose a dark green that blended in with the trees and turned gold in the dappled sunlight. Standing here, I can almost pretend that the past few months never happened, and when I step inside, it'll be just me and her, and we'll be off to the next town.

"And your third request?" the Seelie Queen asks.

Every muscle in my body tenses. This is the part where I find out if my half-formed plan will actually work. Technically, since my third term hasn't been met, I'm not bound by our agreement. It's a loophole that wouldn't hold up to much scrutiny, but it's one I plan to exploit before anyone thinks to stop me.

I look back at Seelie and our friends, willing them to follow my lead. Then I turn back to the Seelie Queen, grin, and simply say, "Bye."

My legs hit full speed before the word seems to reach her ears. I sprint for the wagon, looking back over my shoulder to make sure everyone's with me. Raze is already running, with Seelie half a second behind, slowed by the time it took to scoop an uncooperative Egg up in her arms.

"Wait!" Aris calls, hesitating, but then Olani grabs her by the wrist and pulls her along with us. I'm sure she'd rather do this the *right* way, the *clever* way, but she's stuck with us now.

My boots land heavily on the platform, rocking the whole wagon on its suspension as I fling the door wide. "Get in!" I don't look back again until I'm settled in the driver's seat, flipping levers and testing the brakes and getting the wagon ready for a quick getaway. By the time I do, I see that some of the Queen's Guard have mobilized to get in the way.

Raze knocks one of the faeries aside with a surprisingly effective elbow to the ribs, clearing the way for Seelie. Just as I hoped, the faeries are bound by the Queen's vow not to harm us, which is severely limiting their options in terms of preventing our escape. Raze, Seelie, and Egg pile into the wagon with another heavy thump. Aris and Olani aren't far behind.

"*Stop*," the Seelie Queen commands. If she hadn't promised not to enchant us, the power in the word would probably be enough to turn us to dust on the spot. As it is, it makes my head pound. Time seems to slow in the heat of her golden gaze. No one moves, not even her own forces. "*You will obey me.*"

A black speck moves in the corner of my eye. At first, I think I'm seeing spots. Then Birch appears, his paws lifting off the ground as his hackles raise. He puts himself between the wagon and the Queen, meeting the strength of her glare with his own hateful green one. His tail twitches as his mouth opens to show all his teeth—pathetically small, faced by the force of the Seelie Court, but with the confidence of a full army

Birch pins his ears back and hisses. It's not just a hiss—it's the sound of a dam breaking, a wall of ice crashing down, something primal and powerful released. His rebellion echoes all around us, filling the stunned silence. It lasts just long enough to thoroughly distract everyone from us. Olani, never one to waste an opportunity, drags Aris into the wagon.

"*You impudent little brownie*," the Seelie Queen seethes, so surprised by the betrayal of one of her own subjects that we seem to have temporarily faded into the background of her attention, "I'll boil you from the inside out. I'll rip the magic from your furry corpse. I'll—I'll—"

There's another shimmer of power in the air, and I can tell

it's more than I can sense, because Seelie looks like she's developing a splitting headache. The Queen's fury crashes over us in waves, bent on destroying Birch.

But she can't touch him—because she promised. Because he's one of us.

The wagon lurches into motion. Slowly, at first, but picking up speed fast enough to make me aware that we're very high off the ground, and this platform is not as big as it first seemed.

Aris looks up at me, then back through the open door. "Why do you look so excited?"

Seelie groans. "She gets like this when she's about to do something dangerous."

Birch lets out one last angry howl, then drops from the air and bounds into the wagon. The second his paws hit the floor, the wagon picks up speed. I can't make out the reactions of the faeries around us, because they've all turned into a blur of color.

"*Stop them!*" The Queen's command reverberates in the air like thunder, her fury a flash of lightning.

But I can't watch what's going on behind me. I'm too focused on the path that lies ahead. Faeries dive from our path as we barrel toward the edge, picking up speed with every second.

"Brace!" I shout behind me.

"Isolde, no!" Seelie sounds absolutely horrified. I can practically hear her thinking, *If there's time to brace, there's time to stop before we go careening down a hundred-foot drop*, but that's where she'd be wrong. The time for carefully considered plans has passed.

The edge of the throne room approaches quickly, and then—without so much as a bump under our wheels—it's gone. We're soaring through the air, screams overlapping as the wagon plummets. My scream turns to a laugh, helpless exhilaration at the feeling of flying, even though I know it's going to end with a spectacular crash.

But we're not just falling—we're also moving forward,

carried by momentum. We only fall a story or two before our wheels hit the next platform with a resounding *boom!* and a tooth-chattering jolt. I'm still laughing as the wagon tears across this platform, a vine-woven bridge high up from the forest floor.

"Isolde!" Olani screeches in a shrill pitch I've never heard from her before.

For a second, it looks like we're going to crash straight into a massive tree trunk, as wide and solid as any castle wall. Then I throw the wheel to the right, sending us off another much shorter jump to another bridge below.

"How about a little warning next time?" Seelie scolds, pushing herself up from the floor.

"Sorry!" I'm pretty sure I couldn't possibly look *less* sorry. "We lived, didn't we?"

For a brief, glorious second, I think we've lost them. That we might *actually* get away with this. Then the first arrow thuds into the back of the wagon, narrowly missing the door.

I curse, too busy trying to steer to determine where it came from. It doesn't take long, though. Soon, the faerie steeds appear all around us. Beautiful, terrible horses, some identical to the ones you'd find in the Mortal Realm, and some decidedly *not*.

The faerie hunters have caught up with me again.

I force myself to breathe, not to get caught up in memories of what happened last time. I'm not that scared little fox anymore. I'm not helpless and alone.

"Doesn't that break the agreement?" Raze asks, nearly shouting to be heard over the wind and the rumble of our wheels.

No one responds. The Queen agreed not to harm us, but I suppose the definition of *harm* can be flexible.

I can't keep looking back and forth like this. "Raze, take over," I snap, delivering orders with the confidence of someone who definitely, absolutely, has any idea what's going on.

Raze, to his credit, obeys without any fuss. He takes the

wheel from me and drops into the driver's seat the moment I leave, and I hope against hope that his experience flying will give him the ability to get the wagon to the ground without shattering it and all of us inside.

"There's strong magic coming off that arrow," Seelie says, her brow furrowing as she looks out at the faeries quickly closing in.

I join the others just in time to see Aris yanking the arrow from the door frame and discarding it, letting it plummet into the sea of green leaves moving beneath us.

"It's not an enchantment for us," Aris says. "It's for the wagon. They're trying to slow us down."

Another arrow flies toward us, and while the rest of us flinch back, Olani steps forward, throwing her arms up. Her magic shield blooms in place. Normally, she can only do this spell weeks apart, but the Seelie Court's healing must have restored her reserves of magic along with her health. "That should help," she says through her teeth.

The wagon jolts, nearly throwing us out the open door.

"Sorry!" Raze calls. "Where am I going?"

"Down!" I shout back. "Head to where we came through the realms before!" I don't know if we'll be able to find the spot, but if the rift Seelie used to pull us through is still open, it might be our best chance to leave. I'm not sure if she has it in her to open another portal, and after last time, I don't want to find out.

Another arrow and a sparkling enchantment bounce off Olani's shield in quick succession. The faeries are close enough for me to pick out the individuals attacking us, their faces lit up by the thrill of the chase. To them, this is all some sort of game. My fingers itch to reach for my daggers, to meet their attack with my own, but it's not worth risking the protection I managed to bargain for.

One of the faerie steeds is getting dangerously close—close

enough that if I wanted to, I could probably reach out and touch it. I have just enough time to notice this before its rider spurs it on even faster and it disappears from sight. There's a bone-grinding *crash!* as it smashes into us from the side, making the wagon shake on its wheels. They're trying to shove us off the path.

Birch hisses, and Seelie moves faster than I thought she could. She leans out the back door again, pushing one hand forward. A jet of flame shoots out, narrowly missing the rider, but making the horse rear back and shy away.

"Nonlethal!" I remind her.

"Doing my best!" she replies, turning to aim at a rider attempting the same trick on our other side.

On my other side, Aris takes a deep breath and twists her hands, sending out a shower of sparks that dazzle my eyes. As I blink away spots, I see that it's also managed to blind a few of our pursuers, who are quickly falling behind as they struggle to regain control of their mounts.

We must be getting close to our goal by now, right? I try to take in our surroundings, but it's all trembling green leaves and the snap of branches as our wheels jump from one platform to the next. Seelie and Aris take turns firing off spells as more and more arrows, bursts of light, and unidentifiable trinkets bounce off Olani's shield.

"How's it going back there?" Raze asks. I glance over my shoulder to see him sweating, clutching the wheel like he's afraid it'll escape if his hands slip.

"I can't keep this up much longer." Olani's hands are still raised, holding our shield steady, but there's sweat breaking out on her brow. Egg was able to help her last time, but that was against a much bigger threat. I'm worried that unleashing his flame against the Seelie Queen's forces might be about as helpful as putting a fire out with undiluted alcohol.

"Let me help." Aris stands beside Olani, just like she did

with Seelie in the ballroom. She's spent her whole life studying magic, copying Leira and attempting to master as many forms of it as possible. If anyone can do this, she can.

Olani doesn't seem to reach the same conclusion. "It's a form of healing magic. You don't know—"

"I know enough!" Aris barks back. "And you're about to collapse. Tell me what to do. I can help."

Olani hesitates, arms trembling as she struggles to hold her position. Finally, she caves, and starts mumbling instructions to Aris. I don't catch most of it, and what I do hear goes straight over my head, but Aris is a good student. She listens intently, and within a few moments, a tentative web of her gleaming golden magic is unfurling along Olani's shield.

"Together," she says.

Olani takes a deep breath, then drops one hand. Aris catches it, squeezing her palm tight and holding up her opposite hand, so they almost mirror each other. Their magic combines, shielding us in a radiant glow. It's beautiful.

And I'm definitely not jealous.

Even if I was, I don't have *time* to be jealous.

"Almost there!" Raze announces, but he doesn't have to—a spike of pain rips through me before I even see the Seelie forest's carpet of flawless green grass. The pain is a clear warning, the tug that comes before permanent injury. I close my eyes and fight against it.

CRASH!

With one final wave of force, the *Destiny* hits the ground and skids to a halt, sliding almost in a complete circle as it approaches the tables still set for the interrupted Wintersol feast. I hear the clatter of wheels and gears and the muffled crunch of soft earth, but all my attention is focused within. I dare to open my eyes long enough to see the shimmering rift left behind, the weak spot in the fabric between worlds that Seelie exploited to get us here, and my stomach reels.

"The wagon won't fit through there," Aris points out. "We'll have to go on foot."

They're all moving, dragging me senselessly along with them, when I finally find my voice. "Stop." I sound as unsteady as I feel, barely managing to avoid sinking down into the grass.

Everyone freezes as one.

"The . . . bargain . . ." I manage to get out. I swallow hard, fighting nausea as my body rejects what my mind is trying to do. As the realization of what's happening to me solidifies, as a new plan starts to form in the back of my mind, the sickness slowly recedes. "It won't let me go while I still have unfinished business with the Queen."

Everyone turns and looks at the approaching faerie hunters, the others that have joined the chaos just for the fun of it, the branches still bobbing from our momentum. Splintered wood where the wagon crashed through the walls of their tree houses, and twigs the size of logs showering down from the higher levels of the forest. Just above us, a burning branch drops onto a platform, which goes up as if it was greased for that exact purpose.

We've made an absolute *mess* of the Seelie Court—but at least it will buy us a few moments to sort this out.

"Isolde," Seelie starts.

"I'll stay." The words spill out without thought. We don't have time to argue about it, and I don't see any other way.

Seelie's jaw drops. "Stay here? After all that? Have you lost your mind?" The fire on her fingertips is fading slowly, sparks drifting in the wind that toys with her hair.

I offer a crooked smile, trying to seem more confident than I feel. Birch rams his tiny head into my leg, as if reminding me to hurry. "It's not ideal, but I'll survive."

"I'm not leaving you here," Seelie says, unmoved.

I grab her hands, forcing her to look into my eyes. Maybe I can project some sense into her head. "You don't have a choice.

Maybe this is for the best. I'll stay and talk to the Queen until you get back. I can be very persuasive."

"Do you remember what happened last time you were unsupervised in the Seelie Realm?"

"I won't be unsupervised. Olani will be with me." It takes a second to gather the courage to look over my shoulder at Olani, but I do it anyway. "Right?"

Olani, who's still catching her breath, nods. "I mean . . . it would be irresponsible to leave you alone."

Seelie's thoughts are catching up. It always takes her a moment to wrap her head around a change of plans. She hesitates another moment, mouth pressed into a line, and then nods. "Fine. Then I'm the only one who needs to go to the Unseelie Realm. If it's going to be like that, you should all stay together."

"You don't have to tell me twice," Aris says.

"Whoa, wait a minute." Raze steps forward. Almost unconsciously, we've split into two clear groups: him, Seelie, and Egg. Me, Olani, Aris, and Birch. Raze meets Seelie's burning glare, standing close enough that she has to tilt her head to look up at him. "What happened to not leaving people alone?"

"It's different for me!" Seelie argues, taking another step back.

"You need someone there with you."

"Raze," she starts, voice tight. "Last time—" Last time they were in the Unseelie Realm, he was incapacitated by magic, poisoned, and nearly died. She swallows hard, trying to look as cold and hard as iron. "I need to do this alone."

"Maybe you do," he says. "But I'll be right there beside you."

I groan, cutting them both off. "There's no time to waste. Unless you have a way to stop Raze from following, you can continue this argument in the Unseelie Realm."

Seelie takes a deep breath. Not agreement, but resignation. She reaches out to squeeze my hand, opening her mouth to say something.

"Don't say goodbye," I say with a quick grin. I give her fingers a squeeze, then let them drop. "You'll be right back."

"Right," she says tightly, forcing a smile.

Before they can walk away, Aris takes a decisive step forward. "Raze, wait." In the moment it takes for him to look surprised that she's directly addressing him, she pulls something out of her pocket. Without making eye contact, she grabs her cousin's wrist and forces his hand to open, dropping a simple strand of wooden beads into his waiting palm. "Rowan beads," she says. "To protect you from enchantment. I guess I don't need them anymore, so . . ."

For a second, it looks like Raze might burst into tears. He blinks, then closes his fingers around the gift. "Thank you." Before either of them can struggle awkwardly for something to say, an impossible phrase to make up for years of bitterness and rivalry, he turns away.

Then Seelie and Raze, holding hands and their breath, pass through the shimmering rift. Egg steps perfectly in time with Seelie, so the last thing to vanish is the tip of his tail. My heart squeezes watching my twin disappear into danger, but I don't let it summon worst-case scenarios. Whatever Seelie faces on the other side, she *will* come back.

She always does.

"So what do we do now?" Aris says.

"That's easy." I lean onto my heels, watching the swarm of approaching faeries. "Stall."

chapter twenty

SEELIE

Despite the chill of the unending portal realm, I drop Raze's hand the instant we're through, turning on him. "You shouldn't have followed me."

He looks absolutely stunned, as if this isn't what we were arguing about less than a minute ago. "What? Why?"

"Because it's *dangerous*." I look around, trying to figure out where the magic has placed us. My nerves prickle, but Gossamer is nowhere to be seen. Good. Maybe we can be in and out before he knows we were here.

I'm not sure how I'll find a weak spot in this realm's borders, somewhere we can cross over to the Unseelie Realm without making everything worse, but I trust my magic to guide us. Gossamer made a mistake letting it slip that this place is held together by my power.

My parents are imprisoned by my power. It's a cruel twist,

after all the years I spent running to spare them from the consequences of my uncontrolled magic, as if Fate couldn't help but end up here. Together, and yet still unreachable. My mother and father suffering because of me.

Fighting back the sick anxiety that curls through my chest at the sight of all those unsettling frozen faces, but especially the ones I know, I turn to the open doorway that leads out to the garden. I need to get outside, to see how far this realm's borders go. Raze follows, saying something about how he thinks it's too late to start worrying about a little danger that dies in his throat the second we're out of the ballroom and under the open sky.

No—what *was* the open sky. We're in the same garden we strolled through before, surrounded by an eerie, unseeing crowd. Every icy face is turned up, expressions varying shades of amazement. I look to the last thing they saw before time stopped—a shimmering dome high overhead, its arc swooping down to meet the manor's walls. It's unstable but contained. Colors crawl over its surface like a soap-bubble sheen, obscuring the outside world—if there still *is* an outside world. Maybe, if I get closer, I'll see the rest of Gilt Row moving at the speed of an anthill. Day and night and day and night, as time marches on without us.

Within the dome, the lantern flames are perfectly still, casting even blue light over everything. Above our heads, a firework blooms mid-explosion. The only thing that moves is the hem of my skirt swishing around me and the fog of my breath pluming in clouds. "This is all my fault, and I should be the one to fix it."

Raze lets out an incredulous little laugh. "You really think that?"

I know we have bigger things to deal with right now, but his tone sparks an anger in my chest I can't ignore. I whirl on him, stopping short so he nearly trips over me. "Why are you laughing at me?"

"I'm not?" he says, but it sounds like a question.

"Then what was *that*?" I point at him, a useless gesture I know he'll understand anyway.

He blinks, taking a second to think before he responds. "It's just . . . so . . . Seelie, no one else feels that way."

The anger catches in my throat, choking me for a second. I'm always on the outside, feeling and thinking wrong. Though I've tried to claim my magic, accepting even the strange faerie parts of myself, I can't make that fact stop hurting. "You don't have to say it like that," I finally manage, voice going soft and dark between us.

Raze's eyes widen immediately. "I didn't mean it like that."

"Oh, really? Then what *did* you mean?"

He reaches out, hand dropping onto my shoulder. "That no one reasonable would blame you. No one expects you to do this alone. That's all."

I want that to be true, but I can't accept it. "*No one?*" I repeat, overemphasizing the words. "And you know that because you know everything, right?"

"Seelie," he says. His hand slips back down to his side. "You're deflecting."

"Why would I—"

"Because you can't stand to think that I could care about you?" He says it like a challenge, like it's something we both know but which hasn't been said aloud before now. "I'm tired of pretending you're not avoiding me! Trying to cut me out, because you can't stand the thought of actually letting someone in so you don't have to do everything alone."

I don't know why that makes me angrier than anything else he's said. It feels like the whole world is closing in around me. "Why, Raze?" I say hotly, aware that I'm almost shouting. My voice rings all around us. "Why would I do that?"

He doesn't flinch back from my anger. He remains steady, watching me with an expression that is so tender it cuts straight through every bit of armor I have, slicing into a heart I thought I'd protected. "I don't know, Seelie. You tell me."

"I—" I don't have an answer to that, because maybe he's right. I don't want anyone following me into danger, because the people who choose me invariably get hurt because of it. Every time. I have to stop this spiraling closeness between us before it gets any further. "I don't need your help," I finally manage, but my voice is too raw to be convincing.

"I *know* that," Raze says. "I just wish you'd accept that it's okay to want it."

"*Wanting* things doesn't work out for me," I snap. This conversation feels like it's squeezing me in iron chains, choking tighter and tighter. Forcing my heart to beat faster and my chest to hurt. I feel trapped and overwhelmed, and I know it isn't really Raze's fault, but he's the one right in front of me. My next words are quick and scalding—anything to make him back away. "You make me furious."

"Because you don't want to hear the truth?" Instead, he leans in closer. "Tell me it's not true, and I'll leave you alone."

I grit my teeth, refusing to meet his eyes. Maybe he's right. Maybe he isn't. I can't just *say* something that I'm not certain is the truth, though. When I try, my throat gets too tight and my lips seal themselves. All I can do is glare to the side, like responding is beneath me.

"Interesting," he replies to the silence, and when my eyes finally snap up to look at him—when I see the grin creeping over his lips—I realize he's intentionally baiting me. Trying to get a reaction, instead of letting me win by icing him out. It's not a smug smile, not malicious or cruel—just his constant, infuriatingly good-tempered confidence that we're better off together. Barely a curl, the corner of his mouth sinking slightly into the softness of his cheek.

I shake myself from the realization that I'm staring at his mouth. Which is not so strange, for someone who's often uncomfortable with direct eye contact . . . except that when I force my gaze back up, he's staring at mine.

"Raze, you—" I start, not sure what's going to follow. What shadowed corner of myself I'm about to reveal to him.

But then Egg lets out a pained yelp and streaks over the frosted ground, weaving between frozen forms, until he reaches a fountain, frozen solid and dripping with icicles. He scales the slick stone all the way to the top, leaning out into the open air like he's reaching for something.

"Egg!" Whatever I was going to say to Raze is gone now, replaced by worry. "What are you doing? Get down from there!"

The dragon doesn't even give me the recognition of a defiant hiss. He's just staring up, like we aren't even there. Dark, cold dread sinks down my spine.

Raze swears under his breath. "How are we going to get him down from there?" Egg can't fly yet. I've seen him use his undersized wings to glide a little, but never with only sharp ice and unforgiving stone below.

I turn to him, but he's gone. The spot Raze's voice was coming from just a second ago is empty, nothing standing between me and the cool breeze that plucks at my dress. I turn back, starting to run to Egg, but he's gone, too.

There's no one here but me—and Gossamer, sitting serenely on the edge of the fountain.

"No," I gasp, turning in place again. Trying to ignore him, to look anywhere but at the faerie. The landscape around me shimmers and melts into a brilliant winter day—a flat white sky reflecting the sunlight, the smell of woodsmoke heavy on the air. A familiar sight stands before me, and it cracks my heart in two.

I'm *home*.

My parents' cottage glows with warmth against the gray landscape. I'm standing in Mami's garden, shriveled skeletons of basil and marigold butting up against the defiantly evergreen rosemary. It all shimmers with ice like it's been sugared.

Gossamer gestures for me to sit next to him on the low stone wall that marks the garden's border. I know it's just one of his illusions, that none of this is real . . .

But I numbly crunch over the colorless earth to stand beside him. From here, I can look into the window. Inside the golden glow of the kitchen, I see Papa's dark curls, his head bent over a tray of buns he's twisting into knots one by one. It's too far away for me to possibly be able to smell the kitchen, but the memory of yeast and sugar and the sticky feeling of the dough that nearly drove me to tears all flood my senses. This moment feels surgically removed from time, past experiences and future hopes cutting ruthlessly through my present.

I look over at Gossamer. He's tall and slender, like most faeries, so even with him seated, I can comfortably meet his eyes.

"What did you do to them?" I ask, forcing myself to stay calm. This is all an illusion, so it's possible that Egg and Raze might be standing by watching me talk to nothing.

Or they might be in very real danger.

Gossamer blinks at me for a second, like he's not sure what I'm talking about. "I haven't done anything to your friends, Seelie," he says casually, which does technically answer the question, but is still vague enough that it's not comforting.

"So . . . you're not going to try to kill us?"

"Not right now," he says as casually as though we were discussing future dinner plans. As though he didn't run my sister through last time we saw each other. The faerie is on his best behavior again, which can only mean one thing.

"What do you want?" I sigh, still standing just out of his reach. My hands are balled at my sides, ready to start slinging spells at any moment. We both know I can't, not without shifting the balance of power between us. I still have an iron dagger tucked away, but there's no subtle way to draw it. For now, even though every syllable makes my skin crawl, I have no choice but to hear him out.

Gossamer's mouth twitches, forming a distant crescent-moon smile. "Every time I think I know what to do with you, you surprise me." He speaks with a familiarity bordering on fondness that reminds me of every conversation we've had, of all the time he lurked in my mind. We know each other well, and it makes me feel queasy every time I remember that. "Would you prefer it if I tried to kill you?"

I glare at him, my lips pressed tight. Answering that question from a faerie would be foolish, and I've learned my lesson about bargaining with Gossamer. Several times over.

"Perhaps you'd rather have me begging your forgiveness? For the unpleasantness with your sister. How is she, by the way?"

"Still alive," I grit out defiantly. "No thanks to you."

He shrugs, as if that dismisses the fact that he *ran her through with a sword*, and we're even there now. "Well then. For losing my temper, for the Unseelie forest, for everything that came before that. Would you finally be satisfied with yourself, Seelie, to see the fae bow before you? Would you believe me if I said I regretted it all?"

"You're not saying anything," I say between gritted teeth. He isn't. It's all hypotheticals, thought exercises cloaked in tricky language. Gossamer doesn't feel things as mortals do. He's just trying to get me fired up. "Stop playing around and just tell me what you *want*."

Gossamer blows out a disappointed sigh. "Perhaps I simply wanted to chat."

"You didn't."

"I want to offer you one last bargain. And before you refuse, consider that it might be mutually beneficial."

Absolutely not, I think, but I can't make myself say it. Maybe it's the homesick ache leaking from every inch of our familiar surroundings, or maybe it's the knowledge that I still have to *fix* this mess I've made of all our worlds, and if he offers a way to do that, I have to consider it. No matter the personal cost. I swallow hard, fingers knotting together.

"Ah," Gossamer breathes, a little too pleased with himself. "Now you're listening."

"Stop wasting my time," I snap, because the fact that I'm listening doesn't mean I have to like it.

"Time is a mortal construct."

He smirks, looking over my shoulder at the image of my father in the window. Mami has joined him, sitting quietly at the table scribbling in a journal. The silence between them is companionable and comfortable, a bubble that surrounds them as tangibly as a shielding spell. A bubble where I used to belong. I spent my whole life shielded from the world by their love, until everything came crashing down around me.

"It's a simple exchange," Gossamer says in my ear. I jump at the nearness of his voice—I hadn't realized he stood up. But he's standing behind me, bending to speak at a low volume just close enough to make the hair at the back of my neck stand on end. The same way he did in the Unseelie forest.

My jaw trembles, but I don't flinch. From the corner of my eye, all I can see is the pale smudge of his cheek, his long white hair fluttering in the wind around both of us. "Historically, that hasn't gone well for you."

Gossamer attempts to force a chuckle, which comes out more like a growl. "I am aware." With him standing so close, my magic feels like a stormy sea, waves tossing me and crashing over me, jumping to his presence. He reaches out a hand, fingers moving delicately, and the thread of magic between us moves with him. Both of our gazes follow his hand up and to the cottage beyond. "This is all you wanted," he muses quietly. "A quiet, peaceful life. Family and a warm fire in the hearth. Humble . . . and mortal . . . and mundane."

I swallow hard. He's right, but I won't give him the satisfaction of saying so. All those years Isolde and I spent on the road, I was wishing to be right back here. Before that, when I spent every day suppressing my magic and trying to blend in here in our small village, I just wished I could be like everyone else. I never wanted to be an enchanter.

And now I have the power of a faerie, plus the untapped potential of the world's last firedrake, at my untrained fingertips.

"So that's what I'm offering," Gossamer says. His hand drops. "I went about it all wrong before, offering you the world. Trying to destroy you for not seeing things my way. You don't care about any of that, do you? You just want your peace."

For a long time, I can't breathe. Then I turn to face Gossamer, taking a step back to put space between us. He feels more real than before, now that he's actually *here* and not confined to a voice in my head. There's a faint smell of magic and cold, crisp evergreen sap around him. "So . . . my magic, in exchange for a normal life," I say. My voice feels weak, sounds hollow and high-pitched. "That's it? I just . . . go home?"

It's such a simple solution. So easy—perhaps *too* easy. And I'd be lying if I said I wasn't tempted. Didn't I spend every day of our journey to the Mortal's Keep wishing away the burden of my magic?

But that was before I knew how to use it. A lot has changed since then. Even if I somehow could walk away and leave the open tear between worlds, ignore the cataclysm and Gossamer and all his plans, I'd be giving up a part of myself.

Would I even be *me*, without my magic?

The sound of a hawk's cry cuts through the stillness. I look around for its source, a familiar spot of reddish-brown feathers in the colorless sky.

Raze swoops down, diving toward us. Gossamer sees him the second before he passes between us and throws up a hand, summoning more illusion magic to attack. Without thinking,

I shove him hard, interrupting the spell. After so much magical back-and-forth, it's surprisingly satisfying to feel my hands strike his bony chest, to hear the *thump* of him hitting the ground. As he loses concentration, the illusion around us starts to dissolve at the edges.

Magic rolls down my arms, snapping and sparking over my skin. Tiny bolts of lightning, thoughtful and resentful, clinging to me. I think I've grown to like this power. Even if I was going to give it up, it certainly wouldn't be to Gossamer.

I let myself look at the cottage's warm glow one last time, memorizing the smiles on my parents' faces, before I turn and run.

chapter twenty-one

ISOLDE

Time has never functioned quite right for me, either tumbling forward too fast to track or crawling at a snail's pace to smother me. In the Seelie Realm, it's even worse. I'm used to finding my footing without thought, leaping into action with a new plan every time I meet an obstacle, but now, my hands are tied. Metaphorically.

Though I suppose if I find a way to get myself in any more trouble, it could become very literal.

After being denied another audience with the Seelie Queen (three times), two failed attempts to sneak in to see her (both of which resulted in me finding myself suddenly back inside the *Destiny*, parked on the forest floor between roots half my height, like a child put in time-out), and one fit of frustrated anguish, I'm no closer to securing her help. At least I managed to rescue a set of my own clothes from the *Destiny*, so I don't have to wear that ridiculous Wintersol gown any longer. We've slept and eaten a few times. It might have been days.

If Seelie gets back with the Unseelie Queen's support and I still haven't succeeded, I'm never going to hear the end of it.

We've tried going back to the outdoor feast hall in the hopes it'll get us closer, but both times have been an exercise in futility and faerie nonsense. This time, we eat the food they give us on the forest floor, backs leaned against the wagon, just like old times.

Except that my sister and Raze are missing, and Aris isn't trying to capture and/or kill us.

Speaking of which. Aris wrinkles her nose, pulling in her knees to scoot as far as she can get from me. "Can you eat a little less violently? You're getting crumbs everywhere."

I take a spiteful bite of bread in her direction, ripping it from the crust like a wild animal tearing flesh from bone. Chewing noisily, I roll my eyes and look over at Olani. Olani does a very good job pretending like she's been concentrating on her food the whole time, but I catch the quick shift of her eyes as she looks away from me, battling a smile.

Aris lets out a disgusted sound, tilting her head back to the endless dusk sky. "We get it," she deadpans. "You're very angry."

"And you're the picture of cheer," I reply sweetly. We're technically working together now, but I've had just about enough of Aris's attitude. Her constant reminders that she thinks I'm somehow less than her. The fact that she's always hated me, the memory of all those weeks on the road back to Auremore, is actually comforting. It means that she's not disgusted by me because she knows I'm a changeling now.

We've had time to talk about *the changeling thing*, between our ill-fated attempts to speak to the Queen. To talk about how I had only just found out, and I was going to tell them (okay, this was mostly directed at Olani). About how much we all don't know about changelings. About how learning this doesn't change who I am. It doesn't change anything at all, especially not Aris's general dislike of other people.

"I've accepted the situation," she replies primly, cupping a goblet. She holds it like a bouquet, tucked close to her chest with both hands. "I could get angry at the faeries, or you, or your sister, but there's no point. I'm just as much to blame for all this. And the sooner you accept your hand in it, the better."

"Me?" I flare up defensively, but then the rest of her thought hits me. My head tilts as I shift my gaze to look at her. "Wait, you?"

Olani looks up, too, her tone significantly more soothing than my screech. "You blame yourself for this?"

Aris briefly looks like she'd rather be anywhere else in any of the realms, swishing the liquid in her goblet, but then she screws up her face and takes a sip of the weak faerie wine. "Yes. Obviously. If I'd just done as I was *ordered*, you never would have escaped. None of this would have happened. And even if we get out of it, Leira will know—" Her voice suddenly pitches up, and she cuts herself off sharply.

"We still would have escaped," Olani says. It doesn't seem very comforting.

I stuff the last of my crust of bread into my mouth, talking around it. "Why *did* you help us?" I ask. Aris snorts, obviously annoyed by me even asking something like that, but before she can snark at me, I add, "You have nothing to prove to us. Maybe getting it off your chest will help."

She straightens, then sighs. "I just . . . wanted everything to go back to normal. I *knew* what Aunt Leira had been working toward all this time, but I—I didn't care about that. It wasn't so long ago that *I* was her proudest achievement, her legacy. I was going to inherit everything. I was making her proud. And then the changeling and the firedrake came in and ruined everything." She breathes out a shaky laugh, which only serves to make me notice the slight tremor of the goblet in her hand. "I guess I was never that impressive, after all. I just hope she can forgive me."

Aris isn't my favorite person, but I've never liked a bully, and the instinct to defend her is stronger than my personal feelings. "How can you blame that on yourself?" I say. I know my voice is too harsh. "*She's* the one who made you feel that way. Leira threw you away the second something better came along, but you're going to crawl back and apologize? For *what*?"

"You don't know her." Aris's temper flares, lighting her green eyes. "I was no one. I had nothing. And then, one day, everything changed. Leira chose me, told me about the family I never knew, gave me everything. You don't believe in authority or order, but she has a *purpose*. The greatest thing she ever gave me was sharing that purpose. And then I betrayed her."

It's hard to look past Aris's shiny, frightening shell and see the broken kid she is. But there, laid before me, are all the pieces. "She *used* you."

"Shut up!" She stands abruptly, throwing her goblet to the ground. It drops onto the thick moss with a thump, rolling to spread dark wine in an arc at her feet. "You have *no idea*—"

"No, *you*—"

"Isolde." Olani's voice, stern and sharp, snaps me out of the single-minded frustration narrowing my vision to Aris and each increasingly pathetic thing she says. "We should go train."

We've spent an hour or two each—well, I hesitate to say *day* . . . cycle, perhaps?—sparring and keeping our skills sharp. I'm not sure if we're preparing for another run-in with the Seelie Queen's Guard, or Gossamer, or something worse, but at least it gives me an outlet for my frustration. This time, I know Olani's only suggesting it to distract me from arguing with Aris, and I don't care. I could use a distraction. I leap to my feet, drawing my dagger and stalking deeper into the woods without looking back.

I hear Olani's crunching footsteps behind me, then Aris's mocking voice following. "Yes, go play in the woods. I'll just be back here making an *actual plan*!"

A snarl escapes my throat, anger heating my skin. She's probably right. I'm useless when it comes to long-term strategy. I'm just wasting time until someone more competent sweeps in and figures it out for me.

I keep walking until I've burned the hottest fury off, until I have my breathing under control and I don't feel like growling anymore. Then I whirl on Olani, planting my hands on my hips. "Why are you defending her?"

She stops just short of touching me, shoulders squared and quarterstaff hovering over the ground. Ready to fight. "I'm not. You need to cool down."

"Sorry I can't be as calm as you facing the end of the world. All the worlds. Everything."

My anger only makes her smirk. "Would it make you feel better to fight me?"

"Honestly?" I flip my dagger, adjusting my grip until it feels right. "Yeah, it would."

Without another word, we both jump into action. I have to be careful not to actually cut Olani and she has to remember not to knock me out, but that doesn't mean either of us is holding back.

I duck under her first attack, trying to get past her defense and use her height against her. Olani's staff slashes between us in a diagonal line, and I barely manage to change course in time to avoid smashing my forehead against it. My hands fly up automatically to protect my face, dagger dropping to the ground as my fingers close around the staff.

"Just so you know," I say, teeth gritted as we both struggle to push each other back, "I don't really feel like a pep talk right now."

Olani, who is almost a foot taller than me and significantly more muscular, wins. With a shove, I'm sent flying to the ground. "Good," she says, still smirking down at me. "I don't really feel like giving a pep talk."

I don't try to catch myself, instead rolling with the momentum to snatch up my dagger. The air around my head swishes with quick blows from above. The first sends a spray of dirt in my face, but the second catches my arm. My fingers spasm with pain, and the dagger slips from my grasp. Olani's staff raises again, and I roll out of the way of a blow . . .

That goes wide, because she wasn't aiming for me. The staff swipes across the ground, sending my dagger tumbling even farther out of reach. "You need to work on anticipating others' moves," she says.

"That better not be a metaphor." I don't need a dagger to fight. Instead of scrambling for it or trying to jump up, I twist in place, sweeping one leg into the backs of Olani's ankles. She isn't expecting it, and the silky grass below helps force her feet out from under her, sending her crashing down hard onto her back.

Her staff tumbles down after her, and I reach to pull it out of her grip, but she's too quick. She yanks it close to her chest, hauling me on top of her. If we were pulling punches, I'd make sure my legs stayed clear of her torso, but since we're not, I let my knee land solidly on her stomach, reaching past her head for my dagger. The air whooshes out of her lungs with a pained sound, which might make me feel bad if I was having a better day.

My outstretched arm makes the rest of me too vulnerable—a calculated risk, and one Olani takes advantage of. Her legs lock around me, rolling me roughly over the uneven forest floor. Even cushioned by soft grass, it's a bruising amount of force as we both struggle to subdue each other. My fingers stretch, fluttering over the ground, reaching for one last inch, for the dagger I know is just out of sight.

We land, inevitably, with Olani's weight holding me against the ground. Her forearm over my throat, and opposite hand pinning my arm in place so I can't bring it back to my side. "Yield," she commands, teeth gritted. A fine sheen of sweat covers her skin like dewdrops.

Our eyes lock. And stay locked as I pull my head back and sink my teeth into her arm—not hard enough to draw blood. Just hard enough to hurt. I watch her eyes widen in surprise as she rips her arm away, hissing in pain. In the instant she retreats, before she can retaliate, I stretch and snatch up my dagger. In a flash, my blade is between us, my teeth bared in satisfaction. "You first."

She stares at the dagger in stunned shock for a moment before slumping in defeat, giving me the answer before the words even leave her mouth. She rolls to the side, landing in the grass so we're lying side by side, panting to catch our breath. "Fine."

My dagger drops to my other side, an out-of-breath laugh of triumph lifting a weight off my chest. Instead of immediately picking up for a rematch, we just stay there for a second, staring up at the hazy purple sky. Grass prickles my arm in the fraction of a space between us, rustling with every slight movement.

After a long moment, Olani turns her head a little. Not enough to actually face me, just to look at me from the corner of her eye. "You seem . . ."

My heart pounds, waiting for the end of her sentence. Aggressive? Irritable? On edge?

"Off," she concludes eventually. "I don't know if it's just because Seelie's gone, or if there's something else . . ." Pause. "Besides, as you put it, *everything*."

I haven't really stopped long enough to process my feelings about the whole changeling thing. I've been too busy throwing myself in attempt after attempt to see the Queen and fix all this, like if I stop to think too long I'll get sucked under the surface of my own thoughts and drown in them. I prefer action to reflection. Instead of responding, I let out a long, tortured sigh.

"Or is it the changeling thing?" I shift just in time to see her lashes flutter as she blinks up at the stars. "Sorry if that's insensitive, I don't know how else to put it."

Even though I've caught my breath, my heart is still pounding, its frantic rhythm echoing in my ears. The leaves stir overhead, far-off faeries drifting effortlessly from branch to branch. I swallow hard, forcing myself to speak. "It doesn't really change anything, does it? I'm still . . . me. Knowing the reason why doesn't make me any more special than I was before."

"So you think Seelie's only special because she's a changeling?"

"What? No!" I respond too quickly to even think. That makes it sound like I'm jealous of my sister, like I resent her for being what she is. It isn't her fault that she was easily identifiable as *other*, and it's hurt her as much as it's helped her to understand who she is. I admire her, but I wouldn't trade places with her for the world.

It's complicated, growing up with a shadow the way Seelie and I did. Maybe there's a way to separate my view of myself from the reflection of my sister—but if so, I haven't found it yet.

I close my eyes, smelling the grass and feeling the warm summer breeze. Trying to draw my thoughts together from their scattered sprawl. "I just don't want this to change anything. If I think about it too long . . . I'm not sure I know who I am anymore."

Olani says nothing, leaving space for me to continue the thought without adding any pressure. It's obnoxiously effective.

"And what if I figure it out, and it's something bad?"

Hearing the words aloud makes me realize how foolish and childish they sound. Things aren't just *good* or *bad*. The world is more complicated than that. Still . . . I've always tried to be more good than bad, assuming my pure motives justified my actions. But what if I'm destined never to balance the scales?

Olani doesn't respond with an inspirational speech.

But that's okay. I grew up with Seelie, which means I've gotten good at interpreting silence. Her hand slides over mine, weaving our fingers together in the grass. It's hard to fight the urge to squirm in place, but for a moment, I manage to stay perfectly still.

"If it helps," Olani says eventually, turning to face me, "I've never doubted who you are." Her voice is so gentle, smooth like honey. Maybe she truly means it, but I flinch at the words anyway. I can't forget our long-ago fight, the way she stood there like a wall, unmoved by anything I said. Even if she does trust me, that doesn't mean she doesn't think I'm selfish and impulsive and too stubborn for my own good.

There are things we haven't talked about, weight piling up on the friendship we formed those weeks on the road. I don't know how much more that friendship can withstand.

I can feel her eyes on me, tracing my profile from bare inches away. This is my opening to tell her everything, the point at which it would be least weird to spill all the thoughts I've been holding in, but I can't seem to get it out. My heartbeat refuses to calm down, even when I suck in a breath and hold it in my lungs, waiting for her to say something else. Or maybe she's waiting for me.

Eventually, I do what I do best, and deflect. "We should probably get back to planning, huh?"

She squeezes my hand, pulling me up with her, and then lets go to pick up her staff. "How about one more round first?"

A smile tugs at my lips. "If you want a rematch, all you have to do is ask."

chapter twenty-two

seelie

Raze flies low, just barely ahead and above me, waiting for me to catch up. His change of form seems to have thrown off the illusion that was meant to keep us isolated, and I've never been more relieved to see him. Not that I was actually considering Gossamer's offer, but he was clearly trying to distract me—and it was working.

Around the corner, in a patch of melting ice, I spot Egg. He shivers on the frosty ground, looking up at something I can't see and whimpering. I crouch, forgetting my own safety with the instinct to protect him from whatever it is. The second my fingers brush his scales, I see what he sees:

A full-grown firedrake, just out of reach. I recognize it by its size and the shape of its skull, which I saw bleached bare in the hidden mountain keep where we found Egg before he hatched. This dragon, which watches us with mournful honey-gold eyes but doesn't approach, could be his mother.

Looks like the same trick works on both of us, I think, wrapping Egg up in my arms. The illusion dissolves, and if I thought he was out of sorts before, he fully loses it now. He starts to screech, an earsplitting wail that doesn't sound quite human or animal. I can't cover my ears, though, because he's fighting my grip, struggling to get free. I've mostly mastered the art of holding him without getting scratched or bitten, but his claws still find unprotected skin a few times.

We need to get out. Now. Before Gossamer drags me into another fight I don't stand a chance of winning. I can't forget the Seelie Queen's warning about creating any more portals, or the pain of the last time I tried—but maybe there's another way.

I can still sense that portal to the Unseelie Realm, the first one I made on my own, the one that settled deep into the Mortal Realm before I unleashed all *this*. Maybe I don't need to make a new hole between realms, to destabilize everything further. Maybe I can drag that one closer to me.

I try to close my eyes and focus on the limits of this realm, to feel the magic like I did before. It's made significantly more difficult by having to keep all my focus on not letting Egg run off out of my sight again. Shifting him into one arm, ignoring the way his claws tangle in my hair and his shrieks grate in my ear, I call the portal to me like I once called lightning from the clouds. It's far off, a force I can't fully understand, but I feel the moment it connects. A spark, and then . . . nothing.

"Having some trouble?" Gossamer asks helpfully.

I hadn't realized he'd caught up to us. I can't turn to look at him, but I don't have to, because Raze drops down between us, shifting into human form again. He ignores the fact that he's swaying a little in place and draws his iron dagger to train it on the faerie. "Stay back."

Gossamer looks at him with disdain. "Letting your mortal pet speak for you now, Seelie?"

"Jealous?" Raze asks innocently.

Whatever Gossamer would have said is lost to a choking sound. It looks like he's tensing every muscle in his face, before the look is replaced with an ice-cold rage.

Raze shoots me a look of disbelief, followed by an extremely poorly-timed laugh. He knows that with that one word, he's tied Gossamer in knots—that the faerie can't say no. Because that would be a lie.

It is, I have to admit, a little funny. It would be more funny if I didn't know from experience that Gossamer's anger is dangerous. Something tightens in my chest, that same feeling of the magic being drained from my very veins, and the portal slips from my grasp. Above us, the colors of the dome thrum in time with my heartbeat.

Egg screeches in my ear, scratching at me in his sudden frenzy to escape, and I release him before I can master my instincts. The heavy thump of his landing mingles with a . . . metallic clink? Too late, I realize his renewed panic wasn't random—it was a reaction.

The Gossamer in front of us vanishes, and I whirl around on the spot to face the one that just pickpocketed me. This one must be real, right? He holds the chain that Leira used to drain Egg's strength like it might come to life and bite him, but his smug expression is hardened by a fury deep in his colorless eyes.

Without thinking, I summon a ball of flame to push him away. It appears with a *whoosh!* that blocks out any other sound and a wave of heat that blows my hair back. The blaze rolls over Gossamer, reducing him to a smudge of shadow. Then two smudges. I immediately know I've made a mistake. He just absorbs my magic, using it to make illusory copies that all wear matching smiles as the sparks fade.

That flash of sharp teeth is the only warning I have before they attack, moving as one.

I'm prepared for magic, for some sort of assault on my mind and my will. I'm not expecting predatory speed, claws sinking into my wrist. This must be a copy, because the *real* Gossamer would never lower himself to this kind of attack—would he? If it was Isolde here in my place, she would dodge long before the points punctured her soft tendons, tripping him as she swirled out of the way.

But I'm not Isolde, and I'm not fast or nimble enough to do anything but scream in shock as the warm blood streams down my hand. Flames jump to life in my palms again, and I clutch them like weapons. The Gossamer with his claws sunk into my flesh releases me, barely pulling back in time to avoid getting singed. It's a temporary deterrent, but it won't be enough to hold them back for long. I crouch, searching for my iron dagger with sticky fingers.

One Gossamer grips my arm, trying to restrain me, and the other circles us muttering under its breath. I catch a glimpse of Raze, struggling to calm Egg before he bolts again.

And then everything goes dark.

It's not like cloud cover or sunset. More like a pillow has been placed over my face, smothering even the impression of light. I can still feel the heat of the flames in my uninjured hand, but they cast no light. The faerie's muttering has gone quiet, and for a second I think that this spell has cut off my hearing as well.

Frost cracks underfoot. A hand wraps around my injured wrist, making me cry out as it drags me to my knees.

"Seelie!" Raze. Curse him and his inability to stay out of things. Although imagining it from his perspective, hearing me scream in total darkness would be reason for concern.

"Run!" I call back, struggling against the faeries. Even if I'd been able to reach my dagger, I can't see well enough for it to be any use. I don't know what kind of magic I can do without being able to *see* my targets, either. It's never been a problem before.

I hear the crashing of *very* human footsteps—growing louder.

"Run *away*!" I clarify, too late. Something soft and dense slams into me, knocking all of us to the floor. Cold metal slithers over my skin, and even that brief brush makes my magic flicker and disappear from my grasp.

Gossamer dismisses the darkness just in time for me to watch a loop of the chain fall over my shoulders, tightening with one sharp tug to squeeze my arms and chest. One of the faeries tackles Raze to the ground alongside me with a painful crack as his body hits the stone.

I try to fight back, but the chain's effects are too disorienting, like losing another one of my senses. I twist on the ground, trying to face Gossamer and push myself upright at the same time. All I manage to accomplish is making the chain go taut as he loops it around Raze's wrists, binding his hands together. Raze slams an elbow into the faerie, shoving him back to the ground, but the chains stay firmly in place.

Gossamer starts to laugh, still on the ground. I can feel the chain sapping my strength along with my magic, making it hard to focus on what's in front of me. I can hardly remember why I wanted to fight, much less force my body to obey. Everything feels so heavy. I can't find it in me to do anything but uselessly sit and watch.

"Sorry," Raze manages to mutter. He sounds like he's fighting sleep, words slow and syrupy. "I . . . was trying to help."

"So much trouble for one changeling." That chilled, polished voice is familiar by now, accompanied by a sharp pull of my hair. "But I must say, you collect the most interesting pets. I wonder if your little firedrake will survive the amount of power needed to burn a hole through this realm so I can escape. A shame you won't be around to find out." He wraps the trailing end of the chain around his hand another time and pulls on it roughly, making the links constrict tighter around my chest.

My magic is a stuttering flame in my chest, desperate to escape, but unable to break past the chain's enchantment. Even so, I meet his gaze with defiance. "You *can't*."

He stands in a dizzying rush, winter wind rushing into the sudden gap between us. As he rises, he snaps the chain in the air, wrapping the remaining length around my neck. It's slack for a second, and I try to reach up to grab it, but then he pulls it back *hard*. It snaps into place, digging into the tender flesh of my throat, cutting off my air.

My mouth opens in a useless gasp, my hands raising to claw desperately at my throat. Raze throws himself toward me, but his hands are still bound behind his back, so there's not much he can do besides scream at them to stop.

I try to remind myself how long I can hold my breath, to use those precious seconds wisely instead of panicking, but it's difficult when the remaining wisps of air I had are actively being choked from my lungs, my skin bruising under the pressure. Ironically, even if there was a magic word that could bring Egg to heel, I'm being squeezed too hard to say it. I should be embarrassed, ashamed, furious. I should rage against the idea that it could end like this.

But all I feel is exhaustion.

Gossamer's glittering eyes focus completely on the creeping redness under my skin, the gasping shape of my mouth, the glassy sheen on my watering eyes. He looks almost bored of me, more fascinated by what will be left when whatever makes me *me* flees this fragile mortal shell. Darkness is creeping in around the edges of my vision. Soon, it'll swallow me completely.

Instead of my end, I see flames bloom behind him, painting the Unending Realm in dazzling white light. The pressure on my throat relaxes, freeing me to cough and gasp in a breath as we turn to gaze at its source.

For most of my life, firedrakes existed only in stories. The domesticated dragons I knew were so much smaller than their wild counterparts, their magic muffled by generations of living alongside humans. I could imagine a creature the size of a house, one that soared over the mountaintops and filled the sky with fire, but only in still images like storybook illustrations. They were hunted to extinction—partly for glory, partly for their magic, and partly because mortals didn't like sharing their world with something so much scarier than them.

But Egg isn't a story. He isn't a picture in a book or a daydream. And he isn't the helpless baby that cried every time I left his sight for the first two weeks of his life.

The creature that emerges from the flames shakes the ground when it roars, a vision shimmering with heat. He lifts up onto his back legs, but doesn't slow down, running at the faeries with his wings spread wide, baring sharp white teeth. Sparks fly all around him, settling and starting tiny fires on the forest floor, but his focus is only on the threat. His claws scrape against the shiny floor, bracing, and he pounces.

He rockets into Gossamer, who doesn't let go of the chain even as he stumbles back. It digs in, cutting off my air again as the dragon's teeth sink into his shoulder. My vision is dancing with spots, still swarming black around the edges, so what I see next feels almost like something from a dream.

Egg locks his jaws, ignoring the dark blood that wells up to stain white clothes and white skin and white scales. Gossamer responds with a vicious roar, grabbing the dragon by the throat with one hand—an obvious mistake. Egg's scales start to glow with flame from the center of his chest outward, filling the air with an acrid burning smell as the heat reaches the spot beneath Gossamer's clenched fist.

In that moment, Gossamer realizes what I have known this whole time: Egg is not mine to give away or anyone else's to possess. He is no one's but his own.

Fire pours from Egg's locked jaw, directly into the faerie's flesh. Gossamer's skin goes pale, then black, and then the brilliant white flames burn a hole clean through him. He doesn't even have time to look surprised before the two crisp halves of his body drop to the floor, still flickering with flames that slowly turn the yellow of a funeral pyre.

The chain goes slack. I pull it away in a motion so quick I end up flinging it, gasping for breath and covering the injured skin at my throat with shaking hands. Raze shakes the rest of the chain off, and we stand huddled together, too stunned to speak. Egg's fire turns to the chain's snakelike silvery path, and it catches like a rope soaked in oil. Its magic burns off in a second, leaving nothing but an ordinary, slightly blackened chain on the ground.

Gossamer's delicate features are slack, and he looks so fragile. Mortal, after all. The blankness in his eyes chokes me with an unidentifiable feeling—not regret for him. Regret it had to end like this.

And then he dissolves into nothing, snuffing out the fire, and I realize it isn't over after all.

I look around wildly for the real Gossamer, but this time, there are no tricks and no pointed remarks. He shimmers into view behind us, gasping and clutching at a blackened spot in his chest. He looks frayed around the edges, wilted like something left out in the sun too long. Like something essential has been drained from him. Egg's fire has transformed him somehow, like it's burned off the fuel of the magic he stole from me.

If only it was as simple as directing Egg to keep going, to sink his jaws into the real Gossamer, but I'm worried incinerating a live faerie would be more explosive than an illusion. Besides, Egg is already bounding toward me as he has a hundred times before, yellow eyes huge and filled with worry.

I have to fight not to shrink away in terror. I have always known what he was. He has always been capable of death and destruction, has distributed his fair share of burns and bite marks, but he's never seriously harmed anyone before this moment.

He crashes into my ankles, bumping me back into Raze, then stares up at us expectantly. He's still the same hatchling nipping at fingers, huddled in the crushed remnants of eggshell, who never trusted anyone until he trusted me.

"I . . . think he wants to be picked up," Raze says, the words a little uneven.

I nod, sucking in a shaky breath. We need to leave *now*, while Gossamer is injured and distracted. When I speak, my voice sounds rusty and bruised. "I'll get the portal."

While I close my eyes and concentrate on the spell, Raze lifts Egg into his arms in one smooth motion. Egg must be desperate, because he doesn't even protest. He just cuddles up against Raze's chest, looking almost exactly as he did when he was an actual egg tied on for safekeeping.

Gossamer makes a rattling sound, struggling to right himself.

Raze glances at me, brow wrinkled. "Should we . . . ?"

He doesn't have to finish the question. I know what he's asking. We have an iron dagger and an opportunity—maybe we should take it. But my magic is still bound up with Gossamer's, still tangled in this place. If we kill him now, a swift dagger through the heart, it might destroy any chance we have of saving my parents and everyone else trapped here. The time isn't right. We don't know enough.

My eyes meet Gossamer's, and I watch his face transform to a new kind of anger when I shake my head in response to Raze's question. Insulted to be left alive, like a loose end.

I close my eyes against his glare, tightening my grip on my magic. The portal to the Unseelie Realm comes back to me slowly, then all at once. As it crashes into us, I have a split-second glance of the unmasked pain on Gossamer's face. Then the Unending Realm, and its prisoner, and its pull on my magic, are gone.

PART THREE

A mistake. He's made a mistake.

He never makes mistakes.

Gossamer rubs his chest absently, feeling himself turn to ash again and again. His illusions hold a part of him, and he felt every agonizing moment of its death as magic consumed it from the inside out. He experienced real pain, though the black mark the burn left behind fades like a memory. Perhaps he should keep the mark, as a reminder to himself. A reminder that he should have killed the changeling girl at her first moment of weakness. He should have wiped her face and her defiance and even her memory from all the realms the instant he had the chance. Instead, he let her get away. Wasted the opportunity, just for the chance to speak with her one last time.

Even though she had tried to cut the bond between them by sinking iron into her own flesh. Even though she had refused him at every turn. Even though he was more than capable of securing the borders of this new realm without her. He could have killed her. Perhaps he could have forced her to do his bidding.

But he didn't. Why?

Because he wanted her to choose it. He wanted her to choose . . . him. What kind of contrary, doomed being turned down the kind of power he had offered? What kind of nonsensical creature then proceeded to also turn down the reward she had refused all that power to reach for?

Comfort. Safety. Home.

Gossamer cannot keep the disgust from his face, though there is no one there to see it. He thought they were alike, Seelie and him. Two displaced things, belonging nowhere. If no one Realm claimed them, if they belonged to no one but themselves, why couldn't they also belong to each other?

He hates her. Worse, he still admires her, and it only makes the hatred burn stronger, a fire that laps its way through his veins. They are nothing alike. She is not what he had thought, not the same as him. She has turned him down for the last time.

He is alone.

Alone, here, in a timeless realm that holds him captive with all these useless mortals. He stares at the spot where she vanished, dares to raise one pale hand to the shimmer in the air—

He cannot approach. His ability to weave between realms, to come and go as he pleased like nothing more than a shooting star or a winter wind, has abandoned him in this weakened form. He's trapped, as surely as he had been the last few long centuries. A hundred years hadn't seemed so long to him once. Now it is intolerable. Another moment in this state is intolerable.

He breathes deeply. At least there is still that: the cold burning his lungs, frosty ground stinging his bare feet. All the sensations he had been robbed of in his previous imprisonments. He had hoped to break free of this one with her help, to make her see that they were the same, to see how much they could do together.

No matter. He will do it without her.

He will not give her another chance to join him. He will crush her, like he has crushed so many obstacles in his path. He will make her defeat thorough. He will make it hurt.

His heart beats a too-quick rhythm against his ribs, a bad habit it no doubt picked up from her, *but his body remains motionless. He stares at the spot where Seelie disappeared until he masters his breathing and his pulse once more. He indulges in scrubbing his hands over his face as if to wipe away tears. Though, of course, there are no tears.*

Once he is composed and in control, the traitorous boil of feelings reduced once more to a frozen lake, he moves with purpose and without questioning or second-guessing his impulses. He drapes an arm over one of the frozen mortal figures at the center of the room, releasing her from the enchantment that binds them all.

He told Seelie that he could not hurt them, which was true. At least, it is of every mortal except the one that he happens to have bargained with. The one who owes him.

He watches the pink come back into her cheeks. How she has aged, in the short time he has known her. Hardly twenty years, and already the red-gold vibrance has drained from her hair, small wrinkles appeared in the sinking creases of her face. He knows now that a century is a long time, and still, she will be dead in no time at all.

She comes to life gasping and shuddering, with a raging ripple of magic that attempts to push him away, to claw to freedom. He suppresses the magic with the gentleness that comes from knowing she can't hurt him, waits for her to stop thrashing about like a caught rabbit.

She's a fighter, this enchanter. She spent years trying to bully and bargain the location of the Mortal's Keep from him—the one thing he could not give. But she had managed to bargain for something else, before she was the kind of human other humans shied away from and bowed and scraped to please.

Power.

She had dealt with him for—what else?—power. She owes him so much.

And the time has come to collect.

chapter twenty-three

ISOLDE

My arms are twisted behind me, knees grinding into the dirt, when I spot Birch. He picks his way casually through the clearing, black fur standing out starkly in the pastel clusters of wildflowers. The brownie hasn't left the *Destiny* since it was restored, so he seems exposed now that he is out in the open. With his green eyes locked on mine through the curtain of my messy hair, Birch seems almost . . . urgent.

"Hold!" I call through gritted teeth.

I expect Olani to argue, to tease me about cutting this fight short when she's so close to winning, but she lets go immediately. My weight sinks to the ground, and her hand is already hovering over my shoulder. "Did I hurt you?"

A snort escapes my nose, which only serves to make me feel bad when I look up to see the genuine concern in the depths of her amber eyes. "Oh!" The sound of surprise is out before I can stop it, and I rush to cover it with my next words. "No, I'm fine. It's . . ." I gesture to Birch.

The second the brownie realizes he has our attention, he turns and walks back into the trees. After a few steps, he pauses, looks at us, and meows urgently.

It's obvious we're supposed to follow. Olani and I exchange an uncertain look, but what else is there for us to do? Worst-case scenarios play in my head. Aris has been enchanted, or the *Destiny* is gone again, or Seelie has returned and needs our help. Except if it were any of those things, the brownie would probably use his own magic, probably move faster than his unconcerned trot over the forest floor.

I duck under a branch, holding it back with me so it doesn't smack Olani in the face. "I feel like I was warned against this," I mutter as she passes.

Growing up, it felt like there were rules for everything. Rules for carrying iron, for sharing your name, for offering small gifts, all to avoid faerie mischief. When our father sent Seelie and me outside to play, he would kneel to double-check our bootlaces were secured and remind us of all the rules. *If you see a strange animal in your path, do not chase it. If you see a beautiful horse with no rider, return home immediately. If a cat leads you to the forest, run the other way.*

The fear when we were young was that we would be beckoned into the enchanted forest and slip through one of those spots between worlds. Like our mother did, intentionally, when she confronted the faeries. If your kid finds themselves whisked away to a faerie realm, you're not likely to see them again.

The irony of having that thought *here*, with the light filtering down on me through the structures of the Seelie Court, makes my mouth twist like I've tasted something sour. In this moment, I want nothing more than the chance to tell my parents about this. To see their horrified expressions, to be lectured and hugged.

To have someone else responsible for my safety for once.

Birch leads us back to the clearing where we left the *Destiny*. It looks almost exactly how we left it. Our little fire is almost burned out, twisting trails of smoke over a pile of red embers. Crumbs scattered over the leaves, leftover food from our makeshift dinner sitting out on a rock we've been using as a table. Birch breaks into a sudden sprint, launches himself onto one of the taller roots, and meows, as if pointing out what's different about the scene.

Aris isn't here.

For a second, I feel relief and allow myself to fantasize about all the kinds of danger she could have wandered into—ideally, forms that will keep her out of our hair indefinitely. The feeling is chased almost immediately by a faint flash of guilt. As much as I dislike Aris, I don't think even she deserves to be whisked away into the terrifying oblivion of the faerie world. Then I notice the door of the *Destiny* wedged firmly shut. When I stop, straining my ears, I can hear the muffled sound of speech coming from inside the wagon.

Who is Aris talking to? And why is she trying to keep it secret?

Olani's eyes meet mine, and we form a silent agreement to approach quietly. Maybe Aris didn't lock herself in there by choice. She could be in trouble.

I'm certain that we didn't make a sound, creeping along the forest floor cushioned by thick moss and soft earth, but we haven't even made it to the wagon yet when the door flies open.

Cobweb greets us without so much as a flicker of surprise in his eyes. "Oh good," he says, ignoring the fact that we both automatically drew our weapons. "You're back." Then he returns inside, leaving the door flung wide behind him.

Any chance we had at stealth is blown, so we sheepishly follow. I'm relieved to see Aris standing next to the bunks, arms crossed over her chest, unrestrained and seemingly herself.

Robin is there, too, perched on our makeshift table with their feet drawn up so their whole body forms an awkward little knot.

"What's going on here?" I'm wary, on guard, fingers still restless around my dagger's hilt. Aris's casual demeanor does nothing to put me at ease.

She gestures, as if I should have somehow expected to come back to find her entertaining faeries in *my* wagon. Like they've dropped by for tea. "We're being recruited."

Olani joins us, bringing the wagon to maximum capacity. She can stand without ducking her head in the *Destiny*'s cramped interior, but only barely. "Recruited for what?"

"The Winter Tournament!" Robin makes this announcement with a flourish, releasing their arms and legs from their bunched-up position and narrowly missing smacking Cobweb in the face with the back of one hand. "You're just in time—it's like it was meant to be! And we've spoken with all the other—the other, uh—" At this point, they stumble, looking to Cobweb for help finishing the thought.

Cobweb gently tucks Robin's arm back into position away from his face, as casually as brushing away a bit of lint. "Mortal sympathizers," he says quietly. "There are plenty of us who would prefer not to see the realms sealed off from each other permanently."

"But I thought you hadn't left this realm for hundreds of years?" Aris says, raising an eyebrow.

Robin shrugs. "I like to keep my options open."

"Mortals are . . . fascinating creatures. Always changing, always contradicting themselves. Many of my kind see you all as playthings they'd rather not get taken away, but *I*—" Cobweb hesitates a second, looking almost human in his brief shyness. "I've considered mortals great friends." Because he's staring determinedly in the opposite direction, he misses the affectionate smile that flits across Robin's face at that.

Olani glances at me, and I can tell we're thinking the same thing. We don't have time for faerie games.

"This isn't a *game*," Aris says, voice balancing on the edge between annoyed and offended. "It's how we're going to get another chance with the Queen."

Now I'm listening. The faeries rush through an explanation of everything they've already told Aris. Apparently, besides the feast we crashed into, there are days and days of Wintersol festivities—all culminating in an annual Tournament where teams of three battle it out in three rounds of competition for everyone else's entertainment. The trials are meant to test you mentally and physically, and whichever team is crowned the victors earns the Queen's Favor, which is spoken in title case and could mean anything.

"Favor as in her approval, or favor as in like, an actual favor?" I ask.

Cobweb and Robin look at each other, as if they're struggling to determine the difference, then look back at me and shrug.

"Past winners have asked for power, magic, love . . ." Cobweb says. "It's difficult to explain the influence the Queen has over our realm to a mortal."

I don't think they're intentionally dodging the question. They're so different from Seelie, and yet I see tiny echoes of her in the way they move, the emphasis they place on certain words. Maybe she could have been like that, in a different life.

Aris snaps me out of my distracted thoughts. "Isn't the support of her armies in a war she clearly said she didn't want to be involved in kind of a big favor to ask?"

"She can't exactly say no to the winners of the tournament." Robin smirks, voice light with irony. "The Seelie Court runs on favors and social standing and politeness. Even if she wanted to, she's as bound by the law of the land as the rest of us."

I hate to admit it, but this could work. Even if we don't

win, it would force her to look at us. If Cobweb and Robin are to be believed—and I'm listening very closely for tricky language, but I haven't found any signs they're telling anything but the truth—there is already a large contingent of the Seelie Court on our side. Those who are fond of humans, or at least of messing with humans, and resent being sealed away from the Mortal Realm as much as we do. Maybe, with more time, we could rally them to convince the Queen to help—or we could do this the fun way.

"We used to make mortals fight each other, but then the Queen promised one champion never to do that again, and we've had to make do with volunteers ever since! That's why killing is discouraged in the games. To make it more sporting."

Sporting. More like entertaining—what's the fun of watching someone get vaporized instantly when you could enjoy hours and hours of bleeding out?

Despite my doubts that the three of us will stand a chance against teams of faeries, even without their magic, it's not like we're risking our lives. Faeries value life, in a strange way. They live so long and reproduce so rarely that it's not worth the explosion of faerie-death magic to kill each other in a competition like this—or at least so the faeries reassure us.

"It's not *meant* to be to the death," Cobweb says, with enough emphasis on the word *meant* to cancel out any comfort the sentence was meant to deliver. He shrugs, in a *these things happen* sort of way. "To surrender or injury too great to continue. Sometimes there are some nasty curses in there, but don't worry, they usually wear off in a century or so."

"We'll be dead by then," Olani says bluntly. "But good to know."

"I say we do it," Aris says impatiently, surprising me. She doesn't really seem the kind to throw caution to the wind and risk it all for a plan that might not even work. Then again, besides her life, I guess she doesn't have anything left to lose.

Olani is scowling very determinedly at a single spot on the floorboards, like she's trying to solve a difficult math problem. Probably calculating our odds. "So would I, if I thought we stood a chance," she says, and it's nice to know I was right about what she was thinking. She looks up at the faeries. "If you care so much, why doesn't one of you swap in? Then we'd at least have one faerie on our team."

Now the faeries exchange a look, one filled with a shivery sort of energy that can only mean one thing: They don't want to compete in the tournament, because they're too scared. They want to throw us on the field on their behalf, maybe even with their support, because if we lose, it's no huge loss. Rather than say that, Cobweb's brow markings wrinkle. "You have the changeling."

We all exchange an uncomfortable look. "About that . . ." I say, to break the silence. "I just found out about that when we arrived in this realm."

Now it's the faeries' turn to look uncomfortable. "You thought you were human?" Cobweb asks, which earns him an elbow jab in the ribs from Robin.

"She's *like me*, Cobweb," they say meaningfully. "You know how mortals are. And if the sister was obviously a Seelie changeling, what reason would they have to suspect?"

"Perhaps . . . the faerie bargain made for the child's life?" he suggests in that same flat tone that makes him sound almost bored with the conversation.

Robin waves his words off, offering me a grin instead. "Ignore him,"

I blink, trying to figure out how to steer this conversation back onto a path I know how to navigate. "You mean you're an Unseelie changeling, too?"

"Born and raised!" Robin chirps, ignoring the shift of mood in the room. Their nose wrinkles with a thought. "Though I did hear that the Mortal Realm is different than it was in my time.

I always knew I was a changeling, so I can't imagine how you must be feeling right now. It took years to figure out what being different meant—what was *me*, and what was predetermined."

It's a bit of a relief to hear someone else express the same thing that's been troubling me. I tilt my head, studying Robin closer. "And?"

"And I realized it was all me. I wasn't a human or a faerie, a boy or a girl. I was just *me*." Their smile, which briefly disappeared behind a pensive look, returns. "I still am."

I'm happy for them, but I was really hoping their years of wisdom would offer me a shortcut to that kind of confidence. For now, I guess I'll have to make do with the long way around. "I was never recognized as anything other than 'a bit odd,'" I tell them. "Whatever knowledge they had about the different types of changelings back then . . . it's gone now."

"That's a pity," they say. "You are a truly exquisite piece of work."

The complete lack of sarcasm in that statement makes my cheeks feel a little warm. "Um . . . thanks. But what I'm getting at is, I'm not powerful. I can't do magic at all."

At that, a sharp little giggle, like the trill of birdsong. "Of course you can't *direct* the power! That would be like—like—" Robin stumbles, for once stumped for words.

"Trying to put out a grease fire with a bucket of water," Cobweb finishes dryly. Robin illustrates enthusiastically by miming an explosion with their excitable, fluttery hands.

Aris wears an unmoving expression, cold green eyes and the imprint of a sneer—honestly, I don't even think she knows she's doing it, but it unsettles me for a second how much the expression looks like one of Leira's. "What about her eyes?"

A good question—and probably one I should have thought of. It's common knowledge that a changeling's eyes are the only visible giveaway that they're anything but human. In darkness, they reflect light like an animal's eyes. Like a faerie's eyes.

Seelie's eyes do it, but mine are normal, a brown so dark they're nearly black. Nothing special at all.

Cobweb tilts his head. "I can see how Isolde's eyeshine would go unnoticed. The difference is incredibly subtle."

"Tiny lights, instead of one big one," Robin interrupts, with a huge grin. "I bet your eyes sparkle even in the dark."

"They do," Olani murmurs, then looks surprised she said it aloud. Her own brown eyes flit to the floor, just for a second, before they're drawn back up to mine. "We were in that wagon . . . a long time."

It's an admission of sorts. That she noticed. And there's nothing I can say to that, because isn't it obvious that I noticed her, too? How could I *not*? I've always noticed a pretty face, a melodic voice, a stunning smile. The only thing all the girls and boys I formed brief attachments with had in common was exactly that—they were all fleeting, always formed in clear sight of the ending when Seelie and I would move on to the next place.

But Olani was different. We were on a high-stakes mission together, which made her immediately off-limits. Even when we became friends, when we sparred together and she corrected my form with gentle hands on my waist, when we opened up to each other about our dreams for the future, I didn't want to flirt carelessly and ruin everything. Maybe some part of me wanted more than what we had, but I knew I couldn't have it, because the fact that I actually cared about her, that I didn't want to imagine her disappearing from my life, meant the inevitable split would be worse.

I kept my distance. I was so careful.

Then those weeks on the road to Auremore. Captured in the back of a wagon, bruised by every bump in the road. Hands tied behind our backs, reaching for each other, and her healing magic slowly easing the pain from my broken ankle. Huddling together for warmth as the temperatures dipped into autumn and waking up with her herbal scent in my nose.

Something changed, but we never spoke about it. Then the fight happened, and then Seelie and Raze were back, and whatever it was seemed to have dissolved like morning mist.

This look—right now, our gazes locked in the faerie forest—is an admission that it's not fully gone. And I can't take it. I'm the first to look away.

To her credit, Aris winces a little. She showed little interest in our welfare in those weeks we were prisoners, tied up while Leira dragged us back to Auremore. If anything, she was gleeful at the chance to make us suffer to prove her devotion to Leira Wildfall. Now that we're stranded here together, a team, I wonder if she regrets it.

Is it getting hot in here?

I cross my arms and clear my throat, trying desperately to get back to the issue at hand. It takes a second to remember what that was, but I manage to put together the thought. "So. I'm a changeling. Does that give us any advantage in this competition? Do you seriously think we can win this?"

The faeries hesitate again, but to my surprise, it's Cobweb that answers me. "Yes," he says clearly and levelly and—above all—honestly. "We do."

Aris's eyebrows raise and Olani's shoulders slump with a deep exhale—not defeat, exactly. More like resignation.

"Well then," I say, unable to keep the smirk from creeping up my face. "I don't think a better way to get the Seelie Queen's attention is going to fall into our laps. Sign us up."

chapter twenty-four

seelie

I'm surrounded by quiet and cold, a chill that nestles under the layers of my clothes and wind that whispers between the beats of my heart. I open my eyes, a little surprised that it's just as cold in the Unseelie Realm as back home. It must be winter here, too. Worse, I can actually feel the cold, instead of my skin burning feverishly hot against it. I must have lost more magic in the Unending Realm than I thought.

Egg is the first to break the silence, and he does so magnificently with a chittering screech that splits the air like lightning. I'm not sure when Raze put him down, but he seems calmer now that we're away from Gossamer. If he still has energy to scream, it can't be that bad.

My wrist has stopped bleeding, but my sleeve is sticky with warm blood. Any pain it might cause me is drowned out by the memory of burning magic and burning flesh, blank eyes and horrified screams. I have to wrangle my thoughts, to cross my arms over my chest to keep in what little warmth I have, to actually *look* around at our surroundings and figure out what we're doing.

Yet again, the Unseelie Realm is not what I expected. Far out in the wilderness, it was dazzling, rolling hills of sharp contrast and unsettling beauty. I see scraps of that place in the glaringly blue sky; the bare, pale trees with dark spots that sometimes blink open to watch us; the sharp bite of magic on the wind. But here, the ground underfoot is flat and smooth with a few patches of ink-black moss. Around us, stone structures that don't quite look natural arch up to the sky. Moss fizzes over them, too, and it takes me a second to figure out why it looks so familiar.

Auremore, the city where Raze grew up, is built on the bones of an ancient city that was destroyed centuries ago. In the War of the Realms, which Gossamer caused the last time he tried to merge the realms. Instead of being contained, as it is in the Unending Realm, the magic ran undirected through cities in storms and fires and earthquakes.

And it seems the Unseelie Court wasn't left untouched, either.

I turn to ask Raze what he thinks we should do now, but he isn't looking around, mentally cataloging the ruins. He's staring at me, like he's waiting for . . . something. Before I can ask what, he steps closer, raising a hand to touch what must be a striking red welt across my neck. His eyes slide up to mine, and my heart pounds so furiously I'm sure he can feel it. "You're okay?" he asks. His voice sounds wrong here, too loud and yet too small, a strange echo humming in the air behind it.

I nod. I'm not sure if it's true or not, but I need to be okay. We need to keep going.

He hesitates, not sure what to say. Probably wondering if I'll turn him to ash on the spot if he says the wrong thing. Probably regretting coming here with me at all. I want to grab him by the collar and shove him back to the Seelie Realm, as far from myself as possible. I want to dig my fingers into the fabric, pull him close, and never let go. Mostly, I want to be smart enough and brave enough to know what I want.

I settle for turning and burying my face in his shoulder. It's not a hug, because our arms don't go around each other. I don't know if there's a word for this kind of embrace, a supportive lean like you might get from an affectionate cat. Raze settles into it, one hand running absently down my back, along the unbound mess of my hair. His heartbeat is steady and strong. He smells like sage and leather and sweat.

Finally, he speaks. With my face pressed against him, I can feel the way his voice, not particularly deep, rumbles through his chest. "You did your best back there. We'll beat him next time, for good."

"What makes you so sure?" I straighten, forcing myself to step away from his comforting touch. Without looking down, I can feel Egg sitting near my ankles, warm scales a breath away from my hem.

"Just a feeling." Finally, Raze turns away, leaving me to wonder what that could possibly mean as he takes in our surroundings.

Though the form of destruction is similar to the ruins around Auremore, the remaining structures look more like those around the Mortal's Keep: smooth white stone, elegant curves and impossibly high columns. It's all covered in a light dusting of snow, which shifts and curls in the wind like smoke.

"Think anyone's home?" Raze says after another long pause.

We crashed into the Seelie Court in the middle of a party, without a plan, and were escorted to the Queen as a matter of course. I hadn't considered that there would be more steps to getting an audience here, but he's right—the forest city seems abandoned. I take a few steps on the icy ground, letting the wind run over me without flinching away this time. There's magic in it, I'm certain, and it's not my own. My head tilts back to the sky, numb fingertips clenching into fists as I call, "Hello?"

Hello hello hello hello

My voice echoes back to us more times than it should. Shapes that look like birds, but were too still and silent before just now to be real, launch into the air with cries and the flurried rustle of wings. As the winged silhouettes disappear into the silvery sky, the bare branches of sparse trees shiver, and snow spirals down onto the jagged stone shapes that jut out against the clouds.

I try again, forcing my voice not to shrink with nerves. "We're here to speak to the Unseelie Queen."

Queen queen queen queen

Egg's ears perk, and he stands at attention with a shake that runs from his pointed snout down to the tip of his tail. He only reacts like that to the sound of my voice, but he didn't respond to my shout or the echo. I strain my ears, searching for meaning in the insistent whisper of the wind.

But my mortal senses must be missing something, because Egg is getting increasingly worked up. He spins in place, whines, and points like a spaniel.

"You hear something?" I ask him softly, bending to rest one hand on his spiky head.

The dragon lets out a little whine, trembling with tension as his ears swivel to something I can't sense. Visions of Unseelie monsters and faerie tricks flash through my head. I don't trust anything in this place, not even the wind. But we need to start moving, and I don't have any better ideas which direction to go.

I glance up at Raze, who only shrugs.

"All right, then," I tell Egg. "Lead the way."

The words are hardly out of my mouth before he bolts, tearing across the cold, hard earth so fast that for a second I think I've lost him. I jump to my feet, scarcely breathing, until I spot him just on the horizon, pacing with impatience. He gives us one of his tiny, fearsome roars and waits for us to start walking before sprinting off again, in what I can only hope is the direction of the Unseelie Queen's palace.

It's not quite a run, but we're moving quickly enough that it leaves little breath for talking. Egg stays just within sight, but whenever I start to think we're catching up to him, he's gone again. I can't tell if it's oddly lifeless or if there are hidden Unseelie faeries all around us, holding their breaths as they wait for us to make a mistake.

I refuse to make mistakes this time. I am going to secure the support of the Unseelie Queen and stop Gossamer and put everything back the way it was. I am going to save my parents—and until I do, the scariest thing in this forest is me.

Leaves crunch and branches snap under my quick-paced steps, and suddenly I'm struck by the mental image of my mother, crashing through the faerie realm not so far from here. Blazing with purpose to claim what the faeries took from her. I've always seen her fire in Isolde, but maybe Mami and I are more alike than I thought, fiercely protective and inadvisably stubborn.

Following Egg, we find ourselves in a space that is more castle ruins and less forest, though the wilderness crawling over the buildings never really retreats.

And then I realize I can't see the firedrake. Panic surges through my veins as I look all around, but there's no sign of pearlescent scales. The architecture here is confusing, full of crumbling half walls, stained glass windows suspended in mid-air, and stairs that lead nowhere.

A quiet, distinct yelp draws my attention, and I let out the breath threatening to choke me. Egg is close enough to hear, but with all the echoes, I can't tell which direction the sound came from. I gather my skirts to step over a strangely tall threshold—only to find the floor yanked from under me, flailing as I tumble into nothingness. My scream is short, ending in an *oof!* as I hit the ground again.

No—the ceiling.

It takes a second to figure the room out with my head still

spinning from the shock of the fall, and my joints still recovering from the harsh bump against the stone I'm sitting on now. There's a stone floor, walls choked in flowering vines, and—several feet above me—the threshold I just stepped over.

"Seelie!" Raze catches up, freezing at the spot where I must have disappeared from sight.

I force myself to stand, fully preparing for another drop, but it feels like walking on solid earth. "I'm okay!" I reply, even though my voice is still a little breathless. Slowly, not trusting myself to stay upright, I approach the open doorway, where Raze stands upside down with his boots on the forest floor.

It's all very disorienting. His eyes—which are right at my eye level, now that we're facing opposite directions—widen when he sees me. "*How* are you doing that?"

His amazement soothes the bruises I can already feel forming from the fall. I let out a short breath of a laugh, reaching up for his hand. "Magic." When he just keeps staring, I pull on his sleeve until his fingers find mine and squeeze them tight. "Come on, it's not that bad a fall if you're braced for it. Ready?"

Raze takes a deep breath and jumps.

I don't know what I expected would happen, but holding his hand does *not* allow me to assist him in the flip from up to down. Instead, his weight pulls suddenly on my arm and, rather than tumbling down on top of him as he hits the floor, I let go.

"Sorry!" I peer down at him—now that we're both facing the same way, it's easier to get my bearings. To forget that the forest floor is above us, and the sky below. I can see Egg now, on the same plane as us, circling impatiently while he waits for us to catch up.

Raze is looking around, too, taking in our new surroundings and rubbing the arm that cushioned his fall. "Thanks for the help," he says sarcastically, without any real anger behind it.

After a pause that might be a beat too long, I offer my hand again to help him up. He accepts, and I squeeze our joined hands tightly, leaning into his side with an innocent smile I don't have to force. "Anytime," I reply, voice dripping with sweetness.

There's nothing so different about moving across the ceiling, except when we find ourselves walking sideways up a staircase, parallel to the ground. It's strange, looking to the side where a wall should be and seeing forest floor several feet below.

"Maybe I should fly around to check it out," Raze offers, hands on his hips. "If the path is going to keep doing this."

"No," I say, squeezing his hand tighter. I hadn't even realized we were still holding on to each other, which gives me little chance of figuring out why the thought of him turning into a bird and leaving me here alone fills me with dread. I scramble for a second before landing on "You should . . . save your magic."

"Yeah, you never know when you might need a penguin to slide across this ice." Raze shakes his head with a self-deprecating grin, which makes me absolutely furious. Does he have any idea how annoying it is to watch him constantly downplay his value?

"Don't do that. Don't act like you're useless." I can't seem to get my voice under control. It's angry and far too forceful, and I see him freeze in response. "I mean, a penguin might be useless. But you helped shake me out of that illusion back there, flying around. And even when you're completely drained, you're . . . you."

That makes him pause for a second, eyes searching my face for something. For a second, he's as hard to read as he was when we first met, when every exchange was spiked with hostility. I was so angry at him then, for completely different reasons, that just his touch made my blood rush. His mouth twists in that old infuriating half smile as he says, "So what I'm hearing is that you're glad I'm here with you."

My hand jerks away like he's seared my fingertips with his. So much has happened since our fight in the Unending Realm, but he just *had* to get the last word in, didn't he? "No!" I snap. "I mean—yes, but—you—*ugh!*"

That dazzling argument earns me nothing but a shrug and a smug look. As if I've proved his point for him. Which . . . maybe I have.

It's only then that I actually stop and force myself to wonder why I'm fighting him. Raze is being loyal and kind and encouraging—and *yes*, he's being very annoying about it, but even I have to admit that's not a good enough reason to get this upset.

We stare at each other while I try to work it out, and for some reason, I don't feel the urge to shy away from his gaze this time. My mind isn't there, anyway. It's wandering far away, digging deep into thoughts I've been ignoring for . . . for months now. It's like they've all been piling up, and the second I stop to examine them, the dam bursts and I'm drowning in it.

When I'm with Raze, I feel more like myself than ever. He doesn't treat me like a monster or a myth, and I know I deserve so much worse, and it's *frustrating* and *unfair* of him to just carry on like I don't. With Raze, I'm not a pawn or a terrifying force of nature. I'm just myself—a girl who pushes him, protects him, makes him smile. Maybe even a girl he'd like to kiss. The thought sends my heart dropping down into my shoes, like a stone sinking in clear, cold water. In its ripples, another forms:

I want to kiss him back.

I want more than that, so much more, so intensely that it feels like a yawning hole in my chest. I sink deeper into it, swallowed by the lack of things I thought were silly and pointless when it was anyone else: holding hands, whispered confessions, laughing in the middle of the night, casual touch. I don't know if I'm allowed to want those things, but I do. I want them with him.

Egg must have just realized that he's leaving us behind, because I hear an irritated yelp and the click of little claws as he backtracks to us. We have, at best, moments before the dragon starts trying to herd us like unruly sheep.

My cheeks feel hot all of a sudden, and I break Raze's stare, turning away in a swirl of tattered skirts. Not far. Not out of reach. "I may owe you an apology," I say, trying to keep my voice cool and level, like my ears aren't ringing with the weight of realization.

"May?" Raze repeats, with an eyebrow arch so intense I can *hear it* in his voice.

"I do." I bite the inside of my cheek, anything to distract me from the flush crawling over my skin. "I . . . I wanted to protect you by keeping you away from me, but you're too stubborn to stay away, and instead of being grateful for it, I've been . . . I was . . ." My voice fails, tripping into something hoarse and stuttering.

"Exceedingly difficult?" he volunteers, finishing the thought.

I swallow hard. "Yeah." My head tilts up, so we're eye-to-eye again. "But I am. Grateful. To be clear."

He smiles softly, just enough to make his eyes glitter in the faint light. "I know."

A moment from months ago, in a haze of fevered dreams, overtakes me like an ice-cold wave. Me, sick from magic and blood loss, waking in a room I didn't recognize. Raze, holding up his end of the bargain we made in the Seelie forest, vowing to never make me kiss him again.

I should have known better than to trust the word of a human.

chapter twenty-five

ISOLDE

"Fae of the Seelie Court, we now welcome Isolde Graygrove and her mortals to the Winter Tournament." The Seelie Queen's voice booms, seeming to come from everywhere and nowhere at once. I expected we'd at least be facing the other teams, but this room—maybe it would be better described as a den, a place sunk under the trees with walls held in place by roots, which part in gaps on the ceiling to let a little light in—is empty. Dust floats in the beams of light, the air warm and still in a place that is somehow both cavernous and cramped.

An unseen crowd responds to the Seelie Queen's announcement, cheering and stomping at our introduction. It's strange, to be seen without seeing them in return. I'm not sure if I should acknowledge the Court, wave, or stay stoically still. I can feel my shoulders creeping up to my ears in discomfort.

"I didn't agree to that team name," Aris whispers, coming

dangerously close to a joke. Olani snorts a half-hearted laugh.

"Mortals, your task is simple: Open the lock. Leave the room. Only teams who succeed in this task may proceed to the next." I can hear a smug smile in her voice. What could she possibly have to be smug about? Apparently, plenty, because it doesn't ease up at all with her murmured "May Fate favor you."

In the silence that follows, we all look at once. On the other side of the room, there's a door with a round lock in the middle. Between us and the door, a simple table bearing a simple cup.

I look at Aris and Olani, trying to gauge their reactions. Not that there's anything for any of us to do except approach the table and stare down into the cup. It contains a liquid as clear and green as emeralds, which ripples in response to our footsteps. The ripples make the shape of the key at the bottom of the cup shift and bounce, but the key itself stays still.

"It can't be this straightforward," I say, not hesitating before reaching into the cup to grab the key.

"Isolde, wait—"

Olani's warning comes too late. My fingers reach down to where I should be able to feel the imprint of cool metal, but it's like plunging my hand into an ocean with only emptiness below. The widest part of my hand hits the rim of the cup—which from the outside doesn't look deep enough to contain my whole hand—and stops any further progress. My fingers stretch, straining for the key, but I know it's out of reach.

"Weird." I pull my hand back, shaking the green droplets from my skin.

Aris eyes the liquid and my face, looking equally disgusted by both. "What is it?"

"Great question," Olani snaps pointedly. "Glad we've ruled out flesh-eating acid, at least."

"Sorry." In the spirit of investigation, I touch the tip of my tongue to one of my still-damp fingertips.

Olani immediately sucks in a gasp, no doubt saving her

breath from the warning not to lick the liquid she was seconds away from delivering. "Fate, be with me," she mutters under her breath.

My nose wrinkles, and I stick out my tongue again, this time on pure instinct. Whatever the green liquid is, it's both bitter and sickly sweet. As if someone tried to cover the unpleasant sting with honey, and somehow only ended up magnifying it. "It's horrible," I gag.

"Isolde, that could be *poison*."

I shrug. "Well, they gave us a whole cup of it, so it's probably not strong enough to kill me in one drop."

She makes a helpless sort of sputtering noise, unable to argue with the logic, but still furious. It gives me a strange sort of glee to render her speechless.

Eventually, she gives up and changes tactics. "Let me see." I hand Olani the cup, and she investigates with the cautious and thorough air of a professional—by which I mostly mean glaring suspiciously at the liquid before giving it a sniff. "Yep," she says, mostly to herself, before setting the cup back on the table. "You should be fine, but *don't drink any more*."

I make a face. "Wasn't planning on it."

Aris latches on to the relevant information immediately. "You recognize it?"

"My parents always had some on hand. It's foxglove extract. Good for an irregular pulse. In *small doses*."

"And in a cup full?"

Olani shrugs. "It'd stop your heart before you made it to the door."

"Fantastic, so let's not drink any more," I say, as if it was my idea. I swipe the cup and flip it upside down, sending the poison out in a gush.

Less of a gush, more of a flow.

Okay, something isn't right here.

It pours and pours, and the key never clanks out of the

bottom. When I finally give up and put it back on the table, it's exactly as full as it was when I picked it up. The key hasn't budged.

"Huh." The doubtful hope that getting through the first trial might really be this easy is curdling into something sickening in the pit of my stomach. Or maybe it's just the trace of poison I swallowed.

We all stare at the cup. At the puddle slowly sinking into the dusty earth around our feet.

Eventually, Aris cracks the silence. "I think one of us has to drink it."

"Let's not jump to any conclusions," I say. "There's got to be another solution."

We try taking turns reaching into the cup. We try setting the cup on its side on the edge of the table so the contents spill out, then reaching for the key. We try flipping it upside down on the table without spilling a drop, waiting for the telltale thump of the key hitting the wooden surface.

Nothing works.

"Out of curiosity," I ask when we're running out of ideas, "what would a third of this dose do to someone?"

Olani's eyes jump from the cup to my face. Then back. "You mean . . . if we split it between us." There's a pause, and then a long sigh. "I mean, it's poison. That much won't kill you right away, but it would probably shut down your kidneys. You'd have a week or two, at most." Her voice softens as she says, "It's a slow, painful way to go."

"But you could heal it!" At her uncertain frown, I add, "Or . . . the faeries could. Right? I got stabbed and they managed to fix me up."

"You think that's in the spirit of the game?" Aris says. "Because I don't. More likely we all end up dead, which seems like a waste."

I turn to her, not bothering to hide my irritation. She's had pitifully few suggestions since this whole thing started. "Okay, well, what do *you* suggest?"

Aris waits until she has both of our full attention. She takes a deep breath. "I'll do it. I'll drink the poison."

She seems to be expecting some kind of response, which makes the absolute silence of our shock feel like a painfully awkward void. Realizing we're going to need a moment to catch up, she continues, "There's going to be some kind of combat later on, and my magic is no match for theirs. You two stand a chance with your weapons. I can do this."

"But . . ." My mind stalls, unable to fully understand what she's saying. "But you'd *die*."

"Yes," Aris says, sharp and clean as the cut of a knife. "And you'd move on in the tournament. Which we need to win to get the Seelie Queen's support, to *save the world*. So I'd like to think it would be worth it."

"No. Absolutely not. There *has* to be another solution!"

"Maybe," Olani says. "Maybe not."

My jaw drops. "You're not serious. You're not seriously considering letting one of our teammates *die* for this stupid tournament."

Olani shakes her head, gesturing to Aris. "She has a point. We need to win this."

"But not like *this*!" I burst out, loud enough to echo in the high cavern ceiling. Suddenly, the space feels too small. My chest feels too small, unable to take in the amount of air I need. I don't like Aris, but I don't want her dead. I don't want her to die so I can live. Selfishly, I know that if I let her go in this moment, I will never stop seeing her face.

Olani reads my thoughts in the most irritating way possible. "There are bigger things at stake here than your idealistic worldview."

Honestly, it's just like her to look at this so coldly. Olani isn't a bad person, but the need to *do the right thing* doesn't burn in her like it does in me. She cares about people. She calmly and logically determines what she can do to help the most people, to cause the least suffering. She does that.

And everyone else is just collateral damage.

"I can't believe you haven't changed," I say, surprised at how my voice breaks over the words.

She gives me a hard stare, regal features as cold and unfeeling as a marble statue. "Why would I have changed?"

"Because I was *right*!" I can't stop myself from saying it, quick and fierce and pointed as a blade. I know that she knows exactly what I'm talking about. The same argument we had months ago, the one we keep skirting around, the one that always sits between us whether we ignore it or not.

We were on the road a long time. Indistinguishable days bumping along in a wagon, so close to the firedrake egg—the treasure we'd risked everything for, now tantalizingly out of our reach. Leira warned Seelie and Raze that if they followed us or tried to stop her, she'd kill us. And then she left them there. Stranded, in the uninhabited mountains bordering the Dragon Lands, with no wagon and no supplies.

No one doubted that she'd do it. Sometimes I wondered if she'd have preferred to just kill us all on the spot, and why she didn't. Was it because of some lingering affection for Raze, the nephew she raised as an heir before she abandoned him and he turned on her? Or was it out of fear of Seelie's magic, that she'd be starting a fight she couldn't win?

When we finally made it back to Auremore, she didn't release us. The egg hadn't hatched yet. Her treasure hadn't fully been secured. She didn't chain us in iron or anything, but we were guarded, watched for any hint that we had somehow gotten in contact with the others.

Which, of course, we hadn't. There hadn't been so much as a breath of Seelie's magic, or a suspiciously intelligent bird swooping overhead. We'd been looking for them in everything, with mingled hope and dread, and there was no sign that they'd escaped that harsh stone valley at all.

Eventually, when the golden leaves were falling and each chilly sunset seemed earlier than the last, Olani took me aside. Pulled me into a pantry just behind the main kitchen where no one would think to look for us, where we could speak for a few moments without anyone hearing us over the clatter of pots and pans.

It took a second for my eyes to adjust to the darkness, my pulse pounding in my ears, in the spot on my wrist her fingers were still clamped tight around. I took a breath, ready with a joke about what this would look like to anyone who saw—

"We need to get out of here," Olani whispered.

Anything I might have said shriveled up and died on the tip of my tongue. Finally, I managed, "And give up on the fire-drake? On the treasure?"

She gestured vaguely. Not at the pantry as much as at our whole rotten situation. Too afraid to step a toe out of line, knowing we could be disposed of on a whim. "I think we're past that point."

"Where . . . where would we go?"

"Somewhere she'd never find us. We could disappear."

"But then how would Seelie—Seelie and Raze—find us?" My tongue tripped on his name, even though I'd been comforting myself over and over with the fact that she wasn't alone. There was still someone watching my sister's back, even if it wasn't me. Even if it was a disgraced enchanter who was better at smooth-talking than shapeshifting.

Olani's gaze softened, visible even in the dark. Her brows arched gently, making her eyes look huge and deep enough to dive into. "Isolde," she said, as if that was a response on its own.

"When Seelie comes back, I don't want . . ."

"Isolde," she said again. "They're not coming back."

"You don't know that."

She sighed. "They're *probably* not coming back. And we can't base every action around the assumption that they are."

"Maybe *you* can't." I pulled my hand free from her fingers, which she seemed to have forgotten were still wrapped around my wrist. "Seelie isn't dead. Okay? I'd know if she was. I don't know where she is, or when she's going to figure out a way out of this, but I *know* she's coming back."

"And if she doesn't? You'll stay here until Leira Wildfall decides to kill you? How long can you live like this?"

"As long as it takes."

"You're not worried about your own safety at all?"

"Not at the cost of others!"

"Isolde, be reasonable. Do you really think—"

"It doesn't matter what I think. I *feel*, Olani. And my feelings are *real*."

"You think I don't feel?"

"You're not acting like you do."

"And you're not acting like you have any sense of self-preservation. I'll drag you out of here if I have to."

I snorted. "Good luck with that."

"Then maybe I'll just leave you."

With that, our back-and-forth volley cuts off abruptly. Olani inhaled sharply, as if that could suck the words back. Her face twitched, unreadable as it flickered with the traces of expressions she fought to suppress. She opened her mouth, and I interrupted before I could hear what she was going to say next. I didn't want to know.

"You should," I said, the words less steady than I'd hoped they'd be. "You will eventually anyway, as soon as your heartless logic decides it's *too risky* to stick with me."

There. She looked as stung as I felt. It wasn't as satisfying as I'd hoped. "That's what you really think about me? After all this?" Her eyes and voice softened, but I clung to the cold steel in my heart. I would not be thawed. Not after what she'd said.

"I think after all this, you're finally showing me who you really are. So thanks for that."

Without waiting for a response, I shoved past her, opened the door, and walked away. Fast enough to get out of there. Just slow enough that she could catch me if she wanted to.

She didn't.

We didn't really speak for the next two days, but I was surprised every time I saw her that she hadn't disappeared. On the third day, Seelie and Raze crashed into Leira's study from the Unseelie Realm, injured but very much alive, and the firedrake egg hatched, and the rest was history.

But I was *right*.

Staring at me over a puddle of poison, Olani shakes her head. "I can't believe you're bringing this up again."

"Well, that's who I am! I'm emotional and illogical and I'm never, ever going to stop being upset about it just because you don't feel like talking about it!"

Aris drums her fingertips on the tabletop, tilting her head to look at us. "Am I missing something?"

Olani grits her teeth. "We had an argument. *Months* ago. I'm over it now."

"That's good to know, because you never apologized."

"What in all the realms would I have to apologize for, Isolde? Trying to save you from your careless, mindless loyalty?"

"For trying to tell me that my sister was dead—for not *listening* to me when I told you I knew she wasn't."

"You didn't *know*. You hoped. And the thing that really gets me is . . . I would have *tried* to work with you! We could have figured something out, but you were too damn stubborn to see—" Her sentence ends abruptly, cut off mid-thought with almost enough finality to make it sound like that was all she was going to say. But I know her better than that.

"Then maybe you should have led with that, instead of trying to make me feel like an idiot."

"I wasn't trying to make you feel anything, Isolde. No one is responsible for your emotions except you."

"Just because *you* can turn your feelings off at will doesn't mean the rest of us should have to."

"I can't, either! Go ahead and call me heartless over and over. Say whatever you want about me. You think just because we spent a few weeks together you *know* me, Isolde? You don't know me at all. You have *no idea* how much I feel, all the time, *especially with you*."

Oh.

Oh.

Olani wears righteous fury like fine jewelry, a hard glitter that makes her eyes sparkle and her cheeks glow. Even when I'm the object of that fury, I can't help but be mesmerized by her. The twisted corner of her full lips. The wrinkled slope of her perfect brows. The exhalation as all that pent-up anger slowly ebbs away, leaving . . .

Something else.

In the silence that follows, I forget Aris entirely.

At least, until she sighs and swirls the cup of poison in her hand, and we both break our heated gaze. "This doesn't seem like it's about me anymore, so how about this: You two kiss and make up, and then you can win the tournament in my honor, okay?"

I watch her fingers curl around the cup, shaking a little, as she lifts it to her face. I see her green eyes pick up the reflection of the green liquid, a glow that seems to light them from within until she looks down into the cup, tilts it back, and her eyelashes obscure her irises.

I launch myself across the table at her, knowing I'm too far away to knock it out of her hand, but hoping to stall her somehow anyway. "Stop!"

But before I can reach her, she puts the cup down. The mouthful of poison runs over her chin, a tiny river of green that didn't make it past her lips. Aris wipes her mouth with the back of her hand. "To be clear, this isn't because you told me to." She extends the hand holding the cup toward us. "Is it just me, or does this look . . . emptier?"

It does. The cup is only half full now, instead of to the brim. I can see the key more clearly, tantalizingly close to the surface. Without even meaning to, we've managed to partly drain the poison.

What have we done differently in the past few minutes? Maybe it's because we ignored the cup. Or maybe it was Aris's plan to nobly sacrifice herself. Or maybe . . .

"It's because of me, isn't it?" Olani says. She sounds like all her emotion is spent, and all she has left is the flat sound of exhaustion. That, and a slight raise of her eyebrow as she looks at me sideways and mutters, "Of course she gets to be right about talking about our feelings."

As soon as the sentence ends, the level of liquid in the cup drops—not by much, barely a mouthful. But it's an obvious response. The poison is responding to truth, but not the tricky faerie version of truth. It drains a little with each buried, hidden hurt, things that we don't want to say. It's half emptied itself, because Olani has spilled all of hers.

Which I guess makes it my turn.

I take a deep, steadying breath, clench my fists, and force my voice not to shake. "You were right, too." I can't help a glance at the cup. Another teaspoon of liquid has disappeared. It gives me the strength to keep going, to say, "I—I only said you were unfeeling because it was easier to convince myself you were being callous than that Seelie might have been gone. I was scared, because I knew that—logically—you were probably right. And if you were, I didn't really care what happened to me anymore."

I'm partly tempted to check the progress of the poison, to see if it's still draining, but I'm too caught up in the flow of the words now to look away. I know I have more to say, and I don't need some stupid faerie cup to tell me that.

"You put up a good front, but I do know how much you feel. How much you care for everyone around you. How much you expect of yourself, to protect everyone. I've been treating you like the shields you put up are all there is to you, because I knew if I got to know who you really are beneath the surface I would get too attached and probably get my heart broken." I try for a grin, fumble, and shatter into an expression that reflects far more sincerity than I intended. "But I think it's too late for me now."

I wait, heart pounding, for Olani to respond. Before she gets the chance, Aris's voice brings the rest of the world crashing back down around me. "We're almost there! Anything else either of you needs to get off your chest?" She steps forward as she says it, holding the cup up between us.

The look Olani and I exchange lasts somewhere between thirty seconds and an hour. There is, probably, more to be said. But not here. Not now. I can feel the lightness in my chest where all the bitterness I didn't realize I was holding on to has drained away, leaving only a radiant sort of peace.

However long it is, it ends with Aris sighing deeply. "I'd rather be angry at the outside world than the true source of my problems. Which is either my own inadequacy, or the fact that I've been raised to feel inadequate to keep me thankful for the scraps of approval Leira Wildfall throws my way."

We all hold our breath as the liquid in the cup lowers almost imperceptibly—then stops, leaving a fine sheen of poison over the key. Aris lets out a noise somewhere between a scream and a growl, and—before I can stop her—hurls the cup at the ground. Poison pours out in a trickle, slowed significantly now that it's down to a few drops.

Aris grits her teeth, staring into the cup with fire in her eyes. "Fine. I'm afraid to be loved, because I'm worried I'll lose my edge if I don't have to fight to be the best. Are you happy now?"

Clink!

When the key drops, no one moves. I think Olani and I are both waiting for Aris to act first, not wanting to get in her way when she's this worked up. When she doesn't move, we both bend down to reach for it at the same time and find ourselves caught in an awkward game of bobbing and apologizing and reaching at the wrong times. Our fingers brush as we both grab for the cup, and somehow we both end up holding it as we straighten again. One of her fingers grazes my thumb.

"You should . . ." she says, eyes dropping from me to the key, then to me again.

I freeze, waiting for her to finish the sentence.

But she doesn't get a chance, because Aris snaps, "Actually, go back to arguing. This is worse." She reaches between us, snatches the key, and marches to the door without looking back.

Olani lets go to follow her, only making it a few steps before stopping to look at me over her shoulder.

I'm still standing there, holding the cup like an idiot. I let it drop onto the table, step over the puddle of poison, and join my team. The key fits into the lock, the door opens smoothly, and we're greeted by a crowd of a thousand cheering faeries.

chapter twenty-six

SEELIE

We keep following Egg, watching for spots where the world flips again, until the repetition of it becomes a bit mind-numbing. I remind myself that I'm on the most important mission of my life right now, and I don't have time to get distracted, and yet, I remain thoroughly distracted.

I trip over a small gap and land hard on my flat palms, sending a stinging shock all the way up my arms. I'm still sick from the momentum as I push myself up, just in time to see Raze follow. With his extra height and longer legs, he manages to clear the gap without much trouble, and immediately focuses on helping me get back to my feet.

I should have known this whole Liking Raze Thing was going to be a *problem*. Not because there's anything wrong with him, or because I can't keep cloaking it, but because I have never once, in my life, been able to like something a normal amount. Once my mind fixates on something, my heart jumps in without reservations.

Like the time when I was a child and refused to wear anything except my dress embroidered with daisies at the hem, which my mother refashioned over and over again until it was beyond repair—and then I sobbed for a full day over it. Like the time I found Birch, a sickly and starving kitten-shaped thing, and ignored Isolde's reservations and any concern for my own health, staying up night and day to tend to him. Like the time I decided to perfect my base scone recipe, spent weeks covering every flat surface in the *Destiny* with batch after batch of sweet and savory scones, lost hours of sleep planning the tweaks I'd make to the recipe the next day, totally consumed until I was satisfied I'd done it.

"Are you okay?" Raze asks. Then he's helping me to my feet and turning my hand over in his to check my injured wrist before I can even think to awkwardly crawl away from him. The wounds are still sore, but they haven't reopened. You'd think, from the concern dancing in his eyes like sunlight on fresh water, that he'd discovered a mortal wound.

My throat closes, but I don't snatch my hand away.

Once I'm devoted to something, I'm *unstoppable*. I don't know if anyone would want to find themselves under the force of that kind of caring, and I don't know how to deal with it myself. Getting over this isn't going to be accomplished by something as simple as adjusting the ratio of sugar to molasses.

So I bite back the words that want to spill out of my mouth without permission and act like nothing has changed. Because nothing *has* changed. I try to say yes, I'm just worried, but the words seem too far from my reach, so I end up staring at him blankly.

"Yeah, bad question," he chuckles after a second. I can't believe it took me so long to notice the way he fills in these gaps for me—for everyone around him—that puts people at ease. Even when they're as close to snapping as I am right now. Leira Wildfall is a greater fool than previously imagined if she couldn't see how that skill would be just as beneficial to her would-be empire as any shapeshifter's magic.

The brilliant thought that maybe I should *tell him that*, that maybe no one's ever told him that, strikes me. I open my mouth, stammer, and what eventually comes out is "You're—you're nice."

Raze's brows shoot up to his hairline. "Iselia, is that a *compliment*?"

In his hint of laughter, I hear the echoes of hundreds of mocking giggles—not his gentle teasing, but the combined effect of a childhood of endless social mistakes and ridicule. I know those kids weren't Raze, that he's not like that, but I'm too afraid to misstep any further. "Shut up. Never mind."

I turn sharply, looking for Egg again. I can't see him at the moment, but just ahead, the wall steps back down to the forest floor. He's probably down there already, racing to the horizon. I'd like to feel the real ground beneath me, to be shaded by the evergreen branches and breathe in the scent of the trees, until I'm steady again. Maybe putting space between us will clear my head. I start to pull out of Raze's grip, suddenly overwhelmed by anxiety.

"Seelie, wait." Raze doesn't let go, presumably to stop me from running away. I attempt to keep walking anyway, putting long strides between us, but he doesn't break his grip.

Which is what saves my life.

In my eagerness to return to solid ground, I didn't even notice the windblown snowflakes in front of me drifting upward. I'm falling up again, except this time there's no ceiling above to catch me. Only Raze's hand, which almost slips from mine at the sudden change, which my fingers tighten around automatically as—for the second time today—I hear my short scream of surprise.

My legs kick in the air, all my weight trying to pull me up into the endless blue sky. It's a strange feeling, being so heavy and weightless all at once. Of course, there's no surface for my shoes to push against, nothing but empty air.

"Don't let go!" *There's* the fear I've been delaying, a pathetic scrape in my high-pitched voice.

"I won't." Raze's fingers are locked around mine like a vise. I know he can lift my weight without much trouble, but right now he's fighting to stay rooted to the spot—because if he takes another step to get better leverage, he'll end up falling into the sky, too. He looks up at me, eyes reflecting the bright blue above. "Can you move yourself any closer?"

I squeeze my eyes shut, trying to haul myself toward the one anchored point. I can lift myself a little, but I'm not strong enough to hold myself up by my hands. "I'm trying," I say, just as pitifully. This is so humiliating. After everything I've survived to get to this point, I *cannot* die by dropping into the sky.

Raze is trying, too, his teeth gritted with effort, but something about the change in direction seems to be making me a dozen times heavier. I can't stop my legs from kicking, even though it's not helping at all, and between that and the effort of hanging on, I'm getting tired quickly. He stops pulling, which doesn't change much, and we both stare at each other, fighting for breath.

Then his gaze leaves mine, his head turning one way and then the other. When he looks at me again, it's with determination. "I'm going to swing you that way, okay?" He motions with his chin to a spot on the forest floor several feet away, almost underneath the floating stone he's standing on. "When I give the signal, let go."

"Wait!" I screech, even though he's not letting go yet. If I disappear into the air, will I float away forever, or will I eventually reach another turn and drop hundreds of feet to the ground? I can do a lot with magic, but unlike him, I can't fly. I squeeze my fingers tighter, nails digging into the soft flesh of his palm, too panicked to feel bad about that. "Wh-what if—"

Our joined hands are getting sweaty, making them slippery. Raze's face tenses as he tries to pull me back. "We can't hold on forever. Do you trust me?"

I can't breathe. I can't speak. I look up at his face, wondering if his scrunched auburn brows are the last thing I'm going to see before he launches me into the sky. I see the boy I've fallen with an embarrassing number of times—into Leira's carpet, into dry autumn grass by the *Destiny*'s wheels, into leaf-cushioned forest floor, into a sparkling feeling that might eclipse our friendship.

Surely another fall at Raze's hands won't be so bad.

I clench my teeth and nod, forcing back tears.

He takes a deep breath before he moves. Tugging me sideways is far more effective than trying to pull me forward, and I throw my weight into the movement along with him. It takes everything in me not to bring it all to a panicked stop when Raze starts counting down, but I somehow manage to keep it to an undignified yelp. When I'm swinging at a frankly alarming pace, he barks out a sharp "*Now!*"

We both let go.

For a long moment, I'm weightless. My fingers keep stretching forward, begging to be caught again. There is no up or down, nothing but my pounding pulse and all my organs shifting around uncomfortably.

Then I fall. I'm not even sure which way I'm falling until I slam into the ground hard enough to roll with the momentum, harder than I thought I could withstand. When I stop rolling, I'm vaguely aware that Raze has already launched himself to the ground after me, that he's tumbling just as hard and as unsafely as I did over the pine needles, a wheel of red hair and pained curses.

It would be enough to make me laugh, if I could breathe. But my lungs are empty, and all my fighting only serves to make me wheeze uselessly. It's too hard to move, so I just stay there, staring up at the blurry sky and hurting, until I hear my name.

"Seelie!" Raze drags himself over, obviously in pain, but at least still breathing. "Are you okay?" I want to answer, but I'm still fighting to regain my breath. It's all I can do to lift a hand, to try to nod, to bear my teeth through the pain. He leans over me, gripping my hand hard. "Where are you hurt? What did you hit?"

I don't think it's anything more serious than bruising, maybe a sprain or two, and the breath knocked out of me, but I can't tell him that. He keeps repeating similar questions until I lift the arm wrapped around my ribs to smack his shoulder, gesturing for him to give me a second.

He rocks back on his heels, letting out a deep sigh. "Oh, you're okay."

I shoot him an offended glare as I push myself up on my elbows, wheezing and choking. I'm still trying to gather enough breath to speak when Egg pounces on my chest, knocking the wind out of me all over again in his excitement.

Well, that's more than enough of that. I wrap my arms around him before he can run away. I can feel the frantic beat of his heart through his still-warm scales. "*There* you are," I choke between gasps, torn between irritation and relief. Has he finally let us catch up with him because we almost died, or because we've finally reached whatever he was running to?

Raze helpfully lifts Egg into his arms and helps me to my feet, and I try very hard not to stare at him like he's made of sunlight. It helps that, for once, he's not looking at me. Instead, his attention is focused on something on the ground behind me, eyes going wide. "Whatever he was looking for . . . I think we found it."

I turn, fully expecting a faerie monster or an even more creative death waiting for us. Instead, I see clusters of lacy white mushrooms. As I watch, a gentle blue glow lights them from within, hopping from one mushroom to the next until they form a wide, glowing circle. A circle we've just happened to land in the exact center of.

In the Mortal Realm, stepping into a circle of mushrooms is bad luck. You can leave a small token for the faeries behind before stepping out to negate the effect, but it's little more than a superstition. Still, I can't help thinking that we're not in the Mortal Realm anymore.

The earth shifts beneath our feet, trees and rocks parting as the ground rolls, slowly yawning open to reveal a crumbling staircase, mossy stone delving down into total blackness underground. The opening seems to sigh, brushing my hair away from my face with another whisper of wind. I move toward it as if towed by a line, feeling a strange acceptance of the waiting dark.

Raze grabs my elbow to pull me back. "What if it's a trap?"

I look at him over my shoulder. "Might be." Pulling gently from his grip, I weave our fingers together and squeeze his hand tight in mine. It's uncharacteristically clammy at just the thought of the underground staircase, which makes my skin crawl, but I can bear a little discomfort to comfort him. "But we don't have anywhere else to go. Come on."

Together, we descend.

The blue glow fades quickly, leaving us to navigate by touch. Weighed down by Egg, each of Raze's steps is tentative, while I keep my free hand pressed to the wall to feel our way down. It's a spiral staircase, an unknown number of shallow steps, which makes it kind of feel like we're in an endless cylinder of damp, cold underground air.

"Here, let's switch," I say after hearing a ragged breath he doesn't quite manage to hide. I reach back and gently pull Egg from his arms.

Raze interrupts me mid-sentence. "I can carry him!"

"I know you can. But he's warm. This is purely for selfish

reasons." Even as I say it, I rub Egg's scaly cheek against my own. He allows it, letting out a happy little huff of hot air. His tail curls around me, like a hug, which helps support his weight a little, but not much.

Raze huffs, but he shuffles in front to feel along the wall before reaching back to take my hand. "Now *I'm* cold," he grumbles.

"You'll live."

After a few more minutes, a faint light ahead signals a change. As we get closer, I realize it's just a chunk of glowing green crystal clinging to the stone wall, barely bright enough to illuminate the space of a few steps. But we keep descending, and there's another glowing crystal, and another—all evenly spaced. No more natural than the stairs themselves. Someone has created this passage, and I can't help but wonder if it's just for us.

The journey probably feels longer than it is, due in large part to the total silence. Raze's fear of small spaces is one of the few things that truly suffocates his personality. Even in the dark, I can feel the tense lock of his muscles with every step. I hope I haven't made a mistake leading us underground. I still have so much to do, so much to fix.

Eventually, the eerie crystal glow gets brighter. Without warning, the tunnel around us opens up to an enormous cavern lit in a wash of flat, pale green light. There are dozens of other holes in the ceiling much like the one we emerged from, some with stairs and some without, which give the cavern the effect of an anthill. The space is so tall that we descend at least another two stories from the ceiling to the floor, which makes Raze relax enough to start breathing again, and gives me plenty of time to observe the glowing eyes of the faeries all around us.

A low hum of insect-like hisses and clicks follows us, from the faeries clinging to the stalactites above to those seated all around the room in finery almost indistinguishable from the Seelie Court's: relics of mortal styles from centuries past. Some have wings, or sharp teeth protruding from their lips, or frames far too long and thin to ever be mistaken for human. Some look like us.

But it's the ancient faerie seated on what is very clearly a throne at the end of the cavern that steals my breath away.

It's strange, because faeries don't age as mortals do. Instead of wrinkling, its skin looks faded and translucent and moth-eaten. In places, there's no skin at all, just a bare rib cage with jewel-toned fungi blooming between the bones, skeletal arms folded peacefully in its lap. A spiked crown reminiscent of antlered beetles adorns its pale, hairless head, and dusty wings unfurl behind it. The only thing untouched by time are its silvery moon-glow eyes.

My mouth goes dry as I try to figure out whether I'm meant to stare at this spectacle or not.

Raze's hand drops from mine as we approach. I get the sense we're supposed to bow or something, but since I've never been trained in courtly manners, I settle for bending down to gently place Egg on the ground. For once, he remains where I put him, pinned under the attention of the Unseelie Queen and her Court. He can't possibly know he's a relic of another time, the likes of which they haven't seen in long enough for even their immortal memories to start to fade.

"I wondered when you'd show your face here again, Seelie," the creature says in a scratchy, sibilant voice. "Or should I say 'Guardian of the Last Firedrake, Lady Iselia of the Gray Grove'?"

"It's just 'Graygrove,'" I say before I can stop myself. The impulse to make the correction slips past my filters, overriding the awed silence. "One word. Mother's side Gray, father's side Grove."

"That's how we do it in the Mortal Realm," Raze adds helpfully.

The ancient faerie frowns. "That won't do at all," she says. "A lady of my court must have a fitting title."

Of course this is the Unseelie Queen. Her magic feels different from her sister's, like a cool, enveloping fog. It diffuses everything around us, seeping gently rather than blazing with life. She must have created that path for us—which means she must want to see us. After every twist the Unseelie Realm has thrown us, it feels a bit dizzying to be so close to our goal. All I have to do is request her help, and not ruin everything.

The Unseelie Queen ignores my anxious silence, continuing, "I suppose we could just hand down Briar's full title. Not usually how it's done, but I hardly think she'd mind now. Being dead and all."

My skin goes ice cold, and I think my pulse actually stops for a second. "Briar?" I repeat.

(Blood on my hands, fingers stiff around the dagger's hilt, Isolde's wide eyes the ones that meet mine as the faerie's body drops to the leaf-mulch forest floor.)

"Yes, Briar," the faerie snaps, starting to lose patience. "A well-known courtier. Perhaps you remember running her through with pure iron?"

The chills develop into sweat. "I—I didn't mean to," I stammer, which isn't quite true, but it's not exactly false, either. I only killed Briar because she was going to kill me, right before chaos broke loose and we escaped to the Mortal Realm. I knew the Unseelie Court might remember my crimes. I knew I'd have to pay for it eventually.

"A lie." Her mouth twitches in what might be a smile. "But an unnecessary one. It's been so long since we had a mortal among our ranks. They never last long." I try to comfort myself with the knowledge that, from her perspective, the cheerfully ominous statement would be true of a human who lived a full, healthy life and died in their sleep at ninety years old. It doesn't make me feel better.

"Among your ranks?" I don't realize until the words slip out that I'm echoing again, repeating the things I hear rather than generating my own sentences. I need to be sharper than that to survive here.

"You, changeling, inherited Briar's rank the moment she died at your hand. What do you think of 'Lady Iselia, the Iron Dagger'?"

I can't respond. I think my jaw has dropped. I turn to Raze, who looks equally stunned, but who isn't shut up nearly so easily.

"Sounds kind of intense," he whispers. "I think you should take it."

chapter twenty-seven

ISOLDE

The Seelie Queen's throne room is a buzzing hive, music and jewels and overladen tables all vying for my attention—and I'm absorbing none of it.

I was too dazed by the trial, the crowd, the raucous cheering that followed us as we exited the cavern to focus on anything but putting one foot in front of the other. The only thing that pulled me from the clouds was the full blaze of the Seelie Queen's attention. She saw the whole thing. And I don't know what we did to make her, specifically, angry—but I'd swear that, as we left, she cast a glare on me that hit me like a flash of heat.

Ideally, I'd have time to discuss that moment with my teammates. To see if they felt it, too. If they could guess what we did wrong so we could strategize around it. Instead, we're being swept off to the next trial, without even a second to breathe. The good news is that, after this one, we'll have time to rest.

The bad news is that this one seems to mostly involve being paraded around the Seelie Court like some sort of fancy, well-bred horses.

At least we're not losing more time. Seelie could be weeks ahead or days behind in the Unseelie Realm. I can't even begin to wrap my head around what it might be like for our parents and all those trapped in suspended time in the portal realm.

"You did very well," Cobweb hums, looking faintly pleased, which is the happiest I've seen him.

I don't feel like we did well. I feel like we spilled our guts, left ourselves looking all too mortal and too vulnerable, and now we're being forced to mingle while we're still seasick from the waves we made.

"By humiliating ourselves?" Aris asks, staring both faeries down.

"Yes!" Robin chirps happily. I can tell from the look in their glittering gray eyes that they recognized my sarcasm, and are simply choosing to ignore it. They throw an arm around Cobweb's shoulders, pulling him in tight and shaking him a bit in their excitement—which, to my surprise, the faerie allows. "The Court *loved* it. Every second. I can't remember the last time we had such a display!"

"They're right," Cobweb says, staring at us as if there isn't an ecstatic changeling hanging off his shoulders. "So don't waste the opportunity to secure your place as the favorites. The more they like you, the better chance you win—and the bigger a favor you can ask for when you do."

"*When*," Olani repeats ironically, looking over all our heads at the party beyond. Her shoulders are stiff, fists clenched at her sides.

The Seelie Queen has settled herself at the head of the table, rather than distant on her throne. The faeries of the Court elbow and jostle each other for a seat closer to her side, vying for her attention until she stands, and everything stills at once. "Fae of the Seelie Court. Competitors in the Winter Tournament. Let us all toast to the second task in this Wintersol Tournament." All around the room, glasses raise, liquids in every shade of the rainbow sparkling in the dim light. "Competitors, congratulations on passing the first trial. All of you will be proceeding to the third, but tonight, you have the chance to win once more: make an impression. Catch my attention—perhaps even my sympathy. May Fate favor you." With that, she lifts her glass to the room as a whole, and takes a deep drink.

As the goblet touches her lips, she looks to me once more. Despite the smile fixed in place, something burns in her eyes. And I know—she wants us to fail. No, not just that. She *expects* us to fail.

When I look back to Robin and Cobweb to ask another question, they're already gone. Great. We're on our own.

Of the thirteen teams that started the tournament, only five are moving on to the combat round. Besides us, there's one other team of goat-legged musicians that figured out the trick. The faerie teams were given a different poison concoction than ours, brewed from enough rowan berries to weaken their bodies and magic for at least the length of a human lifespan. Two teams are now down to two players each after sacrificing one of their members to drink the full dose of poison, and the final team is all green and faintly ill, since they all shared the cup.

Aris snorts, eyeing this last group. "Bet they won't be much competition in the morning." Her expression is calculating as her gaze sweeps the rest of the party, missing nothing. After all her years as Leira's right hand, I have to admit that she may be uniquely suited for this challenge in a way that I (immediately infuriating to anyone I perceive as powerful, which is pretty much everyone here) and Olani (who shuts down in large groups of people, turning into a particularly lovely brick wall) are not.

I cross my arms, leaning closer to her. "So, where do you think we should start?"

She begins to consider the question before actually doing a double take, apparently shocked I'd ask her opinion on something. I miss whatever she says next, because I'm wondering if it's really that surprising that I'd let someone else take the lead when we all know I'm out of my depth.

Following Aris's lead, we strike up a few conversations with faeries, all while sipping wine and trying to look like we're having a blast. I'm so distracted trying to figure out why Olani is distracted that I hardly remember any of it and am suddenly startled back into myself at the feeling of a faerie's cold skin on mine.

I force myself not to flinch when she squeezes my wrist tight, sharp edges of her jeweled rings digging into my skin. "You mortals are just so *adorable*," the faerie gushes. "The way you *refused* to consider sacrificing your friends! So noble! Just like those knights in the olden days. Is the chivalry trend coming back around in the Mortal Realm, do you think?"

This last part is said hopefully. No one has ever implied that I might be chivalrous before, and it's been centuries since the idea of noble knights loyally devoted to their monarchs died out. I only have a hazy picture of it in my head from stories, mostly ones where they're hunting down the last of Egg's kind. Still, I try to keep my smile in place and offer a generous "Perhaps."

I know that Olani's smile is fake, but it's almost impossible to tell. I've never seen her *try* before. She's always so perfectly herself that hearing the polished voice that emerges from her slightly-too-sharp expression is like being startled by the sudden appearance of a stranger. "Isolde is being modest. There aren't many mortals like her."

The faerie releases me to peer at Olani, obviously trying to fit her into the story in her head. Wherever she ends up placing her, she offers a satisfied smile. "We must still have some of that armor lying about. You both would look so dashing in something shiny, wouldn't you? And perhaps a defense cloak for the enchanter."

Olani and I exchange a look. Neither of us has ever fought in metal armor, and the unfamiliar weight of it would probably put us in more danger. Aris covers our uncomfortable silence by beaming so bright, I'm not sure she's not putting a trickle of magic into it. "What a wonderful idea! Like something out of a faerie story." She lets the sentence end with a dreamy, homesick sigh, effortlessly disentangling all of us from the conversation as she drifts away with a far-off look. Approachable, but not desperate. She won't reach for help, but she'll make *you* want to reach out to help *her*.

Damn, she *is* good.

Aris's next strategy is to get all friendly with the goat-legged faerie team, assuming that if they're noble enough to solve the puzzle, they will hesitate before attacking an ally in the tournament arena. While she's entertaining them with decorative displays of light magic, something prickles at the back of my neck. I turn to find Robin standing uncomfortably close. My eyes automatically search the space behind them for Cobweb, but this time, they're alone.

"I want to talk to you," Robin says. "Changeling to changeling."

It feels strange to be addressed this way. Besides the whole ageless centuries of living in a faerie realm thing, I'm not *like* Robin. I'm not like Seelie. Any connection I had with the faerie realms must have been severed as soon as my mother carried me out. I'm not special or clever or magical enough to belong here.

But I've never quite belonged anywhere else, have I? It's a feeling I've barely been outrunning my whole life. Especially the past three years of constant shifting location and seeking adventure, chasing down a future I couldn't really imagine. I wasn't moving toward something. I was moving away from the homes that didn't feel like home. The only place I've ever known I belonged was at Seelie's side, and now it seems even she doesn't need me anymore.

"I'll be right back," I murmur to my team. Olani nods, mouth drawing into an unreadable line, and Aris waves me off without looking. I follow Robin, trying to focus on anything but the pounding of my pulse and the thoughts swirling around my head.

"We're not as rare as people think," Robin says, without introduction. They walk alongside me much like Seelie does, eyes focused on the path ahead instead of on me. They hop over obstacles and reach up to drag their fingers along the undersides of dewy flowers, taking in our surroundings with all their senses.

"We?" I repeat.

"You know, unseelie changelings. We're a bit more . . . subtle. Maybe it's a good thing that people don't know about us as much, because humans tend to have real issues with the distinction between *Unseelie* and *evil* and obviously you and I both know that we're not malicious or anything, we're just a bit . . ."

"Different," I finish. Their thoughts may wander a bit, but Robin is obviously going somewhere. I'm hardly going to interrupt to demand they organize their thoughts better when someone is finally, *finally* explaining the magic that makes me and Seelie what we are.

"Right, so, a body woven by unseelie magic and a . . . life force, spirit, whatever you prefer—that is all human. I'll admit, I've never heard of a matching set like you and your sister, but I hear those were extenuating circumstances."

"Our mother is an unhinged force of nature, you mean." Our mother, who traveled to the faerie realm to save her child, who refused to give either of us up and outbargained the faeries.

Robin's easy smile takes on a mischievous twist. "Oh, both courts were buzzing about *that* when it happened." Something out of place and ancient in their voice suddenly reminds me that, despite their appearance, they've been around since Auremore was nothing more than a pile of rubble. They may have grown up in the Mortal Realm, just like Seelie and me, but they chose to pass centuries here instead of a single lifetime back home.

"Wait. If you're an Unseelie changeling, why do you live here? I got the feeling we . . . weren't exactly welcome."

"It's not like that," Robin says. "Unseelie magic is our origin, but we can pledge fealty to whichever court we choose. Even though our vows aren't binding in the same way faerie ones are, they take things like that pretty seriously. I am the Seelie Queen's subject as much as Cobweb, or anyone else at this party. Besides you and your friends, of course. But we're getting distracted. What I'm trying to say is . . . I know how you feel."

"You do?" I'm not trying to be difficult, but the words come out so flat they sound more like a statement than a question.

"You're like me. Alive, because of Unseelie magic. It makes us despise routine and crave change. It makes it hard to live in a world of humans that want you to pick one thing to do and stick with it forever. Instead of the enchantment your sister does, its magic makes us quick and clever and cool under pressure. Most humans don't consciously pick up on it, but they still treat us differently because of it."

"Is that why you decided to stay here?"

"It's one of the reasons." Wistfulness clouds their normally cheerful eyes, as if they're looking at something miles away and centuries ago. I want to ask what's wrong, but we're suddenly right back where we started, illuminated by Aris's false fireworks. The distant look drops from Robin's face as quickly as it appeared, and they brightly say, "Well, that's all. I just wanted to let you know you're not the only one."

I'm honestly not sure if it worked or not. I frown, crossing my arms. "So what am I supposed to do? It's like I'm not a real changeling and not a real human. I can't up and disappear into one of the faerie realms. There's too many people counting on me."

Robin stops, clapping a hand down on my shoulder like an older sibling offering advice. They speak slowly for once, thinking each word over before allowing it to form. "Embrace your chaos. Remember that you're not a broken human—you're a perfectly functional changeling. And if the world tries to shove you into a box that doesn't fit . . . change the box, not yourself."

A dazzling explosion of iridescent light bursts overhead. I don't even realize I've been distracted by it until I look back down, and Robin is gone. I shake my head with a chuckle. Fate forbid me to live enough centuries that I become mysterious and vague.

chapter twenty-eight

seelie

When I sleep, tucked away in what was once Briar's cavernous chamber of the palace, I dream of the Unseelie forest.

I know I'm dreaming, because in the dream, I'm dead. It's *my* body cooling in a bed of dead brown leaves, my blood sinking into the rich soil below. My eyes are wide open, staring at the stars through a screen of silvery leaves, but I can't move, and the creatures are closing in.

I dream of teeth and claws. Iridescent wings and hideous laughter. Hot blood streaking my cold skin. Instead of the pain I expect, there is nothing but numbness as the icy chill claws its way through the layers of my flesh. I am lost, drifting in the darkness.

I don't realize that the whispering and snap of teeth has subsided until the forest's silence becomes smothering, a dark cushion pushing down on my face. The world is completely without sound—and then my heart beats. Once. Then again. Slowly, my pulse returns.

I sit up and find myself face-to-face with the Unseelie Queen. We're still in the forest, far from the glowing gems and underground caverns of the Court. I can tell I'm still dreaming, because when I prop myself up with my fingers digging into the earth, it's still warm and wet with my blood. And yet, as soon as I have the thought, it feels *wrong*. This moment doesn't have the fuzzy, unreal sheen of a dream.

"Are you really here?" I blurt. This wouldn't be the first time one of my dreams was more than just a dream. Faeries seem to regard the lines between waking and sleeping as more of a suggestion than a rule.

"Mortals," she murmurs, almost fondly. "You called to me, and you're surprised I answered?"

Did I call to her? I try to remember how I got here, but of course I can't. The last thing I remember is listening to Egg's steady breathing, trying to get my tired mind under control, to prepare for the path ahead. Dealing with the Unseelie Queen, reuniting with Isolde and the others, winning over the Seelie Queen, and then somehow defeating Gossamer and undoing the enchantment holding the Unending Realm together. No matter how long I lay there, with my eyes wide open and my heart beating like it was trying to escape my chest, I still wouldn't be able to plan for everything that could go wrong.

I wrote my impassioned speech in my head over and over, shifting the words around, hoping to stumble on a magic combination that would secure us the Unseelie Queen's help. Eventually, my burned-out body must have given out and dropped into sleep, and now I'm here.

"Oh," I say a little too faintly. No, that won't do. I have to treat this like the real thing. To summon iron and fire behind my voice. "I didn't intend to summon you, so please excuse any disrespect. But you're right—we do need to talk."

"*Talk.*" On her withered lips, the word drips like toxic mold. The Queen's face puckers for a moment, like she's trying not to throw up, and then she transforms in an instant into a girl no older than fourteen, with the same crest, wings, and silver eyes. The sun rises, casting the forest in blazing light and painting us in stripes of shadow.

The girl scowls, glaring at me. "I already know what she's going to say, and I don't want to talk about it."

She shifts back into the ancient faerie just as quickly, and night falls again. "Well, I do."

Her face softens to one strikingly like the Seelie Queen—ageless yet mature—and for just a moment, the sky takes on a dusky glow. "Like it or not, all troubles must eventually be faced."

"Shut up!" reply two overlapping voices, two overlapping appearances, as day and night flow into each other overhead. The sun and moon of the Unseelie Realm turn to me, capturing me in their gaze.

"You've already enjoyed my sister's hospitality, I see," the ancient Unseelie Queen says, reaching out to touch a flower woven into my hair. It's as fresh as the moment it was plucked, as if it's somehow still alive—at least, it is until the moment her fingertips make contact with it. With that one light brush, weeks pass in the blink of an eye. The flower browns, decays, shrivels to a dried speck. Fear chills my veins. Would the same happen if she were to touch me?

After a pause, I realize that she means the Seelie Queen. A question—a response—anything—stalls on the tip of my tongue, subdued by my racing heart. Luckily, I'm saved from having to speak by the Unseelie Queen's knowing smile.

"That's okay. She doesn't like to talk about me. I understand."

"You and your sister . . . you don't like each other very much, do you?" Seems like an understatement.

The faerie's face looks almost pained. "Oh, no. We love each other dearly. We just . . . shouldn't see each other. It's difficult. I'm sure you understand."

Do I understand? Is pained distance Isolde's and my inevitable end? "What happened?" I ask, not sure if I'm supposed to be holding my tongue or not.

The Queen sighs, and a breeze stirs around us. "When a wolf attacks a child in the forest, no one blames the wolf. It's in their nature to hunt. Blood and bones are their birthright." I try to follow the metaphor, though it feels like my heart and head are spinning off balance. "But when the shiny, well-groomed dog draws blood—then humans grow angry. They're surprised that something lovely and tame still has teeth. That is the difference between my sister and I." Her head tilts, silver eyes burning twin cold spots in my flesh. "I have never tried to disguise the truth of what I am."

I inhale slowly, wondering if I've grown too comfortable here, caught off guard by her casual demeanor. "You're the wolf," I breathe.

"I am change and death," the Unseelie Queen says. "I am the cycle of the seasons, the new moon, the chrysalis. I am nature and all its unpleasant truths. And my beloved, unchanging sister . . . she is a beautiful lie." She scoffs, turning away from me. "No wonder you mortals seem to favor her."

When she puts it like that, it does sound unfair. I don't know how to comfort an ancient force of nature—if I'm even supposed to—so I just say, "We do like order."

That makes her smile. A strangely mortal smile, the one adults always used to favor me with when I was trying too hard. "I know more about you than you think, Iselia. And I know your sister. I see your paths, winding like rabbit trails around my sister's and mine. There's only ever one end."

My brow furrows, my fingers twisting in my skirt. "So . . . why are you telling me this?"

For a second, she's a little girl. The sky flickers to day and back to night so quickly I'd have missed it if I blinked. Then the ancient faerie says, "Because I should have said it to her."

She could kill me as easily as drawing breath. I need to remember that. No good can come from feeling *bad* for the Queen of the Unseelie Realm.

But my stupid mortal heart twists anyway.

"But you're not here to talk about our sisters, are you? You're more concerned with an immediate problem."

I nod, relieved to see we're steering back to the more immediate problem. "Gossamer."

The Queen lets out a breath with all three of their voices. "He's always been a problem. I was all too quick to offer the mortals help last time he started eroding the borders between worlds. I blamed myself. I was always too soft on him when he was young."

The thought of Gossamer young, a child even, seems so ridiculous. I realize I don't know much about the life cycle of a faerie. But still, the Queen talks about him with the same wistful voice she used discussing the Seelie Queen. Like he's family.

I'm not sure what's expected of me, so I stick to the script I've been working on in my head for . . . however long it's been now. "I understand and fully accept my part in what's happened."

The young woman appears, raising an eyebrow at me in the golden afternoon light. "By which you mean the whirlpool of uncontrolled magic pulling at the threads of all the realms, twisting them into a tangle of something new?"

I haven't heard it described like that. My throat goes dry, but I nod. "He's calling it the Unending Realm," I say weakly.

"You made it. What do you call it?" She looks at me almost like an equal, but it's impossible to determine if that's just another manipulation tactic.

I take a deep breath, deciding to present myself as if she's already decided to take me seriously. "A mistake," I say. "I had no desire to encroach on your kingdom or your sister's. I don't even want to rule the Mortal Realm. I just want everything to be set right again. And I'm seeking your support to make that possible."

The Unseelie Queen flickers between forms, looking straight through me with her gleaming silver eyes. The forgotten flower in her hand blooms and wilts and blooms again, twisting new tendrils of green stem around her fingers with each cycle. "It's your spell," she says eventually. "You can undo it."

"Maybe," I say, which is about a thousand times more confident than I feel. "Unless Gossamer kills me first."

"So you mostly need help subduing the rogue faerie."

"Like last time."

"Last time, mortal, was an *unmitigated disaster.*"

"I—I'm sorry, I didn't know. Mortals have short lives and shorter memories. The full story never made it to my generation." Maybe I should have tried to fill the gaps in my knowledge sooner. Now that I think of it, it is strange—that I have managed to kill a faerie, and so has Egg, but the combined force of all three realms barely managed to suppress Gossamer. He was, perhaps, more powerful than average, but *that* much more? I gather my courage and ask, "What happened?"

The Unseelie Queen stares off into the distance, like the memory is appearing before her. "Gossamer was my . . . I don't know if there's a mortal term for it. My ward. A child both charming and vicious, beloved of the Seelie and Unseelie Courts alike. My sister and I both had a hand in raising him, passing him back and forth between our realms. But faerie children grow so slowly . . . one day he was no longer a child, and it took us far too long to realize it. To stop spoiling him and coddling him, and insist he choose which Court to join permanently.

"Back in those days, travel between the worlds was simpler. The separation between realms was a formality. But Gossamer never forgave us for making him choose. He resented all rules and expectations." Her mouth quirks a little. "You may not see a difference between his resentment and the chaos of the Unseelie Court. But even we bow to natural law, mortal. Gossamer did not. Perhaps he could not. But he still had both courts' favor. He turned faeries to his side under our noses, promising rebellion and a new order. To give them dominion over the Mortal Realm, which to some of our kind may as well be inhabited by ants."

I must show my fear on my face, because the Queen kindly adds, "Not to fear. I am old enough to know that ants are a vital part of the environment."

So I am an ant to her. A particularly troublesome ant, but one not worth squashing because I'll be dead soon anyway. Very comforting.

"Gossamer wove bargains that deceived even his own kind. He placed his followers strategically around the Mortal Realm—cities and strongholds, vital ports, trade routes. And then he killed them."

I thought nothing could surprise me at this point, but that does. The sound I make is less like a gasp and more like air being sucked out of me. "His own forces?"

Too dignified to nod, the Unseelie Queen merely raises her chin. "He used the faerie-death magic to create dozens of tiny holes between the worlds. Similar to the one you unintentionally created, but smaller and more unstable. Magic poured through and manifested in floods and firestorms. Humans and faeries alike tried to control the damage, but we couldn't get it to stop until a few of the most powerful mortal enchanters who had managed to escape organized our efforts. Only then did we realize whose fault it was."

Gossamer's. Her own. It's impossible to tell which she means.

"We didn't want to risk martyring him and . . . well, doing what *you've* accomplished. He had gained too much power by then. We only just barely managed to lock him away."

"It was an accident," I say. I hope that she was finished speaking, but even the fear of interrupting can't hold the words back any longer. "All of it—releasing him, creating this—" Words fail me, so I frantically mime an explosion, a tangled ball of yarn, trapped between my hands.

"I always knew he would escape." She still wears that strange near-smiling expression—*wistful.* That's the word. "Sometimes, in the darkest hidden corner of my heart, I even wished for it."

This time, I wait long into the silence, not sure how to respond to that. "And now?" I finally ask, as softly as if I was speaking to my own sister. "What will you do?"

"He must be stopped," the Queen answers, which is a relief. For a second, I thought she was about to turn on me. "However, this is not my quest. I cannot offer my support freely."

"What do you want?"

"What can you offer of equal value?"

My mind races, trying to solve an impossible puzzle. Promising to help us will almost certainly result in some loss within her forces. I doubt that my mortal life, which burns so bright and so short, is even worth one to her.

A ghostly smile smears the Queen's faded features. "As I thought. Perhaps, by the time you wake, you will have something to offer me."

I sink back into the ground, and just as suddenly as the dream started, it's over.

chapter twenty-nine

ISOLDE

I push through the crowd to rejoin my teammates, and quickly realize that there is no team to rejoin. Aris is still holding her audience captive, but Olani—who I *swear* I left standing right behind her, who I promised to return to after that brief conversation—has wandered off somewhere.

I turn around slowly, feeling a bit betrayed that Olani would sneak away without so much as a word. She hasn't gone far, though. I spot her almost immediately, standing near the edge of a puddle of lantern light, like she's trying to hide in the shadows. A breeze stirs the air, ruffling the loose strands of hair around my face. When I push them back behind my ears, Olani is looking up to meet my gaze. I choose to take that as an invitation to join her, slipping away from the group still mesmerized by Aris's magic.

At least, I hope it's an invitation. My heartbeat speeds up as I approach, ignoring the fact that this should be the easiest thing

I've done all day. "Found you," I say once I'm close enough to hear. I keep my voice at a low, soothing register so only she can hear. "You know, it's rude to leave without saying goodbye."

Olani looks straight through me, as if she can somehow sense the hurt I'm trying to cover with a joke. "You left first."

"*I* said goodbye," I say, giving her an exaggerated pout. "And I came right back."

"What if I didn't think you'd miss me?"

"What if I did?"

"Then I won't leave you again."

Promise? my traitorous heart asks, but I clamp my jaw shut before I can say something stupid like that and turn our gentle teasing into a serious conversation. We fall into silence, taking a moment to settle and rearrange our thoughts after the absolute chaos of the day. In the background, the faerie celebration carries on, lit in bursts of color by Aris's show-off-y spells.

"How long do we need to stay for no one to notice when we slip out of here?" Olani mutters eventually. It makes me realize I've never seen her at a party before. On Revelnox, she and Raze were on a mission, sneaking around in stolen servants' uniforms. Our first time in the Seelie Realm, she was so lost in enchantments she was hardly herself, and the months since haven't given us much reason to celebrate. Even on Wintersol, she never dressed up, not even pretending to plan to be in attendance at the ball.

My stomach drops uncomfortably with a flicker of anxiety—maybe she was right. Maybe I don't know her at all. I smother the feeling with a grin and eyes rolled in her direction. Even if it's true, that is one problem I can solve. "Do you have a thing about parties? It's okay if you do. I always try to pay attention for Seelie if something is too loud or crowded, so I'm used to it."

"No," Olani says quickly, defensively. Her eyes keep scanning the chaos all around us, but I don't stop looking at her until they finally drop to me. She sighs. "It's not that. I just . . . don't understand the appeal. Like, isn't it better to spend time with a few people you actually like than surround yourself with several dozen strangers?"

"What if you have several dozen friends?"

"No one likes that many people."

"*I* like that many people! I might even like a couple hundred people. I haven't done the math."

"That's easy for you to say. You're . . ." She trails off. Then she has the nerve to keep moving, as if I'm going to let her leave it at that.

I chase her down, walking carelessly backward to cut her off. I'm sure everyone else can do the work of avoiding running into me without my cooperation. "I'm *what*?"

"You're . . . you know."

"I *don't* know, Olani, but I really wish you'd tell me." I have gotten very good, in the past few weeks, at not touching her unless necessary or invited. But now, with the first trial behind us, I'm feeling bold. Something has settled, and I'm not so afraid of what will happen if I rock the boat of our friendship. If I pull her by the hand until a tree cuts off her escape route, corner her with her back against it, and linger just under her chin to smile sweetly up at her.

Olani rolls her eyes, but she smiles in return. We both know she could push back if she wanted to, that I'm only cornering her because she's choosing to let me. "Well, I was going to say likable, but that's starting to feel off."

"Come on."

"You're . . . cute!" The word sets off a warm glow in my chest, but before I can start feeling too pleased with myself, she adds, "Like Birch."

"How exactly am I like Birch?"

"You just have such a sweet little face that makes people

want to protect you. And by the time they realize that you're an absolute menace who's more than capable of taking care of yourself, you've already got your claws in them."

Neither of us has moved. The branches of the tree at her back shelter us slightly from the party. I can still hear everything, and I'd be able to see the party through the leaves—

If I was looking at the party.

Olani's lips are slightly parted, her eyes bottomless wells heavily shadowed by thick lashes. I've seen similar expressions on other faces, but the way it looks on hers breaks something inside me. I can't keep pretending I don't want this. Moved by that same rush of boldness, I close the space between us until we're pressed together against the tree, raising one hand to tilt her face down nearer to mine. I know what it's like to be near her, have tackled and grappled her enough times to be familiar with the crush of our bodies, but *this* is something totally new.

Something that sends a flurry of frantic, desperate wings fluttering from my heart into my stomach.

"My *claws*," I murmur ironically. My hand rests on her jaw. My pulse beats at a dizzying tempo. "Am I really so terrible?"

Olani inhales, maybe to respond . . . or maybe to do something else. She's so close I can almost *taste* her.

And then we're interrupted by a high, sharp, unmistakably human scream.

My head snaps up to see Aris, still surrounded by the three goat-legged faeries, all red-faced with laughter. I could ignore it, but then I watch her take another swig of whatever they're all drinking before slumping over onto the table, shoulders still shaking.

Curses.

Olani's hand slips from my shoulder, the buzz of her nearness dissipating as her defenses swiftly raise again. "We should check on her."

I wordlessly agree.

Aris's giggles have faded by the time we make it back to the table, but she remains a puddle of soft brown curls, face pressed into the tablecloth, fingers loose around a bright yellow bottle. The faeries are only in slightly better shape.

"Aris? You . . . okay?" Olani shakes her shoulder gently, and she lurches upright—then overcorrects, wobbling in the other direction.

"I'm okay," she says, voice just as wobbly. "I'm *so good*. Look at my new friends!"

She gestures with the bottle, which makes my eyes water as it passes under my nose. I grab for it. "I'm just going to take this, all right?"

"No! I'm fine!" I try to pry it out of her grip, but she's surprisingly strong. Clear liquid dribbles out of the bottle, spilling over her lap and prompting a new round of giggles.

The faeries join in until I snatch one of their bottles away, holding it out of reach to examine it. "What did you give her?" I demand, not caring if I crush whatever bond she's been working on building.

The three all look at me with round eyes, their horizontal pupils stark. "It's good!" one insists cheerfully.

I sample it with as much caution as I used with the poison, wrinkling my nose at the overwhelming sweetness. To be fair, they're not *wrong*—whatever this is, it goes down smoothly, without the burn of something as strong as it smells.

"It's just honeysuckle moonshine," the one I stole the bottle from finally says, reaching for it. "Give it *back*."

I do, focusing my attention on Aris. She manages to push onto her feet, then nearly drops over as it all rushes to her head at once. Olani catches her, and between the two of us, we manage to snatch the bottle away before she can drink any more.

"'S not even that strong," Aris mumbles. "Doesn't taste like anything."

"That's great," Olani says, setting it down like it might blow up in our faces. "But I think you've had enough."

Aris shoves her, but at least she staggers away from the table to do it. "Everyone's always telling me what to do," she complains. Before we can stop her, she steps on her chair, then onto the table. She's so focused on glaring at us that she doesn't even notice her boot knocking the bottle over, or the faeries all clutching things out of her path. "Can't I do what I want for once?"

Okay, so she's fully lost control. Given their innocently shocked faces, I don't think the team of musicians intentionally sabotaged us, but they have no idea how much faerie liquor a mortal girl can take. I reach a hand up to her, which she ignores to turn precariously in place. "I'm a *good* enchanter! My family—do you *know* who I am?" Her hands start to glow.

Olani and I exchange a look. "Uh . . . yeah, we do," she says, trying to support my effort to catch Aris by sort of herding her with outstretched arms.

Obviously in a helpful mood, Aris walks away from us, kicking any dish that happens to get in her path. A ripple of sound follows, drawing more attention with every second, every splashed sauce and crumbled crust. "No . . . do *you* know who I *am*?" She finally stops, turns with her arms outstretched, and collects the light gathered at her fingertips into one glowing orb. "Watch *this*!"

And I do.

I watch in horror as she takes a deep breath, then falls sideways and rolls from the table into the grass. The tablecloth tangles around her feet, and she ends up taking a shower of food and drink and crystal with her. Stunned silence falls in the clearing, a crowd of bright eyes waiting to see what the mortals will do next.

So I do the only thing I can think to do, which is let out a loud whoop and start to applaud.

Mercifully, the goatlike faeries take up the cheer almost immediately. The rest of the crowd follows, and then the music starts with new fervor. Even Olani starts clapping uncertainly as we rush to Aris's side.

"Is that enough of an *impression*, you think?" I mutter, teeth still clenched into a grin.

"It's something," Olani replies.

Aris is groaning into the grass, but despite the fall and the broken glass, she seems mostly fine. Between the two of us, it's not too difficult to lift her to her feet, arms draped around my shoulders and Olani's waist.

"I don't *want* to go," Aris whines, but a lot of the fight seems to have gone out of her with her stunt.

"Too bad," I reply, pushing her hair away from her face, shaking crumbs from the curls—in case she gets sick, not because I feel strangely protective of her. "It's bedtime. We have a big day tomorrow."

At the reminder that tomorrow will still come, whether the sun sets and rises here or not, she groans. She doesn't fight as we drag her back to the *Destiny*, growing sleepier and heavier with each step. We almost make it all the way to the wagon before she lunges out of our arms, doubles over, and empties her stomach into the ferns.

The sight is enough to make me vaguely sick, but Olani's stomach is stronger than mine. She crouches next to Aris, rubs her back and gently reassures, until Aris is done spitting and retching. I stand nearby with crossed arms, trying to look supportive, as Aris looks up with tear-filled eyes. "You can leave me here," she mumbles miserably. "No one will see."

It hits me after a moment—she thinks we only escorted her this far so we'd seem united as a team in front of all the faeries. Not because she deserves to be taken care of, no matter what a mess she is.

"Don't be ridiculous," I say. I approach, trying to avoid

looking at the puddle of vomit soaking into the ground, to put a hand on her shoulder. "Come on, we're almost home."

We help her up and manage to get her the rest of the way to the wagon. She's been sleeping on a bedroll on the *Destiny*'s floor that I think used to be Raze's, and she drops down onto it like a puppet with cut strings. I unlace her boots while Olani wipes her face with a wet cloth and forces her to drink a glass of water. There's something so ordinary and tender about all of it, the domestic motions of caring for someone who just . . . really needs someone.

"You guys . . ." Aris says, eyes welling up again. "You're so nice."

"Yeah, that's us," I chuckle softly, dragging the blanket up around her. "I'm going to leave this bowl here in case you get sick again."

She grabs my wrist before I can pull away, looking up at me with round, shiny eyes. "No, I *mean* it. Don't leave me, okay?"

Olani straightens up the abandoned boots, sitting down next to me on the cramped floor. "We won't," she promises. "You're safe."

Aris falls asleep not long after that, but we're wide awake, trapped in the dim stillness. Birch materializes, then places one tentative paw on Aris's stomach. When she doesn't wake, he makes a big production of walking back and forth over all three of us, digging in his claws for balance, before coiling into a tight ball on Aris's chest. Birch's eyes close slowly, and the resonance of his quiet purr fills the wagon.

Eventually, I whisper, "Think she'll be okay to fight tomorrow?"

Olani sighs and lays back with her hands under her head. There's just enough room for the three of us to lie side by side on the floor, and even though my old bunk is within spitting distance, it doesn't seem nearly as appealing as right where I am. She smiles up at me, a faint twist of closed lips. "Once her body processes the alcohol, I can heal the side effects. She'll be fine."

"Good." Slowly, I lie back, too, preserving the inches between us. "Probably embarrassed, though."

She snorts. "This whole thing is embarrassing."

I don't know if she's talking about what we said earlier, about how many faeries saw the whole thing, or about competing in a silly competition for a chance at saving our world. I'm not sure it matters. My heart is pounding, and it takes a second to realize that it's because this is the closest we've been to alone since the whole poison thing. "Everyone will forget the low points," I say quietly. "When we win."

She lets out a laugh that's more of a breath. "I won't."

I've never liked quiet, but the silence that falls after that statement feels like a soft blanket settling down over us. Our hands find each other in the dark, just like all those nights on the journey back to Auremore.

There are still plenty of things left to say, but I'm not sure I need to hear them aloud anymore. It's enough to stare up at the ceiling in silence, to let the constant waterfall of my thoughts flow away until all that's left is the trickle of awareness that I'm safe in our temporary shelter. It's enough to fall asleep with her herbal scent all around me and her hand clasped in mine.

chapter thirty

seelie

I wake without a start, without the sensation of falling or a sudden kick. One moment, I'm in the forest, puzzling over the Unseelie Queen's words. The next, I draw a deep breath as my eyes open to the dark chamber in the palace where I drifted off. It's still dark, though that's no indication of the time. The still, cool air has the feeling of the quietest hours of night, right before dawn. I don't think I was asleep long, but I feel strangely energized. I sit up, already knowing I won't be able to go back to sleep. Not after that.

The room is another of their underground chambers, with a ceiling high enough to spare us the feeling of a cave-in. It doesn't feel like an indoor space any more than the Seelie tree house rooms did, with the faint blue light of glowing mushrooms and soft yellow-green moss foaming up over the stone. Above me, the ceiling glitters with flecks of gold like stars.

There's a door, a large nest of moss and embroidered cushions, and the nearby trickle of an underground stream that cuts through the room. Egg is still curled up beside me in the nest, warming me with his steady breath.

Raze—who was resting across from me when we fell asleep, stretched in opposite directions—is gone.

I feel a stab of panic, remembering the time I almost lost him in the Unseelie forest. When he was charmed so he couldn't think straight, lured away by the sound of a voice from his earliest memories. I swore I wouldn't lose him here again.

But he has Aris's charm, a small protection against the Court. I don't know how long he's been gone, but I should at least check the room before I give in to the impulse to smash the Unseelie Court to rubble in a frantic search.

I stand carefully, but Egg doesn't so much as twitch an ear. He must be exhausted after the day he's had. I hope he's not permanently traumatized by it. Straining my ears, I can hear a faint humming. A low voice, notes sliding up and down. It would be too quiet to hear, if not for the echoes bouncing around the cave's glittering ceiling. It's hard to determine the source, but I think it's coming from the stream.

This is eerily similar to how it started last time, that enchantment that carried Raze away. I'm too worried to even be angry with him for falling for the same trick twice. I may as well be charmed, for how quickly I scramble to my feet and follow the sound, drawing my iron dagger. I don't care what the consequences are for killing a faerie within the palace itself. I'll do whatever it takes to protect him.

There's an outcropping of rock above a short, sharp slope down to the running water where we both drank and washed our faces before going to bed. I'm not sure where the water comes from or where it goes, and I curse myself for not questioning it more. For not making sure our room was truly secure, walled off from any malicious faeries that might want to harm us while we slept like the fragile mortal things we are.

But as I creep to the edge, something starts to feel *wrong*. Actually, no. What I'm sensing is the absence of wrongness, a void where I expected to feel magic thrumming in the air. I slide down the embankment, bare feet slipping over tumbling pebbles. It's a little brighter down by the water, lit by several varieties of strange glowing plants in addition to those green crystals and thick patches of mushrooms.

It's by their light that I finally spot Raze.

Alone.

I'm relieved that there doesn't seem to be any immediate danger, but I don't let my guard down yet. He's found a comfortable place to lean against the trunk of what could almost be a willow tree, tucked away behind the long tendrils that trail into the water. He sits with his arms propped on his knees, his hair outlined in gold by the tree's strange, shining leaves. It's barely enough light to make a difference, leaving his face in shadow until he turns so I can see him in profile.

I have seen Raze at least a thousand times, in a thousand different ways, but this time—

This time—

It feels like the first. Like I'm gazing on something new, painfully beautiful in the unearthly light. He looks exactly as I remembered, unchanged. It's me who's different. Me who can suddenly appreciate all the small mortal flaws that make him so perfect—messy hair, tired eyes, the asymmetry of his mouth that always makes him look like he's up to something. His eyes are distant, his lips pressed together while he hums absentmindedly.

I freeze, not wanting to startle him, not wanting to turn back. I don't know if I'm welcome at his side right now. I hope I am. Eventually, pushing past the rising guilt of watching him without his knowledge, I open my mouth and speak haltingly.

"I'm—I'm behind you."

Despite my attempt to use the gentlest tone possible, Raze startles. He jumps and turns on me, clutching a hand over his chest, and it's only then I realize I'm still holding the dagger in a white-knuckled grip. I sheathe it hastily, holding up my hands and shushing him like he's a spooked horse.

"Sorry, I wasn't— I didn't— I can go," I babble, words tangling as they all try to leap over each other on their way out.

"Why are you sneaking up on me with a knife?"

I can't help it—I laugh at the high-pitched note of fear in his voice. "I'm . . . I thought you were enchanted! I heard humming, and I was . . . I . . ." I trail off as the laugh dies in my throat.

"Rushing to my rescue?" Raze asks with a single raised brow and a half smile.

"I can go," I repeat awkwardly. I can't tell if he wants me here or not. His face is so guarded, an expression I have to reach back into my memories from months ago to place. I'm not sure if *he* knows if he wants me here or not.

Eventually, he sighs, patting the mossy ground beside him with a weary smile. "No," he says softly. "Please, feel free."

I have to push past a curtain of dangling leaves, glittering like a chain of morning dew, to reach his side. I drop down and try not to think too hard about how I normally sit, folding my hands in my lap.

"Sorry if I woke you," Raze says eventually.

"Oh, I was awake anyway." I study his face, trying to decide if I should tell him about my dream-that-wasn't-just-a-dream. About the Unseelie Queen's bargain, and the puzzle she put before me. It's all just on the tip of my tongue again when he sighs, looking away.

Something is wrong. I don't know what it is, but I can tell it's *something*. Something made more obvious by the fact that he's trying to hide it. I don't know why that stops me from telling him—we need every moment we can get, both our minds working together, every advantage we can find. Nothing can be more important than defeating Gossamer and breaking the curse.

Except . . . somehow . . . this is. Maybe it's selfish of me, but all I want in this moment is to make everything else stop, to create an Unending Realm where it's only the two of us and we have all the time in the world for Raze to feel everything he needs to feel. Technically, I suppose I could do that, but since I'm pretty sure it would destroy everything, I'll just have to pretend. Just for a little while.

"Did you sleep at all?" I ask gently.

"A little."

I frown. "You should try to get some rest."

Raze chuckles, a dry little sound like the snap of twigs. "Why?"

"Because we need to be ready for what's to come, and—"

"No," he interrupts. "*You* need to be ready for what's to come. It doesn't matter how rested I am, I don't think even an entire menagerie of birds would be particularly helpful."

"I'm . . . sorry."

"It's not your fault," he spits. "It's mine. I should have made you take Aris with you. Or Olani. Then you'd at least have some real help. All I can do is stand by and try not to get killed. It's not— I mean, I don't want to be in your place or anything . . ."

"Thanks," I mutter. "Neither do I."

"I just feel so *useless*."

"Raze," I say gently, debating reaching to touch his arm. I decide against it, curling my fingers into my own sleeve instead. "You're not useless."

"I'm not use*ful*," he snaps.

I debate telling him about the dream then, presenting him with a problem he can solve without magic. But somehow, I can tell that this isn't just about that, and if I give him any distraction, he'll take it. And even if it's soaked in bitterness, I'd rather hear how he truly feels.

"Do you have any memory of persuading me that I needed your help? That all I had to do was accept it, and we'd be better off together? Because it *worked*. You convinced me." The words come out impatiently, but I can't help it. If I could grab Raze by the shoulders and shake him until I knocked some sense into his head, until he saw himself like I do, I would. Until they can invent a spell that does *that*, frustration and sweet words spoken harshly is the best I can do.

His jaw clenches as he keeps staring off at nothing. He can't regret all those things he said. He can't wish things were different now. It's too late for that. We're in—*I'm* in too deep.

Impulsively, I grab his chin and turn his head, forcing him to meet my eyes. "Are you mad at me?"

"No, Iselia. It's not—"

I plow on anyway. "Because I know. I know I've kept secrets and taken you for granted. I haven't listened to you, and I've—"

"It's not that!"

"Then what is it?" Raze breaks away first this time, and I chase his gaze, ducking down close to catch his eyes. "Because I'm not like other people, Raze. I can't know what's wrong if you don't tell me. I need you to be honest with me so I can know not to do it again."

"It's not something you're doing," he says, sounding awfully frustrated for someone who's swearing up and down that he's not mad. "It's—it's—*you*! You're driving me crazy."

My heart sinks. Of course. How could he narrow it down to one thing, when I am made entirely of flaws and mistakes and annoyances? My mouth tilts in a smile, the only shield I can pull up over my hurt in time. "What else is new?" I say softly.

"Not like that," Raze says, finally giving in and meeting my eyes. "But—also, partly like that. Like I know you're going to disagree with everything I say, and sometimes I say it anyway, just to hear how you're going to argue with me this time. It's your laugh, and the way your hands flutter when you're excited, and your *hair*." He spits the last word out like he's personally offended by it.

"My hair?" I repeat, struggling to hide a laugh. The Seelie enchantment on our appearances is finally dissolving, and I can already feel my hair snarling in the back, curling up around my ears in the front.

"Why is there so *much* of it?" he snaps.

"Because I don't like anyone touching it." I shudder. My hair has always been long, partly because it helped separate me from Isolde, and partly because it's paradoxically easier to keep it out of my way when it weighs itself down away from my face. The thought of having any less of it is like losing a shield between me and the world. "Especially not to cut it."

"But you let me touch it."

"Yes," I agree slowly. That's true. My mother used to braid my hair for me. Isolde fixed it just before the Wintersol Ball. And Raze touches it absently sometimes, brushing strands away from my face or gently touching the crown of my head. I've never considered why I allow that. "Because I like you. It feels nice."

"It's beautiful," he says hotly, as if we're in the middle of a disagreement. "*You're* beautiful. It's maddening. I want to protect you—not because you can't protect yourself. Obviously you can. It's just . . . when you treasure something, it hurts to see it come to harm and know there's nothing you can do. You want to guard it. Foolishly. Endlessly. Completely."

Those three words thrum in my pulse, lodging in a corner of my mind where I know I'll never be able to shake them loose. *Foolishly. Endlessly. Completely.* It's like he's trying to say something else with them, but I'm too afraid to try and figure out what, because what if I come up with the wrong answer? We've been through so much, and we're only alive because we fought our way through it together. Our survival is linked so thoroughly that I feel like our heartbeats form the same rhythm, like one would be off-time without the other. Of course he wants to preserve that.

Raze's name slips from my lips softly, drawing us both back into the conversation from the uneven paths of our thoughts. I meet his eyes like any barrier there ever was between us has dissolved, leaving nothing but soft blue and wrinkled brows. My voice is quiet, strained with the effort of picking out my next words. "Enough, Raze. Stop teasing me. Stop reminding me all the reasons I need you, and then telling yourself a different story. You brag to everyone about how wonderful you are—except to yourself."

He returns my awkward half smile. "That's because it's an *act*."

"I *know*." I say it without looking away, without flinching. "Forget everything else for a moment. Be here with me. Please." I watch him breathe, struggling to steady himself. "Now tell me what you want to say. As simply and clearly as possible."

"I can't. I feel so *useless*—I don't deserve . . ."

"I'm not that clueless, Raze. I know you're just repeating the same lies you heard about yourself from Leira over and over again in your head, then covering them up when anyone else is looking." I'm almost as surprised to hear myself say it as he looks. I didn't realize that I knew that, not in such certain terms, until I blurt it out. Once I do, I know the truth of it, and it only strengthens my determination to get through to him for once. "And I'm not just disagreeing with you for the sake of it. I truly believe that you are everything you want to be, and more. And that you deserve whatever happiness you choose."

"Do you really mean that?"

"Of course I mean it, I wouldn't say it if—"

"Because if so, I choose you." Everything stops. Suddenly, I am nothing but a thundering heartbeat and wide eyes unable to look away from Raze as he moves so close, I have to tilt my head up to see his face. He isn't smiling for once, intensity carved in the crease of his brows and shadowing the depths of his eyes. His lips form each word carefully, leaving no more room for doubt. "And tomorrow, I'll choose you. And if I could turn back time so that none of this ever happened, I'd still choose you. And if you can't respond to this right now, I'll wait as long as it takes to keep choosing you."

I am split in two halves: one a wreck of nerves and guilt and fear, the other an inextinguishable ember of certainty. With each heartbeat, each second it takes to absorb the weight of Raze's words, the certainty grows. Despite everything, I find all else washed away, leaving the solid ground of confidence and trust—Raze's, and my own.

I'm surprised to find that I can smile.

"Because you love me." It's half statement and half question, a truth I know but need to hear aloud, even in my own faint voice. I look up into his eyes as I say it, realizing he's so close now we're practically bumping noses.

Raze opens his mouth to reply—freezes—breaks into a soft, shaky laugh. "You're supposed to let me say it first."

"Sorry," I say, which is probably not especially convincing paired with a grin I can't seem to hold back.

"Don't be. I love you." His hand lifts to push a strand of hair back from my face, then lingers on my neck. It would take so little to close the distance between us now, but he doesn't move. That infuriating corner of his mouth twitches, making it basically impossible not to stare at his lips. So close, yet maddeningly out of reach—we had a deal, after all.

Without thinking about it, I blurt, "I think I'd like to kiss you now."

The crooked grin deepens. "Then maybe you should."

"Maybe I will."

"Fine."

"Fine." And then, before he can sneak another reply, I do. A wave of something that isn't magic but is just as powerful sweeps over us, pulling both of us under, and I lose track of everything, except that Raze's mouth is on mine and I *want it there*.

Technically, I've kissed Raze before. But this isn't a technicality. This is—

His taste on my lips, indescribably sweet. His hands, firm around my waist, one sliding up between my shoulders, in my hair. They're almost feverishly warm. My own hands feel restless and cold, fluttering from his shoulders to his face to the back of his neck. I can't stop moving, frantic to feel everything all at once.

I've never wanted to be kissed before. I've never been swept away on a current like this, bright and hot and thrilling. For the first time, I understand why people might enjoy this.

"I love you, too," I breathe when we pull apart. "Just—so you know."

His grip on my waist tightens slightly, an ironic note sneaking into his voice. "Oh, that's good."

I hesitate before moving in again, studying every detail of his face—the crack of a grin, flushed skin, shining eyes. The moment freezes, our eyes locked as my hands wander on their own. One slips under the loose neckline of his shirt, skimming over his collarbones, then his chest, until I feel his heartbeat racing just as fast as mine. My fingers rest on the edge of the jagged outline of a scar over his heart, one burned there by my long-ago spell. I inhale to apologize, but before I can, his hand covers mine, pressing it tighter to his chest.

His forehead dips to mine.

And then, wordlessly, he kisses me again. This one is slower, deeper, made of things that have gone unsaid too long and things we're not ready to say yet. Time melts around us, leaving nothing but our uneven breathing and the soft sound he makes when I pull him closer.

He loves me. I've let Raze see *me*, from my daily struggles to the worst tempests of my emotions and my magic, and he still loves me. The realization that I've tried my best to scare him off, but he's too stupidly brave and stubborn to allow it, cracks the rest of the wall I've built between who I really am and who the world gets to see, leaving my heart painfully exposed in a dusty heap of rubble.

And the worst part is that I *like* it. No—I love it. I love that same smug smile I hated, the same unrelenting cheerfulness that made me furious, the same stubborn need to push me that I used to think meant he hated me back. I love his messy red hair, every freckle and scar on his skin, every preening bird shape he takes. I love *him*.

I pull away again. "I don't know what this means. How to do this right."

Another short kiss. "That's okay."

"And if the world ends—"

"Then I'll choose to stay with you as it burns." Raze pulls away in earnest this time, but his face remains scarce inches from mine. Sensing my hesitation at the inaccuracy, he sighs. "Or . . . implodes into magic dust or whatever. Okay?"

I laugh again, partly hysterical, partly delighted that he somehow sensed exactly what I was thinking. "Okay. That sounds nice." I lean in again, driven by a hunger that sits not in my stomach but in the rush of my pulse, and Raze draws back just enough to stop me.

"Sadist."

"You said it first!" I protest.

Raze's hands slip to my ribs, and he pulls me closer, lifting me into his lap. I move easily, shifting my weight to bring us even closer. I shiver despite the warm breeze that wraps around us, blanketing us from the cool underground air. "Maybe," he admits, warm breath tickling my neck. Fate, he's going to kill me. This feeling is going to burn me up from the inside out. "But you're the one who brought it up."

And I don't want to let him have the last word, but I'm afraid that after that, our mouths are entirely too busy to keep arguing.

chapter thirty-one

ISOLDE

I feel strangely exposed, standing in the same dusty expanse that contained the cup of poison and the locked door. This time we can see the spectators just as clearly as they see us. We make a mismatched set—me fidgeting in lightweight scraps of chain mail and leather, Aris poised and still in her borrowed cloak, Olani radiant in a dazzlingly shiny breastplate with matching bracers.

My gaze bounces all over the arena, fighting not to get sucked up into the chaos of the crowd above. This time, the Queen presides over it all. She's flanked by attendants, casting an even glow on us lesser beings, and it takes so much concentration not to stare at her, or to imagine her bright golden gaze on me. I can feel myself getting distracted and fidgety, waiting for the fighting to begin.

"Focus." Olani's voice interrupts my thoughts, disturbing me again with the realization that she can somehow tell when my mind is wandering. Maybe she noticed the tension creeping into my stance that had nothing to do with sizing up our competition.

Our competition—three teams left, since the trio that all poisoned themselves dropped out. Two of the sets are mean, vicious, and have a predator's focus on the wreath. The third is the musicians, who are laughing and shoving each other around as if they don't have a care in the world.

"I'm gonna kill them," mutters Aris under her breath. She threw up again this morning, before we forced her to drink two more glasses of water and Olani helped ease the worst of it. She's standing straight now, not squinting from a headache, and probably won't heave her guts up again, but I think she's mostly interested in avenging her wounded pride.

"I think that's discouraged." I tear my eyes away from the faeries to offer her an irritating smirk.

Aris rolls her eyes expressively, but before she can say anything, the Seelie Queen raises a single hand, and the arena stills, as completely as if she's frozen it in time.

"Fae of the Seelie Court and competitors in the Winter Tournament," she says once more. A cheer goes up, and she allows it a moment before continuing, to absolute silence. "Welcome to the third and final task in the Wintersol Tournament. Your wits and charm have gotten you this far, but now it is time to show off your strength. You all know the rules—whichever team holds the prize when time runs out will win the Tournament and my favor." The cheer at that is even louder. I feel it down to my bones, a vibration that sets my teeth on edge. No one needs this like we need this. The fate of my world and (as much as she doesn't want to admit it) hers—it all comes down to this silly game. I can't bear to look at the Seelie Queen, too afraid she'll catch my eyes in that spiteful stare as she says, one last time, "May Fate favor you."

The low drone of a hunting horn vibrates through the arena.

A sound I know well, one that my body recognizes before my mind does. By the time I place it, it's already over—and I'm frozen on the spot, like some sort of prey animal. I thought I'd recovered from my first time in the Seelie Realm, but a terrified little fox still lives in my chest, and she's the one who calls the shots in terms of self-preservation at the first sign of that bone-piercing sound.

Our surroundings transform, settling over me like fresh-fallen snow. Gone is the Queen and her Court, though I can still feel hundreds of eyes on me. The weight of being watched seems heavier, now that I can't look back at them. Far off in the distance, farther than I thought the arena could contain, a beam of golden light shoots up into the sky, marking the prize we're all after. The warmth in the air bleeds away, and bare trees appear slowly, as if through an ebbing fog. Underfoot, ice crystals appear, and above, the purple sky brightens to a clear, cold blue.

Winter has come to the Seelie Realm—in appearance, at least. I watch my breath puff in clouds around me, trying to remember every scrap of advice about what to do now.

We must have done decently well at the party last night, because Cobweb and Robin woke us at what felt like a punishingly early hour to get us ready. They decked us out in gifts from faeries who had bet a decade of luck or the vibrance of their wings or some other nonsense on us winning. They explained the rules of the combat trial to us: Four teams. Two hours. One wreath we're all competing to secure. But it doesn't matter who gets there first—whichever team is in possession of the wreath at the end of the time will be crowned victorious.

There's no way we can hold it that long, which means we're better off waiting on the sidelines and saving our strength for the end. How do we time it out, though? Moving too soon will ruin our chances, even if we're lucky enough to get our hands on the wreath before it's stolen away again. But if we're too late, we'll still be fighting our way to the wreath when time runs out. It's as much about predicting the actions of the other players as planning our own.

The two teams of Very Serious Faerie Warriors take off immediately for the beam of golden light. The musicians disappear into the trees with barely a sound, obviously hoping to pull off the same strategy we are. We'll have to keep an eye out for them.

I hate waiting, but it's the only sensible thing to do here. We walk farther than should have been possible, based on the size of the arena before the illusion fell into place. Our steps crunch in the snow, which swirls and melts and sticks to our eyelashes, indistinguishable from the real thing.

We find a sheltered spot in the trees where we can still see the distant golden beam of the prize, growing steadily shorter like the wick of a candle burning out as the time runs down. By my estimation, we spend the entire first hour stamping our feet, making no sound louder than the huffs of our breath in the cold. I rub my hands together to chase numbness from my fingers, grinding my teeth with worry about dropping a dagger or missing a mark because I'm too cold for my hands to work.

I'm starting to doubt my own sense of time passing when the goat-legged faerie appears. He's on the other side of the screen of trees, stumbling quickly through the snow and looking back over his shoulders. Apparently, whatever he's running from has him too distracted to notice us. Chunks of ice stick to his fur, and his dark blood melts a path behind him. Most importantly, we realize, when several moments pass without his friends following behind, he's alone.

Aris springs out of our hiding spot without warning us and blasts a beam of light at the faerie. By the time I see she's shielding her eyes, it's already too late. The light bounces off the snow, off the ice, off the nearly white brilliance of the sky, blinding the musician and the rest of us along with him. Bright pain sears my eyes, forcing me to my knees as I blink away stars. The world around me spins, reduced to flashing, dancing lights. I curse, almost in unison with Olani, who wasn't spared, either.

I hear Aris's boots crunching through the snow as she takes off without consulting us, or even checking to make sure we're behind her. She moves as if she's alone in this arena, with no one to defend and no one watching her back.

"Get up," Olani commands, and I do my best to obey, reaching a hand out blindly. My fingers are stiff and stinging from digging into the snow when I fell. After a disorienting moment of swooping through empty air, they land on something warm. A quick zap of healing magic bolts up my arm, soothing my eyes instantly.

Aris and the musician have both managed to sprint out of sight.

"Great," I say, using Olani's offered hand to pull myself up and dust snow off my knees. "Excellent teamwork. No notes."

Olani snorts, and somehow manages to make it sound like dignified disdain. "Come on, we don't want her getting herself killed."

"Don't we?" I mutter under my breath, without much bite behind the words. We're already moving, following the clearly marked path of their footprints in the snow. We weren't blinded for that long, and they can't have gotten far.

First, I think something is wrong. But that feeling is smothered quickly by something lighter. The confidence that we're on the right path, that if I do anything, it must be to take another step and another in this direction. I thought we were bound for disaster, but it's not that bad, really. Actually, this is going pretty well. I start humming along—

Wait.

"It's a trap!" I shout at the same time Olani calls out, "Cover your ears!"

We both stop short, drowning out the lightly plucked instruments with hands clapped over our ears. I hadn't even *noticed* them, just their effects, but now that I have, it's hard to push the melody out of my head. I turn in place, looking for Aris.

There. Lying in the snow, sleeping more peacefully than I've seen her any night at our makeshift camp. Her eyes are closed, head pillowed on her hands as the musician continues playing that awful little flute over her. His friends join in on a lute and a harp from the branches above, so well-hidden I wouldn't have seen them if I hadn't paused to watch.

Even muffled by my hands, bits of the melody hang sweetly in the air, like ripe fruit. That feeling of calm is hard to shake, and I just want to let my hands drop and listen. To be as gently at peace as Aris, curled up comfortably in . . .

"Sol!" Olani's voice snaps me out of it, and I'm not sure if it's because it helps cover the sound or because she never uses my nickname. We need our hands free to fight, but we need our hands to help block out the music. So we just stand there *looking* at each other stupidly while the musicians play on and on and on. "What did I tell you when you were bleeding out on Wintersol?"

"Don't fall asleep," I yawn obediently. But even then, when it was literally life or death, I couldn't obey. What chance do I have now?

Maybe I can cover it with my own voice. I clear my throat and try to recall a song, any song. I come up with nonsense babble from the middle of a tavern song, but as soon as I starts shout-singing, they shift their music to harmonize so it all twines into one honeyed lullaby.

I remember Seelie's face right before she disappeared through the shimmering veil to the Unending Realm. Seelie won't fail. I know it. She's too stubborn, too determined to overcome. She'll manage to get the Unseelie Queen's help, and she'll be back, and I can't fail her. I have to admit, she'd be better in this tournament than I would. She'd sling a fireball at them. Even if she couldn't, I don't know anyone who's better at *not* listening—whether it's because of summoned storm winds whipping around her, her own distracted mind, or the howl of her voice when she's too overwhelmed to speak.

That thought gives me a deranged, desperate idea. I close my eyes and *shriek*. It's a horrible, utterly unmusical sound, one that draws out emotions I didn't even know I *had* and shoves them up through my lungs.

And it works.

They don't *stop*, exactly, but there is no musical way to incorporate a sound like that. It earns me a single faltering rest, during which I drop my hands and fill my lungs and scream again. I don't need to be louder than them, just loud enough to make it sound terrible.

I hope all those unseen faeries of the Seelie Court are enjoying the spectacle, I think, unable to help a small twist of a grin. I don't have to tell Olani to go after the one nearest us first. As soon as an opening appears, she takes a swing at him with her staff. Obviously unprepared to actually have to *fight* in this combat tournament, he nearly drops his instrument in his haste to dodge.

He's fast—faster than most humans, I have to give him that. But she's quick and clever enough to realize she doesn't have to hit him square, as she would most opponents. Olani shifts her weight, feigning another blow toward his hooves, then swooping up between his hands to knock the little flute into the air. It sails over our heads, landing in the snow behind us, and they both scramble after it.

Meanwhile, still screaming, my eyes scan the leaves above. I'd prefer not to kill the musicians, who have gone about all this as peacefully as possible, but I don't have to land lethal blows. I send one knife sailing at the lute player, who automatically holds up the stringed instrument to protect his face. My dagger severs the strings, cutting the music short with a sharp *twang*, followed by the *thunk* of splintering wood an instant before the musician tumbles off his branch into the snow.

By this point, absolute chaos has broken out, the music has come to an abrupt halt, and I realize I can stop screaming. Their remaining team member slings his harp over his shoulder and scurries farther up the tree, nimble as a squirrel, while his friends lie groaning in the snow. Curses. It figures they'd have a backup plan, one more play they can execute even if they're down to one player. Even if we kill the others, they could still win.

I draw my second dagger, take aim as quickly as I can at a moving target, and hold my breath as I throw.

It's a near miss, but still a miss. The harpist jumps from branch to branch—how he can climb like that makes no sense, given that he has *hooves*, but now isn't the time to question how that's possible—and he only looks back for a second.

Aris sits up and, in the same snap of movement, raises her hand to launch a searing ray of light at the rustling branches. It hits at the exact moment the remaining musician pauses to look at his friends, knocking him off his perch. He hits several branches on the way down, making me wince with each one, and lands in the snow with a loud, icy *crunch!*

"Please don't make us kill you," Olani says, with a flat weariness that doesn't leave much room to argue.

The musicians glance at each other, calculating their odds. They start to stand, shaking snow from their fur, and approach us with their hands up—only to vanish on the spot. I suppose the same magic that keeps the faeries from outright killing each other also sweeps them away when they yield.

"All according to plan," I say, gathering my daggers from the ground like dropped fruit. The beam of gold flickers on the horizon, almost too low to see. How much time has passed? How long do we have to get our plan back on track? Without speaking, we take off toward the prize. No more stalling—this is it.

This time, we all move together—Aris in the lead, with me and Olani covering her back. I don't know what we'll find at the center of the arena, but we can't risk delaying any longer.

I hear the conflict before I see it—the roar and snap of magic, clanging of metal and clashing shouts. It's enough noise to fill a battlefield, but when we find its source, it's not even the remaining four players. We have to step over the sprawled form of one of the warrior faeries, a shiny pile of peacefully snoring armor who must have been less lucky than we were against the musicians' charm. The other, an elegant woman I remember from the party last night wielding a bow and a gaze as barbed as her arrows, is missing—probably injured badly enough to get swept out of the arena before ruining all the fun with a faerie-death explosion.

And then there were two. The ground around them is blackened and bloody, snow melted and grass churned into mud. A bubbling gray puddle of goo oozes unpleasant magic. A twisting whip of fire constantly moves the boundaries of their fight, dancing just on the edge of a beam of golden light.

I don't know whether to focus on the fighting or the prize—a glistening wreath of waxy evergreen leaves and holly berries, suspended as if held up by that beam of light. It hovers barely out of reach; close enough that you could grab it with one well-timed jump. It's *right there*.

But there's no way to get to it without going through *them*. As if to punctuate the thought, a heavy battle-axe whooshes through the air, missing its target to bury itself in the ground with a spray of mud.

The axe is wielded by a green-skinned faerie woman as tall as Olani, but bulkier. Her armor, made of tree bark and bits of monstrous teeth and claws, makes her look even more imposing. An antlered helm shadows her face but is unable to cloak the raging golden glow of her eyes as she faces down her opponent.

He's one of the smallest faeries I've seen, like the little men in the stories about cobblers and bakers I heard growing up. His cheeks are rosy, eyes shining in malicious cheerfulness as he dismisses the wall of flame swirling around the faerie woman with a wave of his beringed hands. He isn't wearing armor but more than makes up for it with an overwhelming clash of jewelry, layers of clothes, and multiple hats stacked on his head.

"I suggest a truce," the little man says, blowing a lingering stream of smoke from his index finger.

She swings again, and he barely manages to sidestep. "And why would I agree to that?"

"Because it's down to *us* or *them*. And I don't know about you, but I don't intend to let a group of *mortal* teenagers best me in the tournament."

"Humiliating," she agrees, hefting the axe over her shoulder with an appraising look. "And once they're gone . . ."

"Back to maiming each other," he finishes brightly, grinning like he's genuinely looking forward to it. And that's all the warning we get before they stop attacking each other and start attacking us.

I saw the axe's movement earlier, but I'm still not prepared for its weight as it sings in an arc toward my skull. I try to dodge, and immediately know that I've botched the timing, underestimating the weight of it. Maybe if I twist just right, I can catch it on my shoulder instead—

Olani is in front of me, blocking the blow with a staff raised between both hands. It shudders down her arms, wrenching her shoulders, but she holds firm. Before the faerie woman can lift the axe from where it's stuck, Olani manages to kick her unprotected side, sending her stumbling back a few steps.

Meanwhile, Aris faces down against the other faerie. This time, instead of blinding us all, she tosses a shower of dazzling sparkles that settle on his skin like ash and don't go out until there's an acrid smell of burning. He barks out a surprised laugh before he moves to launch a spell back at her.

His magic is different from any mortal enchanter I've seen, nudged by words in a language I don't understand, the movement of his hands almost an afterthought. I'm braced for fire, for thunder, for a rain of daggers . . . but nothing happens. Maybe his spell has gone wrong.

But that would require luck, so instead, the bubbling goo picks itself up out of the mud and launches at Aris with all the malevolence of an attacking dog. I don't have to hear her scream to know it's as dangerous as one, too.

"Help her," I say sharply. Olani's hesitation is so brief that if I didn't know her so well, I would completely miss it—barely a hitch of her breath before she's moving to Aris's side. Leaving me facing the faerie woman, looking for weaknesses.

That's the trick of fighting someone bigger and stronger than you—using their reach against them, finding what makes them falter, where their armor is incomplete. With Olani, it's her follow-through, the result of years of training herself without a real sparring partner. It always takes her a moment to shift mid-blow, to change plans, and if I'm quick and clever enough, I can use that brief hesitation against her. This faerie *must* have weaknesses. Everyone does. I just can't spot them yet.

This time, I manage to dodge away from the axe as it swings toward me, leading her away from Olani and Aris. She recovers quickly, flexes the weight of her weapon effortlessly, without even a second off-balance. Behind her, a flash of light, a spray of mud, muffled curses. I can't pick up much more than that without risking a fatal distraction.

Another swing at my head, but this time instead of moving away, I duck and press in closer, preparing to strike with my dagger. In the middle of its arc, she shifts the weight of her axe to one hand, leaving the other free to grip my knife arm by the wrist. I open my fingers, letting the knife drop. Trusting the reflexes of my off hand to catch it.

They do. The instant my fingers wrap around the blade's

familiar weight, I know I'll only get one chance. A strike just below her ribs, her fingers still capturing my arm with bruising force. I put all my strength into it, feel the blade slice through layers of leather armor and soft flesh, scraping the bone. I feel the warmth of her blood just before she lifts me by the arm like an unwanted doll and tosses me back into the snow.

I land hard, failing to turn my momentum into useful movement on the icy, mud-slicked ground. The faerie woman glares down at me, my knife still buried in her side in a dark patch of blood. Her eyes glow with fiery fury. I meet them, refusing to yield. Even if it means dying here, in this stupid faerie game. I will not fail.

And then my eyes dart over her shoulder, and my heart sinks. Olani and Aris are immobilized, held in place by some sort of enchantment, and part of me wants to just give in and let it end here. We're beaten.

No. We're not. Not yet. I cage the despair attempting to gnaw at my resolve. I'm still looking for weaknesses, and maybe I've found one—in the form of her temporary teammate, moving slowly behind her back toward the beam of light in the center of the chaos.

"He's making a play for the wreath," I warn her.

"Nice try," she replies, quickly deciding that I'm attempting a distraction—which I have to admit, does sound like something I would do, even if it wasn't true. But this time it *is* true, and lucky for me, the silence behind us seems to sink in to prove it. She can't help letting her eyes dart for just a second over her shoulder before she drops the killing blow.

Even luckier, she forgets me instantly, all her rage turning onto the other faerie. "*You!*" she screams, an accusation in one word. She turns, grabbing my knife by its hilt and yanking it from her own side to send it sailing to the smaller faerie.

Damn.

He knocks it aside with a wave of his hand, trying to look

nonchalant as she approaches. "If you'll recall the terms of our truce—" he starts, still trying to subtly shift back toward the wreath.

"You slimy little mortal-tongued back-stabbing *wretch*!" She charges at him, barely remembering to swing the axe. She looks like she'd tear him apart with her bare hands if he gave her half the chance.

This is my opening—perhaps the *last* opening—to forget about the others, make one last desperate move for the wreath, and hope that it all sorts itself out in the victory lap. I can't outfight these faeries, but I may just be able to outrun them. I push myself up on aching muscles and pause, racked with indecision. Do I go for it, knowing that all the glory of a win and all the blame for a failure would then rest on my shoulders?

It turns out that it's not a decision at all. I couldn't make my legs run past Olani, abandoning her to her fate, even if I wanted to. Besides, I know for a fact that Aris would never let me hear the end of it if I criticized her for abandoning the team and our plan, only to turn around and do the same.

I crash to the ground on my knees, attention shifting away from the faerie conflict picking back up behind us and onto them. I don't know what kind of enchantment this is—glowing strands of magic woven around their ankles and wrists, paralyzing everything except their faces. Even if I could identify it, it's not like there's anything I could do to help. Why did it have to be me here instead of Seelie?

"We're not getting out of this," Aris says firmly, before I can ask. "This enchantment is strong enough to last years. I just hope he remembers to set us free before he asks the Queen a favor."

"It's not over yet," I tell her fiercely. "Olani, any ideas?"

"Working on it," she says between her teeth. I'm not sure if her jaw is paralyzed, too, or if that's the frustration of their situation showing.

A *crash!* sounds from the faerie fight, and I look up just in time to see the axe slicing through another wad of that horrible gray goo. At least they're not looking at us. Maybe we can attack them from here, while they're distracted. I look back at Aris, who has managed to make her fingertips wiggle slightly. "How much magic do you have left? Think you can get them from here?"

I give Aris an appraising look. Like most enchanters, she can only use so much magic before it starts to catch up with her, to demand a price of her body. She's a bit gray, a bit sweaty—but I've seen her fight through worse. She's fought *me* through worse. Then again, by that point, she had abandoned spells entirely and we were punching each other, pulling hair, and rolling around in the dirt.

"I can try," she says, and I can't tell if she's actually in pain, or just pained by the admission. "But I can't really aim like this. And from here, there's a good chance they'd be able to dodge any of my attacks. I'm running out of strength."

"But what if we didn't attack?" We both look at Olani. Well, I look at Olani, and what little of Aris's eyes can move snaps to the side, straining at her periphery.

"We didn't come this far to *lose*," Aris says with a curl of her lip.

Olani's gaze is far away from us, golden light glowing in the warm brown of her eyes. "When did I say we'd lose?"

chapter thirty-two

SEELIE

It's Raze, in the end, who solves the puzzle of the Unseelie Queen's bargain. Of course it's Raze, and of course it's a deceptively simple yet elegant solution. Something every bit as nonthreateningly charming and tempting as he is. When we present it to the Unseelie Queen, a fresh-faced faerie girl in the cold morning light, she doesn't react for a long time. I press my hands into my skirt, forcing myself not to fidget nervously.

My other hand is caught in Raze's, his thumb swiping gently over my knuckles in a way that is obviously supposed to be comforting but is just making me all too aware of every sensation. I don't pull away, though, because his touch is grounding, a reminder of the hours we shared before sunrise, when I leaned my head against his steady heartbeat and finally dared to whisper everything that happened in my dream. One of his arms circled my shoulder, fingers toying with a lock of my loose hair. I held his other hand in mine, just like this. We schemed and debated and perfected the wording of our bargain, only occasionally stooping so low as to shut each other up with a kiss.

The Unseelie Queen studies us with brows slightly raised, like she's trying not to look interested. "You . . . have my sister's vow of service?"

I run back over the proposed agreement in my mind, even though I know I chose and delivered each word carefully. *In exchange for your help defeating Gossamer and repairing the realms, we offer the alliance and support of the Seelie Queen to do the same.*

Perhaps offering her sister's alliance was a bit premature, but we have so few options. *This* is tantalizing, better than a lifetime of smiles or the sound of our voices or whatever foolishness we might offer. It's something she actually wants, for starters. The chance to speak with her sister again, to be on the same side after so many centuries apart. Maybe they can even patch things up, I think a little optimistically, but don't dare to offer.

"We will." I don't know how, but we will. "My sister is working on it." I have no idea how, but I hope desperately that it's true. Between Isolde, Olani, and Aris, there's more than enough single-minded determination to make the impossible happen.

"*That*, mortal, is worth something."

Raze and I exchange a glance, part victory and part confusion, as the Unseelie Queen stands from her throne with the alarming creak of a very large tree falling and a shower of dust. She mutters to herself as she turns and claws at her own throne, clearing away roots and crystals that shatter with a touch. Egg, who until this point has been sprawled at my feet, half asleep and bored with our unimportant conversations, suddenly perks up.

Raze clears his throat. "Um . . . Your Majesty? Should we return to the Seelie Realm now?"

The girl turns a bemused look on us, wild-eyed with all the force of a blizzard. "Oh, no. You may wait here with me until the terms of our bargain are fulfilled."

We both mumble thanks automatically, not wanting to be rude, even in our confusion.

The Unseelie Queen returns to her task, quickly revealing a dull, dusty mirror. It reflects the glow of her eyes, searing spots into my vision.

"May I ask what that is?" Raze tries.

She beams. "You may."

When she doesn't proceed to explain, I sigh, dropping my shoulders. "What is that?"

"This is a looking glass to my sister's throne. A small portal we've kept as long as we've been apart. As soon as her status as your ally is secured, I will know."

I peer closer at the mirror, getting so close that I can see the wrinkle between my brows as my fingers skim its dusty frame. "I thought spells like this were impossible. Wasn't my open portal what started all this?"

The Unseelie Queen's reflection meets my eyes. Her claw-like hands are folded in front of her, her head slightly bowed. "This spell is stabilized by a fragment of my sister's power and my own. It's sustained itself for centuries now without straining the borders of the realms." She doesn't end the sentence with *You useless turnip of an enchanter*, but it's implied. She waves one skeletal hand casually, and the surface of the mirror ripples like smooth water. Its surface frosts over, and then it's more like a window, a thin sheen of magic veiling the image of another world.

I wait for it to clear, heart in my throat. I know time passes differently between realms, but I've barely been gone a day. How much trouble could she have gotten into in that time?

The image clears, and I immediately regret the naivety of my imagination not ten seconds ago. First, we see Isolde: hair tangled and stuck to her face with sweat, face bruised, covered in streaks of blood and mud. Tiny ice crystals cling to her hair and clothes, because she's somehow managed to find the one snowy spot in the Seelie Realm's eternal summer. Her brow furrows as she concentrates deeply on something—a look I recognize from some of our leaner months, the look she'd give a mark right before she pickpocketed them, a door right before she picked the lock.

I have just enough time to wonder where in all the realms Olani and Aris are in all this before the mirror's view turns, revealing them in a melting patch of grassy, dirty snow, captured by some kind of enchantment. They strain against it, but don't seem able to move much more than their eyes and fingertips. A jet of purple flame shoots past them, and they can do nothing but watch it pass with fear reflected in their eyes.

Someone stumbles into view between us and them, quickly followed by the arc of something heavy and sharp. Two faeries, locked in combat, apparently not worried about their attacks accidentally hitting an unlucky mortal. It's enough to shake the ground, to make the floating wreath in the air behind them tremble . . .

I left Isolde alone for a *day*. What has she gotten herself into?

"Oh, the Winter Tournament!" the Unseelie Queen exclaims, excitement battling through the wistful whistle of her voice. Egg, caught up in the thrill of it all, jumps and presses his snout to the cool glass. She gently pries him away, looking briefly like a mortal child wrangling an overexcited dog.

Raze speaks first. "Tournament, like *tournament*?"

I've heard stories of such contests, from the days long before. When mortals had things like kingdoms, and knights, and chivalry. Warriors and enchanters battling it out in an enclosed space for the entertainment of others, for a prize, like some sort of deadly game. Such things tend to lose entertainment value when anyone with valuable survival skills actually needs to use them to, you know, survive.

I suddenly realize I'm squeezing Raze's hand hard enough to cut off the circulation. "That can't possibly mean they're going to *fight* all those faeries, can it?"

"That is exactly what it means," the Unseelie Queen says gleefully, settling into her throne to watch. "And there's nothing to do now but hope Fate is on your sister's side. What a delightful twist to our tale."

chapter thirty-three

ISOLDE

My muscles tense with the strain of waiting for the perfect moment.

This is a kind of waiting I'm accustomed to, one I can force myself to sit still through. Watching for an opening, for the moment when backs are turned and all attention will be off of me, giving me the opportunity to secure my prize. I'm only going to get one chance at it this time. Better make it count.

Time is running out. The faeries are still closer than I'd hoped they'd be, but I might not get another try. This is it. I burst into movement with an explosion of energy, turning every bit of restlessness I'd held back into fuel on the fire.

Time slows—figuratively, in this case. The distance between me and the wreath seems to stretch out three times what it was before, every potential obstacle leaping to my attention at once. *No*, I command my thoughts. *In order. Give it to me in order.*

First, the puddle of gray goo. I leap over it, managing to

catch myself before the mud I land in can send my feet sliding in opposite directions. I have to adjust my path to go around the purple flames, which make my eyes water with an acidic stench. By that point, both the faeries have noticed me. The smaller one lunges for me first, and the woman grabs him by his cloak to pull him back, stomping on one of his hands in her hurry to catch me.

Perhaps if I was a normal human girl, I wouldn't be quick enough to avoid her. But I'm a changeling, too. Just faerie enough to stand up to them. Maybe just faerie enough to *win.*

The faerie woman dives, obviously intending to tackle me. I lower my center of gravity, slowing down enough to throw off her aim, so she slides across cold, wet ground instead. Seeing my chance, I jump up onto her back, using her as an extra step to launch me at the wreath.

The beam of magic around it tingles with warmth, a radiance that feels like approval and applause. My fingers close around the prickly leaves and needles, yanking it out of the air as I crash down. I have to pull it in close to avoid an unknown spell from the other faerie, which barely misses my wrist.

They're both closing in on me. All focus is on me. This might be a good time to run.

But instead, like we planned, I freeze. I freeze in place in the beam of magic like a spotlight that followed the wreath, clutching the prize close to my chest, and I hope that, just this once, the plan will work.

"Bad timing," the woman says, almost sympathetically, pulling back a punch.

Just this once . . .

Her fist flies. I don't move. The instant before she makes contact, a barrier flickers into place between us. Her fist smashes into it, sending a splash of golden light out all around me. Olani's shielding magic, woven through with bits of Aris's light. From between the two faeries, I can see them, faces scrunched in concentration, moving what little bit of their hands are still free to direct the magic.

It's working, but I don't dare to crow with victory yet—or even to exhale. Next, another spell crashes into my shield. It bounces off, narrowly missing its caster. The woman swings for me again, this time with the axe, but it's worse than useless. She lets out an enraged scream as her axe nearly escapes her grip with the force of it, and I remain safely cocooned in light. Nothing they throw at the shielding spell can break through, and they're too focused on wrenching the prize from my hands to figure out how to break the spell.

This shield won't last forever, but it doesn't have to. For a long, heart-pounding moment, I'm invincible.

The horn sounds again. I am still holding the wreath, now slightly crushed and dirty and crusted with snow. The faeries fall back, looking up at the sky in disbelief. We *won*.

I feel the magic drop around me, turn to beam at Olani and Aris—

But before I can grin triumphantly, raise the wreath above my head and shout with victory, the arena disappears. One second I'm standing in the mud, looking over the despairing *losers* of the Winter Tournament. The next, I'm back in the throne room, warm air pressing in all around me.

"Why won't you *give up*?"

I don't recognize the voice at first. It's hollow, almost childish in its devastation, and sends a chill through the room. My eyes search the empty room and land on her—the Seelie Queen, sitting in a heap of wrinkled skirts at the foot of her own throne. If I didn't know better, I'd say she looks . . . defeated.

Is this real, or just another test? I look over one shoulder, then another, but it's only us. Hesitating, I take a faltering step forward. "Are you . . . talking to me?"

"Yes, you vile creature. Who else?" Her head snaps up, glowing eyes focusing on me, cheeks marked by golden streaks. She looks almost as though she's been . . . crying. The heat of her words, as she was before, would have been enough to make my skin shrivel like overripe fruit on the vine. Now it just makes me flinch a little. Something tells me that this isn't how the tournament usually goes. That I've stumbled into something deeper.

Well, good. I'm after something deeper, too.

Steeling myself with a breath, I let the wreath drop. It bounces off my boot, then settles in the grass. It looks strangely out of place, such a clear symbol of winter, overgrown in less than a second by summer's plush green bounty.

"Look, I *know* you don't want to help us defeat Gossamer, for whatever reason. But—"

Before I can launch into an explanation of the greater good, she interrupts. "Do not presume to understand me. You cannot know the mess you've stumbled into. Gossamer isn't just some—some dragon to be disposed of, some villain to be vanquished. He is—was—my family. Just like my sister. Last time we fought him, it tore your world apart. But it tore my *family* apart."

My tongue is ready with a response, but I hold it back, trying to make sense of that revelation. "Your *sister*?"

Her tear-streaked glare shifts, as if she's as confused by my ignorance as I am. "The ruler of the Unseelie Realm," she says, as if that's obvious. Then she looks disappointed in herself for stooping to my level—I do tend to have that effect on people—and tries to gather her dignity. "*Champion*. I did not bring you here to discuss my family. There is unfinished business between us yet. I know what you will ask—my support against Gossamer. And I will admit, you have put me in a position to be unable to refuse it. But first, answer me this: What do you truly want?"

That's easy. "I want to win this fight. To take him down."

"No. What do *you* truly want?" The Seelie Queen's eyes lock on mine, sizzling down to the marrow.

It's like she knows how I'm going to react before I do, like she's wasting my time on purpose. We both know that I don't have the patience for this. "I mean, first off, I'd like for my whole world not to be destroyed. Not to mention my parents. My sister and I have fought too hard for too long not to see them again. I promised her we would. I *promised*."

"You want your family to be together. A noble goal. But trust me, the reality isn't so pretty. Isn't it better this way? To not know how far you've drifted apart, to be able to picture those sunlit days in your mind?"

"Is that why it's always summer here? Because it reminds you of—"

"It is summer because that is my nature," the Queen sniffs, summoning regal disdain back into her voice. "The warmth of long days, the security of abundance. The unforgiving storm wind breaking that which does not bend. You would do well to remember it."

I feel her frustration, boiling off her in waves, mingling with my own. I know she didn't summon me here, grant me a private audience, just so she could whine about the good old days. Even though it makes my eyes burn, I peer at her harder, tilting my head. Trying to see what I'm not seeing. To understand. There's something familiar reflected back at me in her expression, something I tried so hard to keep from myself that it takes me a second to recognize. I don't think she even knows that it's there.

Yearning for something more. Something . . . *different*.

Is that even possible? She's bound to this unchanging realm, as much a part of its magic as it is a part of her. It shouldn't be in her nature to long for the breath of autumn, for the freshness of spring or the bite of winter. For anything other than what is. But I'd swear I see it in her eyes anyway.

I approach slowly, crouching beside her as if she's a friend. As if she's Seelie. Gently, I ask, "What do *you* want?"

She laughs, hollow and brittle. "What do I want? I am the *Queen* of my realm, mortal. I don't get what I want."

"Really? It seems to me that nothing matters except your will, your preference, your image."

"I act for the *good of my people*," the Seelie Queen snaps. "For the good of my realm. And yours, miserable as it is."

"And that's why you won't help us save them. Makes sense."

"You dare to speak to me in such a way?"

"Well, *someone* should! Look around—all your subjects are terrified of you! They're willing to go through all this for a chance to ask for a simple favor. Some of them helped us. They want to fix the realms as much as we do, but they have no voice to tell you that. Maybe you've spent too long away from mortals. Our puny minds can't comprehend your great and terrible power, which makes us just bold and stupid enough to be the ones to tell you to shove it!"

There's a pause after that. I wonder if she's going to incinerate me on the spot or turn me into a frog. I'd be a cute frog, I think. It would be simpler than going through all this. But despite the unrelenting sunburn tingle of her anger, there's no flare of magic in the air. Finally, the Seelie Queen finds her voice again. "I can recall the joys of interacting with mortals," she says, a sigh threading through her voice. "Though I seldom remember them being quite as troublesome as you, Isolde Graygrove."

"What can I say? I'm special." The joke lands like a dead bird between us. After another pause, I clear my throat and add, "The fight ahead won't be easy. But we *need* to try. And we need your help to win. Who knows? Maybe it'll be good for you."

"Optimism." The golden wings of her brow flutter as she meets my eyes again, radiant with the clarity that comes after a good, much-delayed cry. "How very mortal."

With a long exhale, our surroundings melt away again. We're

still in the throne room, but it's changed. Expanded, and filled with a crowd of faerie courtiers once more. The Queen sits regally on her throne, as if the past few minutes between us never happened at all, and I'm standing before her with Olani and Aris on either side. They're still in their borrowed armor, sweaty and streaked with blood and soot, wearing almost identical stunned expressions.

"We did it!" I exclaim, throwing my arms around both of them. Even though it's awkward. Even though it takes them both a second to thaw, to join me in my excitement. Even though, when Aris wraps her arms around the two of us in return, it feels like she's never hugged anyone before.

"Dear mortal guests." The Queen's voice is vaguely amused when she interrupts our celebration, making us and every other voice in the room go quiet. "You three have bested the faeries of my Court and succeeded against each challenge you faced. We now crown you . . . champions of the Winter Tournament."

If I thought the cheers were loud when we came out of the first trial, it was nothing compared to this. The ground trembles, the air around us vibrating with the shouting and stomping of a crowd of faeries. I offer them a sideways look and a triumphant grin, basking in the praise for the moment it takes me to piece together why they're really cheering. Not for us, for our victory—not really. They're applauding as you would after a moving play, reveling in the sheer entertainment value of our struggle.

Most of them, at least. Searching the crowd, I spot Robin and Cobweb, cheering louder than anyone. They're on their feet, whooping and hugging each other. They're surrounded by similar celebrations, including the faerie woman we charmed last night who donated Olani's armor. All the mortal sympathizers, those who want the same thing we do, but have no way to ask for it. Robin spots me looking and shoots me a thumbs-up and an uncharacteristically wide grin.

"What a delight for us, to have mortal champions after such a long separation between our people," the Queen says, not quite managing to sound delighted. "You have won fame and favor. If there is any request you have of me—anything within my power to grant—you may ask it now."

Olani squeezes my hand, then releases me. Aris nudges me forward. We all stand close, still, but I am clearly in the front. I know what I have to do. Every faerie eye and ear is focused on me. I fall from the sheer, dizzying height of victory as the pressure of the moment sinks in. This is another trial of itself. I have to be careful, so careful, what I ask for. I swallow hard, forcing myself to look unblinking at the Queen as I try to formulate the words, to use our private conversation to strengthen my request.

"We ask for your help and support defeating Gossamer and . . . restoring . . ." My voice trails off weakly. I don't know enough about magic to know how to phrase this. Still, I don't want to look away. I don't want to lose the momentum of this moment. "Restoring . . ." I repeat, hoping to summon the right words and failing.

"Restoring the barrier between worlds," Aris finishes for me. Clipped and confident, but not the barely restrained rage and superiority I'm used to from her. She even offers me a little smile in the relieved silence that follows.

The Seelie Queen sighs, a gust of sweet-smelling summer wind that blows our hair back and shakes the branches. "Yes, I thought you might ask for that. Are you sure there's nothing else you would prefer? I could make each of you immortal and give you a permanent place here in eternal summer. I could give you magic beyond your wildest dreams. I could twist the strings of Fate . . ."

"Yeah," I say with a soft smile, speaking directly to the small, unguarded version of herself that she let me see when we were alone. "We're sure."

If it was possible for her posture to be anything other than regally perfect, it happens then. I have to squint through her glow to see the faintest slide of her shoulders as she lets out another breath. "So be it. To honor your status as champions, I will lend my aid to your cause."

"Yes!" My fist pumps high in the air as I bounce on my toes, unable to contain the rush of excitement. For a second, I think I've jumped into a spot that echoes, because I hear my voice thrown back at me—but then it continues in a victorious whoop, joined by another, louder voice. One that almost sounds like it's coming from . . . behind the Queen.

She looks just as puzzled by the sound, the wings that frame her face fluttering as she blinks rapidly, head turning back and forth.

"No," she mutters to herself, like she's forgotten the rest of us are here. She stands slowly, with a groaning sound that might be the ground under our feet shifting to welcome her, and turns to brush aside one of the patches of thick, flowering vines that cover the throne. Curling tendrils of stem rip away to reveal a pollen-coated pane of glass. On the other side, Seelie and Raze have frozen mid-cheer, still clutching each other as they stare up at the Seelie Queen.

"Oh," Seelie says faintly. I'm relieved to see she looks slightly worse for wear, but very much alive.

"We, um, didn't realize this went both ways." Raze releases his grip around her waist, and she drops a couple inches to the ground. He straightens out his shirt while Egg continues running circles around their legs with the obnoxious energy of an overexcited puppy.

Seelie's eyes scan past the Queen to find me, a crooked smile brightening the shadows under her eyes. "Hey."

The sound of her voice—a lighter, breathier echo of mine—releases a knot of tension I didn't realize I was holding in. I smile back, as if it's only been an afternoon since we saw each other instead of a watercolor blur of faerie realm time. "How's it going?"

In the wave of relief that swells to fill my chest, I forget myself, my surroundings, any sense of gravity or decorum. We crash together in a hug, launching ourselves in a shower of squeals as if we're not in the middle of the Seelie Court. Egg joins in, nipping at my heels, and I can't see anything through the tangled veil of my sister's hair, and I know this isn't all over, but I don't care. My sister has returned to me one more time.

"Sister," says another voice, cool as wind over a frozen lake and with the same swishing quality. Significantly less excited about this reunion than we are. I let Seelie unwind from my grip, keeping one arm around her shoulders, and study the face of the Unseelie Queen for the first time. Can't say I see much of a family resemblance. When she smiles, I'd swear dust pours from the creases of her face, like those muscles haven't seen much use in a few centuries. "It seems we have much to discuss."

chapter thirty-four

ISOLDE

I flop down on the *Destiny*'s stage, a platform barely big enough to sit me and Seelie side by side. One of my arms lands across her lap as my legs dangle off the edge. Now that everything has quieted down, I am exhausted. Bone-deep exhausted, sweaty, and missing the winter chill.

It feels like night, though I've lost track of the time again. A few faraway stars gleam in the dusky sky, peeking from between the silhouette of branches. My gaze shifts from the sky to Seelie, her features flickering in the orange light of a campfire. Her eyes drop to mine, and her face softens with a weary smile.

There was a celebration to mark the end of the Winter Tournament. There was planning, negotiating between the Seelie and Unseelie Queens, and catching each other up on everything. And now, finally, there is a strained, tentative peace.

"I missed you." Seelie speaks quietly, one hand brushing a strand of hair away from my eyes.

I grin back at her. "I know."

We should be asleep. We should be resting for the coming fight, like we told the faeries we would when we convinced them to give us a couple hours before just storming into the Unending Realm, magic blazing. We should definitely stop talking, put out our little campfire, and go to sleep, while we still can.

But Fate, it's good to be together again. Not just me and Seelie, but Raze and Olani and Aris, too. The tangled knots of tension that our group has held—for, well, as long as we've been a group—have dissolved, and things are easy and light as they've never been before. As they may never be again.

But we can't escape the idea of *tomorrow*, however abstract a concept it is in a place like this. And because we all know that the worst is yet to come, a shadow hangs over our exhausted relief.

I'd hoped to avoid it entirely, but Seelie is too practical for that. Before I can distract her talking about something else, she shatters our star-drenched silence. "Tomorrow. If I don't make it . . ."

"Don't say that."

"I'm just trying to be realistic. Gossamer's going to be heading straight for me, for my magic, and if it comes down to me or everyone else . . ."

I sit up, turning to face her. "Seelie, shut up. I'm not letting you sacrifice yourself."

"It might not be up to you, Isolde."

I don't know how to express to her that it isn't worth thinking about. That I've never been good at picturing my future, but trying to imagine a world without Seelie in it produces nothing but a swirling void that threatens to swallow up my past and present along with the days to come.

Instead, I say, "Would it kill you to *try* to be optimistic?"

Seelie's smile gains an ironic twist. "It might."

"Well, maybe *I'll* sacrifice myself for *you*. Or am I not important enough for that?"

Seelie blinks at me for a second, and I think I've won. Then she lets out a disbelieving laugh. "Only you could make *dying* some sort of competition, Isolde."

My echoing chuckle is softer, but just as humorless as hers. "I could never compete with you."

"You never had to." She reaches for my hand, gripping it tightly in hers. My vision blurs, turning every star overhead into the streak of a comet's tail. "*If* it comes down to it," Seelie says, "I want you to know you've sacrificed enough for me. The past three years. The chance at a normal life. All the pain and trouble that's followed me, that you helped me shoulder without me even asking . . . it's enough. And if I have to, I'll give you a life in return."

My heart sinks. I study her face, trying to keep my emotions contained. When she realizes I don't have a clever retort, that the fight is slowly going out of me, Seelie continues.

"If I don't make it, I want Mami and Papa to know I did my best. I want Egg to be protected. I want you to be safe and happy. Remember that, okay?"

I bite my tongue to stop myself from arguing with her. There's no point withholding this comfort. We're both going to be just fine. "Okay," I whisper. A single tear manages to escape, and I swipe quickly at it, hiding my sniffle behind another pitiful chuckle. "And Raze?" I ask, because teasing is the only way I know to get through this. "What should I tell him?"

Seelie's face changes instantly. She looks past me to where Raze, Aris, and Olani are sitting around the campfire. Raze and Olani's reunion was less intense than ours, but no less emotional. Now they sit leaning, so they each hold up the other's weight. Their lips move, their words a low mumble only they can hear. Olani says something that makes Raze laugh loudly in her ear, but it must not have been intended as a joke, because she's valiantly fighting a smile in response.

"I'll talk to him." I look back at Seelie to find her *smiling*. Not glaring or looking away, but actually grinning from ear to ear. Practically glowing. Perhaps we haven't caught up on *everything*.

I acknowledge and am fully aware of the dance Olani and I are trapped in—two steps forward, one step back, each hoping the other will break the pattern—but whatever's going on between Seelie and Raze is something different. I guess everything is different for her, sharper and more intense and harder to grasp. It makes sense falling in love would be the same way.

Because, obviously, that's what this is. I can only keep my nose out of my sister's business for so long. Honestly, I'm proud of myself for making it this far, especially when I can see the connection between them as strong as the tension. I tear my eyes away from our friends to look at her, my head dropped almost to my shoulder. "Did something happen between you in the Unseelie Realm?"

For a second, I think she didn't hear me, because she doesn't react at all. She just keeps staring past me, blinking a little too rapidly. Then I see the color slowly creeping up her cheeks.

"It *did*, didn't it?" I poke her teasingly in the ribs. "You're holding out on me! Come *on*, Seelie, tell me everything!"

At the sight of the grin on my face, she pokes me back much harder. "Shh! You don't have to *shout*." But her own smile is creeping back. Her gaze drops to her hands, fingers twisting as she says, "We kissed."

"And? How was it? You wanted to, right? Do I need to kill him before tomorrow?"

Seelie's cheeks are going from rosy to fiery. I'm surprised she doesn't actually burst into flames. "You— I'm— Isolde, *no*. I am *not* discussing this with you." I wait, giving her a long pause.

Finally, she covers her face in her hands, mumbling, "It was nice," between her fingers.

I let out an exaggerated sigh of relief. "Oh, good. I like Raze. I'd hate to have to murder him. For you, I wouldn't hesitate, of course. But it would be a shame."

Seelie groans into her hands. While she's hunched up into herself, I wrap an arm around her shoulders and squeeze tight.

"Well then. You should go . . . *talk* with him while you have the time."

She peeks at me with a sideways glance. "But I—"

"Go on." I shove lightly. Instead of holding her ground, Seelie stumbles off the stage with it. I can tell she's being dramatic, because she follows the close catch of her balance with an exaggerated dark look up at me. There's no real heat behind it, besides the lingering flare of her embarrassment. I give her an innocent look, and she rolls her eyes, unable to hide the quirk of her mouth as she turns toward the campfire and the others.

I watch Seelie walk to them, watch her say a few quiet words, watch Raze take her hand and follow her into the trees. Not too far, hopefully. They disappear into the shadows, and my eyes meet Olani's, and the thought *So, this is happening* passes between us as clearly as if it was spoken out loud.

There's no use pretending I don't want to go over and sit by her side, so I don't. I take the seat Raze just vacated, perched on a mossy log just barely wide enough for us to sit side by side without touching.

Birch is curled up on Olani's lap with his paws tucked under himself. His fur is so black it seems to swallow the firelight, leaving only his slitted green eyes and the pink tips of his ears distinct from the void of his body. Across the dying fire, Aris sits with her elbows propped on her knees.

"Well, looks like it's just the three of us again," she drawls, as if she knows something I don't. "Do you guys want to share any more secrets? Play Questions and Commands? Maybe braid each other's hair?"

When this earns her nothing but a blank look from both of us, she snorts. It might be considered a laugh, in other contexts.

"I'm just kidding. Actually, I think I'm going to go to sleep. I'm . . . uh . . . really tired." With one last meaningful look, and an extremely fake yawn, she stands and walks to the wagon.

Leaving Olani and me. And, of course, Birch. I can't bear to look at her, so I focus on the brownie instead.

"You know how unfair it is that *you're* his favorite?"

Her fingers curve around the underside of his jaw, scratching his soft cheeks. I can hardly blame Birch for the betrayal—I'd be purring, too. "You've mentioned it."

In the firelight, I can almost imagine this is one of those nights on our quest to the Mortal's Keep. That Seelie and Raze are off arguing about some method of enchantment, and our friendship is burdened by nothing but fun and frothy flirtation, and there will still be treasure for us at the end of this journey. If we were out in the autumn woods of the Mortal Realm, a chill breeze would give me a reason to scoot closer. Maybe even to put my arm around her if she shivered, with the excuse of loaning her my warmth.

But then, I think, I wouldn't know the truth of my origin. And Olani and I wouldn't have fought and confessed everything and made up again. I've grown fond of the weight of whatever we're carrying between us. If I'm going to move closer, it will be for no reason except that I wanted to.

Olani speaks before I manage to find the courage. "So what were you and Seelie talking about?"

"Death." I stare at the fire, watching the pulsing red of the embers. Finally, I dare to look up at her, unable to keep a trace of amusement from my face. Is her mind in the same dark place as Seelie's? If it was, would she trust me enough to talk about it? Or is she just as unable to conceive of our permanent demise as

I am? I know that this is all very serious, but trying to actually take it seriously is another matter entirely.

Her knees shift toward me. It's the slightest movement, and might have gone completely unnoticed, if it didn't offend Birch. The cat-shaped creature blinks awake with a start, lets out a loud and disappointed sigh, and launches himself off Olani's knees at top speed, literally disappearing into the darkness.

"*Rude*," she scoffs, watching the tip of his tail vanish into thin air. "I was just thinking about doing the same thing."

"You don't want to talk about it?"

She shrugs, looking off at the distance. "We might die tomorrow. I'd like my things to go to my brother if you . . . if I don't . . ."

"I'll make sure of it," I say, closing a comforting hand around hers.

Olani's glare softens. "Thanks. There's a note in there explaining everything." She pauses. "Well . . . almost everything."

I nod, wondering if I should be feeling something I'm not. If Seelie and I don't make it, then our parents won't be saved, and there will be no one to miss us. It doesn't bear thinking about.

She lets out a little huff of air, the same baffled amusement I'm feeling. "I don't know what else there is to say. It doesn't feel real."

"None of this feels real." I laugh with a shake of my head.

Tension eases with the sound, drawing Olani closer to me and relaxing the sharp angle of her shoulders. Her face tilts nearer to mine, and before I can think better of it, I reach up to tuck back the stray braids that sway between us. So there's nothing blocking me from the sight of her wide eyes, flickering gold in the firelight. That *look* moves through me like a physical force, curling in the pit of my stomach. I take a deep breath past the choking pressure of it.

Now or never.

"If we are going to die tomorrow . . . there's something I'd like to do first." In case there's any room to doubt what I mean by that, I indulge an impulse I've been suppressing for *weeks* now and let my thumb slip to the plush cushion of her bottom lip. Her mouth opens a little with the gesture, and I soak in every detail of the slightly chapped skin under mine, a glimpse of white teeth and pink tongue. My eyes finally drift back up to hers, looking for a response before I move any further. A *yes*, spoken or unspoken. Anything.

"Isolde . . ." Her mouth splits in a smile, and my thumb tracks down from her lip to her chin. She leans into me so that our noses bump, and the only thing separating my mouth from hers is the fact that she's not done talking. Her lips brush mine with each word, sending a warm tingle over my skin. "I'm not going to kiss you just because we might die tomorrow."

I swallow hard. I can't move closer, but I can't move *away*. So I stay there, cheek to cheek, lips barely touching with each shallow breath. "What if there were . . . other reasons?"

Olani's hand slips to the base of my neck. She leans back, and I can't help swaying forward with her until I squeeze my nails into my palm and force myself to go still. Warm summer air fills the gap between us, smoke chasing away her sharp, clean scent. "Then I guess we're both going to have to live through it so you can tell me what they are."

Because . . . I grasp for reasons, but my thoughts feel like cold spring water, slipping through my fingers. I've never felt like this. I don't know what this is. I don't know where to start.

And Olani doesn't give me the chance. She pulls me in, pressing a kiss to my cheek. It's swift and soft and stops my heart for longer than the second it takes her to say "Good night, Isolde."

With that, she's gone. I lose the fight not to watch her walk to the wagon, a sleek shadow outlined by yellow firelight until it fades into the night beyond. I should go rest, too—even if I'm too restless to sleep, and even if time is all wrong here, it's been a long day.

Egg lifts his head when Olani passes, startled awake by her footsteps. I'd almost completely forgotten he was here. His ears swivel around in confusion, like he's trying to remember where he is. Where everyone else is. After a second, his bright golden eyes meet mine, and he slinks over to plant himself on my boots. I'm not sure if it's for my benefit or for his, but the pressure is strangely comforting.

"Well?" I sigh, giving in to scratch his scales behind his ear. "Anything *you* want to get off your chest before this is all over?"

Egg makes direct eye contact with me, flicks his ears as if to brush off my touch, and then drops his head and falls asleep on my feet.

Which, at this point, feels about right.

chapter thirty-five

ISOLDE

It was always going to end like this: with me standing at my sister's side, waiting for her to manipulate the threads that tie the realms together one last time. Our friends at our backs, ready to step through with us and face whatever's on the other side. A small, impatient dragon underfoot.

The assembled faerie forces waiting just behind them are an exciting addition I hardly dared to picture in my daydreams, much less the shining golden eyes of the Queen. I can picture her sister, a matching force in silver on the other side.

The other addition I couldn't have anticipated is the faint smudge of a red mark visible against the olive skin at my sister's throat. I didn't say anything about it earlier, because I was waiting for the right moment.

And I don't think we're going to die today. I won't allow it. But just in case there's a chance I might not get the opportunity to tease Seelie after all this is over . . .

"You know you have something right here?" I whisper, breaking her concentration on the swirling portal in front of us as I gesture to the spot on my own neck.

Her hand flies up to the spot, confusion rippling over her features. And then understanding, and then a truly powerful blush. "No," she says, eyes flicking over her shoulder to Raze. He sees her, fingers still pressed to her throat, and meets her stormy stare with a sunbeam grin. "I wasn't aware."

I laugh, light and uninhibited, so that all the weight of this moment slips away for just a second. *She's going to be fine. We're going to be fine.*

"Well, I'm ready to die now. Is my face red? Any chance the ground will swallow me up?"

When her hand drops, I thread our fingers together and squeeze tight. "I'm happy for you."

Seelie lets the glare drop into an embarrassed little grin, squeezing my hand back. "Thanks." She doesn't let go, and even though she looks composed, I can feel the clenched anxiety in her sweaty palms. The portal outlines her profile in silvery-white light, making her look all too pale and mortal and fragile.

Even though I promised myself I wouldn't, I sneak one last look at Olani. This morning, as I helped her buckle back into her borrowed armor, my fingers trembled. They brushed the curve of her lean, muscled arms, and my heart stopped. Strange, after the amount of touch we've shared—fighting together, fighting each other, resting side by side—that such a small thing could feel like a spark on dry tinder. Olani's breath hitched, her lips parting slightly as she looked over her shoulder at me.

That would have been the moment to tell her all the reasons I wanted to kiss her, I think now, watching her furrowed brow as she concentrates on fixing some invisible flaw in her gear. I could have chased that spark, whispered something sweet and pulled her close to see if the fire caught. I don't know why I didn't. I've never hesitated like this before, never felt like my emotions were winged things fighting frantically to escape the cage of my chest. I don't know what makes her different.

I guess we're going to have to live through this so I can figure it out. My stomach clenches, but I refuse to recognize the feeling as *fear*. This is the moment we've been working toward since we landed in the Seelie Realm. I am not the kind of person who shies away from danger.

Even if, this once, the anticipation of the future and all its terrible possibilities—the full force of how much I have to *lose* right now—feels like a heavy weight around my neck. We've set something into motion that can't possibly be pulled back.

As if moved by that very thought, the Seelie Queen looks to us. This being, a creature whose blood is more magic than flesh, looks to *us* for a signal. If I wasn't sweating before, I am now.

Seelie and I step through the barrier together. Seelie moves first, as if she's parting a curtain for the rest of us, and I follow before I can let myself think about it. Egg darts between us, as if afraid to let her out of his sight for even a second.

I'm blasted by the chill of the Unending Realm, a burst of frigid wind against my Seelie-summer-warmed skin. Tiny glittering ice crystals swirl in the air, illuminated by the ghostly bluish light that fills the hollow husk of Wildline Manor. It seems empty, each step echoing off unforgiving stone.

Seelie and I exchange a look. At no point did any of us prepare for Gossamer simply not showing up. I didn't think we'd have to hunt him down. He seems like the type that can't resist a grand entrance.

My senses prickle, searching for anything amiss. My job is clear—to watch Seelie's back while she gets the two faerie Queens into position, bringing the two portals nearer so they can defend them. Seelie explained it to me like darning a sock, a temporary repair that will work to keep the chill of the Unending Realm out and the magic of their own realms in, so Gossamer doesn't have access to it.

The Seelie Queen warms the air around us slightly with just her presence. Tiny white crocus buds pop up from the floor at her feet. Still, I can't help but notice that her golden glow dims, devoured hungrily by the cold blue jaws of the Unending Realm's magic.

We were prepared for this, I remind myself. Fingers tap over my dagger's hilt. We just need to stick to the plan.

The instant the thought is formed, a strong wind picks up around us, drawing us into the room. I glance at Seelie, who's moving swiftly to a spot a few feet away, where she'll call her existing portal to the Unseelie Realm over to join us. I don't quite understand how all this magic stuff works, but I can tell that the rising wind obviously isn't one of hers. Her brows wrinkle, her eyes settling past me on the top of the grand staircase.

Where Leira Wildfall stands with her hands folded in front of her, unfrozen in time, looking down at us with an unreadable expression on her face. "He was right," she murmurs to herself, slowly descending the stairs. "It was only a matter of time."

He was right. Great—Gossamer's gotten to her already. He claimed the enchantment that froze time, froze people, froze *our parents*, was out of his control, and yet here Leira Wildfall is, as lively as ever. This is, I'll admit, an unexpected obstacle.

And Seelie doesn't, historically, do great with those. Her brow furrows as she freezes on the spot, trying to piece something together. Her lips part, but she can't even form a question, too thrown by this development. Egg seems torn between hiding behind her and standing in front to guard her, and ends up half wrapped around her ankles, snarling in Leira's direction.

"Aunt Leira, whatever he told you—" Raze starts, taking a protective step forward. Something in her distant, unmoved face makes him stop and recalculate. "I mean, you know better than to bargain with a faerie."

Leira's smile doesn't reach her thousand-yard stare. "A lesson I learned too late."

Seelie is thawing slowly, her hands still lifted mid-enchantment. I see the moment everything connects behind her eyes, and her expression shifts to horror. "Gossamer. What did you bargain with him for?"

The rest of us all speak at once in a jumble that basically boils down to a collective "*What?*"

Seelie's brows wrinkle together, her hands wringing in front of her. "I *saw* it. When I was trying to do the memory spell—she was a teenager, and he was still trapped, and . . . they made a deal. What was it, Leira?"

Raze's head turns sharply to her. "And you didn't think to mention this earlier?"

"There was a lot going on!"

Leira looks briefly annoyed that she's no longer the center of attention, before smoothing her face to poised indifference again. "We can fight, if you'd like, Raze. Or you and your . . . *new friends* can surrender now and discuss making arrangements between the Unending Realm and the others."

Raze shakes his head in disbelief. "You should be on our side. You *know* what he'll do to the Mortal Realm. There's more at stake than *us* and stupid rivalries and the Wildline Legacy."

"Unfortunately, my side in this fight was chosen long ago." Leira knows he's right—she must. But admitting that would mean admitting that *she* has ever been wrong. "Long before I could have ever guessed the consequences. Your concern is touching, nephew, but don't worry about me. I'll get what I'm owed in return. You can at least count on faeries for that."

Seelie pins her with that glare that looks straight through people, as if she can take Leira apart with her eyes and figure out what makes her work. The faint hint of sunset glow on her face reminds me that the Seelie Queen is still behind us, struggling to hold the barrier between the realms. This is a distraction. And it's working.

Raze must be having the same thoughts I am, and more

disturbingly, he reacts exactly the same way I'm about to: grabbing Seelie gently by the forearm, looking deep into her eyes, and gently murmuring, "Stick to the plan."

Seelie brushes her palms against the sides of her skirt, where her apron would normally be. Her gaze flickers over all of us, pausing briefly as I give a faint nod. She turns to resume her task, but as she passes me, she murmurs, "Wait here."

I know what she means. She can defend herself—she'd prefer me to wait here with Raze. To keep Leira busy, while she does whatever magic thing she needs to do. There's no way I'm going to argue with her, but at least Egg is following at her heels. Apparently, he's scarier than he looks.

Especially because it's starting to look like there's not much I can do to Leira without getting in the way.

"I'll deal with her." Raze, for once, looks grim. Like he somehow always knew this would happen, and that he'd be the one to step forward and face Leira when it did.

Olani hesitates, obviously wanting to defend Raze, but stilled by whatever passes between them in the last glance they share. Aris seems absent in her own body, shoulders hunched and fingers twined nervously. Her face turns to the ground, as if she can't bear to look at either of them. Maybe it's stupid to let Raze take Leira on alone, but I can't deny that he's earned this fight. We won't abandon him, but I won't do him the disservice of getting in his way.

Leira lunges. Her transformation is smooth and fast, a familiar shape that surges around her as she moves. By the height of her arc through the air, she's a pouncing wolf with reddish fur and snapping, snarling teeth. I didn't expect her to hold back, but knowing all their history, it still feels wrong to see those teeth on a direct path for Raze's throat.

Still, I can't interfere. He can handle this.

Before the wolf's claws sink into him, Raze seems to drop into the ground. A sparrow darts between the wolf's paws, swooping beneath her. Fluttery and tiny and impossible to catch. The wolf turns and snaps at the bird again, circling like a dog chasing its tail. Raze evades easily, not leaving so much as a feather behind as he draws her away from us.

"Why aren't you helping him?" The voice in my ear is cool and genuinely curious, and it sends an icicle spike down my spine. Gossamer materializes at my elbow, between me and Olani, his pale eyes watching the two animals chase each other.

I don't pause to converse, or even to wonder why he's here. I turn and stab all in one motion, burying my dagger in Gossamer's chest. It cuts through smoothly, sinks into soft flesh, and is immediately greeted by a dark, spreading bloodstain.

Gossamer looks down, half surprised, then meets my eyes with a lazy smile. My fist is against his ribs, hand still curled tight around the dagger's hilt. "I suppose I earned that," he says. With that, he disappears.

The wolf blurs, then lands in a pile of coils as a snake with viciously pointed golden scales. It takes her a second to unknot the sinew of her new shape, but this new form is blindingly quick. It strikes at the bird in the air, displaying needle-sharp fangs. Raze barely manages to duck around it in the air. Suddenly, his form's quick, staccato movements seem more like a beacon than a protection. The snake winds up to strike again, jaws angled wide. In this shape, even one bite will fill his veins with enough venom to stop his heart.

Realizing that, Raze flies up out of reach and changes shape again midair. This time, he's some sort of crane, gray with a sunburst crown of feathers sitting atop a long, curving neck. He drops from the air, sharp beak snapping at the snake.

A *bang!* across the room snags my attention. The portal has appeared, a dripping gash between worlds with glowing edges, but Seelie has vanished. Every instinct screams to move, to run toward it and drag my sister back—but I can't move. The snake is faster than me, and I don't want to remind it that I'm here, or to get in Raze's way. Besides, I trust Seelie. She knows what she's doing—right?

Leira twitches back and forth, making another attempt to strike at Raze with those wicked fangs. As she carves angry zigzags on the frozen ground, she seems to be getting slower. He snaps again, this time pinching the base of the snake's skull in his beak.

All it would take is one sharp *crunch*.

But he doesn't get the chance. She's realized her error, turning into a cold-blooded creature here, and is already changing forms again. This time, expanding, so quickly that it's not enough just to let her drop—the crane has to land and back away. When she rears before him, a gleaming golden mare, he's still fighting to balance himself with his wings outstretched.

Even I flinch at the abrupt display of black and white feathers longer than I am tall. The mare doesn't retreat, instead crashing down, clearly trying to crush the crane under her hooves. He dodges out of the way, then runs at her with his wings spread again. As the mare wheels around, ears pinned back, I see a trickle of blood running from her mane, from the base of her skull, where the snake got snapped up. She's injured, but she's not slowing down.

After another brutal charge, Raze's form shimmers again. I've never seen him change shape this much, back-to-back. The one time he came close, he overexerted himself and made himself sick. In his new form, the familiar hawk he favors, I can see glassy-eyed exhaustion starting to weigh on him.

Still, the hawk is quick and vicious, slashing claws over the mare's exposed neck. She lets out a high-pitched scream, a neigh that turns human as she shrinks back to her true form, a hand pressed over diagonal gashes in the side of her neck. Blood runs between her fingers, down her pale chest, soaking into her dress. The injury alone doesn't look life-threatening, but the blood loss might be.

"Don't just stand there!" Leira shouts. Her voice is pulled tight, halfway to a sob. Is she talking to *us*? Her eyes burn and water like a sharp chunk of ice squeezed tight in the palm of your hand.

Raze hesitates, unsure if they've called off the fighting. It's harder to attack her when she looks like herself. If even Leira's shoulders are heaving from all the effort of her expended magic, he probably needs a break just as badly.

"Aris!" Leira shouts, struggling to regain composure with blood streaking her hands. She's stumbling a bit, pressing her wound tighter. Behind me, I sense Aris stiffen, her posture going rigid. "Enough is enough. Do you have any idea how much punishment you're in for, assuming you even survive this? For once in your life, do something *useful* and help me."

There's a silver flash, and something in the air changes, like the pressure before a storm. Seelie is back, looking no worse for wear, with Egg and a creature that can only be the Unseelie Queen behind her. The faerie faces her sister as both stand in front of the portals to their realms. Though they're close enough for the air to hum between them, close enough to speak, they both seem to be pretending the other doesn't exist. Instead, they focus on weaving threads of magic I can't see.

The plan was for each of them to seal as much of the bleeding between worlds as they could, to cut Gossamer and this realm off from their respective sources of magic. Based on nothing but the taste of the cold air, I have to guess it's working.

Seelie doesn't take time to gloat, though. She's already rushing back to us. I catch her before she can run in between the two enchanters, gripping her hand tight. She holds her breath, watching the blood drip slowly from Leira's wound onto the frozen ground.

Raze lands beside her, human again. He looks ill from exertion, but to his credit, he's still standing.

Leira glances at Raze as he shapeshifts, quickly dismissing

him as a target for manipulation. Aris is the one she wants. The one she looks at with round eyes, letting a tremble into her voice. "I see now I underestimated you for too long. It took courage to turn on me. You're finally standing up for yourself. When the faerie and I make our new world, I will make sure there's a place for you. But first, I need your help."

The back of my neck prickles. I'm afraid to turn and look at Aris directly, as if that will frighten her like a deer into the brush. Suddenly, I remember that she fought this hard with us, for this long, so that she could restore Leira from the curse and earn her approval. Maybe she got swept up; maybe we all forgot what this was about for her, but it's all coming back.

Leira's eyes are almost pleading now. Not just commanding Aris—*begging* her. Peeling away layers to reveal that, despite all the harsh words and harsher treatment, she needs her.

Aris breathes deeply behind me. My fingers tighten reflexively around my knives. If it comes to it, I can push aside the memories that flood me now: Aris's voice, trembling with truth over the poison goblet. Her face when she passed out in the *Destiny*, comforted by our presence. The shaking feel of her arms squeezing around me in victory, the first friendly touch I'd ever seen her give.

"It's a shame," Aris says. Her high-pitched voice sounds thin in the cold air, like a whistle of wind disappearing as fast as it comes. I don't want this. I don't want to forget. But she's not looking at me. Her attention is trained fully on Leira. "Your timing, Aunt Leira. Finally admitting you need my help—once I've realized I don't need *you*."

She gathers her hands to her chest, collecting light in the cupped space between them. It snaps back out in a flourish, a more successful version of the spell she attempted right before she fell off a table. A bright line sears across my vision, a thread that connects Aris and Leira.

It all happens so fast:

Leira lets out an undignified yelp and disappears. The bolt of light keeps going, splitting the air in the spot where she stood just a second ago. A squeak draws our eyes to the floor, where a ginger-furred mouse trails tiny drops of steaming blood on the icy ground.

Leira—the mouse—sees it in the same instant we do. Her fur blurs—and then solidifies again. Still fur. Still wrapped around the tiny, fragile frame of a mouse. Her round, glossy eyes go wide, and she lets out another terrified squeak. And Leira Wildfall, the last great shapeshifter of the Wild line, runs away.

chapter thirty-six

seelie

The moment Leira Wildfall has no other allies left, her power and Gossamer's combines. Just as he promised.

All Leira's capability for magic in this moment, all the potential magic she might have used in the remaining years of her life, rushes to Gossamer at once. His face, for a moment, shows nothing but relief. The feeling of finally breaking the surface after too long underwater.

But for Gossamer, a little power is never enough. Rather than sinking in, it rolls off him, nearly knocking me over. His magic and mine are both woven through this realm, bound together, and the sensation as it's magnified rushes straight to my head. We cut him off from Seelie and Unseelie magic for a reason. Everything relied on it.

Another wave of magic, just like the one that tore through the realms to create this place. But this time—it *hurts*. Connected by our magic, I feel everything Gossamer feels, until I can't untangle which magic and which feelings are truly mine. At my side, Egg lets out a little whine as his ears go back.

I fell to pieces once, in the grubby room of an inn on our way to the Mortal's Keep. Then I was so overwhelmed by my senses and my situation that it felt like a gaping wound in my chest. I became an abyss, that *feeling* turning into a swirling emptiness, which turned into a gale of wind inside the room. This is like that—if instead of being pulled in by my emotions, it had all exploded out in a sunburst of excruciating contradictions.

Rage and relief. Sadness and triumph. Hunger and satisfaction. Instead of a windstorm, the fabric of this impossible realm itself shifts around us.

It's not enough, not enough, not enough.

The limitations of this power are pressing down on me, crushing me. I am more than this. I need more than this. If I don't push back, I'm going to collapse.

No—those are Gossamer's thoughts. I can't let him—

Pain and cold. My knees hit the ground. I can't withstand this, can't contain this explosion of power. I've found an unsteady peace with my magic, but years of wrestling with it all flood back in this moment. It wants to *push*, to *expand*. I have to protect everyone—can Egg protect them?

A moment of clarity pierces the fog of feelings. Egg. We needed the firedrake here to burn off the excess magic. If I can secure his help, maybe we can still get this under control before it's too late. He hasn't moved, despite the shivers of fear running down the spines of his back. I don't realize how much his internal flame has warmed me until he suddenly moves away.

I look at Egg, and an unfamiliar creature looks back.

His face is the same: cragged pearlescent scales over a rounded, babyish form. But within his eyes, the soft yellow of a hearth fire, of melted butter and sweet honeycomb, has burned off. He looks at me as if he doesn't recognize me, eyes yellow like sharp glittering gemstones, a house fire licking hungrily up the curtains.

This is *wrong*. He should not have been twisted so quickly, so easily. Not Egg, who napped on my chest and would only eat straight from my hand. Not Egg, who has been bound to me since the moment he hatched by the twined magic of the portal that brought me and Raze home.

My magic, carelessly punching a hole through the realms. Egg's magic, an anchor that tugged me in. And . . .

Gossamer's magic. It was *him*, wasn't it, who created that portal? I took control of it, made the spell my own, but it *was* his. Which means Egg is his creature as much as mine.

No, not Egg. The hard, snarling creature with flame licking at his jaws isn't my Egg. This is the firedrake. A weapon, something to be used for killing and seizing power. As he might have been, if I hadn't been there.

No no no no—

No, please no—

It's too late for thought. Too late to react. The firedrake lifts his head and releases a jet of white flame. Gossamer's silhouetted form raises its arms, as if that will release the storm of emotions I can still feel crushing and pressing.

Sunlight—something this realm, painted in its half-baked shades of blue shadow, was never meant to see—blooms around me. I watch numbly as Aris and Olani raise a shield together, a small dome around all of us.

They don't need to bother. This magic is already all around us, in our lungs, between our fingers. It can't surround us any more than it already has. It can only crash out, overflowing the borders of the Unending Realm—the borders where we left the Seelie and Unseelie Queens, and their forces.

It's too late to warn them, too late to change anything. Gossamer has grown so much stronger than me. The Unending

Realm's magic is hardly mine at all anymore. It's a freezing, bleaching force that devours its way into the faerie realms. By the time the queens realize that their guards are going still and lifeless around them, the spell has already started to claim them.

The Seelie Queen cries out and tries to step away, but her feet are already frozen solid. For the first time, the Unseelie Queen looks sharply at her, just in time to see her lungs seize, silencing her.

"Gossamer," the Unseelie Queen gasps. Her voice is almost lost in the howling wind, but I can still hear a note of almost-mortal desperation. "Don't do this."

At first, I think he's too far away to hear her. But his hands drop, and even from this distance, I can make out the cruel sneer, the triumph at hearing her beg. "Are you afraid of imprisonment? After all those centuries you inflicted on me?" He doesn't wait for an answer she's already too frozen to give. "Don't worry. I'll kill you long, *long* before then."

And with that truth, he claims both monarchs in the same icy grip that holds my parents. I can tell they're still alive, because their outstretched hands are still holding the fragile barriers in place. He'll have to kill them to access their realms' magic again. I know he'll do it, even though the resulting faerie-death explosions might destroy all the worlds. Nothing will be able to protect us—or the other realms—then.

The silence that follows is enough to smother us. A new, thick snowfall that muffles the world's shape. At some point, Aris and Olani dropped their shield.

"This way," Olani pants, practical as ever. I know she's worn out, and just as stunned as the rest of us, but she shepherds us all behind the curtain that once hid the brass cage from the Wintersol party guests. The cage is still here, broken on the floor. We all stand together, shaking from the cold and from everything else, but for a second, the heavy velvet seems to shield us.

Eventually, I have to twitch aside one corner of a curtain to peek out. From across the room, half obscured by the frozen forms of party guests, I see the slope of Gossamer's shoulders, heaving with heavy breaths. We have a moment, just a moment, before he regroups and comes at us again.

Raze's hand slips into mine, warm and alive. How is he still *warm*? How could anything be, in a place like this?

I turn and look at everyone, memorizing their faces, every worried line and gleaming, hardly-held-back tear. This is it. Surrender, or death. Maybe it's too late to surrender, and we don't even need to worry about deciding.

Isolde's cold fingers squeeze my other hand. Her eyes, sparkling with dozens of tiny lights, are just as close to tears as everyone else's, but her jaw is firm. She struggles to start the sentence, and I read a thousand apologies and comforting words in the silence. In the end, she doesn't need to say any of them—I understand.

Isolde cracks a watery version of that smile: the one that always gets us both into trouble.

"I have . . . one last idea," she says, other hand fidgeting with an iron dagger at her belt. "But you're not going to like it."

PART FOUR

Gossamer watches his changeling wordlessly split from the mortals as they slink out from their hidden corner like scolded children. They all stand shoulder to shoulder: the shapeshifter, the one who wields light like a dagger, the healer. The only one who flinches, who fights an internal battle not to reach for Seelie and drag her back to them, is the twin. The second changeling, dressed all in black, a wreck of tired eyes and wisps of short hair mussed by the wind. She stops with the others, and Seelie keeps moving, sailing toward him like a ship to an empty horizon.

She is lovely as only something fleeting can be. The colors of a sunset slipping into nightfall, a flower plucked just before full bloom, a mortal girl who knows she will die before he draws his next breath. Gossamer watches her approach, draped in a dress that was almost as fine as faerie-made before all this started, now ripped and stained and burned, layers of skirts fisted in her trembling hands so she won't trip over them. Her hair is pulled up and back, so there's nothing to hide her face. Her gleaming eyes never leave his, each line in her face hard and sharply drawn.

Gossamer feels his lips curl into a smile, a wild animal's warning snarl. "I should kill you," he says.

The girl smiles back, a soft and ordinary expression, and it's because of this that he keeps forgetting she's a worthy adversary and not some mortal who wandered into the wrong part of the woods. "But then you'd never get to hear my deal."

He's greedy. Always has been. It's not a vice, as mortals think, for a faerie to want to know how much they can hold. So far, Gossamer has found that no matter how much he takes into his grasp, it never seems to be enough. Which is why, even though a warning sounds in his head, the clear and rational thought that Iselia will not bargain away everything she's fought for so quickly, he chooses to hear her out.

"The stakes are higher than ever before. What could you possibly offer me?"

"My magic. All of it. In exchange for the firedrake, and the safety of my family and friends."

"No tricks this time," he hisses. Viper-quick, he snatches her wrist and squeezes until something pops, forcing her to drop the iron dagger hidden in her skirts. It rings against the stone at their feet, but not loud enough to cover her gasp of shock and pain. He freezes, fingers still wrapped tight around her racing pulse, trying to sense any more iron on her. There's nothing but a cloud of magic, intoxicatingly near.

He steps forward into it, slowly letting her wrist drop. Forward, until they're nearly nose-to-nose, her eyes still burning furiously into his.

"It's a deal," Gossamer says, low enough so only she can hear. This is better than dragging the scraps of magic away from her one at a time, better than waiting for her death at his hand or the cruel inevitability of Fate. This is—finally—victory and revenge. Proof to her and himself that while she may have won a skirmish or two, the war was always going to be his.

The shining glee of victory fills his senses as he reaches out to wrap his cold fingers around hers. Her skin is warm, her palm a little damp, her fear a melody in the air between them. He digs his nails into her flesh a little too hard, just because he can.

And then she digs in right back, hauls him even closer, and grins right in his face. "Idiot." Her shift in intonation, the uneven sharpness of her smile, the tiny lights dancing in her eyes. It's all wrong.

Because this is not his changeling.

Gossamer tries to let go, but Isolde won't let him, and it's too late anyway. The deal is already made. He gave her everything she asked for, and in exchange he gets—

Nothing. Despair sinks his soul, crashing down over him in opaque ink-dark waves. He can't have come this far, just to be stopped by such a petty trick. It can't be over. It can't have all been for nothing.

No . . . not nothing. He feels a glimmer of hope, testing the boundaries of this agreement. The vow of a changeling made in a mortal's perfect image, one who can't wield magic, who bears only the scraps of power woven into her very creation. Magic that is inseparable from her hands and hair and wide, unflinching eyes. Her magic.

Magic that is his now.

chapter thirty-seven

ISOLDE

Gossamer disappears before my eyes, leaving nothing but a chill on my fingertips. I have just enough time to realize I've made a huge mistake.

And then I have nothing.

chapter thirty-eight

SEELIE

My braid is heavy as a severed limb in my pocket. Short, loose hairs still ragged at the ends from Isolde's dagger tickle my nose, my lips, get in my eyes. I don't know how she stands it.

I didn't think it would actually work, that even with our hair cut to the same length and our clothes swapped, Isolde and I could be mistaken for each other. As the magic of their bargain seals itself around them, there's a moment of panic in Gossamer's eyes.

Then he vanishes.

I try to gasp, but the knot in my chest is too tight. We can't be so lucky, can we? I try to remember the exact wording we agreed on, to figure out if it somehow banishes Gossamer from this realm or imprisons him. It seems too good to be true.

Isolde slumps a little, then stands up straight. She moves on a slight delay, each bend of her joints not quite lining up as fluidly as usual.

She's in pain. Something's wrong. I break away from the group, unable to stop myself from running to help her any longer. "Where'd he go?" I gasp. "Sol—"

Her head snaps up, her eyes meeting mine, and I stop short several yards away. It feels like my heels are sinking into the frozen ground, like there's a weight on my chest I can't slip off. When Isolde looks at me, it's like seeing a stranger looking out from the windows of your home.

"Not quite," she says.

It takes everything in me not to fall to the ground then and there, to scream and lose control because this can't be happening *again*.

Last time was just practice, the voice of all my nightmares whispers in the back of my mind. *This time is for real.*

Because the thing facing me is not my sister, and it wants me dead.

"Really, Iselia?" Gossamer says in my sister's voice. There's an echo to it, a hollowness that doesn't belong there. "You expected that little trick to work? As if you haven't been playing into my hands with each step you've made."

"No." My voice is almost as unrecognizable, a pained scrape.

He takes a step toward me, fingers flexing and twisting in the air. "*You* released me. *You* created this realm for me. And now you've provided me with the last thing I needed to return to my full power." He glances down at Isolde, wearing my borrowed clothes. The gown looks like it's been dragged through the Dragon Lands, burned and ripped and stained, the full skirts reduced to layers of tattered ribbons, but the remaining pale fabric still delicately flutters in the breeze. "Not the *ideal* form, but it will work for now."

"Leave her alone!" I'm surprised when I finally find the courage to speak, and my voice sounds like the high screech of mountain wind. "She's not part of this. This is between you and me, Gossamer."

It's a weak argument, one that doesn't make any sense, and both of us know it. Even appealing to his pride at this point is useless. Isolde's smirk has never looked quite so pointy. "Not anymore, *Iselia*." The last word is pointed and dripping with venom, because he's been in my head, and he knows that my sister literally never calls me by my full name.

And that, for some reason, is what makes the hot tears spill over, blurring my vision and streaking my cheeks with tingling warmth. Trying to hold them back is impossible, so I just let them fall and wipe away the droplets clinging to my chin with the back of my hand. My grief and my fury are too strong to ignore, too powerful to suppress, so I release them.

And my magic rushes in, power overflowing the hollowness where my heart is supposed to be. We're indoors, with no clouds overhead, but thunder rumbles deep in my bones as the storm within fights to escape.

Isolde could still be in there. When Gossamer took control of my limbs in the Unseelie forest, I was still conscious, still fighting him, even as I felt myself slipping away. I cut into my own palm with the same iron dagger that killed Briar to weaken him enough to take control again. Maybe—if we can find a way to do the same to Isolde—

It'll mean running my sister through with iron. But there's a way to do that nonlethally, right? There must be. As long as I'm breathing, I won't give up on her.

This time is for real.

I push the thought away, but it won't stop echoing in the stormy swirl of my mind. The overflow of emotions burns me from the inside out, boiling through my veins with each heartbeat. I am trying to think of what Isolde would do if the situations were reversed, what trick she would play, what strategy she would form in the moment, but each thought scatters like dust in the wind.

I am not Isolde.

I am only myself. And I can do nothing but rage until my magic swells in the air around us, a force vibrating with enough ferocity to make my bones hum. So much power and nowhere to direct it—not at my enemy. Not at my sister.

I let everything go and just *feel.* I am the frigid wind as it whips around the shapes of so many frozen bodies, and I am the flames that jump up to greet me in my path, and I am the empty void of a future without Isolde that claws a painful hole in my chest. I'm the unending scream in the air, a sound so wretched and pitiful I know it should be embarrassing.

What am I supposed to do now?

It's clear that everyone expects me to unleash my power on the faerie. To use all this magic to save the day, to tear apart the fabric of the worlds until I find one where Isolde is safe. Isn't that what I expect, too?

But when I try, all the instincts that have guided my magic for so long are silent. They don't provide me with a next action, or with the power to execute it.

The wind drops, and so do I. I fall to my knees, barely catching myself on my hands to stop from landing face-first on the stone. Even the weight of standing is too much. I have nothing left to give this fight. Nothing left to give Isolde.

Everything is still and silent and unseeing as I kneel there, shaking, begging my body and my magic to do anything else. But it's useless. I can't stand any more than I can stop the hot streaks of tears that roll down my cheeks to splash my fingers. I'm vaguely aware of footsteps, the rustle of fabric as someone crouches in front of me. Cool fingers tilt my chin up gently.

I stare into Gossamer's eyes, a strange, flat black in Isolde's face.

My nose is running, but it seems he doesn't care about the dampness on his fingertips. He offers me a small smile that is for a moment so like hers that my stomach turns. Then he reaches out for my hand, turns it palm up, and presses something smooth into my grip. I can't move. He folds my fingers so I won't drop it, and I look down to see an iron dagger.

"One last chance," he says in a light, teasing voice. "In case you were thinking of disposing of me as you did Briar."

My hand goes numb, the sickness rolling so far through my body that I have to fight not to gag.

Gossamer is offering me the chance to kill him and my sister both, smiling serenely because he's secure in the knowledge that I won't. Even if it means saving my parents and half of Auremore and all the worlds. He's toying with me, because he knows he's already won.

But what if he's not? What if this is Isolde's last act, influencing him to arm me with iron, to save her from a fate entwined with his? If it is her, I owe her . . .

Anything she'd ask of me. Even death.

Gossamer's grin turns toothy. "Having second thoughts, Iselia?" he whispers.

Fresh tears fill my eyes, blurring my sister's face. It's too unfair to ask me to do this. It's too unfair not to do this. With my free hand, I reach up to cup her cheek, wishing there was some way she could show me she's still in there. To know I'm doing the right thing. My fingers squeeze so tight around the dagger's smooth leather grip that my hand shakes.

This time is for real.

Briar's dying moments replay in my head, a vivid image of what it looks like to run Isolde through with pure iron. I know what I have to do.

Gossamer realizes it the instant before I do. His eyes widen, glassy with fear, as my hand moves—quick and irrevocable as a bolt of lightning.

The dagger clatters to the stone floor between us, leaving both my hands free to grip his face. Giving him nowhere to look but directly in my eyes as my magic blurs the world around us and I delve into his memories.

chapter thirty-nine

SEELIE

I've done this spell before. My magic remembers how. Never mind that both times I've attempted it, it's knocked me out. Never mind that Gossamer is a thousand times more powerful than Leira Wildfall, more stubborn than my father, even fiercer than my mother.

I've done this spell before.

And I can do it once more.

It's a simple process, I try to convince myself, though I know I should be seeing memories and bits of Gossamer's mind, and yet there's nothing but a dense white fog. Gossamer, now that he's taken control of Isolde, is no more than a collection of memories and magic somewhere in her mind. I can remove them, just as I did with my parents' memories of us. As I tried to do with Leira and the firedrake.

The process might kill him—which, in turn, might set off

an explosion of magic that will kill Isolde. Still, I like our odds better with this magic than anything involving an iron blade.

I stand in the fog and wait, calling those memories to me. It's a sensation similar to controlling the wind, invisible currents that twist around me and slip between my fingers. The fog stirs and swirls, and for a second, I think I can make out the shapes of something—*anything*—in the fog. But then it condenses again, an oppressive cloud of stillness that pushes into my lungs.

I push back. The fog doesn't want me to move, but I do. Each step is a battle, struggling to find footing in terrain I can't make out, rough and slippery like climbing a mountain of ice. When I look down, it's harder to see my own boots than it was a second ago. The fog must be growing thicker. I hope that means I'm going in the right direction.

There isn't the howl of the wind or the sound of a mocking voice, no sound but my own breathing. It feels wrong. Leira's mind was a riot of color, a hundred different points in time all clamoring for my attention. Gossamer's mind is too blank, too still to be real. He couldn't function like this. He must be holding back from me intentionally.

Maybe he's scared. He knows I've beaten him before. He knows that, this time, there's no reason for me to show mercy. I try to focus on those thoughts, in case he has any awareness of me, to smother my own fear in deadly certainty.

My foot slips on something, and I barely manage to catch my balance before smacking into the ground. I can feel that I'm looking down, unsteady, but my limbs are even more faint. The awareness that something is wrong here takes a bite out of my forced confidence, sending a shiver through me. Perhaps it's not just the fog. What if I'm fading?

What if I'm playing into Gossamer's hands, each step moving me closer to disappearing entirely?

Well then, at least Isolde and I will be together. While he

wreaks havoc on what's left of the world using both our combined magic.

The fire of determination and hope that pushed me this far is slowly going cold, giving way to the bleak storm of emotion I barely managed to pull myself from. Why did I think I could do this? Why did I think that my magic could ever be more than an accidental force, rising and snuffing out with the whims of Fate? I have held blame for every victory and every defeat, every injury I've caused, everyone I've saved, but maybe none of it was ever my doing.

Maybe I'm nothing more than a tiny boat floating on a tide that I'll never understand. There's nothing special about me or my attempt at controlling the sea that tosses me without a care. I thought, for so long, that the whole world was against me, but now I see the truth—that I was never special enough for that.

And not strong enough to save Isolde. And not good enough to save myself.

Each step becomes heavier and heavier, until I finally give up on dragging the nebulous weight of a dissolving consciousness any further. I want to take just one more step, to keep moving until there's nothing left of me, but I'm simply not strong enough to fight anymore.

I stand, frozen, and watch the grayish outline of my hands get swallowed up in the same white fog that blankets everything around me.

I drop, but don't feel the impact in my knees. There's nothing except the sinking, the emptiness, the all-consuming numbness.

I might well be right back where I started. None of Gossamer's memories are coming to me. And this time, there's no one to drag my body away in the outside world, to save me from the effects of my own magic.

Maybe it's better this way. To simply dissolve. Maybe I can

find a nice memory of Isolde's to take shelter in, let her hold me one last time in this world.

Maybe.

The wind around me gentles. I'm losing the sensation in my limbs, losing any connection to myself, but it doesn't seem so bad. I breathe in deeply, then release the air slowly.

I've waited too long to admit defeat. There isn't enough left of my magic—of *me*—to even call Isolde's memories. For the first time in my life, I am very much, truly, alone.

A single tear—this one cool as a long-forgotten cup of tea—trickles from the corner of my eye, taking its time to run down the curve of my cheek. I know it'll be the last thing I ever feel.

"I'm sorry, Isolde," I whisper, with the last breath I have. Her name echoes all around me.

And then . . .

The echoing doesn't stop. It fades and grows indistinct, and then it's *my* name, repeated back to me over and over again.

"*Seelie!*" cries my disembodied voice.

But it's not my voice. It's Isolde's.

The breath turns into a gasp. Everything I had released zips back to me in an instant, forming a leaden, chilled shape around me. It's heavy and hard to control but it's *mine*. I force myself to stand, to drag my feet another step, to call out again: "Isolde!"

The echo returns, just as faint, but still there. "Seelie!"

My sister is still in here. Still calling for me. And I'm going to find her.

chapter forty

ISOLDE

My sister has come to rescue me, but she can't see me.

Honestly, I thought I was a goner already. As soon as the bargain I made with Gossamer sealed itself, running me over with magic—magic I could *feel*, for the first time in my life, visceral on my skin, which actually explains a lot about Seelie—I knew it was too late for me. His consciousness took control of my face and my limbs with a speed that would have been embarrassing if I didn't at least have the excuse that I'd never had to defend myself from magic before. It was a totally foreign sensation—and then it was over, because there wasn't enough of me left to feel it. Forced out of my own mind, dissolving into nothingness . . .

When a pull called me out of the dark. In that moment, I felt the instinctive certainty that Seelie talks about, like developing a new sense. One that recognized my sister's magic, twining through my memories, and hauled me back enough to cry for help.

Help that may or may not come. Now that I've regained some awareness, I can tell that Seelie is sinking fast. She's fighting it, but I don't know if she's strong enough. Maybe, even if it's too late to save me, I can convince her to save herself.

Gossamer has been suspiciously quiet this whole time. His thoughts, which at first were so loud and overpowering they erased any ability to think for myself, have gone quiet. We're in a blank wasteland—metaphorically, I guess. In the real world, my/Gossamer's face is probably still in Seelie's hands, trapped in a frozen world, waiting to see how all this shakes out.

He's hiding. I had no idea that was something you could do, but his magic is beyond either of us. I'm sure he's hoping this emptiness will be enough to make us fade away, until we're no more than a bad dream, and he comes back to life in my shape wielding Seelie's magic. I don't know how, but I know we're going to stop that, if it's the last thing we do.

"Seelie!" I call again, trying to get a better sense for where my sister is other than *here*. To reach out and grab her hands and will us both to be stronger.

I think I hear my name in the echo of my voice, but it's hard to be sure. I take a step forward, not knowing if it matters which direction I walk. My foggy mind is struggling to remember anything Seelie has said about how she wrangles her magic, to force this unfriendly landscape into submission.

Focus. Focus is always an element. I squeeze my eyes shut and find a thought to latch on to—that last night before we left Auremore. Our seventeenth birthday, stargazing and eating cake and telling the story of how our family came to be. The air was warm and smoky, with a hint of fall on the breeze. Seelie's fingers kept worrying over the silvery enchantment in her skin, and the stars twinkled with promise of adventure.

The memory binds us together, pulling us closer. Now I'm

sure I can hear her voice, hear her calling to me. I can't really run in this metaphorical state, but everything in me screams to forget that and try anyway.

When we were eight, I was the fastest kid in our village. I remember racing in the town square, and seeing Seelie out of the corner of my eye—slowly moving closer to the others playing with dolls, humming and bouncing her doll along the ground. She sat near them, her eyes focused on her own toy, just wanting to be included by being close. They all got up and moved away. She followed. They got up again, and this time someone pushed her into the dirt. I didn't hear what they said, but it made her cry. I abandoned my race and ran to her.

Just as I'm running now, each step growing stronger. I see a silhouette through the fog, slowly taking shape into the same small and defeated girl that cried into the dust that day. I reach for her, call her name again.

And Seelie looks up. She stands, her arms reaching out toward me.

In my mind, I see that same little girl, another day that summer. We walked the riverbank, collecting smooth pebbles and feathers and other tiny childhood treasures. I chattered on the whole time, jumping from topic to topic the same way I jumped between the slick stones and mossy logs, and Seelie followed me the whole time. Our struggles were different, but I grew up used to being misunderstood and cut off and asked to stop talking, and never fully realized the toll it took on me, except in that peaceful moment. Later that night, I cried when I thought I'd lost all those little tokens, only to find that Seelie had removed them from the pockets of my carelessly discarded clothes and carefully organized it all into a neat, straight line.

She has always taken care of me, in her quieter way, as fiercely as I've guarded her. But we're not those fragile little kids anymore. Knowing she doesn't need me in the same way she used to doesn't feel like disappointment. I can see how much she's changed—how much we both have. And I'm so proud of both of us. We have faced impossible odds again and again, but we're still here.

Together.

I crash into Seelie's arms, and she's real and solid to the touch. I can feel the wrinkled fabric of our swapped clothes, her fingers digging hard into my sleeve as she sobs and smiles all at once. I can sense her magic, still pulling me in, like an anchor in a stormy sea. *Our* magic. Two sides of the same coin.

"No!"

The fog disappears all at once, but instead of standing in a memory, we're in a room of pure, smooth marble. This must be what Gossamer's imprisonment looked like, long centuries of captivity that permanently changed his sense of self. A huge pair of eyes opens overhead to glare down at us—then another, and another. All the same cool, clear gray, only varying slightly in size. They keep appearing, blinking open, until the once-blank walls are a constellation of furious gazes.

"Stop that," Gossamer's voice seethes. "This is impossible! You shouldn't be able to find each other. That's not how memory magic works. There are *rules*—"

I turn to Seelie, a crooked smile on my face. "I think he's scared."

She returns it. "Obviously. He just realized we're stronger than him."

And then we move as if we've rehearsed this a thousand times. I'm delighted to find that my spectral form still has her knives—I can worry about them being *that* intrinsic to my identity later, when our lives aren't at risk—and I unsheathe one smoothly, taking aim.

"Wait!" Gossamer's voice thunders, filling the space. "You don't know what will happen! It could destroy her mind—you don't understand the consequences—!"

He couldn't speak the words if they weren't true. And he

might be right. Seelie glances at me one more time, her hands twitching slightly as they do when she's summoning her magic. This is what the spell looks like from the inside, I realize. The spell that stole away our parents' memories of us, memories she captured in a jar, memories we thought were lost forever. They woke the next day and lived their lives for years without remembering us. But Gossamer is little more than a memory himself, no life to return to outside this marble room locked away in my head. It's impossible to guess what will become of him—or me—if we destroy this. I doubt Seelie knows, either.

I nod—I'm willing to risk it. I don't know what will happen, but I know that if I'm going down, I'm taking Gossamer with me.

I pull my arm back and let the knife fly. Years of target practice pay off, and I watch it whistle through the air, directly into one of the first eyes that opened. The instant it makes contact, Seelie raises her hands, and lightning pours into the dagger. The eye bursts, white-gold sparks of lightning shooting out in all directions, until the room is covered in crackling energy. A pained faerie scream, inhuman and high-pitched, splits the air.

Then it all goes dark.

chapter forty-one

SEELIE

The darkness only lasts the space of a blink before we're in the faerie forest again. It's disorienting until I notice the haze around the edges, the slight shimmer giving away the fact that this isn't real—just Gossamer's memories playing out around us. Whatever defenses he had put between me and the memory spell have gone down, and I can feel the overwhelming fullness of a life thousands of years long at my fingertips.

Pulling the memories this time is, paradoxically, easier than drawing out the bonds between us and my parents, or Leira and the firedrake. I don't have to sift through them, because I'm just grabbing everything at once. A century in, it starts getting hard to hold, like an armful of snow. I can't let any trace of Gossamer escape this time. I hang on tighter, pouring all my magic and then more into the enchantment, not caring what the price of calling on such power might do to me.

It is not, as you might expect, the story of a lost and confused faerie child. I see, in the span of generations, a boy who was given everything. Always. And yet, everything was never enough. It wasn't enough for him to take, to have, to hold—he needed to deprive others. Whether it was physical or intangible, something he wanted or not, didn't matter.

Gossamer is a long-limbed not-quite-adolescent, too old to cry to get what he wants and too young to understand why. His sisters are so much older than him and he does not understand why; they rule their own realms and he fits seamlessly into both, unable to put down roots, and he does not understand why. They tell him that the day will come that he must choose which realm he will swear fealty to. That they will both welcome him, and he will still be able to travel back and forth as he wishes.

But it will not be his.

Nothing ever truly is.

He does not cry, this time. He does not cry ever again.

In a blur I feel rather than see, he grows from a small, wild, beautiful child into a tall, cunning, terrifying full-grown faerie, and no one ever steps up to stop him.

It's too much to contain. I may be a changeling, one who has been drawing on the power of a faerie for weeks now, but I am still just a mortal. The scope of a faerie lifetime is too vast for me to understand, much less to compress into a physical form, like the dried forget-me-nots of my parents' memories. It's going to spill over, to explode, and even if I can somehow manage to destroy Gossamer, there's no way I can channel the explosion somewhere safe.

I'm in too far to give up, though, so I force myself to breathe through the panic.

In this dreamlike space, I sense Isolde nearby. "Seelie . . ." she says.

Gossamer is this close to holding the Mortal Realm—a useless, empty place he could have turned into the most spectacular realm of all—when it slips from his grip. It is pulled, taken from him by his sisters and the worthless mortals they allow to command them. For all their words about the fleeting lives of mortals, they still put so much stock in the creatures. He looks at his sisters with the same wide, round eyes that always got him what he wanted, but he does not cry. He knows they won't have the courage to kill him.

He laughs to himself, knowing he will soon be free. Even as his body betrays him and his blood freezes. Even as he turns to cold, unforgiving stone.

Being stone, after all, is not the same as being dead.

"Seelie," Isolde repeats, bringing me back to myself. "Let me help."

I try to protest that there's nothing she can do, but before I get the chance, she grabs my wrist and squeezes her eyes shut. Her brows crease in concentration. The pressure releases slightly, the impossible weight growing easier to bear. Maybe it's because we're still technically battling it out in her mind, and Isolde has power here.

Enough power to make the next few centuries whip past at a speed too fast to really follow—there is magic and mortals and conflict, fire and devastation, and then smooth blankness that goes on long enough for me to start worrying something's wrong.

Then my face. My memories. The invigorating chill of the Unending Realm.

And then we're here again—all three of us, hands wrapped around a ball of something shiny and impossible to hold. A faerie's lifetime.

Gossamer looks at me, eyes almost wide enough to be pitiable. I think this act is so effective because it's not truly an act—at his core, he is a small, wretched creature, who will never stop trying to pull apart anything he sees as a threat. Which is everything. He manages to summon anger, baring sharp teeth and flashing quartz eyes.

"Iselia," he says, voice thick with emotion. "You can't do this to me."

Isolde holds her breath. Maybe I can't. I'm clutching all his memories and his magic now, but they won't budge. Pressure is building again, the inevitable explosion growing nearer with each heartbeat.

Then I realize I don't have *everything*. There is still a scrap of Gossamer's magic left in me, and while it's true that it may be the only thing holding this enchantment together, I can't leave it aside. I know there's every chance I'll lose control or drop dead the second I release the faerie's power.

But I really, *really* hope I won't.

I summon all his magic, that frantic Unseelie hum in my pulse, and pour it into the enchantment. I let it go, like opening my fingers around a handful of sand in a river.

When it's all gone, it doesn't feel like missing something. It feels like something missing has just fallen into place. The ability to hold back the explosion is slipping, but Isolde looks at me with blazing, defiant eyes, holding strong.

"No, I can't," I tell Gossamer. "But *we* can."

I open my eyes to the Unending Realm, my hands still resting on either side of Isolde's face. My vision is full of flashing lights, a growing pain in my head making it hard to concentrate on the tiny sun resting in my hands. The enchantment holding all of Gossamer captive has come with me to the real world unchanged, and my time to do something with it is quickly slipping away.

I can't just release it. I can't keep holding it. I'm afraid of what will happen if I move my hands and lose Isolde's help, but I'm also putting her at risk. I need to find somewhere to put this power, quick, before it can't be contained any longer. The pain is getting sharper, a knife between my eyes. I squeeze my eyes shut against it, my head bowing to mirror my sister's.

Something nudges my arm from below. I gasp, looking up sharply, expecting to see Isolde looking back at me. Instead, I see a scaly snout and bright golden eyes. Egg is once more himself.

Maybe when I fully separated my magic from Gossamer's—when I cut myself from that power—I freed him from its influence, too. He nudges my wrist again, his eyes locking onto my shaking hands. To the violently bright glow of white magic I've managed to pull from Isolde's head.

"What?" The uncontrollable tremor, sparks of pain racing from behind my eyes all the way to my fingertips, is getting worse. I'm going to let go in a second, whether I want to or not, just because I'm losing control of my hands. Black spots are starting to fill my vision, making it hard to tell exactly what Egg is doing in response. He nudges me again, gently insistent, like he's trying to push me back.

Let go.

It's not safe for Isolde. I can't let go. I'm the only thing standing between her and destruction.

Soon, the choice won't be mine anymore. Releasing Gossamer in this form might just give him another chance to take shape. I can't allow that, either. No one can do this but me.

Let go!

In the seconds before the pain blacks everything out, I finally see everything clearly: Would I rather remain in control and doom us all—or finally trust that I don't have to be the one holding everything together all the time, and at least give us a chance at surviving?

I don't know if Egg can absorb this magic. I don't know what will happen if I let go.

But I do it anyway.

The pain disappears so quickly that, at first, I'm left overwhelmed and breathless by its absence. The captured explosion expands, flying up above Isolde's head. I catch her before she can fall, watching it as it ascends over us.

And then stops.

Egg's head lifts to the sky, his wings spreading behind him as he opens his mouth and lets loose a jet of the hottest, brightest flame I've ever seen. It's like watching a comet stopped in the sky, a trail of fire tied to this fallen star above our heads. Egg's fire turns blue and gold as it covers the surface of the enchantment, turning the cold whiteness into a dazzling array of colors.

And then it all explodes.

My vision goes fully white, and then slowly the shadows of the world start to etch themselves in stark black. Briar died in darkness, and while I sensed her magic dispersing into the Unseelie forest, it happened invisibly. Gossamer's faerie-death explosion, ignited by firedrake flame, is a true spectacle—ironically, I think he would have loved it.

I also think there's still a solid chance it's going to kill us all, since I have no idea what the effects of a wall of pure magical energy slamming into a person are, and this time, Olani isn't here to shield us. Isolde is still out cold. I shield as much of her with my body as I can, squeezing her hand tight. Maybe everyone who's preserved in frozen time will be fine. Gossamer said nothing could hurt them like this, didn't he? After we're gone, maybe the faerie queens can find a way to put them all right, and everyone will be okay. The explosion is overhead for now, but the flames will rain down on us before long.

Won't they?

The white of the explosion starts to bleed in streaks of blue and gold. I blink my dazzled eyes to see Egg, still posed with his head to the sky, still blazing with fire. I feel a spark of hope. There's enough magic here to fuel him for ages—but he's so young. Can he really control that much?

Maybe if I help him. If we help each other. With Isolde's head still in my lap, I reach my hands up in the air, sensing the magic's flow. Egg is just holding it at bay for now, but maybe, together, we can *do* something with it. My hands sweep through the air, directing the explosion like a paintbrush. The still-blue flames of the torches around the edges of the room jump to life, turning a cheerful yellow and filling the room with warmth.

The swirl of colors moves in a controlled dance, a thousand sunsets flowing into each other at once. It advances from the edges of the room in, weaving like a needle and thread. Gossamer's magic, mending the holes between the worlds. Knots that previously seemed impossible to untangle fall apart at the magic's gentle touch, guided by my intentions and Egg's strength.

Slowly, color and warmth return to the room. I'm so focused on sweeping the magic through the air that, at first, I don't notice the hum of life. People are waking. I can see them from the corner of my eye, blinking their way from a haze, murmuring in amazement at the swirl of colors. My arms are straining, physical and mental exhaustion threatening to pull me under. I keep going, refusing to leave any detail untouched by the enchantment. Everything will be as it was, and everything will be as it should be.

I lose track of my surroundings after that, all my senses narrowing to the brilliance overhead and the tingle of magic on my fingertips and the weight of Isolde's head in my lap. Just when I think I might black out, it stops. I panic, startling back to alertness, terrified I've lost focus and ruined it all.

I try blinking away spots, but these two remain: gashes between the realms too ragged to simply stitch shut. Like a wound that will heal on its own, I'm afraid that pouring any more magic into the portals will break that equilibrium. They're stable for now, which is more than I could have hoped for.

Egg roars, shaking out his wings one last time. I release the last bit of magic—just enough to explode into a flurry of snowflakes that slowly drift down over us all.

Isolde's eyes flutter open at the cold brush of a snowflake on her cheek. She smiles up at me weakly, and I smile back, ignoring the fact that my vision is blurry and going black around the edges. I'm spent, but I'm alive. *We're* alive.

My head slumps, my eyes falling shut. The tone of the room takes on a strange quality, volume rising until it's all an indistinct blend of faerie and human voices. A heavy hand falls on my shoulder, and I manage to crack my eyes open to see Raze. Olani is with him, wasting no time with her healing magic—one hand on my arm and the other on Isolde's face.

"You did it," Raze says, voice broken with joy, low with awe.

I lean into his touch, letting my eyes close, ignoring the cold tears that have started up again.

It doesn't last long before I'm interrupted by a shriek, the sudden weight of someone's whole body flung at me, and the familiar smell of lavender oil.

My mother's arms around me are stronger than any spell, bringing me back to life. She clings to me and Isolde so tight I wonder if she'll ever let us go again. My father, on the other side, is openly weeping. They didn't pause to notice anyone else, which means we're in a sort of awkward six-person sandwich with a dragon's snout digging into my arm and Aris to the side.

Mami seems to realize this, too, taking a break from repeating our names like a chant to look up at me with bright, tear-filled eyes. "Who— Why— What—?"

Isolde and I manage to glance at each other from opposite sides of our mother, and we both stumble awkwardly with where to even begin explaining.

"Never mind, what matters is that we're all here," Mami says, this time intentionally including our friends in her embrace. They join the *Look* that is already passing between me and Isolde, but the conclusion is the same: Our mother's love is inescapable and just a little smothering.

We stay like that until another flash of light, and the gasp of the crowd that follows, makes it impossible not to look up. Standing in front of the rifts to the Seelie and Unseelie Realms, like two portraits in a frame, are their queens. Their glow is dimmed a little, perhaps because they're each out of their own realm, so that for the first time I can truly see both of them.

The way they're facing each other, faces painted in near-identical expressions of shock, it almost seems like this is the first time they're truly seeing each other. Silver and gold, life and decay, a perfect mirror of wide eyes and wrinkled brows. The Seelie Queen moves first, reaching a hand toward her sister before stopping short, like she's encountered an invisible wall between them.

Then the Unseelie Queen, disregarding any concern for who might be watching, launches herself forward. Arms open, she wraps her sister in a hug that is immediately matched, and both of them let out a cry like the break in the heat before a summer storm. The two faerie sisters cling to each other for dear life, sorrow and joy radiating out from the center of the room. The wave of emotion that ripples out from them is enough to make new tears spring to my eyes. Looking around, it seems no one is untouched by the sheer power of it.

"This is bad, isn't it?" the Seelie Queen sniffles eventually. "I mean, the changeling's bargain remains unfulfilled as long as the realms are entangled like this. We should—should probably—"

"I missed you," her sister laughs, a little wetly. "But I didn't miss all your hand-wringing over the *rules*."

The Seelie Queen sighs and shakes her head. Finally, the two part a little, their glowing eyes searching the crowd around them until they find . . .

"You," the Unseelie Queen says, staring me dead-on. "You tricked us."

It takes a moment for me to realize what she's talking about. I told them my goal was to return everything exactly how it was, and however much I managed to stitch back up the damage between worlds, they still remain slightly entangled. Open to each other, in a way they weren't before. But on the other hand, me leaving two very convenient portals open to the Mortal Realm has given them neutral ground on which to meet for the first time in centuries, so it's really not *that* bad, is it?

I take a deep breath and pull myself free from the group.

"Seelie—" my mother starts, pulling back. Unable to let me go.

Instead of pulling harder, I look her in the eyes—warm hazel, a shade lighter than mine. I manage to hold eye contact for a second before I let my gaze drop to her hand, squeezing my wrist to draw me back protectively. I smile. "It's okay, Mami," I whisper. "I can handle it."

She swallows, forcing down something I know she's dying to say. And then she lets go. Papa offers me his hand, helping me to my feet and giving my shoulder one last squeeze.

I'm pleasantly surprised to find I can stand, though my legs shake and threaten to give out. I test them out with a few wobbly steps toward the queens, all too aware that every single one of the hundreds of pairs of eyes in this room is on me. "I did my best," I say, as firmly as possible. "We defeated Gossamer, and I destroyed the Unending Realm. It's not my fault that some things are just *different* now."

They both frown down at me, and the attention is enough to make my skin start to itch, like standing in direct sunlight for too long.

"But . . . maybe it's better this way?" I finish, unable to stop my hands from fidgeting and wringing together.

A murmur rushes through the room, faerie voices indistinguishable from human ones. I hope they're agreeing with me. A slight rustle draws my attention, and I turn to see Isolde standing beside me, surrounded by our friends and our family. They're too distracted to notice a small black cat making his way through the group, right until he makes his way to Olani and plops himself down on her shoes.

"*Different*," the Unseelie Queen repeats, as if she's testing out the taste of the syllables. "As in, keeping the borders between realms open?"

Isolde nods, swaying on her feet a little. I link her arm in mine to help keep her upright, but her voice is strong as she says, "Our realms have never been truly separate."

"We could see each other," the Seelie Queen muses, giving her sister a sideways smile. "And the mortals, too, I suppose. Better to intervene before they let things get like this again." The slightest brush of her hand in the air has all the grandeur of a huge, sweeping gesture, taking in the whole manor—the whole city—the whole *world*.

"Right," I say. "And . . . changelings shouldn't be forced to choose one world or the other. I'm sure there are others like me, and we could help—you know, translate. To make all the worlds better. For everyone." I realize that we're sort of volunteering Wildline Manor for the center of this new, open system, and glance back at Raze and Aris. "Assuming that's something people want."

It takes them a second to realize I'm addressing them, and then their stunned expressions are comically similar. They seem to have a silent conversation, each asking something and answering it all at once, before Raze gestures for Aris to speak. She turns and beams up at the faerie queens.

"We would be honored to be included."

The two queens give each other another meaningful look before smiles break over their faces—the Seelie Queen's as brilliant as the dawn, and the Unseelie Queen's a quiet, closed-lip peace.

"Then I suppose it's settled," the Seelie Queen says.

"And we owe you thanks, Iselia Graygrove, the Iron Dagger, ambassador to all worlds."

"Oh." I don't need to hear the room's response to the title for it to make my face heat. "'Seelie' is fine," I say, fidgeting with a tiny flame at my fingertips. The movement quiets my mind enough for me to look up and smile, meeting the force of their twin gazes head-on. "Just 'Seelie.'"

chapter forty-two

ISOLDE

The sun sets early in midwinter, but the manor's ballroom is incandescent with light and color. Cheerful yellow candles clash with the pale glow of the portals, lighting up all the long, heavy tables that have been pushed together to make room for everyone at our belated Wintersol feast.

Instead of the rich and powerful, the crowd is mostly made up of the manor's remaining staff: those brave enough to work in a place wrecked by so much magic. Once Raze and Aris decided to hand over responsibility of the manor's daily activity to Mami and Papa, the atmosphere among the servants immediately relaxed. Most of them already have the rules for interacting with our fae guests memorized. Several have changeling children of their own, who are currently sledding with all the other kids in a corner of the room where it's snowing indoors.

Across the table from me, my parents are arguing good-naturedly about whether to go back to our old home in Rurava to pack up their belongings themselves, or to send someone to move their things for them. Birch purrs blissfully in Papa's lap. The *Destiny* has been moved to the carriage house, but the brownie doesn't seem to be in much of a rush to return to it now that he has the run of the entire manor.

Mami even somehow managed to convince Olani's brother to stay for the feast—something about food waste. He and Olani sat talking quietly for ages, with their matching serious expressions and matching sunlight smiles, before he politely excused himself, and she left to see him on his way out. I'm going to pretend that my eyes don't keep sliding to the door every five seconds waiting for her to return.

The Seelie and Unseelie Courts are both represented at the party, though the Unseelie faeries seem mostly content to stare at Egg while he sleeps, basking in his raw power, and whisper about how great my sister is. The goat-legged faeries, who apparently don't hold a grudge, are playing a midwinter ballad with a group of mortal musicians. Cobweb and Robin have somehow convinced Aris to sing along with them. Raze, in the form of an actual robin, perches on top of Robin's head, harmonizing.

It's complete chaos. I love it.

And yet, I feel strangely outside of it all, like I'm waiting for something else to happen. I feel like I'm watching grains of sand run out from an hourglass, unsure if I want it to end or not.

Something bumps my elbow, and I turn to see Seelie dropping down at my side. She's almost glowing, more at home and more herself than I've ever seen her. She passes me one of the two goblets she's holding, but because she's still Seelie, overshoots my hand a little and splashes droplets of the mulled wine inside on both of us.

"Oops," she says, still grinning.

The goblet is warm in my hands, garnet liquid swirling around as I gesture with it. "What's this for?"

"A toast."

I raise an eyebrow. "You know, you could get the whole room to toast with you if you wanted. You're kind of a big deal."

Her fingers trace the rim of the cup. "I know," she says—not too arrogant, not too humble. Nothing but the truth. "But this one is just for us."

"For us," I repeat, smiling at her, forgetting everything else for a second. And there's no need for grand speeches, because it's just us, and that simple toast is enough. We raise our goblets to clink gently together, and then Seelie sips at hers delicately while I throw the whole thing back in one gulp.

"Sol!" she scolds, failing to sound truly stern through the laugh that distorts the sound of my name.

"What?" I grin. "It's *mulled*. It's barely even alcoholic."

Seelie rolls her eyes, sips her wine again, and leans her head on my shoulder. We sit like that in peaceful silence, just watching the party around us. I can't help fidgeting with the cup, my fingers growing antsy for something to do. She fits perfectly here, and for once, I'm the one who's not sure of my place. How can I be so happy and so restless all at once?

After a while, Seelie sighs. She lifts her head to look at me, brushing wisps of hair back from her face. "I know this won't last forever," she says quietly.

"What?" I feel myself tense, surprised to hear the words I've been searching for in my sister's voice.

She shrugs, and even though her eyes turn sad, the smile remains pressed into the corners of her mouth. "I know you're still missing something. Adventure. And I hope you find it. I know things are going to keep changing around here. I'm just happy that we're all here together right now." She lets out a long, contented sigh. "I can hold on to that."

"Seelie, I—" I don't know what to say. I don't know what I can say that my brilliant sister doesn't already know. The sound that finally escapes my throat is somewhere between a laugh and a sob. "When did you get so *wise*?"

"Oh, I've always been wiser than you. I am the older sister, remember?"

That makes us both laugh. Yes, I remember. And I also vividly remember the expressions on our parents' faces when we broke the news to them, mostly because I wanted them to be a whole lot more shocked than they were.

"Olani was looking for you," Seelie says, trying too hard not to look at me. It ends up turning into a crooked, painfully transparent, sideways glance.

I don't even care, because I suddenly realize I've been waiting to hear those exact words. "She's back?" I ask embarrassingly quickly. I've been waiting for her to come back, and I don't think I would have missed it.

"Earlier," Seelie clarifies. She stands, tossing back the rest of the wine. "Maybe you should go talk to her."

"Raze told you to say that, didn't he?"

"Maybe." She offers me one last innocent look before she turns and walks away, almost certainly to return to the shapeshifter's side. Her cheeks are rosy and I'm not sure if it's from wine or warmth or embarrassment, but her smile is too sweet to get annoyed with her. Besides, I have somewhere else to be.

I end up finding Olani in her room after confidently knocking on her door with no idea what I'm going to say.

"Well?" she prompts, reminding me that she's already greeted me twice and I have still said nothing. Instead of trying to formulate the perfect response, I breeze past her into the room.

It's a decently comfortable, if cramped, space, with a small hearth and a rug to cushion the cold stone floors. The room is messier than the last time I was here, clothes scattered in piles and ink-stained balls of paper strewn about like a blizzard ripped through. I wonder if her compulsive neatness had been descending into chaos in the weeks leading up to Wintersol, the weeks we were barely speaking, or if this is a newer development.

"Love what you've done with the place," I say, which seems to make her realize that she can't get rid of me without a fight.

She sighs and shuts the door, turning to face me. "Sorry, I don't get a lot of company. Didn't realize I'd be entertaining."

My mouth slips into a smile. I can't help myself. "You're always entertaining."

"You should be at the party."

"And if I'd rather spend time with someone I like than several dozen strangers?" I ask, throwing her words from the Winter Tournament celebration back at her. My cheeks feel warm, even warmer under the attention as her eyes settle on me.

"Isolde . . ." she starts, stealing all the air from the room. Her thick lashes flutter and her throat bobs as she swallows hard. Looks away.

Then I spot the bag on her bed. The blankets beneath are folded and tucked, crisp as new snow. All the clothes and bundles of herbs and hair wraps radiate from this point, like the strike point of some sort of explosion. The bag is half packed, as if I've caught her in the middle of deciding which of the bulkier items can be rolled up to fit.

Oh. The realization strikes me in the middle of my chest, a strange cold hollow radiating between my ribs. I force my face not to let it show, aiming for any expression other than *devastated* as I turn to look back at her.

"You're leaving." I don't say *without me*, but the words seem to manifest themselves in the space between us anyway.

Olani's hands drop, landing heavily at her sides. She tilts her head, smiling softly. "I promised."

While we were trapped in that strange bubble of time, only an hour passed in the Mortal Realm. Hawn was just outside the range of what appeared, from the outside, like an explosion of magic emanating from Wildline Manor. A wall of shimmering magic kept anyone from entering the Unending Realm until we emerged around one in the morning. Olani found him as soon as she could, and he was so relieved she'd made it, I don't think he would have cared if she didn't explain everything that had happened.

But she did. Because she promised.

And she also promised to return home, at least for a little while. It makes sense that they'd set off as soon as possible, so that news of the disaster in Auremore wouldn't make its way to their parents too long before confirmation that their children were all right. Still, I thought Olani had a few more days to tie up loose ends.

Like me. The person she hasn't exactly been *avoiding* ever since I regained consciousness in the rubble of our final fight with Gossamer, but who she hasn't directly addressed, either. I've almost convinced myself that all those moments we shared, those near misses in the Seelie Realm, were nothing but the result of forced proximity and too much pressure, and now that we're back, we're going to go back to normal lives that don't include each other.

It's been harder to convince myself that I might be okay with that.

"Well." I clear my throat, which is definitely not choking me with emotions I can't place. "Safe travels. Um . . ." I twist the bag's strap absently, as if checking it for holes. I wonder if she's going to miss traveling in the *Destiny*. It's nice having shelter on the road. I think I'm stalling, because the next words I hear out of my mouth are "Tell your parents hello for me," as if I've ever met them and they could possibly care about my greeting them.

Olani takes a quick step forward, capturing my hands. At first, I think it's just to stop me from fidgeting with her things, but . . . she doesn't let go. "Sure," she says with a shrug. "Or . . .

you could tell them."

By the time my gaze jerks up from her hands to her face, a grin is already creeping up her lips. A real smile, with teeth. One that makes her eyes shine like sunlight through amber. It's open and inviting and . . . maybe a little bit hopeful.

"Really?" I say, immediately panicking and latching on to the wrong thing. "I mean, I'd love to go with you, obviously, of course, but like, you don't think they'd hate me for putting you in danger all those times? Because if you think about it, really, a lot of this was my fault, and I don't want—"

"Isolde."

I am fully expecting Olani to cut off my distracted rambling.

I'm not expecting her to kiss me.

She hesitates, swaying in place, just long enough that I could pull back if I wanted to. But I don't want to. We both move to close the distance, skulls colliding in a bony crush. Bright pain sparks behind my eyes, and I can't help but laugh. Olani's laugh is shakier, barely more than a breath, and our second attempt is smoother.

And then everything is soft, and the world goes liquid around the edges. Soft lips, the soft skin of her cheek under my fingers, soft breaths mingling between us. Blood rushes in my ears, the million thoughts that could be distracting me from this perfect moment all scrambled together into an incoherent mess. She's colder than I expected, the soothing chill of a healing balm rubbed on tender skin. I could drown in her sweet, herbal scent.

My knees turn to water, every sharp edge melting until it feels like the only thing holding me up is the magnetic pull of her touch. Olani's hand drifts along my ribs, featherlight, then grips my waist hard enough to tug my body firmly against hers. Like she, too, is afraid we'll collapse if anything pries us apart. I gasp at the sudden hitch, eyes opening to catch a glimpse of her deeply focused expression before her mouth slides deliciously over mine again.

Olani kisses the way she does everything: thoroughly, methodically, unhurried but not slow. We should have done this much sooner. I have wasted so much time, and I intend to make up for every second of it. Still, I can't blame my past self for hesitating, because it makes no sense that I would be the one who gets to kiss the bravest, loveliest, most intimidatingly perfect person I know.

Her nose bumps unexpectedly into mine as she draws away, eyes scanning my face. "What are you thinking about?" Olani asks. Her voice is a little breathless, her eyes dark as they drift back down to my mouth. The sound and sight combined make the blood rush to my face, punch whatever breath I had left out of my lungs.

"You," I manage hoarsely. Which is true, but I search for something truer and cleverer to add so she'll know what I mean. "You are a wonder."

And she is—the rich color of her cheeks glowing as she breaks into a full, radiant smile. Wisps of hair too short to weave into her braids coiling around her face, sunset eyes locked on mine. I think she might be blushing as she looks away, shaking her head and sinking her teeth into that perfect bottom lip, and honestly, I don't know how she expects me to respond except by kissing her again.

Blood tingles in my veins, fizzy happiness pressing against the confines of my skin. I press closer, knocking our knees together and making us both wobble off-balance. Instead of righting us, Olani pushes me back, and maybe this would devolve into an all-out sparring match if the room wasn't quite so small. As it is, the backs of my legs bump up against the mattress, and I let myself drop, dragging Olani down with me in a heap of giggles.

The rare, bright sound of her laughter goes straight to my head. She rolls so we're facing each other on our sides, laughing on a rumpled pile of clothing that was, up until a second ago, perfectly folded. Our fingers slot together easily, like a key in a lock. Our legs fit together, too, ankles brushing as they dangle off the side of the bed.

"You're sure you want to keep me around?" I ask, voice hushed within the fragile space between us. I'm mostly joking, but something tender and aching deep in my chest needs to hear the answer. "I'm just going to keep making trouble for you."

"Oh, I'm counting on that." She drags our joined hands up to kiss my knuckles. As she pulls away, the silly grin slowly falls from her lips. I bite back the urge to ask what's wrong, holding my breath to give her the space she needs with her thoughts. After a moment, she says, "For so long I thought, if I never let myself *think* about . . . what this was, it wouldn't be real. And I couldn't get hurt. But then you almost . . ."

We're both used to danger, blood and blades and close calls. What happened with Gossamer was something else entirely—the total lack of control, my body cut away from whatever makes me *me*. I don't think the feeling will ever stop haunting my worst dreams. I nod silently, prompting her to continue. I don't want to think about that now.

"I thought you were gone," she whispers. "And I realized I hadn't been protecting myself. I'd only been depriving myself." Her voice warms on the next words, head tilting so she's speaking directly into my ear. Her warm breath sends a shiver down my spine. "So yes, I want you to go with me, Isolde. I want us to be together."

With her, I feel the restless stirring that constantly drives me into motion still to a contented thrum. And when silence fills the warm confines of the small room, it's not because she's guarding her thoughts and feelings. It's because they lay between us already, open and unguarded in a fragile kind of peace. After worrying so long that the potential of *us* was an impossible puzzle to solve, it seems now that nothing in the world could be easier.

"I want that, too." To stop the tears threatening the corners of my vision, I close my eyes and kiss her again. Sweet and soft, until the world shrinks down to a bubble made of clean laundry and smooth skin, and I can feel her smiling against my mouth.

I want that, and so much more.

I want to kiss her until she can think of nothing else. I want to travel with her, to fight off anything that tries to hurt her. I want to spend each day getting into trouble so she can drag me back out of it. I want to see everything the world has to offer and to return home again and to do it all together. I want this future, this adventure, with her.

The first part, at least, I can start right now.

chapter forty-three

seelie

I think I'm taking the news shockingly well.

Then again, this is the last morning Isolde and I will have together before she goes off on her adventures, before we both set off on our diverging grown-up paths and everything changes, a morning that dawned frosty and full of promise—and we're wasting it arguing about the ethics of killing a mouse.

To be fair, it's not just an ordinary mouse. Someone caught it in the kitchen before the sun came up, and it passed from hand to hand to hand in its little wicker basket before it finally made its way to us. Raze is holding the basket now, lid cracked open to peek at the gingery-furred creature inside, and he looks a little pale. We've all had a look in the basket by now, and agreed that as far as we can tell, there is something distinctly Leira Wildfall about the mouse. Though we can't agree if it's the light reddish-brown fur, the pointed nose, or the gleam in its beady little eyes right before it tried to bite me.

"Obviously, the logical thing to do would be kill it." Aris glares at the basket with her arms crossed, her feet propped up on Isolde's now-empty desk.

"Right," Raze says, his brows creased in thought. He doesn't sound sure. He sets the basket down, as if not looking directly at it will make this situation disappear.

"After everything that happened, it's a miracle she's not already dead," Isolde adds, the only one of us who's managed to call the mouse *she* instead of *it*. Isolde sits cross-legged on her bed, wedged between Olani and the pack stuffed to bursting with her things. Birch is curled up in her lap as if he knows this is his chance to say goodbye, motionless except the twitching tip of his tail. "I mean," Isolde continues, "isn't it what she deserves?"

I don't know. I don't know if it's our place to decide what Leira Wildfall deserves. I know she'd have killed us in an instant if the situations were reversed, but isn't that kind of the whole point? That we're going to use the power and influence we've wrenched away from her to be *better*?

Egg snorts sparks, as if to underline the point I haven't managed to speak aloud. He's getting unsettlingly perceptive.

"Maybe you could keep it here," Olani says. Her arm is draped over Isolde's shoulder, fingers toying absently with the fabric of her sleeve. "Like . . . a pet." When everyone turns to look at her in surprise, she frowns at us. "What?"

Isolde smirks, holding her gaze. "That's not very practical of you."

"Well, maybe I'm tired of always having to be the practical one." She turns to Raze, Aris, and me. "You can keep yourselves alive without my guidance at this point, I hope."

"I hope so, too." Raze cracks. As if he's not going to miss her, make me suffer through all the jokes that he's saving for when she returns, and then talk her ear off for three hours straight when they get back. Good. We can be miserable together.

"What if I don't want a pet mouse?" Aris snaps. "Those little hands . . . disgusting."

"I don't think anyone wants a pet that took delight in torturing them for the better part of a decade," Raze adds.

"Not true," Isolde says mildly before shooting him a wicked grin. "Some people have birds."

Raze's jaw drops in overexaggerated offense, and he lets out a sound that is not going to help him in avoiding the obnoxious-parrot allegations. I would laugh if I wasn't so deep in thought about the immediate problem.

"The thing is," I finally say, slowly, "that if Leira is still *in there*, somehow, and we could restore her . . . she might have useful knowledge."

"Hand her over to the faerie courts?" Isolde muses. "Let them sort her out?"

That feels excessively cruel—which might be just the right amount of cruel. We all let the thought sink in, but we know the final decision is down to Raze and Aris. Then even Aris turns to him, waiting for her cousin's judgement.

I can see Raze fidgeting, his fingers drumming on the basket, his discomfort growing at the thought of every possible solution. Raze takes a deep breath, straightens his shoulders, and says, "I say we— *Oh!*"

My gaze snaps from him to the basket, but I'm already too late to see the twitch of movement that must have caught his eye. The basket tumbles to the floor, where it lands with the lid flopped open. The yellowish mouse inside hops out and makes a break for freedom.

Before any of us can react, Birch is off Isolde's lap and leaping after it with supernatural speed in an unbroken streak of glossy black fur. He descends on the mouse with the inevitability of nightfall, plucks it up in his sharp white teeth, and snaps its neck in one smooth motion.

Absolute silence fills the room as Birch trots off with his prize, tail flicking contentedly behind him.

The Unending Realm is gone. Gossamer is gone. And now Leira Wildfall is gone.

Perhaps she'll be mourned eventually. Once the scars have healed a little. Right now, though, there isn't time for anything more than a stunned moment of silence before we all start moving to get Isolde and Olani packed up and on the road before the weather turns. The past is dead, and we are alive, the future stretching out before us like a smooth, unmarked stretch of snow.

I try to order myself not to think about snow, but it's too late. By the time everyone has gathered outside the manor to see Isolde and Olani off, the last patches of blue sky are already blotted out by thick, pale clouds. As we stand around the *Destiny* in the same courtyard where Leira once hosted a Revelnox festival, where all this began, the first fluffy flakes begin to fall.

"Sorry," I say, holding out a hand to catch one. It's a slow, gentle snowfall, not too wet or icy. Mostly air, really. "I think this is me. I'm nervous."

Mami shivers, and Papa pulls her closer to his side. They both look up, unmasked awe in their expressions as snowflakes catch in their lashes and melt on their cheeks. "Seelie . . ." Papa says. There's an apology in his voice. An apology for all the years they told me to hold back my magic, believing it the only way to keep me safe. An apology I know, and one I'm not ready to hear yet.

They've only just begun to know the new me. The real me. I don't think they're quite ready, either.

Isolde tosses her bag carelessly onto the *Destiny*'s stage, turning to me. Behind her, Olani rolls her eyes and picks up the bag, setting it inside with her own—all stacked perfectly parallel, of course. "No need to be nervous," Isolde says. "We'll be back soon."

She doesn't say *how* soon. It's only a few days' travel home for Olani, but Fate only knows what trouble they might find on the way there and back. Especially if Isolde's the one driving.

This will be the longest we've ever been apart. It's far from the worst thing we've survived, but the thought makes the air around me feel a few degrees colder. Despite Isolde's cheerful grin, the excitement tapping in her fingers that she can't hold back, I know she feels it, too. The strain of a string that ties us together, being tested for the first time.

It's strong enough to withstand it. We're strong enough. That doesn't mean it's not going to hurt. She's ready to leave now, and I'm . . . not. Maybe, once everything settles down, we'll all go out on an adventure together in the wagon, camp out in ruins and chase down treasure as more than just wary allies. The thought cheers me, like an extra layer against the creeping loneliness of the cold.

It's a long, lingering goodbye. Aris stands by with her arms crossed, as if it's mere coincidence that she happens to be here. Egg scurries over the ice-slicked cobblestones, chasing snowflakes and melting them with mere proximity. We talk about the weather, about Olani's family and what kind of greeting Isolde can expect, about all the things Mami expects Isolde to remember to take care of herself.

Eventually, we can't drag it out any longer. Isolde forces Aris into a hug, which she accepts with less reluctance than I'd expected. Next, Mami clasps Isolde's hands in hers. Their heads bend together, words that aren't secret, but aren't meant for me.

Olani stands in front of me and Raze with her arms crossed. "Keep him out of trouble, okay?"

A trembling smile finds its way onto my lips. "Same to you," I laugh, nodding toward my sister, who's now squeezing both of our tearful parents in her arms. "If such a thing is even possible."

"Hey!" Raze complains, dropping my hand. "I'm right here!"

"I know." Olani wraps him up in a hug nearly tight enough

to lift him off the ground. "And I hope you know, you're like the fifth brother I never wanted."

He accepts the hug, and I laugh at the contrast—this time Olani is grinning ear to ear, and Raze is the one scowling. "You're too sweet, Olani."

She drops him, and I rush to take his place. Apparently, sometimes you have to initiate contact for people to realize that their touch isn't unwelcome. I'm working on it. And working on not going strangely, stiffly limp when someone hugs me. I'm fairly sure this one is successful, because Olani is still smiling when we separate.

Then there's only one goodbye left.

Isolde and I stand, face-to-face, like each other's reflection in a mirror. Faintly, I realize that everyone has drifted away, giving us a moment to ourselves. I stare wordlessly at my sister's familiar features, trying to capture every detail of this moment. We're both smiling, both on the verge of tears, both fighting against the wisps of hair whipping into our faces.

"Sorry." I sniffle when the first tear finally rolls down my cheek. I wipe it away on the back of my hand with a wet chuckle. "Hair in my eyes."

"Of course," Isolde says.

"I don't know how you stand it."

Then she finally reaches for me, ruffling my hair between her fingers. "Don't worry," she says, voice thick despite the smile that won't drop from her lips. "It'll grow back."

We throw our arms around each other. I don't try to stop the tears, but it's not wrenching sobs. It's strangely peaceful, letting the tension flow away with my twin's thin arms squeezing me tight, her ribs under my grip, my face burrowed into the cloak covering her shoulders.

In the end, we don't actually say goodbye. My throat is too tight to allow the word, my teeth clenching to hold it back.

Instead, when I finally unwind from Isolde, I catch her eye and say, "Be careful."

She's halfway up the stairs by then, but she looks over her shoulder. Her black cloak swirls around her in the wind, snowflakes glittering against the darkness. She grins and wipes a tear away, leaning precariously yet perfectly balanced. "I'm always careful."

The wind picks up around me as the door slams shut behind her and the *Destiny* whirs to life. I hear the rumble of its mechanics, watch the wheels slowly start to turn. As it begins to move, I hear Isolde's muffled laugh.

I watch the enchanted wagon pass through the manor's gates, picking up speed as it takes to the streets of Gilt Row. I watch until it crosses the bridge over the Harrow River, until even the faintest glint of emerald-green paint on the horizon is swallowed by the rest of the city of Auremore.

Even when it's gone, I keep standing there. Not hoping to glimpse it again, not wishing I could pull the wagon back through sheer willpower, but just . . . feeling. Waiting for this new sensation to settle in. I don't look back when I hear footsteps, don't look back at the gentle touch of my father's hand on my shoulder.

"We'll all be together again soon," he says.

"I know," I manage to say through the lump in my throat. And for once, I don't doubt it. Three years, both faerie realms, and a disproportionate dose of misfortune couldn't keep our family apart.

The moment passes. Mami and Papa give me a quick squeeze, but I'm not ready to turn and walk back to the house. Not yet. So they go on without me, within reach but not hovering too close for me to breathe.

The tightness in my chest, this new ache, doesn't loosen. But eventually, I find that I can still breathe around it. I turn and see that Raze is still watching the horizon, too—or watching me. It's impossible to tell. His hands are shoved into his pockets, shoulders drawn up around his ears against the snow.

Egg crashes into me, jumping up so his front paws rest on my knees and his head bumps against my legs. I laugh and bend down to scratch his scales, breathing deep as his blazing warmth chases away the chill spreading over my skin.

Raze extends his hand toward me, and I accept, threading our numb fingers together as we turn. The manor's silhouette looms above us, glimmering with magic, overwhelming with promise. Even with Isolde gone from my side, I am far from alone.

Finally, I find my voice. "You waited for me."

"I told you," he says. He looks at me sideways, and this time I don't shy away from meeting his eyes. "As long as it takes."

"I'm in love with you," I say, cheeks stinging from cold and from smiling so hard. "Foolishly. Endlessly. Completely."

It takes Raze a second to place the words as his own, but when he does, he bursts into a delighted laugh. He tries to pull me closer and lift me in the air at once, and only succeeds in losing his footing in an icy patch. I scream as we go down, but there's nothing I can do to stop our momentum. We hit the ground hard, my elbow landing square in his ribs, our legs tangled together.

At least Raze is there to cushion my fall. At least he can't be too seriously injured, because he starts wheezing with laughter before he's fully regained his breath. It's a contagious laugh, one that only builds as mine joins with it, piercing the snow-choked air around us.

"We have," he gasps, "to stop doing that."

I choke on another giggle, trying to push myself up. "I think it's too late." He pulls me back down, crushing me to his chest in a hug. I wrestle faintly against it, eventually giving up to finish my sentence against the warm skin right below his collar. "At this point, we're just Fated to fall over and over again."

We eventually pick ourselves up and make our way inside,

snowmelt dripping behind us. The main door is too grand, too intimidating, so we slip in through the servants' entrance to the kitchen—the same one Isolde and I snuck through all those months ago.

The cooking fire is a low, steady heat that reaches to the corners, the kitchen's frantic pace slowed to the gentle hum of a winter beehive. We huddle close to the oven's glow until we're mostly dry and warm, and I close my eyes and picture the hum of activity in the manor.

Upstairs, my parents—two people as unrecognizable from the versions they were when we were last together as a family as Isolde and me—discuss plans for the future in low tones. Somewhere else, a girl with light at her fingertips shrugs off the shadows of her past. In a warm spot, in the last rays of winter sun, a creature shaped like a black cat dozes, safe in the knowledge that no one is going to chase him away with iron and salt. In the former ballroom, two portals swirl with constant, shifting energy. They snap at each other like lightning, the unending flow of their magic slowly, irrevocably changing their surroundings.

We all have adjustments to make to allow each other back into our lives. It will be slow, building like the snow slowly starting to collect on the ground, and then one day it will fall into place.

I don't have to fix everything right now. I just have to wait and see what happens. And so, I decide, my eyes hovering on the gleaming copper pots that flicker like treasure in the firelight, I'm going to do what I always used to do when I couldn't think clearly, when things got to be too much, when I needed to settle my mind.

I'm going to bake—to soothe myself with the predictable reaction of air and heat and sugar.

It's been so long since I took the time to bake something that I'm afraid I won't remember how. I spent my months in the manor with my mind and magic overworked, consumed by caring for Egg and worrying if Leira would let us live another day. There was no time for routine, for sweetness, for the rhythm of losing myself in a task. There's time now.

Raze helps—and by *helps*, I mostly mean makes a mess and gets in the way. He asks questions and listens when I go off on long-winded explanations, comforted that the knowledge of how to make something sweet, something frivolous and fun, hasn't left me. Once the custard is set, we sprinkle each tiny, perfect cup with sugar that rains down like glittering snow. I summon a flame at my fingertips and show him how to toast the sugar so it darkens and caramelizes, stopping just short of turning black and filling the kitchen with smoke. I finish half the batch, while Raze directs Egg in scorching the other half.

"You're burning them! Ease up a little!" I scold, unable to stop myself from laughing. A breeze follows the arc of my hand, dispersing the smoke starting to curl around them. Raze does nothing to defend himself, just watches me laugh with an extremely self-satisfied look.

The laughter eases into a small ember of happiness in my chest, a warm smile as I meet his gaze. He reaches up and tucks a piece of my too-short hair that's escaped its knot behind my ear, warm fingertips brushing my skin. There's something about the way he looks at me that feels like more than just *looking* at me.

"What is it?" I ask, too breathlessly content to be self-conscious.

Raze smiles, leaning down so our faces are almost close enough to touch. "You look so at home."

"I *am* home." I push up onto my toes to kiss him, and a soft wind wraps us up in the scent of burnt sugar and hearth fire.

My home isn't a single place, a single person, a single realm. My home lives within me, in the bittersweet ache that comes from feeling too deeply and seeing too much. My life is a single thread, weaving between the realms since its first moment. It may join and separate from other threads, twist inextricably into them in some spots, and pull almost to breaking in others—and yet it remains itself. A single, shining line, unbroken and unending.

author's note

This book is an imperfect metaphor for neurodivergence. I hope that you'll excuse any inconsistencies or inaccuracies that served its primary purpose of telling an engaging, magical story that may or may not be relatable to some readers.

When writing Seelie, I drew from my own lived experience as an autistic teen (more on that in the Author's Note of book one!). Even while drafting the first book, which is fully from Seelie's point of view, I knew Isolde was somehow different. Her personality and dynamic with Seelie were partly inspired by my own bold, brilliant sister. About a week after I added the twist about Isolde's changeling identity, my sister called and informed me that she'd just been diagnosed with ADHD, and everything fit together.

I didn't know much about ADHD at the time, but I was happy for my sister, because I knew how much finally finding the right description for how your brain works can change your life. Two years later, right around the time I started writing this book, I (along with my doctor) realized how my own ADHD had been masked by my autism. Writing Isolde and exploring the differences between how she and Seelie think was oddly healing. Women and other marginalized people have been historically undiagnosed. It wasn't until 2013 that one could be diagnosed with both ADHD and autism, despite the significant overlap between the two.

"Attention Deficit Hyperactivity Disorder" itself is a bit of a misnomer. Most individuals with ADHD experience hyperfocus in addition to executive dysfunction, and are as likely to be inattentive (spacey and daydreamy) as hyperactive. The disorder can more accurately be described as the inability to regulate one's attention. To those who don't experience it, that seems like a moral failing. I would like to assure you that it's not.

Sure, Isolde is classically hyperactive and impulsive—but she's also quick-witted and compassionate. She is magically adaptable (or at least, that's how it seems to my brain!). She's the calm in the chaos and the chaos in the calm.

ADHD and autism aren't the only forms of neurodivergence, but they're the ones I have experienced firsthand. I've tried to represent them faithfully and lovingly in this book. Thank you for going on the journey with me, and I hope that if you're familiar with these challenges, you're also familiar with the joy of being your undiluted self.

acknowledgments

If you're reading this, it means I've overcome the Second Book Curse. I can't thank you enough for going on this journey, whether you waited through the nearly three year gap between books alongside me or just picked up book one a week ago. Sharing my words with you is an immense privilege.

Words can't express my gratitude for Olivia Valcarce, who I'm convinced was fated to be my editor since that random pitch contest in 2020. Life took the weirdest path possible to make that happen, but this book wouldn't be here without your encouragement, brainstorming sessions, and brilliant feedback.

I will always be thankful to my acquiring editor, Stephanie Cohen, for seeing the potential in and helping me shape Seelie's story. Thanks are also in order to Alyssa Miele, my Quill Tree Books editor, and all the HarperCollins team members who helped create this finished product. Mona Finden, the cover illustrator for *Unseelie* and *Unending*, will probably never know how much her absolutely flawless artwork inspired me. Thank you for your attention to detail and making Egg the cutest little guy in the world.

Thank you to Victoria Marini, my agent, for always fighting for me and going above and beyond any expectations to make things come together for this book. As I say in almost every email, you're the best.

Andrew Joseph White, H. E. Edgmon, Emily Lloyd-Jones, Amparo Ortiz, and Lyndall Clipstone—thank you for your kind words. Katie McNamee, De Elizabeth, Taylor Grothe, and Clare Edge, thank you for the encouragement along the way. Catherine Bakewell, thank you for being my Emotional Support Writer Bestie.

This is the part where I realize I owe gratitude to too many people to name, so let me just say—thank you to everyone I thanked in book one, and also everyone I forgot to mention in book one (my bad!). To my family and friends, thank you for putting up with me throughout all of this. I love and appreciate you all.

At the end of this story about sisters growing up and going their separate ways, I would be remiss not to thank my own sister, Samantha, for being my best friend forever. Thank you for reading the first draft of this book instead of doing your Very Important Law School Homework.

And last, but never least, eternal thanks to my husband, Sam, for always pushing me to give my very best and being with me every step of the way. You are the best reader/creative partner/cheerleader/rival/friend that anyone could ever ask for. All right—who next?